THE
MUMMY
CACHE

SANDY ESENE

BLUE BENU
—PRESS—

Published by Blue Benu Press, Seattle, Wa

Cover design by Mariah Sinclair

978-1-7328105-6-3 (Ebook edition)
978-1-7328105-7-0 (Paperback edition)
978-1-7328105-8-7 (Hardcover edition)

For
Linda, Lynne, and Chris
an amazing goddess triad

PROLOGUE

1075 BCE

During the reign of Hedjkheperre Setepenre Smendes
First month of Akhet, the season of inundation, day 23

*Very adverse: It is the day of causing the heart of the enemy of Re to suffer.
Anyone born on this day will not live. Do not listen to singing or watch
dancing today.* —*Egyptian Horoscope Calendar*

The sky was silvering on the horizon, heralding a new day and banishing the last glimmer of starlight along with any hope of saving her beloveds. The sands of time had run too fast until none remained. Soon Re would emerge from his nightly journey through Nut's celestial body and cast his brilliant rays upon the red and black lands, bringing forth the day that would forever mark Hatshepsut's shame. This coming dawn didn't hold the promise of a fresh start, but instead the sharp knowledge tattooed on her immortal soul that her beloveds would pay the ultimate price for her actions.

In the desert valley below, low-ranking wab priests scurried about in their stiff linen kilts, setting the stage for the coming blasphemy. They had lined up the coffins of the guilty, removed their lids, and set to sanctifying the ground with sacred water representing the four cardinal directions. The priests were readying the space between the mortal and eternal realms in preparation for the rites to banish her beloveds from the afterlife. Cursing them to spend eternity in nothingness—as if they never existed.

Hatshepsut crossed her arms over her chest. Her mind whirred away to find any last-minute way to stop the awaiting catastrophe. She prided herself in always finding a way, but this situation had her at a great disadvantage. She stood alone on the high bluffs above the army of priests and the numerous scandal-seeking courtiers waiting in the wide valley below to whet their morbid appetites.

The high priestess of Hehet, the primordial Goddess of eternity and the immeasurable, emerged from a gilded palanquin carried aloft by temple guards, then stepped onto a platform below. Transporting the priestess and her regalia from the holy sanctuary in the city of Waset to this remote spot was no small feat. At least they didn't have the harsh desert sun on their backs as they traveled in the dark of night. Hatshepsut was gladdened by the fact that they wouldn't be so lucky on the return trip.

The high priestess stepped out of the conveyance and walked to the sacred altar that had been transported from the temple to this barren landscape. Her head was cast downward, and her gait lacked her usual proud grace, as if she were one of the convicted. She paused in front of the large stone altar and was swarmed by attendants who anointed her flesh with sacred oils. The priestess lifted her gaze to the surrounding cliffs appearing to search for something or someone, paying no heed to those around her, like a thoroughbred accustomed to the persistence of flies. Hatshepsut was certain the high priestess Akh-Hehet had been warned of her escape by now. Could it be she was trying to locate Hatshepsut with her visioning powers? There was a time she counted Akh-Hehet as a friend, but what friend would take part in this desecration? Dangerous times made for excruciating choices. Friend and foe—the necessity of survival in the royal court often blended the two in confounding and dangerous ways.

A swift breeze carried the sweet scent of lotus and the sharp fragrance of cedar oils from the valley below. Or was it purely a trick of the mind, a sensory memory of the thousands of sacred rites she had experienced in her mortal life as princess, priestess, queen, and ultimately pharaoh?

Over a lifetime of countless seasons, where she had seen everything under the sun, the atrocity laid out before her was unimaginable. Four of her beloveds lay in wait to receive a punishment they did not earn. One was her dear father, a great pharaoh who ruled hundreds of years ago. He loved her equal to a son, raising Hatshepsut to rule. Alongside him were the recumbent forms of her nephew, who had become a great king after Hatshepsut's reign, her lover, Senenmut, and her absurd half-brother husband. Their mummified remains lay in the valley below, coffin lids pulled off, exposed to the eyes of the unworthy. Their ancient corpses were surrounded by priests and nobles in macabre jubilation. Their long-dead bodies were bound in bitumen and funerary wrappings, defenseless against this most heinous of punishments—the dismemberment of their souls.

As an immortal, Hatshepsut would never face the weighing of the heart in the hall of Osiris. To banish her beloveds from their well-deserved afterlife in the Field of Reeds was the only punishment the king could inflict on her. The pharaoh, Smendes, had imprisoned her and intended to drag her here to witness the unholy rite like a disgraced enemy of their beloved country, Kemet. Smendes and his priests were impotent in their ability to punish her with death. Instead, they craved to witness her suffering with greedy eyes.

With the help of a palace guard who had owed her much, Hatshepsut was able to escape her bonds. She fled to the place they planned to take her, but at least she would be there on her terms. She would not give them the pleasure of her tears.

The location for this foul act wasn't lost on Hatshepsut. Smendes had chosen this exact spot for its proximity to her house of eternity, Djeser-Djeseru, which lay on the other side of the cliff face. Once the Ba-souls of her beloveds were severed, their bodies were to be cached away like discarded wine vessels —not in the tombs constructed for their eternal rest, but in a rough-hewn shaft of a tomb abandoned by a semi-important noble.

Although the priests had laid out the many coffins of the convicted, Hatshepsut had her eyes trained on one in particular. It was the plain cedar coffin of her lover Senenmut. He was the one the others used to draw her into the ill-fated scheme concocted from the Field of Reeds. They needed someone who still walked among the living. Senenmut pleaded with her to do one small thing for him. Turns out it wasn't so small. If she hadn't agreed, neither she nor her beloveds would be here on this most miserable of days.

Hatshepsut leaned against the rough sandstone as ceremonial music drifted up the cliffside. Drums thudded like a heartbeat, grounding the rites in the earthly realm as the sweet chime of the sistrum called to the Holy. Many temple dancers surrounded Akh-Hehet, who stood in front of the large stone altar with a golden statuette of the Goddess adorned in glimmering ceremonial regalia. They swayed to the sounds as they shook their sistrums, causing the small metal disks to play against each other.

Akh-Hehet clutched a ceremonial adze in one hand and an obsidian dagger in the other. She raised them to the sky and invoked her Goddess to use her as a vessel as the sun breached the horizon. Its golden rays surrounded the priestess in brilliant shafts of light, following her as she walked to the line of coffins, like a holy spotlight.

The high priestess knelt and placed the adze to the mouth of the first coffin holding the great Pharaoh Ramses II.

Her four beloveds were at the end of the line. *Of course—they were saving them until the end.*

The high priestess spoke. Her voice reverberated through the valley, amplified with the holy force of her Goddess. The cliffside shook with the voice of the Holy One. A scatter of rocks tumbled past Hatshepsut into the valley below as the high priestess condemned the first pharaoh in line, Ramses. "This mouth was open, but I have cursed thy mouth and thy teeth. I close thy mouth. I close these, thy two eyes. I have closed your mouth with the instrument of the Gods. You shall not walk or speak; your body shall never again be with the great company of the Gods. You will never live again. I command the Ba-soul of the forsaken, our great ancestor Ramses, son of Seti, Usermaatre-Setepenre, rise to me . . . the primordial one demands an audience."

A shimmering bird form embodying countless points of light rose from Ramses's chest and hovered in front of the high priestess. Akh-Hehet grabbed it. The Ba's wings beat hard to escape from her grasp. She raised a long black blade against it, pausing as the ceremonial music thrummed faster and louder. The obsidian blade sliced down, severing one of the bird's wings. The wail of a thousand jackals filled the air.

Hatshepsut's hands flew to her ears at the deafening sound. There would be twenty more such screams during this unholy rite. She willed her hands to her side and stood tall. She would witness each atrocity and allow her pain to forge every vile moment into an unbreakable armor of resolve to one day make her beloveds whole again.

CHAPTER ONE

2021 CE

First month of Shomu, the season of summer, day 10

Very adverse: It is the day the White One of Heaven proceeds upstream to be at the front, among those who rebelled against their master in the Delta.
—*Egyptian Horoscope Calendar*

The streets of Cairo buzzed with excitement. Today was the Royal Golden Parade of the Pharaohs. With great fanfare, the Egyptian government was transporting twenty-two pharaonic mummies from the old salmon-colored museum in Tahrir Square to their new home at the National Museum of Egyptian Civilization. The recently built NMEC had opened for the very first time a few weeks before this grand event was to take place.

Hattie had watched the army of workers conscripted to make the elaborate procession happen over the past few months, reminding her of a time when farmers were called from their fields to build the pyramids for their pharaoh. She assumed the modern-day workers would be paid in something other than a ration of bread and beer.

A shimmering haze of anticipation hovered over the city. From the coffee houses of Old Cairo where small cups of strong coffee were being drunk, to the small shops in the souk selling every imaginable trinket, to the shiny urban center bustling with frantic workers, the coming parade was all anyone could talk about. Their thoughts and words were calling the procession and its fanfare into existence like a powerful spell.

Hattie was invigorated by the strange energy raining down around her. The populace was electric with anticipation for this grand celebration honoring their ancient past. She was jubilant for a very different reason. For Hattie, this wasn't about bringing attention and honor to the ancient past but about righting a wrong from the past.

The parade had yet to start. Hattie went to the old Cairo museum in Tahrir Square on a mission to locate the mummy of her lover Senenmut. It wasn't that she wanted to pine over his remains—she needed to know where to find him quickly once she received her long-awaited delivery later at the NMEC.

She found him stashed away in a dark and unvisited corner of the mazelike old building. His remains weren't going to be transported with the others. As a nonroyal, he was deemed unimportant.

A small spark of hope lit within her as she leaned over the glass case that contained his mummified remains. Hopefully soon he would be once again enjoying the delights of the Netherworld. Hattie tucked the location away in the back of her mind for later and then headed to the museum's main hall. She wandered into the melee, getting lost in the crowd of event staff and performers who were a part of the night's extravaganza.

Being alive for three millennia taught her a thing or two about the ways of deception. Because she was a notable of Cairo society, she could have easily gained a much-coveted ticket to the exclusive affair, but that would have taken all the fun out of it.

Hattie watched the opulent performance in the stately main hall of the one-hundred-year-old museum. The cavernous space was lit by projections of the night sky interspersed with images of the pharaohs who were going to be relocated. Their likenesses were projected onto screens stretched across half-moon arches at either end of the high-ceilinged room. Dancers drenched in gold and flowing white linen erupted around the mammoth seated statues of Amenhotep III and his Great Royal Wife Tiye. Like a river of shimmering color, the performers poured through the great hall and out of the building.

Hattie followed their progress to the outer courtyard, where she spied the brightly lit, pimped-out sacred barques the Egyptian Ministry of Tourism and Antiquities contrived to house the royal bodies. Modern ideas of regalia were strange to her. The vehicles were decked out in a style that would have made a Las Vegas casino mogul proud, but not an ancient pharaoh of Egypt. The design consisted of large, garish, illuminated black and gold wings of protection on each side of the vehicle. Crowning the top of the conveyance was a box resembling a copy of a gilded Ark of the Covenant in a 1980s adventure movie. She assumed this is where the divine flesh of the pharaohs would rest as they traveled on this odd journey to a place they wouldn't have imagined in their wildest dreams as a final resting place.

She grabbed her phone to memorialize the moment, wondering if her beloveds would be mortified or impressed with the knowledge their bodies were once housed within these strange, modern contraptions. It was hard for her, living for all these long centuries, witnessing the evolution of technology, to judge what might be viewed as awesome or awesomely profane.

Hattie walked past the strange queue of vehicles awaiting an unseen signal from the event staff to move out.

Having had her fill of the fanfare, she decided to return to her dahabeeyah anchored along the Nile. Living close to the blessed waters rekindled her love for her homeland with each new dawn and gave her a sense of freedom. The traditional Egyptian wide-bodied sailboat allowed her to live as she pleased in great comfort.

She left the old museum to the extraordinary percussive sound of a hundred drummers marching in step down the cause-way, announcing the coming procession of the pharaohs to their new home at the NMEC. With a light heart, she strolled to her boat to slip out of her street clothes and into something worthy of a gala celebrating those of her pharaonic lineage.

～∿～

The limo darted between cars like an elegant dancer moving through an erratic soundtrack of blaring horns, loud mufflers, and the occasional yelled curse that made Cairo traffic both exhil-arating and hair-raising. The rules of engagement on Egyptian roadways must have been inspired by the turbulent primordial waters of chaos.

The Pyramids of Giza rose in the distance beyond Hattie's tinted windows. Seeing their grand bodies stripped naked, exposing their rough interiors, was a great desecration of their original majesty. Hattie remembered how glorious they once were, faced with bright-white limestone and capped with gold. Once sacred ground was now a destination for flocks of sunblocked and sweat-stained tourists, cooing in amazement and leaving a trail of droppings in their wake, like so many pigeons.

The driver pulled onto a long causeway leading to the National Museum of Egyptian Civilization near Fustat Park. This pre-opening gala and fundraiser was a chance for the well connected to mingle with the mummies before they were placed in their new digs below the main exhibition space. Unlike the other attendees, Hattie couldn't care less about the new glass and granite climate-controlled mausoleum built to display the possessions of those who were long dead. No, this event was the first step in returning the justice and balance of Maat to her beloveds and fulfilling the promise she made centuries ago in that desolate desert valley.

When they arrived at the entrance of the new museum, Hattie stepped onto the red carpet. Cameras flashed as she walked by. The paparazzi leaned over the barricade to snap a shot of her glorious body in her gold-and-lapis-beaded dress. Once they realized she wasn't a movie star or head of state, their heads swiveled down the line to the newly arrived attendees, thinking she was of no importance. *If only they knew.*

She stepped into the museum's lobby and through an arching silver tunnel to the main exhibition space. Upon entering the massive room of smooth grey stone, she was handed a flute of champagne. Unlike her usual approach to events, she had arrived early. There was a smattering of finely dressed people milling about. She took a sip as she strode to the concrete rim in the center of the room. It encircled a gigantic hole cut from the floor exposing the lower level. Projections of tomb goods and depictions of the afterlife played along the rim's interior. Hattie peered below into the dark exhibition area. It was so strange to think her beloveds would rest there for eternity, in a sterile and temperature-controlled museum and not the tombs built for them as their houses of eternity—as if they were a sideshow, and not former kings of Egypt.

All around her, extending from this central cutout, the royal mummies were set around it in a starburst pattern. Each rested upon a gilded dais. It broke her heart to see them on display, the sacrilege of their royal faces being exposed to the gawking stares of these well-heeled looky-loos. The mummies' coffins lay open, allowing the heavy-hitting donors to get up close and personal with the royal ones. Hattie gazed down into the oddly serene face of the one nearest her, Ramses II, or Ramses the Great as he is commonly referred to in modern times. He was a ruler who lived centuries after she shed her mortality. Although it pained her to see him exposed in such an undignified way, she was grateful the first mummified face she was to gaze upon wasn't that of her father, nephew, or brother-husband.

Hattie leaned in close and wondered how the professional museum staffers felt about this setup with these ancient rulers' bodies exposed to all and sundry. She guessed the request to have them displayed this perilous way, or more likely, a demand, came from high up the chain of government. There were most likely a lot of museum staff on edge.

Hattie scanned the room to see if Maspero had arrived yet.

He appeared out of nowhere as if her thoughts called him forth like an unwilling ushabti magically awakened to do his master's bidding. He was handed his glass of champagne as he entered the space. His crisp white suit made his already pale complexion look absolutely pallid. The strange little man probably hadn't slept in weeks in anticipation of their meeting.

Maspero was a withering and spiritless bureaucrat—nothing like his ancestor, Gaston Maspero. The cruel fates of the universe managed to leave him bereft of any visible signs of his forefather's essence. Hattie experienced a few interactions in the

1880s with the French Egyptologist. Whatever views a person might hold of Gaston's legacy as one of the first director generals of excavations and antiquities in Egypt, he had the balls of an Apis bull next to his descendant.

Hattie caught Maspero's eye and waved him to her. He awkwardly waggled his pale fingers at her momentarily before halting and shoving his hand in his pocket. It was as if his tiny little brain just remembered their meeting was meant to be clandestine. He seemed clueless about the art of being unseen. His eyes darted around the room as he neared Hattie. To be seen slumming with the likes of her in her modern assumed persona as an antiquities dealer open to questionable sources wouldn't do his reputation any good as a forthright agent of KHNM, an agency overflowing with a bunch of self-appointed do-gooders priding themselves in keeping humanity safe from the Gods. As if that were possible.

Maspero was blissfully unaware of the powerful substance he was handing over to Hattie. They were tears of an actual God and not the useless ancient unguent he thought. Even considering his ignorance he was no knight in shining armor. If he were true of heart, nothing could entice him to hand over an artifact from his agency, especially something as ephemeral as personal gain. The fact he held his ancestor's reputation in such high esteem that he would stoop to steal from the mighty KHNM on a promise to clear a centuries-old scandal no one cared about, showed his true colors. If he was foolhardy enough to swim into her net of lies, Hattie would be more than happy to have fresh fish for dinner.

She shook his cold, damp hand, holding it a little longer than was custom. She wanted to feel the slight quake of nervousness within him. "I assume you brought it with you?"

He leaned in close and spoke in a low whisper. "Could you keep it down, please? How about we go somewhere private?"

Hattie had no intention of making this easy for him. "If you are seeking discretion, it would probably be best served for us to meet in plain view of everyone to see. If you and I slink off into a dark corner . . . well, you know how tongues like to wag."

He reached into his interior suit pocket and pulled out a gold-toned cigarette case emblazoned on both sides with the profile of Nefertiti. He held the garish object out to her. She had seen thousands of them in the tourist souk stalls. "No thank you, I quit that habit eons ago."

"It is my gift to you. I think you will find the inside particularly well rendered. And it would look lovely with your ensemble."

His beady little eyes bored into hers to punctuate his intended message.

There was no way anyone with a moderate amount of sense would think the cheap atrocity would do anything whatsoever for the beaded masterpiece she was wearing. She pushed a small latch and the top popped open, revealing ten small vials within.

He leaned in close and whispered, "I had to remove the liquid from the vessel. I figured this would be the best—"

"You fool. What have you done? I asked for you to hand the whole object to me, not parse it out in takeaway containers." Hattie closed her eyes against the burst of fury pulsing through her. Why did she always have to deal with such fools? She breathed in deep. No crying over spilled God's tears. If he'd ruined the contents by removing the tears from their ancient vessel, there was nothing she could do about it now.

"I just thought—"

She hissed through clenched teeth. "Our deal wasn't for you to think. The deal was for you to bring. Simple as that. If I needed someone to think, I wouldn't have involved you." She clicked the case shut and then put it in her evening bag. "Come with me. We've got work to do."

"I thought we were done. I gave you what you wanted."

"There you go thinking again. Not your best look. If you've compromised everything with your ideas . . . You'd better pray you've not."

"Or?"

"Our deal will be off."

"But, you promised you'd give me the materials that would clear my ancestor's name."

Hattie inched closer to Maspero. "If you've messed this up, your dead ancestor will be the least of your worries. In fact, I can arrange for you to meet him."

Maspero managed to go a shade paler, verging on translucent.

"We have mummies to find, but we might as well start here with Ramses II. Now, I want you to listen carefully, and I will tell you exactly what we will do. We will locate specific mummies. You'll run interference should anyone approach us while I empty a vial of the liquid you brought onto their lips."

"Wait a minute . . . you want me to do what?" Maspero crossed his arms and huffed indignantly. "I don't know what type of ridiculous New Age hocus-pocus you are into, but I didn't sign up for this. You enlisted me to bring you what you needed. That was my part of the deal. You can do whatever you want with it, but I won't in good conscience help you introduce a foreign liquid onto the mummies of thousands-of-years-old pharaohs. Whoever it is you think you are dealing with—you are mistaken." With a huff he turned to walk away.

Hattie grabbed his arm. His eyes flashed with surprise at the incredible strength of her grip clamping down on his fragile mortal frame. She smiled pleasantly at him. "You will do as I ask. I know exactly who you are. A thief, of the worst kind, someone who would steal from his people. I know of a hundred and one ways to burn you on this. You better smile now. I think others in the room are starting to take note of our conversation."

An uneasy smile crept across his face. "As soon as we are done with this fool's errand, you will give me the information we bargained for, right?"

"Of course." Hattie never had any intention of honoring her end of the deal. She didn't possess the information he wanted, but she knew enough about his ancestor to make it appear as if she did to reel Maspero in. He had been an easy target and was still useful. "When I am certain you've not disabled the magic by rehousing the fluid. Then and only then will I give you what you asked."

"And when will that be?"

"As long as it takes. Of course, I'll need to get my crystals and aura aligned first," she quipped.

Maspero's eyebrows knitted together as if he was trying to divine her tone as serious or sarcastic. Hattie left his side and went to the mummified body of Ramses the Great. She retrieved the cigarette case and pulled out a vial. "No one is looking now, but if someone comes by, start up a conversation."

"About what?"

"I'm sure you'll conjure up something interesting to talk about. Think of it as an opportunity to use all your fancy degrees."

Hattie gazed into the coffin next to her, taking notice of Ramses' serene expression frozen in time by the alchemy of the embalmer's art. His arms were crossed over his chest as if he were still holding the crook and flail of kingship. The liquid Maspero had acquired for her was the Tears of Isis, one of the most powerful magical substances in existence. She uncorked the first vial and poured the shimmering pearly liquid onto the valley of his mummified, pursed lips. It streamed down each side of his face, giving him the undignified look of a prolific nighttime drooler. Traces of the magical liquid vanished instantaneously.

She looked up from her work. Maspero was doing his meager best to try and look nonchalant. "One down and nine to go. Next on my list are Thuthmosis I, II, and III." Hattie led him away toward the other mummies. He followed her like an obedient servant as they wove through the display of king-filled coffins. She searched for the remains of her father, brother-husband, and nephew-stepson.

Maspero quickened his pace to keep up with her long strides. "What exactly are you trying to accomplish with this dabbing?"

"That information is way above your pay grade. Keep an eye out for the Thuthmosid kings."

Maspero halted at a coffin to his left. "How about Hatshepsut? She's right here."

Hattie peered down at the body stretched out before her who was most definitely not her. A wave of sadness and loss washed over her at the memory of the person who lay before her. It was her dear lady-in-waiting, Nefer-Ra. Her sudden demise was simultaneously earth-shattering and convenient. That day Hatshepsut decided to change her life's path from a mortal pharaoh ruling the red and black lands to an immortal in a state of self-exile.

She had grown tired of the ins and outs of ruling her homeland. Her nephew-stepson Thuthmosis III was ready to rule. She had no desire to step aside and become irrelevant. Nor did she anxiously await her so-called glorious reward in the Netherworld, which would equate to spending an eternity with a bunch of patriarchal blowhards who firmly believed a woman could never be an acceptable ruler.

Hatshepsut escaped both fates with the help of a young

magical protégé who was apprenticing for her high priest. He wore the sidelock of youth and trailed behind her like a palace kitten. It didn't take much, only the promise of a fun game, to get him to create a strong glamour upon the lady-in-waiting. It made her appear to be Hatshepsut to all who laid eyes upon her from the moment the spell was cast through her mummification and entombment. This allowed her the freedom to flee the country of her ancestors and find the flame of immortality. She never intended to return as she promised him. Hatshepsut knew the youth's participation alone would buy his silence. Who would ever admit to such a heinous crime? She had an inkling of guilt at using his innocence, but years later as a powerful magician, he found a way to turn that painful screw back on her. "Let's move on to the others."

"But you said you wanted the Thuthmosid Kings. She ruled as a king, you know. Shouldn't you include her? I would think, you being a woman and all, you would count her in that column."

Hattie despised having her own life mansplained to her, which she found happened frequently in academic circles by unwitting professors of the male persuasion. "You are thinking again. I would suggest—"

"Maspero?" A tiny woman decked out like a campy fifties housewife dolled up for a fancy cocktail party swept in with a cloud of perfume permeating the area around them.

The odd little man went from shocked to noticeably uncomfortable in a flash. "Why Gini, how is it you are here?"

"I was wondering the same of you. Tell me, Maspero, who is this divine creature with you? You'll have to introduce us." The woman looked at the mummy before them. "Oh, Hatshepsut." She smiled up at Hattie. "One of my absolute favorites of the ancient ones. Girl power and all, you know." The woman didn't stop to breathe and barreled on. "I do so love your beaded dress, dear, a little risqué for me. Where did you have it made?"

Maspero crossed his arms and scowled. "Gini, might I introduce you to Hattie Shepard the CEO of—"

"Shepard's Antiques and Auction House. I know of you," said Gini.

Hattie shook the hand of the odoriferous vision standing before her. She caught a slight whiff of the immortal. Her pulse quickened at the threat of discovery. "You have me at a disadvantage."

"Sorry, Gini T. is my name. I'm the librarian of the Chicago House in Luxor."

"Glad to have met you. If you'll please excuse us, the director of the antiquities department is expecting us."

A sly smile pulled across Gini's face. "Of course, it's never a good idea to keep him waiting."

Hattie made a mental note to do some research into this librarian when she had the time. It wouldn't be a bad idea to get an understanding of how large the breach might be to her current identity. "It was great to meet you. If we hurry, we won't be too late."

Maspero stood like a startled white rabbit. Hattie took him by the arm and led him through the now packed exhibition space toward a ramp leading to the lower level, where the director was holding court. "We'll have to pop downstairs and make an appearance to the director. We can part ways here, to keep your reputation intact, but keep a sharp eye for when I head back upstairs. When I return we can continue with the anointing."

"You can't be seriously thinking of continuing with this."

"Don't worry your pretty little head about the particulars, Maspero. We have work to do."

CHAPTER TWO

Boxes and packing materials were strewn around Buxton's office as if a hurricane had blown into the basement of the Metropolitan Museum of Art. The cause of the disorder was far less interesting and far more depressing. If Alex were in a glass-half-full mood, she would think of this as a fresh start, a new beginning. However, today felt anything but. KHNM was ordered by the Gods to vacate the headquarters they'd inhabited for over fifty years—by midnight. Not exactly a situation that seeded optimism. The legal order issued by the Gods' law firm bearing the grim news had just arrived that morning. And if the move wasn't enough of a downer, as of six o'clock in the evening, the agency still had no idea where they were relocating to.

The situation was not only a bureaucratic headache, but also an extremely dangerous one. Over the centuries the Keepers of the Holy and Noble Maat amassed magical artifacts and hadn't done a great job of keeping track of them. The thought of such a rushed job in locating and packing all the objects in the New York office felt like a disaster waiting to happen. Everyone was on tenterhooks, including Alex. As she moved through the process of trying to gather everything, she couldn't stop the thought train of terrible things she knew could occur. The possibility of an artifact falling into the wrong hands or a mishandled object with undiscovered powers blowing someone to bits or magically turning them into a ushabti was disturbing, to say the least. Alex couldn't decide which scenario was worse, but those worries combined with the fact they didn't yet have a place to put everything made her feel like she was traveling between Scylla and Charybdis on a sinking ship about to catch fire.

Everyone in the room hurried around packing what they could before the allotted time ran out. A strange sense of déjà vu crept up on Alex. It wasn't too long ago that she stood at the same spot packing her mentor's personal effects when he was presumed dead.

The elderly director of KHNM was carefully wrapping the powerful artifacts he kept a personal watch over for decades. They were stored in his magically warded and deceptively elegant curio cabinet. Luke, the agency's archivist, was observing Buxton's actions closely while taking quick inventory notes. Aside from the positives of Buxton not being dead or held captive by a power-hungry magician as in the recent past, the mood of the room was particularly glum.

Bruce, the Met's maintenance man, and coerced sentinel, stood by the office door. His usual easy smile and open friendliness were replaced with the pained discomfort of having to monitor his friends while they prepared for their departure like common white-collar criminals. The Metropolitan Museum of Art was sad to see their strange and secretive friends pushed out of their facility. The Met hadn't taken too kindly to being told by the powerful attorneys hired by the Gods that they would be expected to, under threat of liability, witness the agency's hasty departure. The museum skirted a fine edge of the command. Instead of using their security guards for the distasteful job, they assigned the friendlier option of Bruce to oversee it.

Alex walked to the cabinet Buxton and Luke were working on. "So much to do with such little time."

Buxton set down a small blue faience Osiris statue and grabbed some archival packing materials. "That reminds me, Luke. Did I ask you to get a hold of Ms. Winifred?"

"You mean the registrar of the European branch?" asked Alex. She had never met Ms. Winifred, but she heard wild stories about the spicy registrar. It struck Alex as odd that Buxton wouldn't have called her himself.

"The very same." Buxton carefully wound the small figurine in soft gauze. He nodded toward Luke. "One ushabti, faience, in the form of the God Osiris, powers unknown."

Luke moved his pencil down the list on his clipboard. "Check. No, you didn't, but I can give her a ring."

"Confound it. I thought I had. There's just been so much going on." The old man set the ushabti down and sighed. "She'll need to charter a jet to get the artifacts from the European branch to wherever we are moving to. Also, I need her to come with them. With the rush we are in, proper care is not being taken. We'll need her expertise to sort everything out once we arrive at our hypothetical new storage facility." Buxton dusted off a large velvet box as he spoke. Its hinges creaked with age as he opened it. Inside lay a glorious golden diadem with the head of a cobra as if frozen in motion as it readied to strike. Radiating from the cobra figure were embedded bands of lapis lazuli, carnelian, and turquoise. "Cleopatra's crown, gold and mixed semiprecious stones, powers awesome, requiring powerful containments."

Luke ticked another box on his clipboard. "Double check."

"Have you heard anything further on a place for us to store all this? I mean aside from the local self-storage area down the street?" asked Alex. The Met graciously offered the use of one of their storage facilities. Although their spaces had an acceptable level of security, it wouldn't do to have powerful magical artifacts within reach of civilian mortals.

Buxton sighed. "No such luck. Gwen is following up on a lead with one of Jorge's old contacts."

Gwen. Another complication Alex didn't want to think about. She never understood how Buxton was so willing to trust her. It was a short blip ago Gwen was in league against the agency. She, along with her recently dead boyfriend, Jorge, and the magician Idris Niru, had attempted to hoard and wield powerful ancient magic. It didn't help the situation that Alex played a leading role in Jorge's demise. Although, if looked at through a clear lens unclouded by emotion, Jorge sacrificed himself for Gwen. Alex was merely a cog in the clockwork of fate that moved Jorge toward the moment of his death. If anyone was to blame, it was his partner Idris. But Gwen would never see it that way. Whenever Alex was near Gwen, she could feel the anger and hatred radiating from her like a bright flame. However, Buxton asked Alex to trust him in the matter. She would do her best, but her mind wasn't free of lingering doubts. "Where should I start?"

"Luke and I can finish packing my office. Why don't you go to the machine room and help Thorne and the others there? All the shattered pieces must be closely accounted for."

The small annoyances were piling up. The last thing Alex wanted on this day of days was to have to deal with Buxton's assistant, Dr. Roberta Thorne. Their relationship was always prickly. It slightly smoothed out when Alex was her boss as interim director while Buxton was missing. Alex shot a knowing glance at Luke in the hopes he might jump in like a knight in shining armor and save her from the perils of Thorne. All she received in return was a mischievous smirk.

"You know where to find me if you need help with anything," she said hopefully as she turned and walked to the door. Bruce was standing at his post by the doorway acting as overseer of the works. His expression softened as she came close. This had to be hard on him. As a maintenance man and a daily familiar face, he was a great friend to them.

"Oh, Alex," Buxton called out.

Alex turned to him, hope rising for a reassignment.

"I almost forgot. The litigants are sending two observers to watch over us as we move and store our goods. I believe they should be here any moment."

"The litigants" was Buxton's code for the Egyptian Gods when they were in mixed company. Mortals like Bruce had no idea of the work KHNM did or about the literal existence of the Gods. "Do you know who they are sending?" Alex could think of a few possibilities, some more pleasant than others.

"As per usual, they were quite opaque. I'm sure all will be revealed in short order. If they show up in the machine room, please send them here. I have a few things to say about this observation process."

The so-called machine room was a large hidden space underneath the Met. It was a KHNM-only portion of the square footage they occupied at the museum. In the lingo of KHNM and its agents, the space was known as the God machine room. It was built at the same time the Temple of Dendur was installed at the Met in the 1970s. The cavernous space was cut from the granite layers below the museum before the temple was installed. This underground structure held the most powerful object in KHNM's care—a containment system that once held the Egyptian Gods' remaining powers when they walked the earth as Immortals. It now lay as a shattered mess. The destruction stemmed from a bungled thievery attempt by Jorge and his accomplice Idris Niru in their pursuit of magics more powerful than they, or anyone but the Gods, had a right to. It was up to KHNM to figure out what to do with the heavily coated magical shards.

"Okay, boss." Alex made a mock salute to Buxton and turned right into Gwen.

The redhead was flushed and breathless with excitement. She pushed past Alex and moved toward Buxton. "My connection panned out. We have a place to store everything. And it might work for a long-term commitment."

Buxton set down the object he was holding. His expression relaxed a little. "Just in the nick of time. Where is this place?"

"It's a little patch of desert due north of Las Vegas—Area 51."

CHAPTER THREE

H attie gazed up at the great sky Goddess Nut's celestial body arcing over the dome of night and decked out in brilliant shimmering stars. The blessed waters of the Nile lapped against the small skiff Hattie and her two servants occupied. An evening breeze whispered across her lotus oil–drenched linen shift, causing her to shiver. She breathed in deep, feeling alive and full of hope for the first time in a long time.

It had been ages since she donned the ceremonial garb of a priestess. A large gold collar necklace embedded with lapis lazuli, turquoise, and carnelian rested heavily against her skin. It was the one her father gave her when she entered the Temple of Amun for the first time in her ritualistic role as the God's Wife. It was so large and ostentatious that modern eyes would glaze over the fine workmanship and assume it was fake.

Hattie chose this traditional ensemble in the hope that paying homage to the Goddess Satis, with all the proper respects, might amplify her case. It was a logical choice to come to Satis's most sacred site on Elephantine island and attempt to wake her beloveds. Stories from the time before humans tell of how Satis stole the heart of the God Khnum from his consort, the Goddess Hehet, the Goddess who aligned herself with the Pharaoh Smendes in banishing Hattie's beloveds. If any God or Goddess might be amenable to undoing this spell, it would be Satis, Goddess of the Nile, Huntress, and eternal foe of Hehet.

. The clothing would serve her well if they were caught breaking into the temple located on the small island in the middle of the Nile, surrounded by the modern city of Aswan. The ultrasheer fabric showcased Hattie's shapely body beneath, which the male guards would be ill-equipped to ignore. Her ensemble could give her suitable camouflage hinting at a less than serious trespass, allowing them to think she was just another well-heeled tourist espousing "cute" New Age tendencies.

Tonight, everything had to go according to plan. After countless disappointments and failures, only two things stood in her way. The magic and the moment. Did the Tears of Isis she and Maspero anointed the mummies with still possess their ancient powers although they'd been transferred into vessels corrupted by the modern world? Even if the primordial magic within the tears was still potent when she had anointed the selected mummies, would tonight's spell magically connect to them? Then there was the other issue of them successfully breaking into the ancient sacred temple of Satis undetected.

At her feet lay a burlap sack. A small twitch came from within. It held the slumbering juvenile gazelle she stalked earlier. Poison from the arrow she used was slowly spreading through its young body, ensuring a peaceful and painless sacrifice.

"Mistress, ready yourself for landfall." Hattie's porter Thabit stood tall and proud near the edge of the small craft as he navigated them toward Elephantine island.

He and his muscular twin brother, Zuberi, Hattie's steward, made her existence easy and pleasurable in countless ways. Given to her as a gift many years ago, they were once stone sculptures carved when the Romans ruled a grand empire. Their finely sculpted bodies had been animated with conjured souls. It was lucky for her they were not made of older Egyptian statues, as the styles of her time were stiff and undefined. Both Zuberi and Thabit were so realistically rendered that they could pass as mortal-born humans. Their endless devotion to her and unwavering loyalty was as deep as the quarry from which they were unearthed.

Zuberi cut the engine close to shore and then slipped the anchor into the water. Once the boat was secured, both men slid soundlessly into the Nile. Thabit reached the edge of the boat and gently grabbed the burlap sack with the slumbering gazelle and carried it to the shore.

Zuberi waded toward Hattie. He held his arms out like a muscular bench for Hattie to slip herself onto. Grabbing his shoulder for support, she swung herself sideways into his arms. His hand curled protectively over her thigh, holding her steady as he waded to the ancient nilometer yawning down into the water. Her dangling toes dipped into the holy river. A sense of comfort washed over her. Could it be a sign the Goddess Satis would be on her side tonight?

Hattie rested her head against Zuberi's broad chest, inhaling the familiar metallic scent of earth and stone. A flame of desire lit within her as she recalled his divine offerings from earlier in the day. She wondered whether, if she was successful in restoring her beloveds to their afterlife, Senenmut would approve this arrangement she had with Zuberi and Thabit. Hattie wasn't sure it mattered anymore. She still loved him, and always would, but she wasn't certain their passion could survive a couple thousand years of separation.

In the time before Senenmut's Ba was banished from the afterlife, Hattie would meet him in the space between the mortal and immortal realms. Immediately after his Ba was severed, she moved heaven and earth to try to get those meetings back, but over time her concern became less of an obsession to regain what was, and more of a need to set her beloveds free from their after-life banishment.

If all went as planned tonight, Senenmut would come to her in the in-between world, but she wasn't sure what would happen when they saw each other—if anything.

Zuberi gently lowered her onto the upward sloping nilometer that stretched from the riverbank to the temple site above. Hattie glanced at the night sky as she ambled up timeworn stairs, steadying herself against its stone walls. Her hands rubbed against the ancient rough grooves that were used to measure each year's inundation levels of the mighty Nile, informing the priesthood how fat or lean the year's harvest would be.

The entire island was an active archaeological site as well as an open-air museum for tour groups during operating hours. Scattered along its small acreage were ruins of temples spanning thousands of years. The sacred space they were visiting was in the heart of it all, as it was built in predynastic times. The site was closed, but Hattie knew she couldn't count on that alone. Some dedicated Egyptologist might be working late.

Hattie motioned for the brothers to come close. "You two walk ahead of me and make sure no one is around. If all is clear, make the sound of a hoopoe." It was the call of a marsh bird they used frequently to signal one another.

She waited for their call in the narrow corridor. Two familiar all-clear coos filled the night air. Hattie caught up to them at a metal security gate. They had already broken the lock. It made a yawning sound as Zuberi pulled it open. They froze in place. Hattie's ears strained to hear any stirrings close at hand.

Zuberi motioned his brother through. Thabit carried the large sack with reverence in honor of the sacred offering within.

Hattie followed the sand and rock-strewn pathway to another small metal door protecting the subterranean predynastic sanctuary. This was a temple built by the worshipers of the early Egyptian faith before the kingdom had come into its full power. The cultic niche embraced three large red granite boulders lying in situ. The ancient ones believed that within this sacred spot lay the mythical source of the life-giving Nile.

Hattie had visited this temple as a princess, priestess, queen, and king. She built her temple above it when she ruled as pharaoh. A sense of disjointedness settled over her at the strange reality of having once ruled and worshiped in this sacred chamber and now being barred by a locked door put in place by mortals to whom this space did not belong. This place was built long before the pharaohs ruled. The ancient worshipers of the Goddess Satis, the personification of the Nile, built this altar as a mud-brick enclosure for their adoration of the Goddess. Over the centuries this ancient place of worship became buried in sand and forgotten.

While Zuberi worked at the chain with a hacksaw, Thabit gently laid his burden down and then tugged at the metal door. Their awesome strength would make quick work of opening the secured door.

Hattie walked to the end of the corridor to check and make sure they were still alone and undiscovered. The moon was high and bright in the sky. Its light gave a silvery-blue glow to the landscape around her. A gentle breeze blew in from the north, filling her nostrils with its sweet smell. *May this night be blessed.*

A loud clang startled her.

"Come, mistress, it is time." Thabit was at her side. He hooked his arm in hers and led her into the small temple. Passing by the first massive boulder jutting into the space, she rubbed her hand over the rough surface and felt the powerful ancient magic within. The spiritual residue of five thousand years of worship in this small and unassuming place was astoundingly thick. The next stone didn't push out into the space as far as the first boulder and was fronted by the holy altar that was inscribed with sacred hieroglyphs all along its edge. The altar looked like a large stela whose core was carved out, resembling an upended elongated horseshoe. Fronting the altar lay a mud-brick offering table. The third and last of the large, rounded boulders stood apart a bit from the middle altar stone. In ancient times water from the Nile flowed into the sanctuary through the gap between the altar stone and this one.

Hattie turned to Thabit. "Bring in the sacrifice and place it on the altar."

Zuberi helped his brother extract the small dying creature from the burlap sack and with great reverence placed it on the altar. Both men backed away from it, heads lowered.

Hattie walked over and checked its pulse. It was very weak. She didn't have much time before it crossed to the other side on its own. "I need you to stand guard while I call to the Goddess. No one can interrupt. If someone tries, you must stop them by any means."

Zuberi and Thabit put their hands over their hearts and dipped their heads in silent acknowledgment, then exited the sanctuary. Hattie hoped their defensive services would not be needed and the gazelle would be the only necessary sacrifice tonight. She didn't relish offering up this small creature to the Goddess, but she knew if the Goddess smiled upon the offering, the fawn would move on to a glorious afterlife in the Field of Reeds and run wild in the Immortals' benevolent company.

Kneeling before the altar Hattie cleared her mind and navigated her thoughts toward the golden path singing through her royal blood—an immediate connection to the Gods. She laid her hands on the red granite stone before her, feeling the magic pulse beneath its surface. Losing herself in the rhythm, she was drawn deep into its power like a great Benu bird to its own flame of renewal. The comforting warmth of magic spread from her extremities and poured into her core, filling her completely. A gentle tug at her heart formed a thread that twined up to her mind, weaving her consciousness with the fabric of the immortal. "Oh Goddess Satis, Mistress of Elephantine, She Who Runs Like an Arrow, and Goddess of the great and mighty Nile, she who drew the mighty Khnum's desire away from the primordial Goddess Hehet . . . hear this call."

The happy sound of trickling water filled the air. Hattie opened her eyes as water slowly burbled into the chamber through the gap between the rocks. The water pooled near her held an otherworldly shimmer, as if a film of crushed diamonds floated along its surface. She cupped a small amount in her hand; the electric prickle of magic played against her skin. Holding the liquid over the gazelle, she dipped her fingers in and sprinkled the creature with it. She reached into a small leather sheath strapped to her side and pulled out a gold-hilted obsidian blade. Inhaling deeply, she filled her lungs with the heady scent of the Goddess, whose sacred presence filled the room, then pulled the sharp edge across the soft fur of the gazelle's neck.

Its blood spilled out, mingling with the water. "O Goddess near, She Who Pours, Mistress of Elephantine, She Who Shoots Arrows, Protector of the Pharaoh and the Southern Border, please accept the honored offering of this young gazelle. May it be a boon to you in the Field of Reeds, where you preside. May it grow, thrive, and frolic in your keeping and bring you joy for eternity."

A wisp of opalescent essence drifted up from the gazelle's wound, forming into a shimmering doe. It glanced at Hattie and then bounded into the divide where the water had come from.

A spark of hope sprung in Hattie's chest. The goddess had accepted the offering and was listening. This long journey might finally be resolved. "O great and Immortal one, I ask you to unmake a spell. A spell conjured by the Goddess Hehet through her priestess many seasons ago. A spell most unholy in the sacrilege of denying eternity to the just and noble worshipers of Maat. I have anointed those wronged with the Tears of Isis. Please, Goddess, restore and repair their Ba-souls so they may return to their rightful place in the Field of Reeds and so you may best your rival for Khnum's love once more."

The warm energy within her ignited to a bright intensity, making her heart feel as if it could burst from an impossible amount of joy. A faint golden haze formed into a likeness of the Goddess in the niche of the altar and then blinked into nothingness. Hattie sat back on her heels as the water retreated through a narrow gap in between the rocks. The coolness of the small sanctuary enveloped Hattie; the Goddess was gone.

Hattie called Zuberi and Thabit inside. They collected the mortal flesh of the gazelle and carried it to the boat. Once they arrived at the dahabeeyah, they would sail to a remote location, unseen by others, and give it a proper burial.

As she boarded the small boat, Hattie was certain the Goddess had heard her, but had she been successful in freeing her beloveds, or would they continue to be trapped in the curse keeping them in the eternal void?

CHAPTER FOUR

A fter leaving Buxton's office, Alex strode through the museum to the place where the God machine was held, underneath Dendur Temple. She walked down the gently sloping ramp leading to the giant jewel box that protected the temple from the elements with its numerous glass panes.

Outside, dusk was starting to fall over Central Park. The sandstone temple looked peaceful painted in the soft hues of the dying day. It was after hours and unlike many nights throughout the year, the Metropolitan Museum of Art hadn't rented this space for a corporate party or gala. It was at least one lucky thing for KHNM as they were hours away from the God-imposed deadline to vacate the premises. It wouldn't do for their enforced move to be witnessed by civilians.

The temple was a gift to the United States in 1965 from the Egyptian government. They wanted to thank the nation for the help it provided with moving several ancient temples to higher ground before the Aswan High Dam was completed. It took some time to find a home for this enormous gift. The Met built this space and installed the temple brick by brick in this custom built enclosure.

At the time KHNM was greasing the wheels of this process on both continents to locate the tomb here at the Met. The massive building project would allow KHNM to donate a large sum toward the construction, allowing the agency to build a subterranean storage place for the God machine underneath the temple.

The God machine had been in Egypt since its creation. This took place during a time in ancient history when the religion and language of Egypt were dying, and the Gods were losing their power. To stave off ever-diminishing powers, the Gods decided to store what remained in a magical orb and walk amongst humanity as Immortals. KHNM, the Keepers of the Holy and Noble Maat, was created to keep the Immortals in check as they lived in the mortal realm. Over time, they were drawn to places in which their worship could revive them. Eventually, they ended up relocating to the United States, where there was a constant enough interest in the Egyptian Gods to keep their names alive, feeding their power. England and Germany were close to the top but didn't have the population to support as comfortable of an existence for the Immortals. The gift of this temple to the Met was a great cover for the move to take place.

Alex walked past the reflecting pool that wrapped around the temple and toward the platform upon which it stood. She remembered the first time she was there with Buxton. It wasn't too long ago that the magical world of KHNM and the Egyptian Gods were an unknown universe to her. It was shocking to think how much her life had changed since then, after only a relatively small amount of time had passed.

She reached for her djed pillar pendant as she neared the small pylon in front of the temple, rubbing her fingers over the horizontal lines depicting the spine of Osiris. It was a symbol of strength in ancient Egypt, but this one was a magical keycard of sorts. This wasn't the pendant her father gave to her as a child. That one was magically reclaimed when she used it to unlock a portal to the Netherworld in Abydos. The sacrifice of the last physical tie to her father was hard to make, but it had to be done. The whole of humanity was at stake. This djed pillar was a replacement key the agency made for her so she could access the God machine room.

She gazed at the ancient stones of the pylon towering over-head, then closed her eyes and said the required words. "Khnum, Creator of Man, Lord of the Crocodiles, keep me safe." The familiar jolt of energy shot through her. She opened her eyes and scanned the cavernous space she found herself in, hewn from the granite layer below the Big Apple. In the center was where the once-pulsating God machine was housed. When it held the power of all the ancient Egyptian Gods, it looked like a giant plasma ball. Now it was a broken globe encased in scaffolding and sealed off as workers in bright-orange magical hazmat suits broke it apart into manageable pieces. It wasn't the ideal way to handle magically saturated material, but they were running out of time.

The state of the God machine was caused by Jorge Trinculo and his partner, the immortal magician Idris Niru, who damaged it in their pursuit of its great power. In hindsight, KHNM should probably be giving thanks to Jorge for breaking it. It would be much easier to pack the small pieces than the machine's massive original form.

The thought of Idris sent a rush of anxiety through Alex. The stress didn't stem from the magician himself, but from the fact that he was currently trapped in the primordial book of magic. The book of magic she borrowed from its guardians. Guardians who also happened to be Alex's ancestors. If the book wasn't returned to its home in the lost oasis in a fortnight, its powerful magic would be lost forever.

Disappointing her newly found ancestors was certainly troubling, and there was no way Alex wanted to go down in the history of the lineage as the bumbling fool who lost one of the primordial books of magic, but that wasn't what scared her most about ruining the book for all eternity. It was one of the four books made when the mound of creation rose from chaos. It was the book of water magic. Water is life for every life-form on this planet. If the book wasn't returned in time, the repercussions for humanity could be devastating.

The sands of time were diminishing quickly. Alex had brought up the subject several times with Buxton, but he insisted the move was an all-hands-on-deck situation. He framed it as a potential sacrifice of one magical object for the many under KHNM's protection. Alex would have to bring it up again before leaving New York. She needed to make it clear just how important it was that she go to Egypt once they arrived at Area 51. If the answer was still no, she would go anyway, whether Buxton liked it or not. It was the least she could do to honor the promise she made to her ancestors.

A sharp crack made Alex turn. Luke and Gwen arrived.

"I thought you were helping Buxton, Luke."

Luke untucked a clipboard from his arm. "He sent us here to supervise the logging and packing of the shards. Now we know where we are going, he has gotten a second wind, thinking he can finish his office on his own. Buxton is worried that the recovery of the shards is taking too long. He figured Thorne and the others could use the help."

Alex bristled at the fact Buxton sent Gwen, a veritable civilian, to help with the hazardous magical material—and to supervise no less. Alex didn't trust Gwen's intentions. She was willing to guess her purported desire to help KHNM was a façade, no matter what Buxton said. KHNM had caused her great pain. Her interest in the agency seemed more of a Trojan horse.

Luke ran his hand through his wavy blond hair. "On the way from Buxton's office, I was trying to explain to Gwen about the God machine. Apparently, Idris didn't share the history of it."

Gwen folded her arms across her chest. "Oh, I don't know, Luke. I think you did a fine job at explaining it."

Alex shifted her gaze to the God machine. "We should see how the demo is coming. It doesn't look half done."

Alex led them toward the large tent in the middle of the space.

"Thorne called Buxton's office saying it took them a while to figure out how to cleanly cut the material, but they were now moving more quickly. He sent us here to lend a hand and get the process moving faster now that they've got a rhythm down."

"You know we only have a few hours left before we need to vacate."

Luke nodded. "We wouldn't want any of this powerful magic to be left behind."

"It would be bad if any of it landed in the wrong hands, right?" asked Gwen.

Alex doubted Gwen possessed the capability to distinguish between who would qualify as right or wrong, given her past associations, but kept the thought to herself.

A bright light flashed from within the enclosed area. One of the orange-clad workers fell from the scaffolding.

Luke shoved his clipboard into Alex's hands. "You two stay put. If something went sideways, the fewer people in there the better." He charged off and darted into the tent.

Standing alone with Gwen made Alex wish she could have

followed Luke into the tent, whatever the danger inside might be.

"Alex, there is something I need to talk to you about."

"Anything." Gwen was paying the bills, after all.

Gwen looked into the distance. "I'll just speak plainly. I don't like you. Nor do I like your father. I never met him, but as you know, I have my reasons. What I'm going to say isn't an attempt to make nice. I think it would be best for us to stay clear of one another as much as is possible."

Alex pulled her hands behind her back and clasped them tightly. It seemed likely Gwen might say something Alex might take exception to. Buxton wouldn't like it if their benefactor ended up with a black eye. "Of course. Was that it? If so, I've got things I need to see to, and I'll do my best to stay out of your way."

"No. That is not all. You must understand, the only reason I am talking to you now is because of a promise. A promise I've made to Jorge. I would just as soon see you and your family burn for what you did. But this has to do with your dad—"

Luke appeared through the plastic barrier. "Everything is . . . okay." Luke's statement turned up into a question as he eyed the two of them. "One of the electric saws became stuck in the God machine shell. The friction created a brilliant combustion of magic, which propelled the worker backward. He's a little scraped up, but he'll be fine."

A sharp crack sounded again, making Alex jump. It came from the direction in which she arrived earlier. Buxton was flanked by Salima and Niles. Salima stood ramrod straight in her highly tailored business suit, while Niles slouched a bit in his. Of course they would be the ones the Gods would send to babysit the move.

Alex sighed. It was going to be one of those days when the

ghosts of yesterday reemerged to haunt your present. Being face to face with Niles in all his Godly perfection was the last thing she wanted to deal with today. Especially because he had ignored her since she last saw him. At the time, he was in the form of a bird flying across the Western Desert holding Aah-Ha the ushabti in his talons to return the little guy to his original master. As Niles flew past her there was a moment where she felt connected to him once more. She had been hopeful he would return to her from the Field of Reeds somehow, but when the dust cleared, he never did. If he cared for her as he professed to her father in the Netherworld, why hadn't he reached out to her in any way?

There were so many things left unsaid between them. That alone would have made this moment uncomfortable in the company of others, but adding the fact that the Gods, who were his family members, wanted her dead made it downright unbearable.

Niles was engaged in conversation with Buxton as they made their way over.

Alex quickly averted her gaze from Niles and landed on the other object of her discomfort, Salima. The last time they were together, they were standing atop a giant rearing snakehead Alex was battling in the Netherworld. A situation Salima may or may not have been instrumental in creating. At the time it was believed that Salima was working in the interest of KHNM to thwart her father, Re, in his attempt to kill the other Gods and hoard their power for himself. Alex always wondered if Salima had been working against KHNM the whole time. Alex would probably never know. Salima was a slippery beast. Just when you thought she was on your side, she would pull the rug out from under you—then return later to help beat the dirt from it.

Buxton firmly believed that Salima was true to the cause of

KHNM and that things would have been much worse without her intervention. It seemed Buxton had a personal blind spot in wanting to see the good in those around him. Was he duped by Salima? Had she been on the side of her father all along in his quest for power?

Ever since the Gods returned to the Field of Reeds, Alex had wondered from time to time what had happened to Salima after that last escapade. Did they lock her up for her participation in the murderous scheme? Did she serve any penance for helping her father Re try to kill them all to attain the Aten-hood? Or, as the fickle creatures they were, did they just let bygones be bygones and she saw no punishment? Alex wouldn't put it past them. They were fighting for the stabilization of their existence now. They would most likely justify almost anything to save their skins.

"A picture would last longer." Salima's tone dripped with disdain at Alex's apparently overlong gaze.

She was about to toss out a sharp barb at her old frenemy when Buxton touched her arm, signaling in his gentle way to suck it up.

"Glad I was able to catch up with the three of you. I was just bringing Niles and Salima around to see the progress we're making," said Buxton.

Niles reached out and shook Gwen's hand. "You must be Gwen. Buxton has told us much about you. It is great to finally meet you."

A red blush crept up Gwen's face. "And you must be the ever-notable Niles Greene. Or do you prefer to be called Thoth, now you've returned to the Field of Reeds?"

Damn his Godly good looks and charisma. His deep, rich voice sent a rush of gooseflesh across Alex's skin. Bringing forward the memory of that moonlit night at Luxor Temple, lips brushing against hers as he pulled her close . . .

"Niles is just fine. That's what my friends call me."

Gwen stifled a demure giggle, pulling Alex out of her reverie.

Luke suppressed a laugh by coughing loudly into his hand, then said, "Salima, Niles, Buxton mentioned that you would like to witness the work being done in cataloging the God machine fragments. If you'd like to follow me, I can show you the completed work so far."

A look of unease shadowed Niles's face. "Of course. Lead the way."

Luke took his charges to the plastic sheet covering the God machine as it was getting hacked apart. He held the tarp for Salima, who went through first. Niles took a backward glance at Alex before entering. His expression was unreadable as he ducked in.

Buxton looked at Alex knowingly. His warm brown eyes gave her comfort. He knew her pain. "Well, I guess I will leave you to it and finish packing my office. Gwen, could you come with me? After you left, a logistical snafu presented itself regarding the moving vans gaining access to the train depot to transfer the cargo. I think Alex and the rest will have this covered."

Gwen frowned at being pulled away, making Alex wonder if it was because she wanted to get her hands on the God machine, or because she was irritated she couldn't finish their conversation. "Of course."

Buxton and Gwen made their way to the portal.

Seeing Niles brought both good memories and bad feelings. She needed to find a way to get him alone to talk. Was she more like Buxton than she wanted to admit, believing too much in the goodness of those around her? Was the glimmer of love she felt for Niles only fool's gold?

She watched Gwen grab her djed pillar pendant and say the magic words that would transport her up to the exhibition space of Dendur Temple. She couldn't help but ponder how odd it was that Jorge's fiancée was KHNM's financier. Odder still was this mysterious conversation Gwen was so anxious to have. What on earth could Gwen want concerning her dead father?

CHAPTER FIVE

T habit and Zuberi prepared her bath with oils of cedar and myrrh to cleanse her body and spirit and wash away the magical residue from calling to the Goddess. Hattie relaxed into the tub of warm scented water. Zuberi knelt behind her, deftly massaging the tension from her shoulders, the enlivening scent of mint oil on his hands wafting up as he worked her flesh. Using magic depleted her. Over the years her boys learned how to get her in working order after a magical encounter with the Gods. Hattie leaned into his broad chest, closing her eyes as she breathed in deeply.

It was time to go to the in-between place to see if the Goddess Satis answered her call by repairing the severed Bas of her beloveds. It would be strange after so many centuries to see Senenmut again. Would he be waiting for her in their ancient and secret meeting place in Nut's celestial house? And what expectations would he have after being trapped in a void of nothingness for centuries? Would he see her as if they just parted yesterday, or would he have felt the passage of time like her?

Hattie had led many lives since she last saw him. She had no idea what to expect.

The in-between place was created by the Goddess Nut specifically for Hatshepsut and Senenmut. She took pity on Hatshepsut, who roamed the earth as an immortal, the former pharaoh who longed for her dead companion and lover. Nut understood what it was like living under a male-dominated system and sympathized with Hattie's choice to become immortal. Nut had existed in that same patriarchal system since the primeval mound rose from the waters of chaos. The Goddess recognized that, even with all her great accomplishments as king, Hatshepsut would always be an outsider, much like herself, who alone held up the heavens and was forever separated from her brother-husband, Geb. The creation of the celestial hideaway for Hattie and Senenmut had been a request the Goddess couldn't refuse, no matter the peril it might have put her in with the other Gods.

Long before Hatshepsut chose immortality, Nut had witnessed, from her dwelling in the heavens, Hatshepsut's struggles as she became princess, priestess, queen, and pharaoh. Witnessed her strengths and losses while fighting against the power of the men around her as they tried to tear her down. Nut knew all too well the contempt for female power that was embedded in their culture and the barriers and admonishments hurled at She-who-ruled-as-he.

As pharaoh, Hatshepsut always felt favored by the Goddess. Sometimes late at night she would wake from a deep slumber and wander onto her balcony as if called by the Goddess. Standing there under the brilliant shimmering starshine of the Goddess's heavenly body, she would make a silent prayer to Nut. Waves of warm energy would cascade through her, filling her body with the spiritual light of the benevolent Goddess.

Hatshepsut would return to her bed and sink into a deep sleep replete with glorious and beautiful dreams.

Hattie opened her eyes at the sound of a door opening. Thabit stood in front of the bath holding a large plush towel.

"Perfect timing." Hattie emerged from the warm embrace of water. A breeze drifted in from an open window, whispering across her skin and filling the room with the earthy scent of the Nile. Hattie steadied herself by holding on to his shoulder while exiting the massive tub. No sooner had her feet touched the plush rug than she was enveloped in a thick cocoon of a sumptuous and thirsty towel. Thabit gently worked at drying her off.

"Anything further you need from us tonight, mistress?" asked Zuberi. His voice held a suggestive and hopeful lilt as Thabit slipped her arms into her finest linen robe. If it were any other night, she would call them both to bed, but tonight was like no other night. Tonight, she would reunite with Senenmut.

If their love was eternal, as they professed countless times, it was possible once they gazed into each other's eyes that the years would peel away and things would go back to how they were. If their feelings hadn't survived the centuries, she hoped Senenmut would at least agree to be her link to her father in the Field of Reeds once their afterlife was restored.

Hattie walked past Zuberi to her bedchamber. "Please gather my star-net dress and have your brother fetch the blue lotus oil. I have a rendezvous tonight." Hattie wondered if Senenmut still had the old streak of jealousy she always found so tiresome.

At the wet bar she poured herself some chilled rose-scented water into a cut crystal glass, enjoying its delicate aroma as she took a sip. Sheer curtains between her suite and the private deck billowed inward, calling her toward them.

On a large balcony spanning the aft portion of the boat, Hattie leaned against the mahogany railing. She gazed at the night-darkened landscape stretching out before her. Silhouettes of palm trees were barely discernible in the distance. They looked like paper cutouts lining the great and mighty Nile. A deep love for her homeland welled up within her. In this remote location, far away from the glare of city lights, she could almost believe she stepped back in time, before cell phones, cars, and indoor plumbing.

The sounds of Zuberi and Thabit returning snapped Hattie out of her reverie. Thabit carried a vessel crafted from a hollowed-out gilded ostrich egg filled with lotus oil. Zuberi reverently held her dress across his forearms, its crystals sparkling brilliantly, betraying the powerful magic within.

It was knit by the Goddess Nut herself, made to help Hattie locate her secret lover's niche in the cosmos. The beads were made of celestial starshine woven into a fine netting that hugged Hattie's every curve. The millions of small crystals flashed with a fiery brilliance as if they were freshly plucked from the sky for this garment.

The boys joined Hattie on the balcony as she shed her robe. They set their burdens down and poured the rich scented oil onto their hands and rubbed it into her skin. The heady fragrance brought back many memories of the nights she spent with Senenmut.

Once they anointed her flesh, Hattie lifted her arms to receive the dress. The cool crystal beads scratched pleasantly against her skin as they slid down her body.

Zuberi bowed slightly to Hattie. It was endearing that after all they three had been through and done together, he still took his role as her steward seriously. "Anything more, mistress?"

"I need you both to guard my door tonight. My body will continue to rest in this bed as my Ba travels a great distance. No one may enter this room before I return to my body. When my journey is complete, I will emerge from the room to inform you."

"We will await your return, mistress," answered Zuberi. Both brothers turned and left the room.

It was time.

She left the deck and lay on the silk coverlet of her bed. It had been a long time since she performed the rite. Would she remember how? Hattie focused her mind on a vision of bright divine light, feeding it slowly from the well of her immortality. The bright glow sent a charge of magic through her, splicing an infinitesimal wedge between her physicality and her soul.

In her mind's eye, she could see her luminous spectral form start to separate from her body. She kept her focus laser sharp. This was the hardest part. When she would acknowledge and release the fear of her Ba never returning to her body, to trust it would return, then free it to rise into the cosmos. It was like trusting a wild and loved creature to return home. She filled her chest with air, imagining the breath within her body was supporting her Ba moving upward farther and farther, through the roof of the dahabeeyah and into the night sky.

Ecstatic joy filled her breast as she rose higher, pulling away from the Nile and the emerald-green fields bordering it. At this altitude, it looked like a finely made diorama. Her speed increased as she floated farther up. In the blink of an eye, she was looking at the African continent and then the blue, green, and white marble of Earth. The sharp metallic smell of ozone enlivened her as she flew upward.

Soon her feet landed on the velvet-soft pouch created by Nut in the heart of the Isis-Djamet, the constellation of a female hippopotamus. The Goddess located this secret tryst chamber there in a fit of humor. The constellation had long been associated with Isis of the moonlit night, mother of the festivals of the sky.

The celestial pocket was woven from strips cut from dense cosmic matter and stardust. Its surface resembled a soft black fabric covered with minuscule shimmering crystals. Hattie reveled in the spangled darkness around her. It had been a long time since she stood in the cosmos waiting for her lover. There was a little catch in her heart at the thought of the glorious times they had here. How they would fall into each other like two halves reunited with their whole. Once spent from making love, they would lie together, gazing at the universe, giggling and chatting like happy children.

She turned at a strange sound as her heart leaped in anticipation. Instead of her lover striding toward her, a large doorway appeared. It looked like ones she had seen in tomb paintings depicting a gateway to the afterlife. Above the door were two lions seated back to back with the hieroglyph for horizon separating the two regal cats. The symbol's shape resembled two rounded mountains with the sun rising in the valley between them.

Something was wrong. No one but herself, Senenmut, and the Goddess knew of this place.

The door creaked open. A wrinkled old man wearing a deep scowl stepped through the doorway that automatically slammed shut behind him. He threw a rough linen sheath dress at her. "Drop the whore's clothes. Put this on and follow me."

"Just who do you think you are, telling me what to do?" She kicked the garment resting against her feet. The man looked familiar. He possessed the proud bearing of a pharaoh, but that wasn't much help—so did ninety percent of the population of the Field of Reeds.

He was plainly irritated by her lack of recognition. "Your

honored elder. You might know me as the original uniter of the two mighty lands."

Hattie scrolled through her mental Rolodex of the three-thousand-year fraternity of pharaohs. "The first recorded smiter-in-chief?"

The old man puffed up with self-importance. What on earth was Narmer, the first king of the two lands, doing here? "How did you know how to find this place? Is Senenmut okay?"

He pointed at the garment near her feet. "Never mind about him. For now, he is . . . all right. Now She-who-ruled-as-he, I command you to replace your garment with the one I brought." He looked down his nose at her. "It would be untoward to travel in whatever it is you're wearing."

"And if I don't?"

"Your boyfriend will have his Ba wings re-clipped."

CHAPTER SIX

Alex sat in her well-appointed sleeper compartment. She had breathed a sigh of relief when the cargo was successfully loaded from the moving trucks onto the train the night before. Gwen had managed to arrange a private train, so both staff and the collateral could be moved together to their new temporary headquarters. This train would take them to the Las Vegas train yard, where they would pick up the cargo brought by Ms. Winifred from the European branch of KHNM. Just before the midnight deadline, Buxton was informed that the privately owned train was not authorized to enter the secured site of Area 51. They insisted both cargo loads would need to be transferred to a government-issued train for the final leg.

Yet another delay had put Alex on edge as if she were trapped inside an hourglass as the sand spilled over her. At least the train was making excellent time, and having made the decision to go no matter what gave her a sense of personal agency.

It wasn't surprising that Jorge, Gwen's dead lover, had a connection with both an old-money adventurer with an interest in high-speed trains who just happened to have a luxurious retrofitted train on hand or that Jorge also knew an Air Force general sympathetic to the agency's plight who was amenable to KHNM taking temporary residence at Area 51.

She leaned against the thick velvet pin-cushioned backrest which would be pulled down to make her bed by the attendants when she left for dinner. The ornate fabric was an eruption of intertwined florals in varying tones of green with gold highlights. She imagined it was inspired by a steam-heated Victorian conservatory packed with leafy exotic plants. Her roomette was paneled with rich dark wood that was punctuated by wall-mounted sconces dangling with crystals that formed mini chandeliers. The sun was setting on another day. The bright light caused brilliant tiny rainbows that refracted from the crystals and danced around the room.

Gazing across the desert landscape, Alex realized it was time she put on her big girl pants and left her room. She had done a good job all day at avoiding everyone since they loaded the train. As she had nowhere to go, Alex did her best to block out the thoughts of the book and luxuriate in having no commitments by sleeping in and taking her meals in her room. Everyone deserved a day off now and again, and she couldn't remember the last one she had.

Alex slept like the dead as of late, even with the stress of moving. The fact she was experiencing uninterrupted sleep was disappointing. She had hoped Niles would choose to meet up with her in her dreams, as in the past. She missed the pleasant tiredness after spending the night dipping and darting through the sky with him in their bird forms.

Recently the only odd sleep-related occurrence she experienced was waking with strange and random thoughts that felt like Egyptological-themed fortune cookie sayings. The one that greeted her this morning was a graphic dream of someone cutting out the tongue of a crocodile. Once the offending organ was completely removed, the dream morphed into a hieroglyphic text stating this was an adverse day, apparently for the God Sobek. Alex chalked it up to a subconscious mishmash; bits and pieces coming together to form a decidedly confusing output. Or maybe the universe was trying to tell her to stay in her room.

Putting superstitious musings behind her, Alex realized it was nearly dinnertime. She figured it was time to step out of her comfy cabin and into the emotional minefield that was waiting for her outside the confines of this small refuge. It wasn't like her to hide away from life issues, but between the continued opaque situation with Niles, Gwen's well-earned hatred of her, and Salima's past betrayals, the thought of facing any or all of them was overwhelming. The one person around who wasn't a challenge or heartbreak waiting to happen was Luke.

Alex exited her room, then pushed the button for turndown service and followed the narrow corridor toward the dining car. She grabbed the metal door handle and slid the door aside, entering the odd in-between area that joined the cars. This space gave Alex the willies—being able to see a small sliver of the rails and ground as they sped past filled her with vertigo. It was as if the fast-moving ground below could pull her to it by an unseen force.

As she stepped through the threshold, her sense of smell was assaulted by the industrial oil of the workings. Feeling a bit light-headed, she looked at her feet, paying close attention to not trip over the slightly raised lip between the two compartments. The door across from her slid open, drawing her attention to it. Damn it. Of course, it was Gwen.

"Oh, it's you." Gwen's tone was as if her path had crossed with a complete and utter heathen. But then again, it made perfect sense given her feelings for Alex.

Alex reached out to the strange accordion-like walls to steady herself against the swaying motion of the train. She blurted out the second thing that came to her. "Hey, Gwen. Great train." She added it to her future stupid things to say list. She guessed saying something stupid was better than something snarky.

"I am glad I ran into you. I've been keeping an eye out for you but have somehow managed to miss seeing you. I asked around and everyone assured me you made it on board before we departed."

Alex ignored the not-so-hidden insinuation that she should have been more visible during the train ride and wondered what made Gwen think it was her job to keep tabs on Alex. "I know we never had a chance to finish our conversation the other day. You had a question for me. Maybe we should step inside the salon?"

"No, here is great." A sly smile spread across Gwen's face as the no-man's-land they were standing in jostled from side to side.

"Go ahead."

"Jorge made a promise to your dad in the Netherworld. He swore if Phillip was able to get him and Buxton back to the mortal realm, he would spring for an ancient Egyptian burial. Replete with ushabtis and all the proper grave goods. Jorge has said no matter what he thought of Phillip . . . and his offspring, he was bound by his promise."

"Well, that is awfully—"

"If you say *sweet*, I'm going to knock your block off." Gwen's tone was all business. "I am only doing it because he asked me to."

The present tense of Gwen's words took a few clicks to sink in. Had she misspoken, or did she mean to talk about Jorge as if he were still alive? "But how is he asking you to do this? Now that he is, well . . . gone?"

Gwen glared at Alex through eyes filled with tears that were on the verge of erupting down her flushed face. "He visits me in my dreams. You wouldn't understand."

"You'd be surprised," Alex mumbled.

A sharp glint shone in Gwen's eyes like a temple cat who just cornered a mouse. "Of course, you've come back from the Netherworld too. Like Jorge did. So do you have dreams like these?"

Alex was mentally present enough to not flinch at the unexpected connection Gwen made between Alex and her return from the Netherworld. She was feeling off-balance suddenly, and it had nothing to do with the fact that they were standing in the unstable in-between. Gwen's knowing look sent shockwaves through Alex, making her wonder if Gwen knew about the price the Gods had put on Alex's head—death by the hands of Niles upon an appearance of a Netherworld power.

For Alex, there was no way Gwen could be trusted, regardless of whether she was true to KHNM or not, because of her unadulterated hatred for her. Gwen would always be a danger to her either way. If the news spread she was meeting Niles in her dreams and now having these new strange fortune cookie dreams . . . If it got back to the Gods, it would at the very least increase their monitoring of her, and in the worst-case scenario trigger her death sentence. "Uh, not me personally. I've heard of it through Akh-Hehet. I know she can have similar visitations." The words came out far less naturally than Alex would have liked.

Gwen tilted her head, as if she was trying to weigh the truth of what Alex said, then quickly changed the subject. "Think about Jorge's promise. I'll need to start making the arrangements soon if you decide to do it." She brushed past Alex and went into the sleeper car.

Standing in the wake of Gwen's departure, Alex was deeply troubled with dueling unpleasant thoughts. One had to do with the distinct possibility she may have given Gwen dangerous information to chew on. The other was broaching the subject of her father's reburial with her mother. After her father died, her mother did her best to hide Alex from KHNM's reach. As time progressed, and Alex joined the agency, her mother's hatred of the agency morphed from an overall denial of what KHNM did to seeing them as a group of delusional fools who put her daughter in dangerous situations. No matter how many times Alex tried to show her definitive proof of the magic and the Gods' existence, her mother would make up an alternate reason or explanation for it that reconfirmed her biases. Alex did her best to shake off both thoughts while moving through the bordello-red salon car. Passing through the exaggeratedly plush interior that screamed desperate Valentine's Day fantasy, she ruminated on how well her conversation with Gwen went.

The swanky dining room was muted compared to the salon car. It was drenched in hues of dark blue. Tasseled shades were pulled down against the darkening sky. A rectangular crystal chandelier ran the length of the car, sparkling in the lamplight as if the ceiling were open to the brilliant desert night sky.

Sitting in a large booth in the shape of a crescent moon was Luke. His elbows were resting on the oblong table with an ice bucket and the telltale orange label of Alex's favorite champagne next to him. Luke raised his glass in greeting. It was odd to see him sitting in this elegant room alone, save an entire bottle of champagne. His granola-bar-eating California-boy life ethic didn't embrace much drinking.

"What are you celebrating?" Alex slid into the booth.

"Would you like a glass?" He lifted his arm to call the waiter over.

Alex contemplated the chilled bottle. "Tonight is a night for bourbon."

The handlebar-mustachioed waiter nodded. "Buffalo Trace?"

Alex smiled. Of course that is what they would have on this train. "Please." Alex's gaze returned to Luke. "Really, why the Veuve? I don't see you as a party-of-one champagne drinker."

"Salima was here."

"Oh, that explains the cinnamon." Alex thought she smelt the fragrant and spicy aftermath of the Goddess-in-her-Immortal-form's wrath. The scent was strong; she must have left moments ago, or she was really angry. "Why was she angry? Usually, champagne has a way of cheering people up."

"Well, she was perfectly happy until she learned she needed to relieve Niles from a double shift of watch duty."

With perfect timing, the waiter slid a cut crystal glass with two fingers of a golden amber liquid in front of Alex. She took a deep pull of the fiery drink. "Oh shit. I completely forgot." Buxton had asked that she, Luke, Salima, and Niles take turns in keeping an eye on the cargo while in transit to the pickup point for the European cargo and on to Area 51. Alex was supposed to relieve Niles.

"Yeah, she was none too pleased with you. But then again, you always have a way of getting on her bad side."

"And which side is that?"

Luke raised his glass again and laughed. "All of them?"

Salima was the anthropomorphic form of the Goddess triad of Hathor, Sekhmet, and Bastet. Dealing with her was never a simple task. One constant Alex could always count on was Luke's sense of humor. His even-keeled approach to life was a breath of fresh air in the close quarters of inter-agency drama.

"I'll drink to that." Alex clinked her heavy cut-crystal low-ball glass against his delicate flute.

Leaning back, Luke ran his hand through his hair. "It was a shame she went storming off. We were actually having fun. I think the Veuve was working its magic until Gwen let it slip she was hanging out with Niles for quite a while in the cargo hold. He'd asked if Salima would relieve him."

Alex didn't like the way Luke said "quite a while." It made it sound like Niles and Gwen were making out in between the packing containers. There was a time not long ago when Luke made it clear he had feelings for Alex. Luke was a dear, kind, and hunky man, for an archivist—but she couldn't shake Niles out of her heart. Truth be told, she'd never really tried.

Luke's complexion was slightly flushed from the champagne, and his eyes took on a faraway stare as if he was trying to work out a mental puzzle. "You know, she was a lot of fun. I was enjoying her company for once. Before she stormed off, that is. I think I was about to crack the mystery of where she was all this time. Since she teamed up with her dear old dad and attempted to kill all the other Gods, I mean her family, and usurp their power."

"Well, hopefully you can resume that conversation with her another time. I'd like to know that myself. It is strange they would send criminal number one here from the Field of Reeds to keep an eye on the agency. I've often wondered if, in the capricious world of the Gods, she or Raymond ever paid a price for what they did. Maybe I'll never know. Too high above my pay grade. Speaking of which, I should probably go make nice with her."

"If I were you, I might let her cool down. She was pretty steamed." Luke chuckled. "Finish your drink, then go. You'll be thankful you did."

Alex took a sip. "Yeah, I hate the thought I let Buxton down. I don't know what I was thinking. As of late, I can easily get stuck within my own mind. Speaking of which, have you noticed Buxton acting a little distracted? I've chalked it up to the move, but maybe it goes deeper than that. The other day I had to tell him where his keys were, like a hundred times."

"You really don't know?"

"Luke, really?"

"It's Ms. Winifred."

"The registrar from the European headquarters? What about her would put him in such a state?"

"He's old, Alex, but not dead."

"You mean they . . . ?"

"Were an item some years back. I don't know the specifics other than there was a scandal that nobody, not even the gossipiest of KHNM agents, would speak of it, and I've never felt impertinent enough to ask. Buxton is such a private guy. I heard inferences it had to do with their age difference, but that would be less than scandalous. As soon as it was decided she would close up shop there and come to the US, Buxton has been acting like a flustered box of kittens."

"Is that why he is joining us later? Putting off the inevitable?" asked Alex.

"One can only guess. But as you know, he does have a lot on his plate. Who knows how accurate our insights and guesses might be into the heart of our dear old friend? Either way, he will have to face the music eventually. The European team will be meeting us at the switch-up point so we can load their artifacts before we head to Area 51. It is also rumored Ms. Winifred will be traveling with two of the hunky agents from Rome with whom she is rumored to be in a relationship. Apparently, they dropped everything to escort her to America."

"Awkward?" Alex tossed back the remainder of her bourbon. Her head was starting to swim in a warm and welcome way. "Wow, an actual KHNM thruple. Who would have thought? I had no idea this agency was so freewheeling. This Winifred sure gets around."

"Ms. Winifred to you. I hear she can be quite formal. Which is odd, as she is not much older than you and me. And by the way, that is a rather narrow and sexist viewpoint there, Alex."

"You're right, must be the bourbon talking. The heart wants what the heart wants, and who am I to judge? I hope this European trio doesn't break our dear friend's heart."

"Don't underestimate Buxton. He is tough as nails."

Alex stared into her empty glass as she rocked it along the curve of its bottom edge. "Speaking of tough critters, guess I should see what she-of-three has to say to me."

The waiter placed a BLT in front of Luke.

"BLT and champagne for dinner. Interesting way to roll, Luke." Alex slid out of the booth, then grabbed half of Luke's sandwich. "Promise me you'll forgive me if Salima kills me."

Luke winked at Alex as she turned and walked away.

Alex smiled to herself as she bit into the salty, bacony deliciousness. Maybe if Salima didn't kill her, she would return to the dining car for an actual meal. Grabbing the handle, she slid open the door to the red-velvet womb of the salon and walked to the cargo hold.

CHAPTER SEVEN

Hattie made Narmer turn his back as she slipped out of her star-crystal net dress and slipped the not-so-fine linen sheath over her head. She didn't do this due to a sense of modesty but in a desire to deny his leering eyes the pleasure of her glorious naked flesh. The dead pharaoh impatiently tapped his feet.

"You can turn around now."

Her face must have shown displeasure at the burlap sack–level quality of the garment Narmer provided. "What, too plain for you? Maybe I should have brought you a starched linen kilt and a smiting stick? Would that make you feel more powerful, princess?"

So this is how it's going to be.

This was the exact reason Hattie decided to forgo eternal life in the Field of Reeds, even if it meant spending eternity alone. By donning the traditional garb of the pharaoh and ruling as king, not queen, Hatshepsut acquired many haters, especially other pharaohs. It was Senenmut who warned her she might want to make a concerted search into the possibility of immortality over the afterlife. After he died and arrived in the Netherworld, he received a small taste of what she would be in for. Ancient Egypt was a highly conservative place, where originality and straying beyond the well-established lines weren't generally embraced. She broke one rule. A big rule. A woman should never be pharaoh. She made it more egregious by being good at it. Hatshepsut threatened their masculinity and power. So much so that they did their best to wipe any knowledge of her and her rule from the history books.

"That would have been great. But I'll make do." There was no way in hell she was going to let him know he had riled her up. She let his literally antiquated ideas of womanhood disappear in the ether of the thousands of years that separated their lives. Hattie adjusted the scratchy garment.

Narmer thrust his hand toward her. "Take my hand and don't let go, no matter what."

"Awwww, you care." Hattie tilted her head and blinked in an exaggerated manner, channeling her inner docile gazelle.

He stiffened and grabbed her hand. "Living in this modern world has somehow managed to make you even more disrespectful to your elders than you already were." Narmer opened the door with his other hand.

Waiting for them on the other side of the doorway was a golden boat resembling a ceremonial temple barque. Its body was shaped like an elongated crescent moon with a square shrine taking up the middle. The decorative ends of the boat fluted outward like stylized lotus blossoms. Instead of being made of papyri bundles, this boat appeared to be forged from pure gold, with inlays of ivory, carnelian, and turquoise. Flowing below was a silvery blue ribbon of a celestial river stretching out into the distance as far as Hattie could see.

As soon as they were both on the boat, the door slammed shut and disappeared.

Hattie wondered where this dead pharaoh was taking her. If the lions and the horizon symbol over the door were any indication, she guessed he was taking her to the Netherworld. Maybe Senenmut sent Narmer to collect her here. Maybe he couldn't travel so soon after the spell was broken. Hattie took it all with a grain of salt. Narmer seemed out of sorts, but harmless. Throughout her immortality she had learned to expect an occasional intrusion by the supernatural or the Gods themselves.

Hattie and the cranky old man stood hand in hand looking out into the dome of the universe. She was filled with both the wonder of her surroundings and the ridiculousness of the situation.

He led her into the small shrine sitting atop the boat. Inside was a large throne. "This was meant for one, but I think it will do for us."

Hattie sat next to him.

"Close your eyes."

"And you'll give me a big surprise?"

Narmer sighed.

Hattie closed her eyes.

A sudden shift in gravity made her stomach lurch. Her eyes immediately flew open. They were falling fast and vertically. The celestial river turned into a cosmic waterfall. She glanced at Narmer—not a hair on his head shifted at the high speed. It was as if they were encapsulated by a protective force field as they fell.

"Close your eyes. It'll be better."

Hattie shook her head. If she was going to plummet to her death, she would much rather see what was coming.

"Suit yourself. Just don't let go, or your Ba will be lost forever in the expanse of space."

Hattie tightened her grip on the old man. "A little warning would have been nice."

They were gaining speed. The star field turned from pinpoints to pinstripes of warp speed. The strips of light swirled together into a pinwheel with a pulsing glow at its center. As they plummeted forward, a violent force pulled her insides in all directions. She pressed her free hand against her midsection as if to hold herself together. The pain was so great that she wondered—if they continued to go faster, would her body be torn apart?

"You will want to close your eyes. This is when it gets weird."

"Great."

"And this time, whatever you do, you don't open them. The closer we get to the light, the more its intensity will grow until it liquefies your eyes."

Hattie clamped her eyes shut; her skin felt as if a million tiny scarabs were scampering across it. It took everything for her to suppress the urge to let go of Narmer's hand and scratch every inch of her body. A high-pitched wailing pierced her ears. Against her closed eyelids, she could sense an intense and hot light surrounding her. She clamped her eyes against the insatiable urge to open them.

"You can open your eyes now."

The boat was moored in front of another door. Except in this case, instead of two lions and the horizon hieroglyph, two donkeys were facing each other as they stood on their hind legs. She was right about where Narmer had taken her. The donkeys were symbols of the God Set and his protection of Re during his journey through the Netherworld.

Narmer dropped her hand then stepped out of the boat onto a platform fronting the door. When he opened it, bright daylight cut through the darkness that surrounded them. She shielded her eyes against it as she followed him through the door.

Hattie was standing near a rocky path running along a high mountain. It startled her that the mountain was one familiar to her. In the desert valley below lay her beautiful mortuary temple Djeser-Djeseru, Holy of Holies. Instead of the reconstructed sun-bleached ruins that stood in modern Egypt, the temple and its grounds were whole, as if the last stone and dab of paint were laid hours ago, and its gardens were teeming with life.

"How can it be?"

"In this realm, every sacred place built by the kings of the Two Lands has a perfectly rendered double here." Narmer nearly spat the words out, as if it cost him to acknowledge she was once among his rarefied ranks.

"It is more beautiful than I remember."

Narmer looked down his nose at Hattie. "You'll get no time for sightseeing or traveling down memory lane. This is a business trip, plain and simple." He turned and followed the pathway toward the other side of the mountain, away from Hattie's mortuary temple.

Hattie paused. She couldn't help but gaze down at the wonder she and Senenmut had built together. Her house of eternal life celebrated her many accomplishments as pharaoh and was meant to be her everlasting resting place. A living memorial where her name would be spoken until the end of time. She breathed in deep, hoping to catch the scent of the myrrh and incense trees planted there, but to no avail.

Narmer turned back and crossed his arms. "We don't have all day."

Hattie resisted the urge to push him down the rocky slope as she followed Narmer along a barely discernible pathway. For being old and dead, the predynastic pharaoh was pretty nimble.

She was struck by the fact that he was so old-looking. She always assumed when a pharaoh went to the Field of Reeds, they would revert to their most youthful and vigorous stage of life. An after-life populated with bare-chested, muscular godlike men and women living for eternity as their idea of perfection, like tomb paintings come to life. She never would have expected any of them to look as elderly and withered as Narmer did. However, she wasn't about to inquire further with he-of-the-most-sour-puss.

"What was that we traveled through? Was it a wormhole or something?"

"Or something."

Hattie mumbled under her breath. "Super helpful."

"I don't know that I agree with the idea of bringing you here, but I was the only one who could. Hopefully, you can be useful to us."

Hattie wondered what the other location choices might have been. "How did you do it?"

He stopped and then faced Hattie. A spark of pride gleamed in his eyes. "Well, princess, let's just say being the first to unite Upper and Lower Egypt has some perks. I've existed here longer than the others. You could say I've got superpowers, in a way. So, mind your p's and q's, and by that, I don't mean your pharaohs and queens. And on that note, never doubt that in my mind you will always be the latter, you were never the former. As the Greeks would say, know thyself. In your case it would be as an abomination before the Gods."

The urge to push the nasty old thing off the mountain increased a thousandfold, but as he was already dead, would it be worth it? She still needed to return from the Netherworld back to the mortal realm where Thabit and Zuberi were waiting for her, and she probably needed Narmer intact for that to happen.

She let the insult slip. "Whatever lets you sleep at night, old man."

It became clear Narmer was leading her to the rough-hewn tomb where her beloveds were stashed all those years ago. Apparently, in addition to sacred temples, tombs of the dead had replicas built in the Netherworld too.

Hattie followed Narmer down a dark shaft cut into the mountainside on a long rope ladder. She struggled to steady herself as the motion of Narmer below caused it to sway. At the bottom was a golden flicker of torchlight playing against the rock. Smoke billowed up past them.

She dropped to the gravel-strewn floor as Narmer grabbed one of the torches from the wall. He motioned her to follow down a sloped hallway, past a smaller burial chamber. She was familiar enough with the tomb's plan to know they were heading to the larger and last burial chamber.

Roughly twenty or so regal faces glanced her way, but that wasn't what shocked her. Beyond the well-dressed and royal crowd were her beloveds—bound like captives.

CHAPTER EIGHT

A lex moved through the sleeper car to the cargo hold where Salima was likely still steaming. As she passed between the two cars, she nearly knocked Gwen over. Despite the physical contact, Gwen maintained a self-satisfied grin as Alex passed by her. Alex's heart dropped like a stone. This was not a good sign. Whatever it was that caused Gwen to run down the hall to tell teacher, it couldn't be good for Alex, no matter how you looked at it.

Alex was tempted to lock herself into her comfortable cabin and ignore all the drama-filled assholes. Instead, she found herself standing in front of the secured storage car. She took in a deep breath before holding her hand up to the digital recognition scanner.

The door opened with a swish. Her nostrils were immediately assaulted by the strong sweet scent of honey. Alex's mood plummeted even further. The overpowering scent did not bode well for Alex.

When Alex first became involved with KHNM, she was part-nered with Salima. It took her some time to figure out that this agent with epic mood fluctuations was none other than the Immortal form of the Goddess triad Hathor, Sekhmet, and Bastet. Whenever Salima was angry and feeling her most Sekhmety and warrior-like, she exuded a fiery cinnamon scent. If she was in touch with her inner Hathor and was in the mood for love, the fragrance notes edged toward clove. To date, Alex never experienced the fragrance of contentment signaling her Bastet state. Could this be it? And if that was the case, had Gwen just told Salima something that made her very happy?

Following the scent, Alex went deeper into the car, past the numerous crates piled high that created a beige wall on either side of her. Salima would most likely be at the end of the car with the container holding the shards of the God machine. Out of the magical objects they were transporting, it was the only one containing the physical remnants of the Gods. It was powerful beyond measure. Just the sort of thing that should never make it into the wrong hands.

Alex approached Salima with great caution. As a Goddess, Salima never felt obliged to lean into any of the usual niceties of polite society. She moved about the world like an entitled princess with the strength and power of a goddess. She was hard to make heads or tails of. Just when you felt like Salima was on your side, she would do something unpredictable. Alex was never sure where her loyalties landed—with the Gods, KHNM, or solely on the side of Salima. The fact she was sent by the Gods to watch over KHNM's move was perplexing given her question-able history with the agency.

Alex wondered through all of this why Buxton still held an apparent unending amount of trust for Salima. *If she is working for the Gods to undermine the agency, why on earth would he have assigned her guard duty?* Whenever Alex asked him, she was never able to get a straight answer. The last time she brought it up was the one time Alex could remember him completely shutting her down. It was as if he took her inquiries into Salima as a personal affront.

Salima was leaning against a large black box containing the God machine shards, hands crossed over her chest. "Glad you could make it."

"Better late than never?"

"I was surprised you missed your shift. You are usually such a rule follower."

"Thank you for covering for me."

"Oh, don't worry about me. I've just resettled in. Why don't you go and do whatever important things you were doing that made you forget your shift in the first place."

Alex let Salima's observations slide over her like a misspoken curse. "Well, I'm here now to relieve you. I am sure you have things to do."

"Or you could go to your cabin and sleep. You will need it when we get to our destination. Unlike you mortals, I don't need my eight hours."

Salima had a way of doing things for you and making you pay for it eventually. "I appreciate you covering for me, but I'd rather do my time, thank you."

"Your new boss lady had a different take on the matter."

"Gwen is not my boss," Alex answered a little too sharply. She was irritated with herself for letting Salima get under her skin.

"Just following the money, my dear. In my experience, the one holding the purse is the one in charge."

Alex rubbed the back of her neck. "Yes, she is our benefactor at the moment, but in this mission, she is mostly an observer."

"Believe what you want. To the casual observer, it looks like Buxton is deferring to her every whim. Whose train is this? Why, a friend of hers? Where are KHNM's new digs? Oh yeah, they just happen to be in a place where Gwen's old lover had connections. Like it or not, Gwen is the only one keeping your beloved agency together. It doesn't matter to me what you do—if you want to stay, go ahead and stay. You'll just have the great joy of my company."

"Why are you so determined to stay? If I leave, I owe you nothing for this."

"Agreed."

Salima must be up to something, but Alex was tired of her games. Alex turned to leave the car. As she walked away her ears pricked at Salima mumbling to herself. Against her better judgment, Alex took a bite. "If you have something to say to me, just say it."

"If I wanted you to hear it, I would have said it so you could."

Alex shook her head. "What is with you? I'm feeling a passive-aggressive vibe from you, which is a distinct deviation from your normal aggressive-aggressive approach to engagement."

"I was ordered to stay here. No matter what you say or do I will be standing exactly here."

"Ordered?" Alex never imagined anyone would ever dare to order the great Goddess triad around.

"My family doesn't trust you and your kind to not screw the pooch on this one. The power in these God machine shards is beyond your comprehension. With your track record, they felt leaving you to watch over this load would only bring failure."

Being out of favor with the Gods was something Alex was used to. She knew all too keenly how fickle-hearted and irrational they could be. They couldn't ever see beyond their best interest and came up with narratives that allowed them to hold on to whatever ideas suited their purposes.

Not so long ago, Alex defeated one of the Gods in their attempt to enslave humanity and managed to locate the lost covenant that existed between the Gods and KHNM. Both successes didn't change the fact she was a fly in their ointment. Nothing she could do would ever be viewed by them as right.

If Buxton was correct, the Gods' strong aversion to her stemmed from them being sent back to the dilapidated Field of Reeds against their will by Alex. In addition to this grand faux pas she made while saving humanity, a belief among the Gods took root that Alex had gained a superpower by besting Raymond. That was what most threatened them about her. So much so that they put the conditional bounty on her head. If any powers surfaced, Niles had to kill her.

This time she didn't bite. Alex waved her hand and said, "Enjoy." As Alex approached the cargo hold door, Salima called her name. Alex turned to see the Goddess standing in the center aisle with an unreadable expression.

Salima raised two fingers to her eyes and flicked them at Alex. "Mind your step. There are eyes everywhere."

CHAPTER NINE

Beyond the cluster of pharaohs dressed in fine linen kilts, Hattie's father, brother-husband, nephew, and lover were bound like captives. They were on their knees with their hands tied behind their backs. It broke her heart to see these regal men treated in a manner reserved for the nine enemies of Egypt. How could their brethren do such a thing?

One of the pharaohs was gagged and apparently in the middle of an indecipherable rant. It was most likely Ramses the ninth. He had initiated the scheme that landed her beloveds, as well as most of the Thuthmosid kings and Ramesside kings, in the after-life slammer. From his easy life in the Field of Reeds, he'd gotten into a lather believing Ramses the eleventh was looting and dese-crating tombs of the pharaohs while claiming to be restoring them. He rallied a group of like-minded royal dead and hatched a plan. Even if the others didn't buy the story of Ramses the eleventh pillaging pharaonic tombs, most of the pharaohs felt he was a weak ruler by allowing the priesthood to become strong and were more than willing to deny him an afterlife.

To execute their plan, they needed someone who was still

rattling around the mortal realm. They made nice with Senenmut, who was desperate for their approval. Living for all those centuries with a clique who wouldn't give him the time of day took its toll. It didn't take much to get him to talk Hattie into acting as their legs on the ground. The idea was presented to her at a time when Hattie was particularly bored in her immortal life. She viewed it as a fun diversion that could potentially help her lover for the expanse of eternity. The plan was a simple one—to block Ramses eleven from the afterlife for his presumed crimes by disabling his tomb's false door.

But even the best-laid plans go wrong. They were caught. Both a temple priest and a squeaky wheel in the Field of Reeds had informed the Gods. Smendes, the new king, gave swift justice to those involved in the attempt at desecrating the sacred rights of the afterlife afforded to a pharaoh. He wanted to make an example of them, so no one would try it again. Especially when the time came for him to be called to the Field of Reeds. He wanted these punishments emblazoned on the memories of all.

He proclaimed that all the current dead pharaohs involved in the crime were relegated to a tomb that was more of a dumping ground than anything. It didn't have a false door or tomb goods. The pharaoh, taking no chances the prisoners might find a way to wander between realms even without the false door, had their Ba wings ritually clipped. Hattie was an immortal and couldn't be killed, so the Gods thought it appropriate her beloveds would pay the price for her actions, though they played no part in the debacle.

Narmer led Hattie into the large tomb. The pharaohs who hadn't played a role in the escapade parted, revealing a woman. It was Queen Ahmose-Nefertari, wife of Ahmose I. She was a part of the original conspiracy. Why wasn't she tied up too?

Hattie doubted it was due to the pharaohs' gentlemanly manners.

Narmer left her side and joined the pharaonic crowd. Aside from the continuing rants of Ramses nine, the only other noise in the space sounded like soft snores. Narmer stooped and shook an old man. "Djoser, wake up."

The elderly sleepy-eyed pharaoh stood among his cohort. Like Narmer, all the Old Kingdom pharaohs looked elderly, whereas the later kings were in their idealized state. Maybe it had taken a stretch of time for the Gods to figure out this whole afterlife thing.

Hattie was familiar with their faces and names, although she never had the chance to meet most of them. She ruled as a Horus-on-earth, and therefore possessed a kings list directory magically emblazoned upon her mind. Not only did she know who they were, but she also knew the ins and outs of their reigns. It was likely one of the many reasons the kingdom lasted for such a long time.

Narmer stepped forward. "So, princess, I guess you would like to know why I brought you here?"

Hattie nodded toward her bound beloveds. "At the moment, I am more interested in how you felt justified in treating your fellow kings in such a brutal way. To bind them as if they are enemies?"

A few in the small crowd looked disconcerted.

"And stop calling me princess."

"Would you rather I call you by that abomination of a name you wander the modern world with?"

Hattie loved the fact her name not only referred to her birth name, but was similar to one of the names of the seven enemies of Egypt—the Hatti, or the Hittites. It was a little thing that brought her great amusement over the years. Banished from her afterlife, although by choice, the patriarchal systems of Egypt and the need for her to rail against them always made her feel like an enemy of her own country and its conservative structures. "Yes, Hattie will do. I know some of you did your best to wipe my memory from the annals of history, so it seemed fitting to assume the name of an enemy of Egypt. What about the bonds? Release my beloveds at least. They do not deserve this treatment."

"We will release them when you do everything we ask."

"And if I don't?"

"Their Ba-souls will be cut anew, and they will be once again banished from the afterlife and into the eternal void." Narmer sneered at Hattie.

"Hear us out, please," interjected someone from the back of the pharaonic crowd. She recognized him as the Pharaoh Sneferu, the first pyramid builder. He had a kind, jovial face. "All we ask right now is that you listen."

"Can you at least unbind them? It is disgraceful to see them like this."

Narmer crossed his arms. "No."

Sneferu made a slight tsk-tsk sound. "Narmer, I think all the smiting you did when you were alive soured your soul. I don't see why we can't at least let the poor men stand. We can keep their hands bound."

"And Neferkare's gag?" Apparently, Narmer was tired of hearing whatever Ramses number nine had to say. Hattie surmised that it was probably so confusing in the Field of Reeds with all the Ahmoses, Ramseses, and Thuthomids running around that they would call one another by their more uncommon throne names.

"Of course. If we do, they all must stand silent, or all be rebound."

Dozens of hard glares flashed at Ramses the ninth.

"So be it." Narmer clapped his hands and from out of the shadows came several servants in loincloths. They worked at unbinding the captives and lifting them from their kneeling positions. The prisoners stood slowly. They must have been bound for a long time.

Hattie was surprised to see that Narmer's ushabtis were so large and humanlike. "Those are quite the ushabtis, Narmer."

"They aren't ushabti." Narmer looked satisfied at her apparent confusion. Before Hattie managed the question, he supplied the answer. "In my day, the pharaoh's best and most trusted servants chose to join him in his eternal life."

In the far corner, where the captives were getting untied, Ramses II put his nose in the air. "That was before the poor hacks realized they could take part in the afterlife with the proper burial."

Narmer stalked over to the once great ruler and looked down at him. "Say what you will, it all came down to loyalty. Be silent or you're getting your legs bound again."

Her father stood. "Blessings be upon you, daughter."

"Silence!" Narmer screeched.

Hattie's brother-husband wore his usual tired expression on his inelegant and wide face. As usual, Hattie was less than happy to see him. At least he wasn't able to say anything.

Senenmut attempted to shuffle toward her, with a gleam of emotion in his eyes.

"Not so fast, lover boy." Narmer held up his hand, instantly halting Senenmut's forward motion. "Do you want your legs tied again?"

Senenmut shook his head.

"Stay put."

He shambled back to where he was.

"Is that staying put?" Narmer yelled. His temper seemed to have a fine hair trigger.

The old man Sneferu came close to Hattie. "Let me explain why we are here, and why Narmer brought you to us."

Narmer and Sneferu appeared to be playing good pharaoh, bad pharaoh in this scenario.

Hattie nodded in the direction of Queen Ahmose-Nefertari, who was standing next to her husband. Why was it her great-great-grandmother was getting special treatment? Was it because her husband was one of the co-conspirators? Hattie nodded in the queen's direction. "Why is she free? She was a part of the conspiracy. Why is she not bound like the others?"

A self-conscious blush flashed on the cheeks of the great-great-grandmother Hattie had never met.

"We need you to procure something for us. Something that will help the current situation we find ourselves in," said Sneferu.

"Being dead?"

Djoser shook his head, muttering something to himself. The only word that made it to Hattie's ears was *disrespect*.

Sneferu continued. "Ever since the Gods have returned to the Field of Reeds, things have been terrible."

"The cat is no longer away, so the mice have to return to the life of courtiers. My heart weeps for your pampered dead souls. If one of you could show me the way back, I have a full schedule of important things I need to do, like getting a long massage from my attendants." The words fell from her mouth without a thought for Senenmut. She glanced at him, bound with the others against the tomb wall. His expression was as if the pharaonic prisoner next to him just let loose the evil wind of Set.

Narmer stepped forward. "I expected as much from someone as selfish as you. You have only ever cared about yourself."

Her father, nephew, and Senenmut moved in unison toward Narmer, as if to defend Hattie.

Sneferu held his hands up. "Stand down. I don't want to have Narmer's men bind you again."

Hattie poked her finger into the chest of Narmer. He was much shorter than she imagined he would be. "You have a lot of nerve. Why do you think I would ever go out of my way to help any of you? The whole reason why I've not been living here in your plush Netherworld existence with all your ushabti servants, hunting and fishing in the marshes as you are surrounded by heavenly birdsong and inhaling the sweet north wind, is because you patriarchal bastards would have made my afterlife a living hell. You would have done everything to ostracize me and make me miserable. I have absolutely no reason to do anything for any of you."

Narmer's face raged with a sharp fury.

Sneferu gently pulled her away from Narmer. "Let's cool this down. Let me explain. I am guessing from what you know of the Field of Reeds, we must seem like a bunch of petulant spoiled children, but let me assure you we are not. For the two thousand or so years the Gods walked among mortals, they neglected this place of eternity and impoverished it by the lack of their magical will. Now they are back, powerless and destitute, and they expect to live as they did before. They have conscripted every one of us to the task of refurbishing this realm."

"So you are actually being asked to do some work? Is that the issue here? That your eternity of forever blissful relaxation is over? If it is, I couldn't care less."

Hattie's father spoke up again. "Hatshepsut, listen to them. We were only given this second chance by their grace."

"I was the one who acquired the Tears of Isis; I was the one who "woke" you all—why are you giving them the credit for it?"

Queen Ahmose-Nefertari spoke. "How do you think you were able to find the tears? Didn't it seem the least bit odd that after centuries of searching you finally found what you were looking for to restore your beloveds' afterlife?"

Ahmose interjected. "We infected your dream state with information to help you find it. My dear wife has the information we need to help us with our plan. She needed to be woken. We figured if you were able to wake your beloveds, it would become an enticement for you to do our continued bidding."

"What is it you would have me do?" Hattie figured she owed it to her dad to hear them out. If there was one person in her life she fully respected, it was him. He had raised her, not like every other royal princess, but as a strong woman who could rule. If he hadn't died abruptly, he would have installed her as king instead of her sniveling brother.

Ahmose lovingly tucked a strand of hair behind his wife's ear. "As a token of my devotion to my dear wife, I commissioned a set of ceremonial vestments for her. This set included a diadem, a collar necklace, and a sistrum. These objects were not only inlaid with the finest stones set by the masterful hands of temple artisans, but they were also imbued with the strongest of magics that allowed her to hone her powers as the Second Prophet of Amun, the God's Wife and Divine Adoratrice."

"I gained a certain reputation for my magical prowess and resurrection abilities. This work I did over the years imbued a magical patina on these objects. After I died, my reputation was great, and I was worshiped as both Mistress of the Sky and Lady of the West."

Sneferu interjected. "We need you to get one of these items for us."

Hattie motioned with her hand across the room. "You orchestrated this to return jewelry to a pretty lady?"

"Not quite," said Sneferu. "We know where one of these objects is today. As we speak, it is traveling across the country you know as the United States and making its way to your so-called Sin City."

"Vegas? What is something like that doing in Vegas?"

"It is on its way to Vegas. Don't you even try to listen?" Narmer was truly getting into his bad cop role.

"It is on a train. It is in the possession of an organization you may be familiar with, KHNM. They've been in place since the Gods—"

"I am familiar with them."

"They are in a time of transition and have to move their head-quarters westward to a place called Area 51."

"It would have been nice if you'd asked me to do this a couple of weeks ago. I had a contact in KHNM. I could have negotiated a twofer. There is no way I can get into Area 51. As a military installation, their security would be top-notch, especially as it has known its own controversies and mythos over the years."

Narmer leaned toward Hattie, allowing her to fully experience his stink eye. "That is exactly why you need to retrieve it before they reach their destination."

"And how do you, a bunch of dead pharaohs, happen to conveniently know this?" There was still so much that didn't make sense. Anticipating Narmer's belittlement, Hattie clarified. "I mean, how do you know where this object is now?"

"We have ears everywhere." Narmer's tone implied not only the statement but a threat behind his words.

"All of this for jewelry?"

Ahmose-Nefertari shook her head. "After I died and was deified, the priests at Karnak used these relics over the centuries to perform ceremonies, thickening the magical patina. This went on for another thousand or so years before—"

"Before our great land was invaded by Cambyses." Narmer's curtness left no question regarding his feelings about the Achaemenid ruler.

Ahmose cleared his throat. "Let my wife speak her piece."

"The priests knew things were not going well and decided to take the sacred relics they could gather before Cambyses's army reached Thebes. They bound the objects magically and threw them into the sacred lake at Karnak Temple, the Most Sacred of Places. After reaching the temple, Cambyses's army found the hoard. He selected from it my regalia, one object for each of his wives. When he left Egypt to deal with a rebellion, he sent the treasure with his army as they moved out to destroy the Oracle of Amun at Siwa Oasis."

"The lost army of Cambyses? What does that have to do with your predicament?"

Sneferu's expression relaxed at Hattie's interest. "If someone possesses one of these three adornments, it will lead the person to the lost army, as they are magically linked by a powerful spell."

"But I still don't see how I can locate this one item that is being transported."

"We have it on good authority the item KHNM has in its possession is the ceremonial sistrum. When you are in its presence, if you start singing the hymn of Amun Re, it will start to shake."

"And if it is the diadem that is in their possession?"

"You'll be out of luck, as will your beloveds. Diadems make no music." It was as if Narmer wanted Hattie to fail so he could mete out the punishment.

"But why do you want this sistrum? Is the magic within it that strong?"

"No, we need this so you can find what we really need."

"Oh great—this job isn't a one-and-done? You have more for me to do."

Hattie's father pushed past the other captives. "Listen to him, daughter. If you do this and succeed, not only will I and the others have their days of eternity restored, but you will also be ensuring your beloveds will live a life better suited to a pharaoh. I ask you to do what you are asked, for me."

Her father could always find the words to reel her in. She owed this to him, her nephew, and brother-husband for jeopardizing their afterlife. If she could get this done once and for all and free her beloveds, it would be worth it. What was the cost to her but a little time and effort? It was the least she could do. "I suppose I do have some free time on my hands. But you still haven't answered me. What is this second object you need?"

Ahmose-Nefertari stepped forward. "If the prophecy is correct, when you find the sistrum, it will lead you to an artifact that can bring the Gods to their knees."

CHAPTER TEN

On the way to her roomette, Alex thought briefly about heading to the dining car and having something to eat and a nightcap with Luke, but she was feeling oddly tired. It must have to do with all the relaxing she did earlier in the day. Her body couldn't be allowed to get used to this type of lifestyle, but tonight would be an early one.

She slipped into her silk pajamas. The cool fabric soothed her as it slid across her skin. After pouring herself a finger of bourbon, she leaned against the cabin window. A brilliant blanket of stars spread above the vast desert landscape as it rolled by. She took a sip, enjoying the fiery burn.

Was the spangled star field above the place she sent Niles and the others to? She wasn't clear on where exactly the Field of Reeds was located. Was it up in the heavens like Western culture believes, or was it tethered to the Netherworld, or on a plane all its own? She also wondered if Niles was mad at her for sending him and the other Gods back, like the Others were. Had that been the reason why he acted as their lawyer in the lawsuit plaguing the agency? Was it why he was there keeping tabs on

KHNM? She knew he was tasked with killing her if any powers came to her. If that was the case, why was he avoiding her? If that was his task, she thought he would be constantly watching her like a hawk. At their new zero rate of communication, she would most likely never know.

Alex tossed back the rest of the bourbon and settled into her bed. As she sunk into oblivion, her mind soared over a vast sunbaked desert. Her wings caught an updraft from the wadi below, pulling her high into the pale blue sky. Her heart was light as she flew.

It had been a long time since she dreamt like this. The act of flying made her giddy as she dipped and dove in the air. Lining the wadi were high cliffs and a mountain whose peak resembled a pyramid. Recognizing its unique shape, she knew Hatshepsut's mortuary temple was close.

When she flew over the temple, Djeser-Djeseru, she noted that instead of the beige-on-beige reconstruction of the temple ruins, as one would see today, it was surrounded by a lush garden. Before this information could sink in, large talons gripped her body from above. Her little bird heart thumped against her rib cage as she struggled to free herself.

Nile's deep voice reverberated through her as he loosened his talons. "Not to worry. I need to talk with you."

Alex rolled her tiny little eyes. "You could have found a much less dramatic way of doing so. Like maybe knock on my door on the train." What she wanted to say was, "Glad you finally made some time."

"I wasn't certain you'd let me in. You've been avoiding me, you know."

Alex's feathers bristled. "I've been avoiding you? The nerve—"

"Just kidding. It's that we shouldn't be seen together. I can explain. We'll be at our destination shortly. Hang tight."

Having no other choice, Alex relaxed into his talons that gently held her. The upside of being bird-napped in her sleep was that at least she would get some answers.

Niles gently set her onto a small opening in the cliff face directly opposite Hatshepsut's temple. When he landed next to her, Alex rammed him with all her might, pushing him off the cliff. She peered down with amusement as he plummeted awkwardly for a bit before he righted himself and flew back to her.

"I guess I deserved that."

"Oh and much more, Bird Boy."

"It has been a while since anyone has called me that. I was pleased when Salima let that one go. Thanks for bringing back an oldie but a goodie." Alex knew he hated the nickname Salima had given him. He preened his feathers back in order. They were tufting out irregularly from the unexpected plunge. "I'm surprised such a small bird as you would have enough strength to knock a big bird like me over."

The last time they'd flown together they were both birds of prey. Alex wondered how it was she fit so snugly in his talons. She must be in a different bird form. "What bird am I?"

"You are a swallow, with beautiful blue plumage, I might add."

"My plumage is no concern of yours." She laughed. "Do you happen to know why I am a different bird than I've been before? I assumed the form I took had something to do with a spirit animal or something."

"I don't know if that is necessarily the case. Magically induced states are unpredictable at best." Niles blinked his falcon eyes and instantaneously changed into a large ibis. His tall white form was hunched over, trying to fit in the small space they occupied.

Alex blinked her eyes and thought of a falcon. Nothing happened. "How did you do that?"

"I am a God, you know."

He never tired of pointing that out. "Whatever. There is one thing I've never understood about you. As Thoth, why are you sometimes represented as an ibis and sometimes as a baboon?"

"Because I like to monkey around." In a blink of an eye, he changed into a baboon, knocking her into the wall of the small space they occupied. His bristly fur felt strange against her feathers.

"Come on Niles, seriously?"

He switched back to falcon form. Niles looked as self-conscious as a bird of prey could at his fumbled attempt at humor. "It's a long story."

"I bet. Your explanations usually are."

"Whatever. You are likely in that form for a reason. Maybe the cosmic power knows something you don't, and it could be fortuitous for you to be smaller now. Or it could be it knows you aren't currently on the hunt for anything, so there is no need for you to be a bird of prey. But I'm not exactly a walking, flying magical rule book."

"I know. You're a God."

"Exactly." Niles bobbed his bird head up and down.

"What are we doing here?"

"Firstly, we are meeting in secret. Secondly, I have some recon to do for the family. I thought I'd kill two birds with one stone." Niles, as an ancient Egyptian, could never pass up a good or even a not-so-good pun.

"You are doing odd jobs for the other Gods now?"

"Like keeping them from killing you." His eyes narrowed.

"We don't have much time. The longer we stay on this plane together, the more likely someone will notice and think I am colluding with the enemy. Which could break every deal I've made to keep you alive. You know I'm supposed to be watching you to see if any magical powers crop up. Why do you think I have been keeping as much distance as I can between us?"

Alex gazed at the vast desert landscape, not wanting to meet his eyes. "Well, you've dragged me into a Netherworld dream. What do you want to say to me?"

"It's not what I want to say. I have an important question for you." He leaned in close. "Look at me, Alex. I need to see your eyes when you answer. I must know if you are telling me the truth. Your life hangs in the balance."

Before turning her head, she saw movement in the valley below. There was a dust cloud following a line of men dressed like servants holding bundles. "It looks like we have company. What would they be doing here, in the middle of nowhere?"

"Damn, that is my other reason for being here. The other Gods are a little paranoid that the pharaohs are up to something. Those look like Narmer's servants."

"You mean ushabti, right?"

"No, he and a few of the early dynastic kings brought their courtiers and servants to their own eternity."

"Those multiple burials around the kings were actual sacrifices?"

"Yeah, they decided to stop it after a few rounds."

"Did they grow a conscience about killing their supporters?"

"No, the Gods decided the Field of Reeds would get far too full if everyone brought their entourage."

"Of course, how could I think the Gods would ever do anything outside of their self-interest?"

Niles squawked indignantly.

"The falcon doth protest too much. Why are you, I mean we, here?"

"The Gods have gotten word from a reliable source that several pharaohs have been seen leaving the precinct of the Field of Reeds and meeting in odd places. These sorts of actions draw the minds of my family straight to rebellion. I was sent here on what I thought was a wild goose chase."

"Rebellion? Why on earth would the pharaohs in the Field of Reeds have anything to complain about? Don't they laze around all day eating honey cakes and drinking beer while their three-hundred-and-sixty-odd ushabtis do the work?"

"That is what one would think, but things have changed and not for the better."

"What, the Netherworld ran out of gilded furniture and imported wines?"

"They've been put to work, and they don't like it."

"How can that be?"

"When the Gods—"

Alex interjected a cough that came out as a strange chirp at the way Niles conveniently edited himself from the group in question.

Niles started again. "When my family decided to bank our powers and walk among mortals, the Field of Reeds went into a state of disarray. Now we're back, and with most of our powers still depleted, we don't generally have the means to do any improvements . . . To keep us in the custom to which we are used to, the pharaohs were brought into service."

"You've got to be kidding."

"If only I were." Niles's tone was wistful. "Now you know why the Gods, I mean my family, are out for your blood. This state they are in is your fault. You are the one who banished them, I mean us, from the mortal realm and back to the Field of Reeds."

"But Raymond was trying to kill you all. One of your flesh and blood was attempting to commit familicide."

"You should know by now the Godly narrative always bends to the will and needs of those in power."

They both watched in silence as the servants made their way up to a cleft in the mountain where they unceremoniously dropped their packages.

Niles spoke out loud, but more like he was talking to himself. "What on earth are they doing? What interest would they have in the old tomb that used to house a pharaonic mummy cache? And why would they be supplying it with pillows and carpets?"

"Servant slumber party?"

"Well, whatever it is they are doing, I'll have to keep an eye on it. For now, I will report as if I saw nothing unusual. I'd like to get a handle on this before something potentially simple turns into a bloodbath. As you know all too well, my family can be compulsive and tends to respond in a scorched-earth way when non-Gods mess with the social fabric. And forever is a long time to endure deep social fissures."

"What is your question for me?" Alex turned toward Niles. The sharpness in his eyes gave her a start.

"Have you been experiencing anything strange since you defeated Raymond? Any powerful sensations or abilities?" His gaze softened with a questioning look, as if her answer could potentially bring him down on the sharp side of a razor.

"No, only dreams."

"Like when we meet up like this?"

She nodded, then immediately felt pangs of guilt. Her dreams of late had been different than their meet ups. While she weighed her words, Niles quickly jumped back in. His tone was a little brighter. "There is no need to worry about our dream time together. It is a common occurrence for mortals who have traveled between realms to experience a thinning of the membrane between time and space. It is more like a gift than a power. You can flit around as much as you desire, but you hold no magical powers as your Ba travels between the realms."

"Well, that's a relief." She was immediately struck by her own lie. These half-truths wouldn't bring her any relief.

"Were you worrying about it all this time?"

"Not exactly. The thought crossed my mind, but it didn't fit with what I would imagine a superpower might be."

"You would do yourself a dire disservice to believe you have any idea of what the Gods might consider a power. It could very well cost you your life. You should have asked."

Alex wanted to knock him off the ledge again. "And just who would I have asked?"

Niles dipped his feathery head down. "Touché."

A silence stretched between them. Alex knew she had to mention the other dreams but didn't want to complicate things. Especially if those complications would end in her death.

Niles nudged her. "I am sorry it is something you've been needlessly worried about."

"It was just today. Gwen approached me about wanting to rebury my dad. Apparently, it was something she promised Jorge. He visits her in his dreams. I let it slip I knew something about it but tried to cover it up by mentioning I knew of it through Akh-Hehet. I don't know if she believed me or not, but at least now I know it doesn't matter."

"This time it may not have mattered, but you need to keep yourself sharp when dealing with Gwen. After everything that has happened, I can't imagine she has your best interests in mind. That leads me to my original question. Any other strange happenings since your journey to the Netherworld?"

Had he guessed that she was holding things back from him? It was now or never to come clean. She knew he'd promised her father years ago that he would protect her, and she knew he would do anything in his power to do so, no matter what he'd promised his family. "Aside from this, I've been having other dreams, and strange ones at that."

Niles leaned in. "Tell me more."

"It's like I've woken up in an Egyptian-themed fortune cookie factory that produces opaque and nonsensical statements. I am starting to wonder if they are stress dreams. I think the sole power these dreams might give me is the ability to initiate inane party conversations. The last one I had was of someone cutting out the tongue of a crocodile and hieroglyphic ticker tape stating it was going to be a bad day."

"Hmmm. Maybe it is your subconscious working on your innermost feelings about Thorne."

"Very funny."

"It doesn't sound like anything to worry about, yet. But keep me posted if this develops into something more."

"So you can kill me?" Sarcasm peppered her words.

"Don't, Alex. I've made a deal. I have to keep it. Unless I can figure a way out. The last thing I want to do, Alex, is kill you." He leaned into her.

Alex drew close. Their beaks nearly touched when a barrage of rapid knocks on her cabin door pulled her back into her body.

CHAPTER ELEVEN

After agreeing to do the pharaohs' bidding, Hattie was escorted out of the Netherworld by Narmer. He took her to a plane of existence where her Ba could return to her body.

With the artifact already in transit, it didn't give her much time to gather Thabit and Zuberi and everything they would need for the mission. It was late morning in Luxor when Hattie made it back into her body. That meant it was already late evening in Las Vegas. The window of time to steal the artifact was narrowing with every passing minute.

Once she promised her father she would seek this object, she couldn't fail. Making a promise to others of her blood was an unbreakable bond. If they ended up getting to Vegas after the cargo was transferred, Hattie had no idea how she could infiltrate the security parameters of Area 51.

The whole plan rested on the secret portal between Luxor and Vegas that the pharaohs were certain existed. If everything went as expected, they would end up in Sin City around two or three in the morning. A perfect time to move unseen, but also cutting it close for Hattie and the boys to extract the artifact stored at the train yard before the agents of KHNM showed up to load them into their train.

Her Ba settled into her body. She opened her eyes to the hand-painted ceiling above her bed depicting the night sky. Its gold leaf glimmered as the morning rays of sun touched them. Hattie slipped out of bed and threw on some street clothes. After checking herself in the mirror, she retrieved Thabit and Zuberi. They were waiting outside her door, like two loyal and protective hounds.

Hattie filled them in on the situation as they packed a few essentials. With the selected gear in hand, they left the dahabeeyah and headed to the Old Winter Palace Hotel. It was a short walk down the Corniche bordering the mighty Nile to the hotel.

The midday sun beat down as they walked up the ornate curvilinear ramp fronting the vintage salmon-and-cream-colored building. Along the walkway were large urns with hot pink bougainvillea and cypress. This stately hotel opened in 1905 and played host to celebrities, royalty, and heads of state.

There was a time when Hattie reserved a permanent suite of rooms at this hotel. It was during the heyday of the "discovery" of Tutankhamen's tomb. She found the modern mortals' ideas of discovery to be endlessly entertaining. As if it had been lost all this time, only to be "found" by the sheer genius of these foreigners. For centuries the tomb and its contents were camouflaged from intruders. Tucked away with care and intention so the deceased could enjoy their deserved afterlife. It always begged the question—exactly how long does someone have to be buried for their sacred place of resting to be acceptably ransacked?

It gave Hattie great pleasure to harass the likes of Carter and his financier Lord Carnarvon as they puffed out their chests at what they'd found, acting as if no other century in the history of humanity other than the current one mattered. Modern culture has a strange proclivity in forgetting these were sacred places, not curiosities that were put there for their voyeurism.

Flanked by Thabit and Zuberi, Hattie strode through the portico into the tiled lobby. In the center of the large airy room was a floral arrangement that could make a nice nosegay for the colossal statues guarding the pylon of Luxor Temple. The heady scent of rose and lily filled the air around them.

Hattie had grave doubts about this part of the plan. She didn't understand how the instructions she had would get her from Luxor, Egypt, to the Luxor hotel in Las Vegas, but she was willing to give it a try. The cadre of pharaohs seemed certain in their claims that their information came from a trustworthy source.

Supposedly Horatio Diogenes, the anthropomorphic form of the God Horus, held a suite of rooms at the hotel in perpetuity. When Horatio and the other Immortals walked among humanity, the one-time music industry mogul wanted the best of both worlds. He mainly lived in Vegas, but often missed his homeland. He used some of his magical capital to create a portal in one of his rooms for easy access. This earth-based wormhole allowed him to easily travel between his two homes. The agreement for the room was set to continue throughout the hotel's existence. Although he didn't have any use for it anymore, now that he was once again a permanent resident in the Field of Reeds, it lay at the ready.

A prim-looking attendant was behind the front desk. When Hattie spoke the password the pharaohs gave her, the clerk's eyes sparked with amused judgment. Hattie wondered what lascivious leaps the young woman's mind made at the thought of two men and one woman asking for a key to a room that held its own scandalous mythos of the man who kept it and his unbridled appetites.

Key in hand, they walked through the salon, with its red silk walls and plush velvet chairs, and on to Horatio's room.

Upon entering the room, Hattie was overwhelmed by a profusion of gold and cream fabrics. The windows facing the Nile were draped in heavy acid-carved gold velvet. Hattie imagined when they were closed, all daylight would be blocked. In the center of the room lay a large mahogany bed with a fabric-covered headboard that matched the drapery.

"Why don't you guys close those curtains while I look around for this portal? I'm hoping when the room is fully dark, we might be able to see magical residue."

Near a large seating area was an ornate table with detailed scrollwork. At the center of its top were carved shapes echoing the inset squares of a false door. Hattie sat on one of the chairs facing the table as the room was shrouded in darkness. Zuberi took the seat next to her, and Thabit stood behind her. She scanned the room for clues but saw nothing. What had she thought? That there would be a massive glow-in-the-dark arrow or something pointing to an open cosmic portal? She rubbed the table to try and pick up on any magical residue, but there was nothing.

Hattie wandered to the main entrance and turned on the lights. A large mirrored wardrobe caught her eye. It looked large enough for a human or two to stand in. Hattie climbed and felt along the smooth wood interior for a latch. Nothing.

"Mistress, come out here."

She opened the door and took Zuberi's hand.

"Look into the glass," said Zuberi.

The mirror on the front of the wardrobe shifted from

reflecting the room around her to a substance resembling a pool of water. The liquid stayed within the frame of the mirror and didn't spill out over the floor. Its surface rippled as she placed her palm on it. The small wave cascaded outward. She no longer saw the room she was standing in but a very different one. This room had bright-white linen, sleek contemporary furnishings, and a startling orange and blue mural behind the headboard. She craned her neck. The exterior wall was slanted at a peculiar angle.

"I'm going through. Zuberi, put your hand on my shoulder and walk as close to me as you can. Thabit, you do the same to Zuberi. I am not sure how long this portal will stay open, and I don't want to leave either of you behind."

She felt Zuberi's hand on her shoulder and then walked through the mirror. As she moved through the portal, the sensation wasn't what she expected. Based on the way the substance moved on the surface of the mirror, she thought it would be thick and sludgy, but the in-between space of this portal felt as if she was walking through a dewy mist. Gooseflesh dotted her skin. Hattie stepped onto the stiff industrial grey carpeting of the new room. With no time to lose, they exited into the hallway and rode slanting elevators down to the main lobby atrium. The doors opened to reveal a tiled floor. Its pattern looked remarkably like the tile in the lobby of the Old Winter Palace, a white base with black squares that met at each of the corners. That is where any similarities ended. This air-conditioned tourist trap couldn't have been more different from the opulent and storied hotel they stood in minutes ago.

Hattie had never met Horatio Diogenes but knew she would like him. She smiled at the blatant irony of his choosing the cheesy Luxor hotel in Las Vegas for his home away from home. How he must have enjoyed the servants hard at work while erroneously wearing the nemes headdress of the pharaohs when the hotel opened.

They were in the heart of the pyramid. The atrium was terraced with inward-facing rooms rising at an angle toward the apex. Initially, Hattie assumed the portal would have involved the massive beam of light that shoots out of the hotel's top at night and not a random wardrobe, as the Gods were prone to grand gestures by nature.

Thabit and Zuberi's eyes were wide in wonder as they took in the massive enclosed interior space. Thabit stopped walking as he looked around. "This land must have many farmers."

"Why do you say that?" Although the boys had been in her company for centuries, they were relatively green to the rest of the world. She only took them outside Egypt on rare occasions. Zuberi was always the more guarded of them and was far less likely than Thabit to let his naivete show.

"It must have taken so many to build this place."

Zuberi laughed. "I doubt that is how this place came to be, brother. Let's see which pharaoh they've made this dubious tribute to."

The trio walked past two monumental statues. "I don't think they are honoring anyone in specific, except maybe the God of blatant commercialism." To Hattie's eyes, the statues didn't resemble any pharaoh in particular and looked to be an approximation of pharaohness in general. Although in reality, did any of the pharaohs' statues ever truly resemble the kings they portrayed?

Zuberi came to a dead stop. "A Mesopotamian ziggurat? What in the land of the dead is that doing next to an obelisk?"

Hattie crossed her arms. "If we are successful in our mission, we can spend all the time we want wondering about this place and what type of madman dreamt it up, but time is slipping away."

"Of course, mistress." Zuberi looked a little embarrassed at his loss of self-possession.

"Just wait until you see the sphinx outside. I think it might be bigger than old Khafre's."

"Humans," Zuberi muttered as he followed her outside and to the taxi stand.

The driver gave Hattie an odd look when she said she wanted to be dropped off at the Las Vegas train yard in the middle of the night. His expression lost its jaded edge when she handed him a huge tip with the promise of five times the amount if he hung around until they returned. After holding out for double the original offer, he agreed to stay. For an hour.

It had been several decades since passenger service stopped in the city. It must have seemed unusual for a woman in the company of two buff men asking to be left in a bleak and deserted landscape. Maybe he thought she was a sex worker or a female entrepreneur with a damsel in distress fantasy, needing to blow off steam with a couple of hired men.

The train yard was in an industrial area on the north end of town. After scaling the security fence and dropping onto the asphalt, Hattie assessed the situation. The low energy of the yard felt like a sleeping giant who would wake just before the rising sun, along with the arrival of the early shift workers. If the info the pharaohs possessed was correct, the warehouse they were looking for would be beyond the long line of cargo containers. It would be in the center and oldest section of the rail yard, a large brick warehouse harkening to a simpler time. All the other buildings they passed by as they traveled deeper into the compound had beige industrial siding.

They were running short on time. It would be a few more

clicks before the sun would rise and KHNM would be rushing around the train depot to transfer their waiting cargo. After centuries of less-than-aboveboard adventures, Hattie knew it was best to stand back and scope out the situation instead of rushing in. When they located the warehouse the pharaohs described, Hattie paused to get the lay of the land. Eventually, two portly security guards appeared. Their attention was more attuned to the animated conversation they were having than the area they were responsible for. It was a good sign.

Hattie and the boys stayed in the shadows, making their way to the front of the warehouse. Its façade was dimly lit by old incandescent light fixtures angling out from its exterior wall. This warehouse wasn't on the top of anyone's list for upgrades. They would have to get in and get out as soon as possible. She saw two guards, but there could be more. This was the time of the graveyard shift. Hattie hoped that translated into a quiet time with less staffing, but she wanted to assume nothing. She and the boys would have to be on high alert.

The old warehouse had glass windows up high for ventilation. She checked the door and found it locked. Up was the only way in. Hattie pointed to a large crate in front of the building. "Thabit, climb on that crate and let Zuberi stand on your shoulders. I think I can reach the windows if I stand on Zuberi's."

"Why don't you let us break the door down? Then we could go together," asked Zuberi.

"I think that would draw the guards' attention. When I get in, I want you to check the rest of the building, keeping a sharp eye out for the guards' return. If you see them, make the call of the hoopoe, and I will hide."

"Of course, mistress." Zuberi made a short bow and then climbed up his stone brother.

As Thabit and Zuberi were initially sculpted from stone, they weren't literally brothers. Their sculptor created their forms of marble sourced from the same quarry, and they were brought to life by an ancient spell centuries later. The only brotherhood they shared was serving Hattie for all these years. Since they were made of stone originally, the properties of that material enhanced their incredible strength. They could stiffen their flesh into a solid mass that would be impossible for a flesh-and-bone human. This had several benefits for Hattie. In this case, it was the ease with which she was able to scale their bodies.

She stood on Zuberi's shoulders and slipped her upper body into the bottom half of the ventilation window's slanted pane. Grabbing onto the frame, Hattie turned herself over until she was looking up at the warehouse's ceiling. The metal lip dug into her spine as she slowly pulled herself up to sitting. She hated having to move in such a cumbersome way, but she was up pretty high. A fall would be treacherous. Hattie could feel a thin grip above. Below was a small ledge that jutted out from the wall and led to a large pipe. If she could get to the pipe, she could shimmy down it to the ground floor. Hattie's core burned as she slowly extracted her lower body from the mouth of the window and onto the minuscule ledge then carefully edged her way to the pipe.

A small piece of the ledge crumbled away. Her foot shot downward. Unable to right herself, she plummeted to the floor. Hattie's heart raced as she braced for impact. Instead of the concrete floor, she landed in someone's arms. Her eyes flew open, and Zuberi was looking down at her. "How'd you . . . ? I told you to check the perimeter."

"Aren't you glad we didn't?" He gently tilted her out of his arms.

"How did you get in?"

"We were checking the perimeter—"

"As commanded," Zuberi added.

"And the side door happened to be open."

"Well, now that we are all here, we should get busy. From the looks of it, we have our work cut out for us." The store-house was extremely large. She was overwhelmed with the prospect of trying to find a relatively tiny sistrum somewhere among all these boxes. The pharaohs had mentioned the KHNM goods were contained in roughly sixty boxes. All the other freight must belong to whoever else rented this space. There were two sections with rows of boxes flanking each side of the warehouse. Both areas were stacked nearly to the ceiling. In between the thick stacks was a large aisle most likely for cargo retrieval.

She assessed the situation and paced in front of the cargo. "I am willing to guess whoever manages this warehouse would strategically stack their inventory so they can bring in a forklift to reach what they need quickly. It is likely the boxes we seek are at the front, as they will be retrieving and loading them today."

"What next?" asked Thabit.

"Remember that old hymn to Amun Re?"

Zuberi crossed his arms. "How could I ever forget? It was practically drummed into our heads while we lived in that temple."

Before the boys were brought to life, they were originally sculpted to grace a great temple. They stood in place for centuries, witnessing the sacred rites over many years. "We will each sing a verse of the hymn in praise of Amun Re, and while we do, the others will listen for the sistrum."

Zuberi crossed his arms. "If we are reciting the entire litany, we will be here all night."

"And well into the morning." Hattie chuckled. Of all the Gods, Amun Re was pretty impressed with his titles and encouraged the practice of saying them all. He had hedged his bets on being thoroughly praised.

Aside from any thoughts Hattie might have about his lack of humility, she owed a thing or two to the old God. Amun Re was Hattie's God-father but not in the way the term is used among mortals. She used the God to create her own creation myth. Every pharaoh claimed to be Horus-on-earth, but Hatshepsut took it further. Ancient Egypt was a patriarchal society, and a royal or noble woman's place was the temple or the harems, not the kingship. That a woman should rule outside of short-lived necessities was unacceptable.

Hatshepsut was her father's favorite. At an early age, he recognized her intelligence and taught her not to be a princess, but to rule. Unfortunately, he died before this unconventional plan could be put into action. After his death, she was relegated to the role of queen and married to her brother, who ascended to the throne. Hatshepsut was better suited to rule than her brother-husband but was left on the sidelines solely because of her gender. When her brother-husband died, she took the throne and invented an imagined birth story for herself. It involved Amun Re entering her mother's bedchamber, and Hatshepsut was the direct result of that divine union. She used this fiction to proclaim that she was the rightful ruler and lord of the Two Lands.

"We will have to do the best we can. I will start the hymn, then you two will take the third stanza." It was the duty of the practitioner who held the closest association with the Gods to start the prayer. As a former priestess and pharaoh, it would be her voice that would open the channels between the realms.

Hattie reached inside her jacket and pulled out three sticks of incense. These weren't the run-of-the-mill fragrances one would find in a metaphysical bookstore. They were made by an Egyptologist whose field of study was the smells of ancient Egypt. One smelt of myrrh to call forth the Gods, one of blue lotus for their pleasure, and the last was the scent of rendered duck fat for their appetites. She lit them all. Scented smoke twined upward, making the utilitarian space smell of the Holy of Holies. She hoped their fragrance would help awaken the magic sistrum.

Hattie cleared her mind and began the hymn.

> *Praise of Amun Re!*
> *The bull in Heliopolis, the chief of all the Gods,*
> *The beautiful and beloved God*
> *Who giveth life to all warm-blooded things,*
> *To all manner of goodly cattle!*

Zuberi took up the chanting baton.

> *Hail to thee, Amun Re! Lord of the thrones of the Two Lands,*
> *Thou who dwellest in the sanctuary of Karnak.*
> *Bull of his mother, he who dwelleth in his fields,*
> *Wide-ranging in the Land of the South.*
> *Lord of the Mezau, ruler of Punt,*
> *Prince of heaven, heir of earth,*
> *Lord of all things that exist!*

As Zuberi took up the next stanza, Hattie strained to listen over his low baritone for the tinkling sound of a sistrum, but there was nothing.

When his brother finished, Thabit's voice quavered with emotion as he sang. All those years as a temple decoration and witnessing the rites for centuries made him a closet true believer.

Alone in his exploits even amongst the Gods,
The goodly bull of the Ennead of the Gods,
Chiefest of all the Gods,
Lord of truth, father of the Gods,
Maker of men, creator of animals,
Lord of the things which are, maker of fruit-trees . . .

Hattie did an internal eye roll at the names Amun Re claimed for himself as she readied to start her next verse. He truly was the hero of his own story. As the thought crossed her mind, she heard a minuscule sound like a distant wind chime. Hattie motioned to the boys for them to keep singing as she followed the sound. She focused her energy on trying to locate it. Craning her neck toward the sound, she realized it was coming from a dicey location at the tip-top of the stack of huge boxes.

She pointed up, indicating which direction they'd have to go. The boys stopped singing and searched for any handholds they might use to climb the tower of boxes. Hattie stepped back, noticing that a few of the front-most stacks didn't reach to the ceiling. A possible solution flickered in her mind. "Feel like building a pyramid, boys?"

Their eyebrows pinched together in confusion.

A smile pulled across Zuberi's face as the idea dawned on him. "One like Djoser's, right?"

"Exactly, a staircase to the heavens."

"Or in this case, the ceiling." It didn't take them long with their extraordinary strength to get several boxes in place, allowing them to climb to the top. The cargo boxes were so large Zuberi had to reach down for Hattie and pull her up. All she needed was a whalebone corset and a large-brimmed hat to feel like a Victorian tourist scaling the great pyramid with her dragomen.

They were nearly at the top when Hattie heard voices outside. She put a finger to her lips. Hattie quietly pulled herself to the top level and lay down. The boys followed suit. Hattie's heart raced as the voices came closer. The door opened below. A beam of light flashed here and there.

"Should we take a look-see? It looks like the door was left unlocked," said the more portly of the two.

"Nah. Everything looks in order. It'd take a forklift to get these boxes out."

The flashlight darted around again. "I bet Stewart on the earlier shift forgot to lock it after running for the toilet. You know how he does."

The other guard laughed. "Yeah, that boy needs to change his diet. I don't want to go anywhere near the blast zone."

"Me neither. It smells like he tried to cover it with a weird-smelling air freshener."

"A little smoke and mirrors, right?"

Their combined laughter trailed into the distance and then cut off as the door slammed shut.

Hattie stood. "That was a close call." She looked at her watch. "It is nearly sunup—we need to get cracking."

Thabit cocked his head. "You mean singing, right?"

"Of course."

"Do we need to start from the beginning?" asked Zuberi.

"I think we've already opened the energy between realms. Let's pick up where we left off. You two take turns singing, and I will listen for the sound."

Zuberi and Thabit sang softly. *"Maker of pasture, who causeth the cattle to live . . ."*

Their voices blurred into the background as Hattie concentrated on hearing the sound.

The little tambourine-like noise was coming from the box on

which she stood. Hattie moved over so she could open it. Within the large cardboard box were several smaller boxes.

The boys stood by her as they continued their chant in praise of Amun Re.

She carefully pulled each small box out and placed them in a pile next to her. At the bottom lay a small rectangular box from which she could still hear the gentle chime of the instrument.

"I think you can stop singing now." Inside the box was a soft velvet pouch holding the sistrum. The golden sistrum jangled as she held it aloft. The movement caused the small disks pierced by horizontal rods to chime against one another. She replaced the sistrum inside the pouch, pulling its tassels tight, and then tucked the small instrument into her jacket. Hattie made a cursory effort to put the small boxes back into the larger one and taped it shut to camouflage the intrusion. It was a good thing Zuberi had reminded her that where there were boxes, usually tape was required.

With the sistrum in hand, she could tick off the first order of business for the pharaohs. Now all she needed to do was find Cambyses's army. Hattie was uncertain how exactly this delicate instrument would help her. She sighed as she climbed down the pyramid of boxes.

When she reached the concrete floor, the boys had already climbed down and started shifting the boxes from the pyramid blocklike steps to the original flat wall of the stacks. It was a thing of beauty to see their manly forms working together putting the large boxes back in place. Since they found the sistrum on top of an interior stack, Hattie hoped it might take a while for someone to discover the cargo was compromised, giving them time to escape. The whole escapade was successful but took far more time than she thought it would. So far, they'd been lucky, but as dawn crept near, would luck hold?

CHAPTER TWELVE

The heavy knocking that had pulled her from her Netherworld dreamtime with Niles turned out to be Luke. They'd just arrived at the Vegas train yard, and she needed to get moving.

They had a small window of time to load the European cargo and then continue to Area 51. Only KHNM staff and those with a need-to-know clearance were allowed to progress to the final destination, as they were traveling to a super-secure military base. The creature comforts and helpful stewards of the vintage train would be replaced with an ordinary passenger car and military personnel.

It didn't take long for Alex to toss her few belongings into her bag and head out. After depositing her stuff into the new spartan passenger car boasting rows of pleather seat pads, she went to the warehouse to meet the head registrar of the European branch, Ms. Winifred, and her two assistants.

It was rare for Alex to be up at the crack of dawn, but when she was, the atmosphere between the dark of night and dawn always felt a little magical to her. The dewy moments before sunrise always managed to wash away the tired residue from the previous day. Even the oil-fuel smell of the train yard seemed refreshed as the sun broke over the horizon.

Alex slid the warehouse key into the heavy metal door, but the lock wouldn't turn. She jangled the doorknob to shake out whatever was hindering the ancient mechanism. It still wouldn't budge. She thrust her shoulder against the door with all her might. It gave way with a violent jolt, swinging inward and propelling Alex onto someone who was standing on the other side. Alex's momentum pushed both bodies to the concrete floor with a great thud. The other person's flesh gave in as it took the brunt of Alex's weight. It surprised her to not hear any cracking of bones.

Unharmed, Alex leaped up to check the person sprawled on the floor. A shaft of morning light illuminated the floor of the warehouse and revealed an extremely attractive woman with wide, intelligent brown eyes who was miraculously sitting up. Standing above her were two classically handsome men who looked like statuesque bookends.

Alex extended her hand to the woman, realizing with great mortification that she must be Ms. Winifred. "Are you okay?" It was a good sign that she stood without taking Alex's hand.

"Yes, I am surprisingly well. A little shaken, but I'll be fine." She was moving around as if to assess any unnoticed initial damage.

As the woman interrogated her physical state, Alex broke the awkward silence between them. "What a way for us to meet. I am a little early. You must be Ms. Winifred from the European office. I am Alex Philothea." She knew she was talking fast, but the fact that she just mowed over the registrar for the European branch, and ex–love interest of Buxton, made her a bit off kilter. She wanted so badly to make a good impression on Ms. Winifred.

Ms. Winifred tilted her head, then spoke in a tone that held great authority. "Yes, I wasn't expecting you yet. I need to run out and grab some paperwork. You stay here. My assistants and I will be right back."

"Of course." Alex fiddled with a pen on her clipboard. "Maybe you should stop in and see Buxton and have him check your injuries. As I am sure you know, he isn't a doctor, but he's good with that kind of thing."

"I'll be sure to." Ms. Winifred pushed past Alex and left with her well-formed assistants trailing behind.

Alex took stock of the canyon of boxes before her while she awaited the registrar's return. There were more boxes than the forty or so she was expecting. She hoped they didn't have to shift all the cargo in the warehouse in the next couple of hours. Unless Ms. Winifred possessed a magical artifact that could quadruple their staffing, there was no way they could manage it, let alone have enough space in the cargo hold for it all.

The door to the warehouse opened. Instead of Ms. Winifred and her assistants, Luke, Gormund, and Salima walked through the door. Her heart lightened at seeing her friend Gor.

Luke's expression shifted from his usual easygoing smile to a frown as he took in the wall of cargo behind Alex. "We are supposed to load all that in two hours?"

"I sure hope not. Ms. Winifred will fill us in. She left a few minutes ago to grab some paperwork. Hopefully it includes a manifest for far less than is here."

Salima put her hands on her hips. "I'll check out the boxes." She stalked through the canyon of cargo.

Alex leaned down and hugged Gormund. "It's been a long time. Good to see you, Gor." She stood back and looked at her squat friend who was the anthropomorphic form of the God Bes. He was as wide as he was tall, making him look like a short double-wide demon, especially when he smiled and flashed his pointy teeth. In addition to being a God, he acted as a liaison between the Gods and KHNM. He had a knack for showing up just before trouble started. She hoped that wasn't the case this time. The agency had enough to worry about with the ongoing litigation by the Gods and losing their New York headquarters.

After the time Alex and Gormund saved humanity together, she felt slighted at his seemingly intentional absence from her life. His lack of reaching out to her had made her doubt their friendship, but now she knew it was just a part of who he was. Aside from his all-consuming duties of protecting the slumbering priestess Meyret, he didn't have much time or interest in small talk or other general niceties of human sociability. He was for the most part a hermit who enjoyed his work and his solitude. Seeing him here made her wonder what enticed him out of his den in the scrublands of New Mexico. If a café in the middle of nowhere could be called a den.

In the distance, the rumble of the loading dock door being rolled down thundered through the warehouse. Soon after, the piercing beep of a forklift signaled the warehouse coming to life.

Gormund's expression brightened. "Well, speak of the devil. Winifred, it is so good to see you."

Alex turned to see a woman flanked by two men. Her mind spun. They were not the trio she had nearly taken out with the door earlier. This woman was lovely in a bookish way, chestnut-brown hair pulled into a bun with loose curls framing her face, not at all like the svelte woman with raven locks she literally ran into earlier. The two men who accompanied her were handsome but more akin to sexy professor than Greek god.

The woman held her hand out to Alex. "Winifred Soane. Glad to finally meet you. I've heard a lot about you through the years. Let me introduce you to Theo and Bradley, my assistants."

Alex shook their hands, then moved closer to the newcomers, as the forklift noise made her shout. "Sorry if I appear stunned, but just a few moments ago I met a woman I presumed to be you and your two assistants."

"What the—?" Salima's voice came from above. Everyone's gaze turned toward her as she stood atop the cargo boxes. "Looks like the cargo has been compromised. One of these top boxes is secured differently than the others. This won't look good in my report to the Others." A lilt in her voice telegraphed a certain amount of pleasure at reporting KHNM's failure.

A realization dawned on Alex that the woman she knocked over and her studly helpers most likely stole something from the KHNM cargo. They would have to move fast to apprehend them. The trio left two shakes ago. Maybe there was a chance. "Winifred, Salima, start getting all this cargo packed into the train. We have less than two hours to load up. Luke, Theo, Bradley, we'll need to try and intercept the thieves. Look for a woman with long black hair and two buff dudes."

The warehouse door opened to reveal Niles, grinning. "You rang?"

Alex rolled her eyes. "You can come along too. Luke with me, we'll head left. Bradley and Theo, right. And mister buff here can shoot down the middle."

Gormund put his hands on his hips. "What am I, chopped ibis?"

"I was saving you for last. You get the building's perimeter. No time to lose."

And they barreled out into the rail yard.

Luke and Alex were able to eventually ascertain their quarry had fled. They spoke to a yard worker who saw the trio escape and jump into a cab. After rounding up the others, they made their way back to the warehouse. Ms. Winifred hadn't lost any time and was doggedly working to get her freight into the waiting train before their set departure time. She stood with a clipboard in hand, ticking boxes off her manifest as the forklift driver moved them one by one.

Alex studied Ms. Winifred as she walked toward her. She hadn't given any thought to what this supposed heartbreaker of Buxton would look like, but the competent woman who stood before her didn't match the snippets of info Alex had heard. Winifred was younger than Buxton but possessed the aura of an old soul. Alex imagined she most likely came from her mother's womb asking for a pen and paper so she could properly record her emergence into the world.

Nor did she imagine the woman standing in front of her as someone who would be in a polyamorous relationship. But then again, what experience did she have in knowing anyone who shared that lifestyle? Alex was a little ashamed of her presumptions. Ms. Winifred was drumming her pencil against her lips as Alex approached.

"You've made a lot of progress, Ms. Winifred."

"I think we only have a few more boxes to go. You might want to get your people to board the train so we can leave as scheduled. The government-issued conductor was here a few minutes ago and held a typically regimental attitude regarding any deviations from the agreed-upon schedule."

"Were you able to sort out what was taken?"

"I have a few guesses, but we won't know for sure until we can go through the objects against the manifest. Which will have to happen when we arrive at our destination."

"Well, thank you for all you've done, Ms. Winifred. It's great to meet you. I can't wait to hear all about the European branch."

Winifred placed her hand on Alex's arm. "Call me Freddy. All my friends do."

"Of course, Freddy. See you on the train." Alex left, wondering about what Freddy had just said. Why was it that no one at KHNM called her Freddy?

———

Alex rested her head against the train window and watched the vast desert whiz by. The decor of the passenger car couldn't be further from the luxurious quarters they had gotten used to. Instead of velvet brocade and marble-topped tables, this car had an aesthetic that screamed public transit. The bench seats were covered in flat, thick vinyl that would stick to the back of your legs on a hot summer day. The table between the long bench seats sported a utilitarian greyish-green Formica. Despite the dowdy decor, the train raced through the desert at a fast clip.

Luke sat across from her and was digging deep into an Area 51 website. Alex couldn't believe he was giving his attention to the online narrative about the military base. "Have you found anything about little green men yet?"

"Hey, don't knock it. I'm gathering intel."

"I sincerely doubt there is anything close to reality published on those digital rags."

"It is never a bad idea to get the lay of the land, Alex. Think of it as an unreliable, but interesting, travel guide. I am learning everything I can about the strange land we are going to. To fully understand a place, you have to understand its mythos and folklore. It seems often the most out-of-this-world stories stem from misinterpreted facts or events . . . Is everything all right, Alex?" he said, his tone turning from lecture mode to soft and caring.

"That is a subject jump. I guess, why do you ask?"

"Oh, I don't know." Luke paused and closed his laptop. "It just seems like you've been different since we left Egypt, and I was wondering if something was going on."

"Different, how?"

"It feels like you've been less here, if that makes sense, and . . ."

"Spill it." She was surprised to hear Luke felt this way. She was unhappy and stressed out as of late, and maybe she was unknowingly taking it out on those around her.

"Inflexible. I know you're under a lot of strain with the move, helping Buxton with the lawsuit, and then Niles shows up."

Niles walked into the passenger cabin. As per usual his timing was perfect in the most horrible of ways.

"You say that as if it is a bad thing, friend." Niles leaned over the table and rested his knuckles on the speckled Formica, his tone less than friendly.

Alex never let on to Niles that Luke had harbored feelings for her. But Niles seemed to sense something between them and didn't like it. Alex had no idea how Luke felt about her now. When they last spoke of it, they agreed to remain friends.

Luke started jamming his possessions into his backpack. "I'm gonna go find Salima and Ms. Winifred. I think we need to work out some things with the cargo before we arrive." He slid out of the booth, slung his bag over his shoulder, and made his way through the passenger car.

Niles sat in Luke's spot across from Alex.

"Nice going, friend."

Niles shrugged his shoulders. "What?"

"You know."

"I can't help myself. There is something about him that irritates the heck out of me."

"Like being one of the nicest people on earth."

"I guess that makes me nice-intolerant."

"Whatever. Just try to be a little less of a jerk to him. I know you and Salima were sent to watch over us, but you don't have to be an ass."

"But maybe I enjoy it." His cocky smile slowly faded as he took in Alex's pointed look of disapproval.

"I'll do my best."

"Promise?"

Niles clasped Alex's hands, which were resting on the table. "I promise."

Gormund burst into the cabin. He scooted in beside Niles, bumping him next to the window, making Niles release Alex's hands. "Awww, how sweet to see the two lovebirds singing songs of promise."

"Not what you think, Gor," said Alex.

"How do you pretend to know what a God is thinking?" Alex was certain Gormund's smirk was intended as jaunty, but the reveal of his pointy teeth gave it a very different vibe. Fortunately, she knew him well enough to look beyond the sharp pearly whites.

Alex glanced at her watch. "We've been traveling for about an hour now. I think we should be there any minute, but I don't see any buildings or anything in the distance."

"That is rather strange. You'd think the evidence of a military base would be cropping up by now," said Niles.

In the distance Alex could see what looked like a vast cleft in the landscape. "Up ahead there is a gaping canyon. It looks like we are heading right at it."

Gormund noticed it; his eyes went wide. "And no bridge."

Alex braced herself as the train lurched forward. Their speed increased greatly and the landscape around them became a beige and brown blur. "Is the conductor going to try and jump the canyon?"

Gormund rubbed his hands together. "Never expected this level of excitement when I volunteered."

Niles caught Alex's gaze. "That seems a bit daredevily for the US government, but hang on tight just in case."

The train sped forward and fell into the jagged canyon.

CHAPTER THIRTEEN

After returning to the Luxor hotel with the sistrum in hand, she discovered that neither the keycard nor the password from the Old Winter Palace Hotel worked for the room in Vegas. She found no interest in assistance from the suspicious front desk clerk either. It didn't come as a shock that the pharaohs hadn't provided Hattie with a return trip to Egypt. It looked like she and the boys would be spending some more time in Vegas.

With no quick way back to Egypt and needing a safe space so her Ba could travel to the Netherworld for her meetup with the pharaohs, she needed a room. One thing was for sure—there was no way she was going to sleep under this pyramid of glass and hollow tributes to her homeland. Hattie and the boys made their way down the strip to Caesars Palace. It would be far less exasperating to stay somewhere in which a culture other than her own was being "honored."

At Caesars, Hattie booked one of the villa suites. It contained an overabundance of square footage fit for a celebrity and their entourage. It was vastly more than they needed, but she longed for its small private pool. After the train yard adventure, she wanted to soak in deep water and not deal with the hoi polloi. The many-chambered and luxuriously appointed suite brought back memories of her days as a king. The staff here were far less numerous and fawning, but just as attentive.

Being of a certain age, Hattie had known too many toga-wrapped Romans to count, including Julius Caesar and Mark Antony. It disgusted her the way they strolled about, cloaked in their colossal egos and a commanding sense of their own exceptionalism. She didn't shed a tear when Rome fell.

Zuberi and Thabit followed her through the large double doors into a circular atrium with a domed roof and a fountain burbling away at its center. The waters were dancing over a standing statue of Venus. Up ahead stretched a long hall dotted with numerous hanging glass lantern-shaped light fixtures. The bright light of the main living room glowed in the distance. On either side of the main corridor were two marble hallways leading to the many chambers in the suite. Moving forward she paused to look at the fountain. Hattie was struck by the fine workmanship of the goddess statue. It was so lifelike, making her wonder if the rumors she heard were true.

"What is it, mistress?" Zuberi asked.

"I've heard a story about the statues at this hotel. It might be true, or like most things in Vegas it may be fool's gold."

Thabit put his hand in the fountain's stream, letting the water flow over his fingers. "I do love a juicy rumor. What is it?"

"They say when the clock strikes midnight the statues here come to life. They simply walk off their pedestals and party with the mortals."

Thabit's expression brightened with excitement. "Do you think it's true?"

Zuberi crossed his arms. "Now, Thabit . . ."

Hattie had never witnessed Thabit smile so big. "It may be. As you both are aware, many things in this world are extraordinary, much like yourselves." She wandered down the main hall to the living room. It boasted floor-to-ceiling windows overlooking a courtyard with a pool available to the exclusive residents of the villa suites. It was complete with a Roman temple folly and palm trees.

"Garden of the Gods. That is what they call this." Hattie slid one of the glass doors open and stepped onto her veranda. Scattered around was enough lounging furniture to host a sizable cocktail party. The blue tile of her small private pool shimmered in the distance, enticing her into its cool, welcoming waters. Zuberi and Thabit stood on either side of her as they took in the sight of sunbathers and swimmers around the communal pool in their colorful and scanty swimsuits. Lounging under tall palm trees were tanned and toned socialites, and in the far distance, in the less exclusive area beyond, lay a sea of cellulite and sunblock.

"Mortals' ways are strange, mistress," said Zuberi.

"How would you both feel about investigating whether or not that statue rumor is true?"

Hattie knew Thabit was barely containing his excitement. "But don't you need our help in readying yourself for your pharaonic meeting?"

"You guys can prepare me for the ceremony and leave in plenty of time to find out the truth."

Zuberi looked perplexed. "But won't you need us to guard your body while you travel to the in-between?"

"Nobody who would care knows where we are, and these high-dollar suites have pretty tight security for the high rollers who stay here. I think I will be fine to let you off guard duty this one time in a couple thousand years."

"Oh, thank you!" Thabit was nearly vibrating with excitement.

"Do me one favor. If you find they do come to life and there is a big party, be back before dawn. I intend to book us on the first flight home."

"Anything else, mistress?" asked Zuberi.

"Report back anything out of the ordinary."

"You mean other than statuary that are not us coming to life?"

"Yes, Thabit. You never know what kinds of information these beings might hold that could be helpful to us down the line. Like your knowledge of priestly life from the Greek temple of Amun helping us find the sistrum."

Thabit looked at the ground.

Hattie guessed he was saddened at the reminder he wasn't human. She put an arm on each of their shoulders. "You know, I am thankful for you both every day. I can't imagine I would be anywhere near sane without the two of you by my side."

Zuberi placed his hand on his heart. "You honor us with your words. We praise your name to the heavens in gratitude for what you have given us, and . . ."

"A family. Something we two were never made to have," Thabit added.

Hattie hugged them both. The three of them had become a small family unit over time. She depended on them as much as they on her. "Let's get inside and get me purified for my big meeting. After that you guys are free to get your party on."

~~~

Hattie's Ba landed on the same rock-strewn mountainside in the Netherworld that Narmer transported her to earlier. Since she had already been escorted to this exact spot by a Netherworld resident, her Ba transported her directly back to that same location. No one was waiting for her, but they probably figured she would have no problem remembering where the Netherworld copy of the tomb where her beloveds were dumped centuries ago was. In the valley below lay her mortuary temple. It pleased her to see its former glory, unlike the bleached-out reconstructed ruins that stand there today.

As she picked her way down the rocky slope, it occurred to her there was another more likely reason no one was there to escort her. Since the pharaohs were working against the Gods, which of them would volunteer to conspicuously stand in the middle of nowhere waiting? The Gods had eyes everywhere, and the last thing a clandestine uprising—or whatever it was the pharaohs were up to—needed was the piqued curiosity of the Holy Ones. She grabbed the rope hanging from the opening and shimmied down the shaft to the subterranean tomb and toward the flickering torchlight. The sistrum jangled in the bag slung over her shoulder. As she neared the end, a low hum of voices echoed from the tomb shaft.

The pharaohs were waiting for her in a smaller secondary chamber close to the entrance. This time there were far fewer of them. Only Narmer, Sneferu, Ahmose, and his wife Ahmose-Nefertari were there. Aside from the dead queen, the only other hostage present was her father. He stood a little to the side and away from the others. At least he was no longer bound. The other pharaohs probably saw him as their ace in the hole, as her devotion to her father was well known.

"Where is everyone else? Did your little rebellion lose supporters? Or is there a big holiday celebration going on in the Field of Reeds?"

"If you are asking where your lover is, he is with the other captives, bound in the rear chamber."

Hattie realized every day for Narmer must be a bad day. His sleeping platform must have possessed no "right" side from which to rise. Since they were dead, Hattie wondered if they slept at all. Narmer must have been just as miserable as a mortal as he was in the afterlife. As they say, a crocodile never sheds its skin.

Sneferu stepped toward Hattie. The gaze of his warm brown eyes softened the sharp edge of Narmer's words. "We have not lost any in our fellowship. Last time we figured it would be important to show you our numbers. This time a smaller group felt safer. The Gods have eyes everywhere."

Hattie pulled the sistrum from her bag. "Speaking of which, I guess we should get down to business. I have what you asked for. What's next?"

All the royals, even her father, came near to take a closer look. A spark of fond recognition warmed Ahmose-Nefertari's face at seeing her old instrument.

The crowd of dead royals stared at the artifact as if they couldn't believe she was able to retrieve it. Hattie cleared her throat. "I don't mean to be rude or anything, but how do I use this artifact to find Cambyses's army?"

Sneferu looked away into the distance. "You know the funny thing is—"

"We don't know." Narmer's expression was hard, almost daring Hattie to get angry.

"You don't know?" Hattie jammed the sistrum into her bag. "You sent me on this fool's errand. For 'We don't know'?"

Ahmose-Nefertari brightened. "I have an idea."

Her adoring husband gushed at her. "Let us hear it. I am sure it is brilliant."

"Me too," muttered Hattie.

"Go to Egypt, see where the holy relic leads you."

"That's it?" Hattie shook her head. "You know this is the most harebrained scheme. This goes way beyond the genius plan that stripped my beloveds of their eternity. This whole idea stinks like rotted flesh. I wash my hands of it." She brushed her hands together. "Goodbye, Father. Maybe your friends here will come to their senses and set you and the others free to enjoy your well-deserved afterlife in the Field of Reeds. I'm out."

She spun on her heel and stomped away. Halfway through the passage, her father's voice boomed, calling out a name she hadn't heard in over three thousand years, "Khnemet-Amun-Hatshepsut."

His tone stopped her in her tracks. It was *the* name, her name, the one he would call when she had blatantly disobeyed him. As always in this situation, his voice held an odd mix of anger and pride, as he raised her to be independent.

"Please." His voice wavered. "Do this one thing for me. Go to our homeland and try at least. See if you are led by the artifact."

His emotional tone bored deep into her defenses and her natural disinclination to help the self-righteous pharaohs who had schemed her into this ridiculous scenario and held her beloveds captive. Hattie couldn't let her irritation at these men, who were using her like a pawn, color her judgment and leave it to chance that they would free her father, nephew, lover, and brother-husband from captivity. She would need to at least give it her best shot. She owed her beloveds that. But this was the end of the road for her. Hattie meant to make it clear for everybody in the room. Their lack of planning wasn't going to turn into her eternal emergency.

Hattie turned to face them. "If I go to Egypt, and the instrument leads me straight to Cambyses's army and this artifact you desire, we are done. Right?"

Sneferu nodded. "Correct."

"That is all great and good, but what concerns me is the lack of clarity you have for your plan. To call your instructions to 'just explore and see where the magic leads you' vague is a vast understatement. You have no plan. You have no reason to think this will work. I need a guarantee. If I do this and am true of heart in my attempt to fulfill your wishes, there must be a point when you all admit defeat and remove the threat of my beloveds and free them to their deserved afterlife."

Narmer snorted. "What a selfish little princess you are. It is disgraceful you would put limits on what you would do to save your own flesh and blood."

A brilliant flash of anger scorched through Hattie. "Some might say binding and keeping your own pharaonic blood as captives is not only disgraceful, but a desecration to the holy sanctity of royal blood."

"Why you . . ." Narmer stormed toward Hattie. Sneferu held his arm out, stopping Narmer's progress.

"We need to cool things down here. There is truth in what you say, Hattie. But troubling times call for troubling actions. I see your point and agree to the idea of a potential future capitulation if need be."

Ahmose-Nefertari stepped forward. "But how do you measure the unmeasurable? How will we know when to call this to an end? There is no way we will be able to measure her heart's intent."

A look of discomfort shadowed Sneferu's face. "There is a way. A pair of golden cuffs were forged by the Goddess Maat. Once they bond with their wearer, it will reflect the purity of their intentions. I think this instance calls for that *friend* of yours."

"That I should use my mortal world connections for the use

of this undeserving one." Narmer shook his head, looking none too pleased with the thought. "If it is the only way, so be it."

Sneferu brightened. "Narmer has a connection in the mortal world, who we know possesses these cuffs. Hattie, if you agree to bind yourself to the cuffs, once you believe your avenues of discovery are exhausted, signal us. You will need to wear the cuffs while we question you. The artifact will project to us whether you are true of heart. If it proves you are, we commit to ending our agreement with you."

Hattie wanted to leave no doubts hanging about. "I need to hear you all swear by blood oath that you agree with and will uphold this agreement."

Narmer unsheathed a small dagger from a belt around his waist and passed it around. Each of the colluding pharaohs sliced a gash in their left hand. The golden essence of the dead pharaohs rose to the surface of their palms. Each held their hand aloft while Sneferu spoke the oath. Hattie felt the strong bond of oath magic weave a cord from each of the pharaohs to her.

"So where are these cuffs?"

"They are in the mortal world. Once you arrive in the sacred black land of Egypt, we will see they find their way to you."

"And what if they don't?"

"You are free from our bond," said Sneferu.

Hattie gazed over at her dad. "Here goes nothing, I guess."

"Thank you, my beloved." Her dad's voice went soft with love and pride.

Hattie dipped her head in a small bow. "Of course, my beloved." Hattie was overcome at hearing the admiration in her father's voice. Something deep broke inside her, and it was as if the centuries of shattering loneliness she experienced throughout her immortality washed over her. She wiped a stream of tears from her eyes as she neared the rope ladder rising to the entrance. She was glad her father didn't see her weep. To this day she prided herself on being his tough, unbreakable one, his favorite.

She climbed to the exact spot on the cleft of the mountain where she had arrived earlier and closed her eyes. Before the magic pulse of teleportation surged through her, a terrible thought floated across her mind. She had a sick feeling she knew exactly who Narmer's mortal-world contact might be.

CHAPTER FOURTEEN

Alex's stomach sunk as her body plummeted downward with the train. An inexplicable lightness filled her as if she was floating in zero gravity, then everything went dark. The light free-floating sensation shifted in a second to the heavy substance of her own gravity as she thudded back into her seat. Her eyes opened to darkness. The lights in the train car had gone out. In the far distance, she could see a bright glow. Feeling around her, she grabbed her scribe's bag and pulled out her phone. Both Gormund and Niles shielded their eyes against the sudden light.

"Sorry." She redirected the light toward the window. The train was moving through a dark void that didn't include the customary tracks one would normally expect to see. "Looks like the Air Force has requisitioned themselves a wormhole."

Gormund smirked. "Or maybe it was paid in ransom by one of the alien nations they are currently holding hostages from."

"Phooey, Gor."

"Are you saying you don't believe aliens exist?" he asked.

"I believe it is completely possible there are other life forms in the universe and we might get visited by them someday. But do I believe that this barren patch of desert has been continually irresistible to alien life since the 1950s? That, I sincerely doubt."

Mischief sparkled in Niles's eyes. "In playing the Devourer of Soul's advocate, I would have to point out that up until a very short while ago, you were unaware of many miraculous things."

"Like sitting across the table from two anthropomorphic Egyptian Gods?"

"If you are thinking broadly, yes, but in truth, I was really only referring to myself."

Gormund barked a laugh and then slid out of the booth. "You are too much, Niles. I'm going to find the others for our impending arrival. I suggest you two lovebirds do the same."

After Gor's small and stocky form passed through the metal door, Niles leaned over the table toward Alex. "Alone at last."

"Are we ever truly alone? From what I hear, the Gods have eyes everywhere."

"As far as I know, they are not watching me that closely. Of course, they do have my collateral in case I should fail."

"Collateral? What did they make you sign over?"

"My word, Alex. A God's word is binding. I could no sooner disobey what I am charged to do than . . ." It was as if Niles thought better of whatever he was going to say. "Let's just say I cannot break my word."

"Why have you been avoiding me like the seven plagues if you don't think they are watching you closely?" Alex was tired of being a moon in his orbit, close enough to be in his gravitational pull but feeling like a vast expanse of space stood between them. She wanted nothing more than to have some uninterrupted alone time with him beyond the KHNM drama to sort out what there was between them. Was it an infatuation or something more? He placed himself in grave danger time and again to shield her from the wrath of the other Gods. Was it love driving him to do so, or was it only because of a promise he'd made to Alex's father all those years ago? Her heart could never find purchase when it came to him. No matter what he felt for her, Alex's feelings hadn't changed one iota since that night at Luxor Temple, where he kissed her for the first time. She needed to know where to place those feelings, or to work at ridding herself of them.

Niles leaned back and crossed his arms over his chest. "Salima has been asked to report independently of me. I figure the less you and I are seen together by anyone, the better. Since you and Salima have an unpredictable relationship, I don't know how much I can trust her. The last thing we need is for my family members to be questioning my loyalties or my ability to do what I've been tasked with." He laid his hands over hers.

The familiar electric thrum of his touch sent a wave of desire through Alex. She gazed into his fathomless blue eyes encircled with a shimmering ring of golden stardust, making them look as if they held an entire universe. "We could always meet in our dreams."

"A dream itself is but a shadow. I yearn to wake with you."

They leaned over the table toward one another. Niles's hand drifted to Alex's neck, making her shiver as he softly stroked her skin. He edged in closer, his soft lips grazing hers. The cabin door banged shut. Her eyes flew open, and Alex pushed away from Niles. The room brightened, revealing the train was no longer in motion, and a blue-white station light illuminated the platform below.

Luke stood in the doorway with his hands thrust into his pockets. "I was sent to fetch you. Everyone is gathering on the platform."

Alex stood tucking stray hairs behind her ears. "Has Buxton arrived?"

"You'll know it when I do." Luke turned on his heel and walked through to the next car. Alex followed with Niles trailing behind her. It was strange for Luke to be so short in his response to her. She thought he was okay with how things stood between them, but maybe she was wrong.

Alex looked at the handful of KHNM agents who gathered on the platform. It was amazing the amount of work the agency was able to accomplish with such a small staff. She took in the utilitarian depot around her. It, along with the beige and brown buildings of the base, sat in a wide valley between two stands of mountains. At the end of the rail line was a massive warehouse where workers were getting ready to unload the cargo.

She was pleased to see that Buxton had arrived. Her feelings about seeing his assistant Roberta Thorne were far from what Alex would describe as pleased. Thorne had been staying in New York City to tie up some loose ends for Buxton. She must have concluded her business earlier than expected.

Thorne had never liked Alex, and she never knew why. Thorne was an agent of KHNM for many years and thought the world of Alex's father, but when it came to Alex, anything she said or did earned a look of disapproval from Thorne. Even when Buxton was lost in the Netherworld and Thorne was her assistant, her pointed barbs, although a little less sharp-edged, were always flying in Alex's direction.

"Jeeves!" Luke rushed off the train and over to a large dog kennel standing between Buxton and Thorne. Jeeves was Luke's miniature schnauzer, making Alex wonder about the expansive kennel size. Although, in a way it made sense—Luke loved to spoil the little pup. She guessed it was most likely outfitted with a memory foam cushion, a non-spill water dish, and a curated collection of the little guy's favorite toys.

Niles paused before exiting the train. "I'm going to check on the payload." He grazed his hand against her arm and whispered into her ear, his warm breath tickling her neck. "I will find a way for us to be together." Without a second glance, he passed through to the next car.

She hoped he would find a way.

Alex dashed down the metal steps and hugged Buxton. "Good to see you, old man." His presence always had a grounding effect on her.

Buxton righted his spectacles. "Old man?" Alex had taken to calling him that since his return from being lost in the Netherworld. For some reason, it felt right. Buxton motioned toward Luke, who was gently pulling Jeeves out of the kennel. "Now that is an entirely different story, grey beard and all."

Alex chuckled at Buxton's joke. "Yes, Jeeves has a luxurious one at that."

The dog was oddly subdued. In usual circumstances, when Jeeves and Luke were parted for any length of time, the schnauzer's extreme vocal welcoming ceremony, complete with stub wagging and hind-leg dancing, usually went on until the little prince either sufficiently chastised Luke or welcomed him home. Alex was never clear which was the case. But Jeeves lay limp in Luke's arms.

Alex moved close to inspect him. "Is he okay?"

Thorne placed her hands on her hips and looked down her nose at both of them. "I've kept him on tranquilizers for the trip. Making his transition less stressful. I am sure he is fine."

Luke shot Thorne a blistering look. "You tranquilized him like this all the way from New York?"

Alex knew exactly what he was thinking. It wasn't the dog's comfort that inspired her to dose Jeeves. Thorne was ill-equipped to care for any living thing, even herself. Alex often witnessed how punishing she was to herself. It made her wonder what had damaged Thorne so.

Luke looked down at the sweet fur ball in his arms. "If there is something wrong with him, Thorne . . ." He clamped his mouth shut as if he thought better of saying the threat out loud. Silence widened between them as he stroked the small dog.

"Why are you here, anyway?" Alex's words came out sharper than she intended.

Buxton chimed in. "I figured we needed all hands on deck. I decided to temporarily shutter the New York residence. With our offices closed at the Met, I don't know if it is worthwhile keeping it attended to, with everything else going on. If worse comes to worst, we could always sell the place. I think the sale of a townhouse facing Central Park and the Met could potentially fund our new headquarters. That is if we prevail in the lawsuit, and the residence is determined to belong to us and not the Gods."

Alex's heart sank at the thought of the beautiful residence being up for sale. She had been a part of KHNM for a brief period, but that house managed to become home for her. She could only imagine how the others who had been around much longer felt.

Gwen alighted from the train looking vexed at the sight of them all standing around. "Alex, Luke, the others need your help with the cargo off-loading. I've just heard from the General. He will be meeting us here, Buxton, and will personally take the three of us to our quarters. He is an old friend of Jorge's and is very interested in meeting you. The soldiers will bring the others along once everything is unloaded."

Alex flushed with anger at Gwen assigning any sort of task to her. While KHNM did owe Gwen for securing this temporary home for the agency, it appeared that arriving at this new

promised land gave her lofty ideas about her place within
KHNM.

Buxton must have sensed Alex's irritation and spoke quickly.
"Thank you, Alex, for helping the others. I appreciate it."

Alex took the meager verbal ointment Buxton offered,
knowing they were in an impossible situation and that they all
needed to take it on the chin here and there.

Luke kissed Jeeves's head behind his bushy silver eyebrows
and eased him into the kennel. The metal door rattled as he shut
it. "Can you keep an eye on him, Buxton? Make sure he is okay?"

"You can depend on it."

It took some time for those who stayed behind to unload the
cargo from the train and pack it into covered Air Force trucks to
transport them to the new KHNM temporary residence. Alex was
surprised at the number of soldiers the General allocated toward
this end. Jorge must have had a solid friendship with him for
Gwen to receive such a strong outpouring of assistance.

Each person in the KHNM party rode shotgun in a soldier-
driven truck. At first, Alex tried to make small talk with her
driver, but his answers were invariably monosyllabic. Maybe the
soldiers at Area 51 were more buttoned-up than others on a
more conventional base given its super-secret reputation.
Outside the passenger side window, a large flat basin surrounded
by jagged mountains stretched on into the distance. The caravan
of agents and artifacts was heading toward one of the great
peaks. The truck jostled as it climbed higher on a long, dusty
road, switching back on itself as they gained elevation.

Nearing the summit, Alex saw a gate up ahead. Instead of the
expected red-and-white-striped military gate blocking access, it

was an ornate wrought-iron affair. A matching twelve-foot-high fence ran as far as she could see in either direction. Her truck was the first in the caravan. The driver jumped out and pushed a button on an intercom panel. After the gates opened wide, he hopped back in and continued. After rounding a particularly tight switchback, a truck just like theirs came right at them. On a cliff like this one, the only way forward was through the other vehicle or rolling down to the desert basin below. She grabbed onto her driver's arm. "Stop the car!"

As if in perfect lockstep, the oncoming truck came to an abrupt halt as they did. Alex breathed a sigh of relief. The driver smirked as he opened the door and slid out of the truck. The driver in the truck in front of them exited his vehicle at the same time. She wondered how they would make way for one another on this narrow road. Then it hit her—her driver was walking toward his reflection. They must be facing a massive mirror. Alex scanned the area but couldn't tell where the mirror began or ended. Near the driver was a white post with a red button. When the driver pushed a section of the mirror away, a Bavarian chalet complete with an alpine forest was revealed. They drove past the house and into a tunnel cut from the mountainside.

Alex stepped out of the truck. The temperature change was astounding. It felt thirty degrees cooler than the outer environment. The impossible fragrance of pine from the surrounding forest was refreshing. As she took in the scenery, her sense of wonder must have been radiating brightly.

The driver laughed. "Germans, right?"

Someone with more bars and stars approached Alex and shot a withering look of disapproval at her driver.

Luke, Niles, and the others were walking toward her with gaped mouths.

Her driver stiffened and then saluted the approaching officer.

The man put his hand out. "Colonel Sanderson, at your service. I am instructed to bring you and your envoy to Schliemann Haus, where you can be united with your party, meet your host the General, and unpack. The soldiers have orders to move your cargo to the secured bay beyond this area. Your Ms. Winifred and her assistants are keeping them on task. Apparently, something went missing in Vegas. She wanted to stay behind and check against her manifest. You can be certain your items will be handled with the greatest of care."

Luke did a double take. "Schliemann Haus?"

The others gathered around as Colonel Sanderson explained. "Helmut Schliemann was a resident here when the base first opened. Command hired him for a top-secret mission that ultimately failed. The documents about the project were recently declassified. We now know his initial project was exploring aircraft invisibility. He was a thought-to-be mad genius brought over after WWII. The only way the government could entice him to work on the project was to build him a taste of his homeland."

"So he was one of *those* Germans," said Luke.

"Dr. Schliemann was many things—eccentric, genius, and kind, but not a Nazi. If that was what you were trying to imply." The colonel's complexion reddened in anger as he continued walking toward the large Bavarian-style house complete with green shutters and balconies exploding with bright red and hot pink flowers. "His methods as a scientist were suspect, and he had a bull-in-a-china-shop approach, but he certainly knew a thing or two."

Luke chuckled.

"You find something I said funny, young man?" The colonel's face pinched as if he'd smelt something bad, and he quickened his pace.

Alex double-stepped to keep up with him. "Sorry, colonel,

archeology joke. There was a Heinrich Schliemann who discovered ancient Troy. And he was known to have roughly the same approach in his chosen field."

"By blasting through nine levels of archaeological strata," added Luke.

"You know the tunnel your cargo is stored in? Well, let's just say Schliemann had a fondness for explosives. Maybe they were related."

"Small world," said Alex as she strolled down the unbelievably mossy, grassy wild terrain in the middle of an arid desert. Alex was enchanted by the colorful low-growing alpine flowers carpeting the ground beneath their feet. Out in the distance, beyond this fantastical landscape, it looked as if the desert mountains across the valley below were capped with snow-packed glaciers. The colonel cast his gaze in that same direction.

"It's an optical illusion. Think of it as an image overlaid on the surface of the box that encapsulates this environment."

"Incredible." Alex stopped to take it all in. Niles stood at her side, sharing the moment.

The colonel placed his hands on his hips. "I've heard tell, sometimes it snows in here."

"In here?" asked Luke.

"You see, we are in what you might think of as a massive square biosphere. The technology was created by Dr. Schliemann. It was a part of the failed mission he was hired for. The government built the house, but the tech supporting this environment was created and implemented by the doctor. He was using the space around the house to test his theories of invisibility. The life-sized alpine terrarium we are now standing in is created in part by the material surrounding it. The panels translate the sun into the needed moisture and shade levels to mimic the climate needed for these trees and flowers to thrive."

"And the outside is a mirror?" asked Salima.

Gormund laughed. "Now we know where Salima will be spending her time."

"Very funny, little man." Instead of getting angry, Salima playfully bumped Gormund with her hip.

The relaxed attitude Salima showed at Gormund's smart-aleck remark made the point blood really was thicker than water. Salima would have been puffing outbursts of cinnamon if Alex made that comment.

The colonel pursed his lips. "I wouldn't call it a mirror. If it were a mirror that size, it would draw attention to the landscape as a big, shiny object instead of camouflaging it as this does. The material seems to absorb and mimic the landscape around it, but it isn't a true reflection. But we should get inside the house, your people are expecting you."

"Seems to?" asked Niles.

"Yeah, Schliemann died, and we've not been able to figure out the technology, try as we might."

This green lush jewel box was nothing short of amazing. "But the tech appears to work, so why did the mission fail?"

"Ground testing is very different from flight testing." The colonel opened the heavy wooden door to the sound of ten thousand cuckoo clocks marking the hour coupled with the sharp bark of a schnauzer.

Jeeves bolted past Alex as she stepped inside. Each of the foyer walls was plastered with countless clocks making their unique sound. Jeeves flew back past Alex into the house and charged up the main staircase. About halfway up he continued to accompany the clock sounds with his high-pitched chirp. His tranquilizers must have worn off.

Admonishing Jeeves's singing with each step, Luke pushed through the door and up the stairs.

Alex was pleased to see the little guy had recovered from his heavy-handed dosing from Thorne. As soon as Luke caught up with the dog, he scooped him into his arms. The cacophony of the clocks halted. The silence was deafening for a moment as their ears attempted to recalibrate. It was unbelievable how many clocks lined the walls, each unique in its design. "What's with the clocks, colonel?"

"Yet another oddity of the old doctor. He had a fondness for them."

"Obviously," Gormund mumbled under his breath. Luke walked down the stairs, Jeeves happily licking his face.

The colonel cleared his throat. "Let me show you to the library. I believe that is where your people are waiting for you." They passed by a large living room with cross-paned windows looking beyond the immediate grounds to the snowcapped mountains in the distance.

"Do those clocks go off every hour?" Alex was getting a headache thinking about it.

"Oh no, that would be utter madness. Only every third hour."

"And that's not considered mad? I think it will drive me cuckoo." Luke's tone held much less mirth than his wordplay did.

"You'll get used to it. Before you know it, you won't hear them at all."

Alex sincerely doubted that. "That includes the a.m. hours?"

"Yes ma'am, but thankfully the sleeping quarters have been thoroughly soundproofed."

"Do you keep them running as an homage to the original resident?" asked Alex.

"No, they cannot be shut off. A few decades ago, somebody took the time to disable them, and the whole ecosystem shut down. The cuckoo clocks appear to be an integral element of keeping this place running."

"This whole snow globe we are in is like a giant clockwork?" asked Salima.

"Deep in the mountain behind us is a contraption Schliemann contrived that no one can figure out. It appears to be a type of Rube Goldberg machine on an infinite loop."

They arrived at large wooden doors. The colonel slid them open and stepped aside. "Here are your friends. If you do not require anything else, I will return to the base."

Buxton walked over and shook the colonel's hand. "Thank you for everything. You've done a bang-up job at making us feel welcome."

Colonel Sanderson smiled briefly. "Your personal items should be brought along shortly and will be put into your assigned rooms." He pulled out a piece of paper and handed it to Buxton. "You will find a house plan with your assigned rooms. Dr. Buxton, you will of course be staying in Dr. Schliemann's suite."

Buxton unfolded the house plan. "I will defer that honor to my second in command."

Both Thorne and Gwen perked up.

"Alex, would you do the honors, and take the big room for me once more?"

Both Thorne and Gwen noticeably slumped.

Alex always found this deferment of any hint of luxury to be a bit odd given Buxton's expensive tastes. She was fairly certain it was an impulse borne out of his own code of chivalry. "Of course."

The colonel clapped his hands together. "And with that, I will be off. Please do enjoy the house and the grounds. The kitchen is well stocked if you experience pangs of hunger. But do not, under any circumstances, go into the basement where the main clock-works are. That level is off-limits to every one of you." He paused for a moment, making eye contact with each of them to seal the deal. He saluted them and turned on his heel to leave. A few paces out into the main hall he halted. "Oh and Alex, since you are staying in Dr. Schliemann's suite, don't be surprised if you have a late-night visitor. Rumor has it he likes to visit his old rooms."

Alex doubted the German scientist roamed the halls of the house. She hoped the colonel was keyed into cosmic truths, as she was hoping for a visitor tonight, but certainly not in the form of a German ghost.

CHAPTER FIFTEEN

The small yet deep pool was the perfect place to wash away the transcendental residue she acquired from traveling between realms. Hattie was glad she sent the boys off to party with the hotel's statues. It was a win-win situation. Not only would they have fun, but she could enjoy complete and satisfying solitude. Her arms were flung back against the pool's edge as she listened to the distant murmur of conversations bubbling up from the exclusive poolside below and the sweet night breeze as it ruffled the leaves of the potted jungle surrounding her.

She closed her eyes and let her mind drift away to centuries ago, when she was king of Egypt. Back when she needed to present herself in male drag for her official duties. Dressing as a man gave her both a sense of strength influenced by her exposure to the powerful men who surrounded her throughout her life, and profound anger. An anger rooted in the fact she needed to make a charade of her sex in order to rule. After performing her ritualistic and kingly duties, she would strip down and swim naked under the moonlight, for all the Gods and men to see her for what she was, a powerful woman.

Laughter, the soft chatter of voices, and the clinking of crystal broke through Hattie's reverie. The sounds were too close to be coming from below. Hattie pushed away from the pool wall and climbed the steps leading out. Water cascaded down her body and dripped onto the tiled floor as she reached for the thick white hotel robe. It embraced her with its plush softness as she shrugged it over her body and tied it shut.

Inside were Thabit and Zuberi, but they were not alone. There were two women and a man with them. They were all huddled around a mahogany bar, their joyful camaraderie reflected in the mirror on the wall behind it. Hattie was a bit put out that her steward and porter had the temerity to bring the party back to her. For all they knew, she could still be in between realms, putting her in grave jeopardy. Hattie tamped down her anger. Her room was far from where they congregated, and it had been centuries since she'd witnessed them this enlivened and joyful. It wouldn't be the worst thing to give them a pass on this indiscretion.

As she thought about it more, they might have done her a great favor. If these guests were the enlivened statues, chances were they might help Hattie sort out who Narmer's connection was in the mortal world. Hattie hoped she was wrong, but it was likely that these enlivened statues were created by the same magical hand who brought Thabit and Zuberi to life. If her guess about the identity of Narmer's mortal-world contact was correct, it couldn't hurt to have an in with a couple of his other creations. Although the thought of dealing with that snake made her skin crawl.

As Hattie stepped through the threshold, all eyes turned to her. Zuberi's eyes went wide. "Sorry, mistress. We thought you'd be exhausted from your travels and would be deep asleep." Zuberi, who appeared to be stone drunk, was not his usual articulate self. "I mean, this place is so big, and your room is far away, we figured we would not be disturbing you."

"It is all right. I am glad to see you are enjoying yourselves." Thabit had his arm around one of the women, who was nearly as beautiful as moonlight shimmering on the Nile. Zuberi leaned in toward a man who exuded agile strength and possessed a smile that could be considered a weapon of mass distraction. One of the women who stood a little apart from the others appeared to be along for the ride and not partaking in the fun and games. "Please introduce your friends to me."

Thabit squeezed the woman next to him. "Well, this here is Venus. The other two are Minerva and Apollo."

"It's a pleasure to meet you all. I am Hattie." She walked to the bar.

Minerva gave Hattie a look of appraisal. "Thabit and Zuberi told us about you."

Hattie wondered what exactly that meant. Over the centuries, the boys had gotten good at making stuff up about her on the fly, as Hattie's long life could be difficult to explain. She wondered if they'd told the truth this time.

Apollo propped himself against the bar. "Please call me Paul. I was modeled after Apollo, but it never felt right to me to go by the God's name. Paul suits me fine."

Both Venus and Minerva shared a look, but neither shared a different name for themselves.

Zuberi poured a flute of champagne and slid it across to Hattie. She took a sip as she considered the group of enlivened statues. "What do you say we move to the salon area? I'd love to learn more about you all."

Minerva polished off her champagne and pointedly set the

flute on the bar top. "We should probably get going. You know the rules, guys, we only have a few more hours."

"Aw, Minerva is always the party pooper. I'm not going back one second earlier than I have to. I want to enjoy my freedom while I can." Venus pulled Minerva toward the large living room area. Her captive didn't put up much of a struggle as she was dragged into the adjacent room and onto a chaise lounge. Zuberi supplied her with a fresh flute of champagne.

Paul walked alongside Hattie and grinned at the sight of a grand piano. "Do you mind if I play?"

"I couldn't imagine anything more delightful." It was a small lie. Hattie could imagine several delightful things Paul could do, but instead of making any suggestions to that effect, Hattie curled up in the velvet embrace of a settee. There were many types of seating choices set facing each other at comfortable angles. The space was designed for conversation. Thabit stretched out on one of the long couches, and Venus cozied into him as he wrapped his arms around her. Zuberi took a moment to top off everyone's champagne, then sat with one leg flung over the other in a puffy chair with an unobstructed view of the piano. The soft tinkling of music filled the air with Paul's masterful playing. The song wasn't one Hattie had heard before.

As if reading Hattie's mind, Minerva spoke. "He writes them, you know. Everything he plays is something he has dreamt up while trapped inside his stone self."

"It's quite good. When you are not free to roam the hotel, you are fully conscious?"

Venus nuzzled Thabit's chest. "It is rather cruel, but it is what we know. It makes our time outside all the more precious."

Zuberi looked lost in thought as he watched Paul play. "When Thabit and I were not as we are now, we were housed in a temple for Amun-Re. The rituals and ceremonies performed seasoned our stone beings and permeated our internal matter, but we possessed no thoughts. We didn't know we were imprisoned in the stone that gave us form. I guess that could be seen as a blessing."

"We were stone and stone was all we were." Thabit's eyes were cast down at Venus's radiant face as he stroked her arm.

Having known both Zuberi and Thabit for centuries, she wasn't surprised at their answers, one being practical and the other a dreamer.

Venus looked into Thabit's eyes. "I would trade anything to sleep in a blessed void in between. It is sheer torture to not be able to move. Yet you see streams of people passing by you all day laughing, talking, shopping, kissing." Thabit leaned down and kissed her.

"To be a constant voyeur may sound romantic, but I agree with your brother, Zuberi. You were both blessed with your ignorance." Minerva placed her champagne flute on the table next to her. "Exactly how did you know of us? We have never run across other living statuary. They mentioned you heard a rumor about us."

Hattie wasn't sure how much to tell them; for centuries she had lived by lies and subterfuge, never able to share her true story with anyone. It was hard for her to feel safe in telling the truth. "Well, it was more than a rumor. You see, I . . ."

Zuberi sensed her hesitation. "Mistress, we have told them you are an immortal. Please forgive us for our transgression. I know you live in the safety of secrets." He placed his hand over his heart.

"I understand your instinct. You've never run across your kind. We will discuss this later, boys." The fact the boys shared some of her life story felt oddly freeing to her. "It was centuries ago. I had a certain relationship with another immortal, a magician who brought Zuberi and Thabit to life. They were his gift to me. We parted soon after on rough terms. As I travel through the world, I hear whispers of other work he has done. I understand his magic has become ever darker over time, and that doesn't surprise me. I can certainly imagine the perverse thrill he has experienced in the knowledge of the eternal prison he has created for you."

"You know our creator?" Minerva's eyebrows peaked up.

"I am all but certain the man who created my companions is the same one who breathed life into you all."

Paul stopped playing. "If you can call this a life."

Zuberi walked over and rubbed Paul's shoulders. He leaned into Zuberi's touch. "Oh, that's nice."

"When you wake, what do you do?" asked Hattie.

"We enjoy our time as much as we can. This is the first time in a long time we've had others to hang out with." Paul started to play a more upbeat tune.

"The last immortal we spent time with disappeared not too long ago. He would come into town from time to time and throw wild parties, after which he would disappear. But it's been a year or so since we've seen him."

"He would usually come around that frequently?" asked Hattie.

"I think he lived here for part of the year. His cover as an immortal was as a music producer or something in the entertainment world," said Minerva.

Venus pouted. "He threw the most outrageous parties. I miss Horatio."

"Horatio Diogenes?" Hattie wondered if they knew they were partying with the anthropomorphic form of the Egyptian God Horus who recently returned to the Field of Reeds with the Others.

"You know him?" Venus sat up from Thabit's embrace. "Is he okay?"

"I can't say I know him personally. I have heard of him, though. 'Okay' can be a relative term. I don't think you will be seeing him anytime soon."

Venus leaned into Thabit. "I guess I won't be needing to access his suite at the Luxor anymore. We would sometimes stay up all night together and—"

"You have a key to his suite?"

"It's not exactly a key. There is a password I use at the front desk. The people there remember me."

"How could they not?" Thabit smiled and squeezed her.

Minerva rolled her eyes. "They will give any of us a key, not just Venus."

Hattie perked up. Maybe there was a quicker way home. "Any of you feel like an off-property adventure?"

"Why would you want to go to his suite? Yours here is much bigger and more luxurious."

"There is a cabinet in his room that can transport us to Luxor. It would be a great boon to me and the boys if you could see a way of getting us there."

"I'm in. It'll give me more time with Thabit," said Venus.

Thabit smiled broadly.

Minerva shook her head. "But time is getting short. If we don't return before dawn breaks, you know what will happen."

"We'll just have to be sure to get back in time," added Paul.

Hattie sensed Minerva was the more cautious of the three. "I don't mean to put you out, but if you can, I'd appreciate it."

Minerva had a calculating look. "If we do this for you, will you do something for us?"

"Of course, what would you like?"

"Will you talk to our creator about freeing us?"

Hattie figured it wouldn't hurt to promise this. Most likely she would be heading straight toward him on her pharaonic errand. "I will do my best, but no promises. We split on bad terms. I don't know if I will be able to move him."

Venus flashed a radiant smile at Hattie. "I know you will do what you can."

It was a long shot, but Hattie would give it a try. "You've got a deal."

CHAPTER SIXTEEN

L uke and the others followed Alex into the library after Colonel Sanderson left them. Buxton, Thorne, and Gwen took seats in high-backed intricately carved mahogany chairs with fine needlepoint-work seat cushions next to a roaring fire. Alex walked past them to take in the detailed scrollwork on the massive hearth—a glorious celebration of the woodworker's craft. She rubbed her hand over the smooth wood as the pleasant scent of the fire and the erratic cracks and pops relaxed her. She looked at the dancing flames and was intrigued by the idea they were seated by a roaring fire in the heart of the Nevada desert during the hottest part of the day.

"I see you have an appreciation of fine craftsmanship."

Alex turned toward the voice. A stranger was sitting in the fourth chair, nearest the fire. He must have entered the room while she was fire gazing. He was about Buxton's age or older. He had a helmet of grey hair and a dark unibrow and a mustache that crossed his face like charred fuzzy caterpillars. Alex guessed he must color them but couldn't understand the advantage of doing so.

Buxton crossed his legs. "Everyone, gather round."

Luke and Salima sat at opposite ends of a love seat situated beyond the armchairs. Gor wiggled himself in between them, smiling at Luke's discomfort as he wedged himself in. Niles stood behind Salima, his hands resting on the love seat, pointedly looking everywhere but in Alex's direction.

Buxton cleared his throat. "I would like to introduce you to the General. The agency has much to thank him for. He was the one who generously worked with Gwen to find this new temporary home for us."

"Anything for friends of Jorge. I worked with him years ago on a project. He met Herr Schliemann before he passed. The two of them quickly became as thick as thieves. I think the old man would be happy you are all here."

Alex wondered how much Gwen told him about Jorge's relationship with KHNM, because it was around ninety-nine percent unfriendly.

Luke crossed over to shake the man's hand. "I'm Luke. Good to meet you, General . . . What shall we call you?"

The old man tilted his head and considered Luke for a moment, as if wondering what kind of dolt this was who worked for the agency. "General."

Alex shook his hand. "Alex Philothea, glad to meet you, General."

"You are the one who will be sleeping in the old man's bedroom?"

"I will be staying there tonight. After that, I'm not sure."

"Scared of a little ghost?"

Alex let the General's patronizing tone roll off her. "No, I have some business to take care of, and I expect to leave tomorrow. Right, Buxton?"

Buxton nodded toward Thorne. "Of course. I've had Thorne

arrange everything now that we are here at our temporary head-quarters. You'll be flying out tomorrow evening. I was hoping the General could loan you a car so you and she might drive to the airport, as I am doubtful Uber has clearance to come to the area."

The General laughed. "Yes, and that would be an expensive fare, for certain. I can arrange something."

Alex wanted to clarify the situation. "Thorne will drive me there and return to the base, right?"

"I thought she would travel with you. I know there are issues Chicago House is experiencing with the lawsuit. I think another pair of hands in Luxor might be good to have around while you return your book."

"But don't you need all hands on deck here to unload and catalog the objects?"

Thorne was unusually silent. As a know-it-all she was always too willing to throw her opinions around. Alex knew it must be killing her to be talked over as if she weren't in the room. But she was also aware enough of her own desires to stay quiet and let the others sort it all out.

Niles chimed in. "I have to go with Alex. You know of my charge, Buxton. Thorne should stay with you here and help."

"I hate to lose the manpower here, but I suppose the three of you must go. I need someone who can smooth things out for the staff of Chicago House while you two are searching for the lost oasis, to return the book of magic."

Alex glared at Buxton.

"That is my decision, Alex."

The General chimed in. "It sounds like you might be gone for a while. I think it might be best to have one of our drivers drop you off instead of leaving one of our vehicles unused at the airport. Just let me know what time you three will need to be picked up."

"Make the reservation for four." Gormund sat up. "Since I've been to the lost oasis before, I can help Alex find it."

Salima rolled her eyes. "No, my brother. You know as well as I, with Niles gone, the Others will expect you and me to stay put so we can oversee the processing of the KHNM artifacts, magical and otherwise."

Gormund crossed his arms and puffed out his cheeks, making him look like a petulant demon.

Alex caught the General's glance go between the slender and elegant Salima, with silken hair as dark as night and dazzling emerald-green eyes, and the double-wide dwarf. He would probably be astounded if he knew the truth.

Buxton rubbed his hands together. "Well, I guess we've sorted that out."

The door to the library burst open. Ms. Winifred, clipboard in hand, glided into the room with Bradley and Theo trailing behind her. Her assistants hovered outside of the main circle of furnishings, each clasping their own clipboard against their chests. Alex studied Buxton as Freddy sauntered through the room, noting that his expression shifted from warm recognition to discomfort. His gaze moved to an unseen puff of lint he was vigorously brushing off his pant legs.

Freddy stood with her body positioned in the opposite direction from where Buxton was seated. "Well, we now know what went missing. The only question is, why?"

Alex had never seen Buxton so flustered. "And what exactly is missing, Fr— . . . Ms. Winifred?"

Freddy looked at Buxton as if he sprouted three heads. "Well, Dr. Buxton, it appears the item taken from the train depot the other night was a sistrum dating back to Ahmose-Nefertari. The object itself is believed to have great magical energies within. The queen used it in temple rituals in her role as the Wife of

Amun, and after she died, the sistrum's use continued for centuries, coating it, as it were, with a load of holy magic. Although this potency was noted by the agency, we had yet to find any magical uses for it."

"It did make a lovely sound." Theo piped up from the conversation cluster hinterlands.

Freddy smiled at her assistant. "I am willing to guess whoever took it has an idea or two about what to use it for. From the evidence they left behind, they were definitely looking for something specific."

Luke leaned forward. "I recall a note in our database about that object. It was part of a set of regalia Ahmose-Nefertari used as ceremonial garb."

"Yes, the sistrum had a diadem and a collar necklace as its mates. It is believed the three items stayed in the Gods' house after her death, but after that, it gets tricky and becomes more word-of-mouth than provenance. I am guessing you've heard of the hoard of Karnak?"

Alex caught Freddy's eye. "Isn't that from when Cambyses's army was advancing toward Luxor, and the temple priests at Karnak hid the religious relics in the sacred pool?"

"You are right. But as the story goes, their efforts were for naught. Cambyses strode into the city, heard about the hoard, and quickly located it."

"There must have been traitors in their midst." Thorne looked pleased with her ability to bring forward a hint of negativity.

"To save your own life, maybe you'd do the same," Freddy chided. "It's easy to sit in this well-appointed library and look down on the actions of others, but the ancient world was a cruel one, and I can see how secrets then might not be so easy to hold."

Alex loved that Freddy called Thorne out. "What did Cambyses do with the hoard?"

"He sent it off with the rest of his army."

"The army that was lost in the middle of the desert? But if no one has ever found the army, how was it the sistrum was in KHNM's European archives?"

"Not all the pieces went with the army. He took three, one for each of his wives," added Luke.

Freddy crossed her arms. "The sistrum is valuable as an object from antiquity. I think it could command a decent price at auction. But it isn't a masterpiece or something that would bring in a fortune. I don't see why someone would take the trouble to steal it from an organization that has gone well out of their way to be unknown."

"That might narrow down the suspects," said Alex.

"Maybe it was random."

Salima looked down at Gormund. "I don't know. The scene of the crime looked far from random."

Luke went into pure archivist mode. "I can't imagine why someone would specifically want that object. I'm not sure why we've kept it all these years. KHNM has run every test imaginable and hasn't found any magical properties. It was an object that was once thought to have magical powers, but either lost them or never had them to begin with. It was never deaccessioned from our collection of magical relics. If I recall correctly, we had another object from this jewelry triad. It may have been a collar necklace. I'll have to check our database and see what I come up with."

Gwen, who sat across from Buxton in one of the four armchairs in front of the fireplace, had a perplexed look on her face. "I have a vague recollection of Jorge talking about Cambyses's army and an artifact from it with one of his friends. It was one of those ancient mysteries he would have loved to have solved. It might have been Herr Schliemann he was talking to. General, do you recall Jorge and the doctor talking about any of this?"

A flash passed over the General's face as if the conversation had taken an unexpected and unwanted turn. "Herr Schliemann was a man of many interests. It wouldn't surprise me if this subject was something they would have talked about. But I have no recollection of any talk of artifacts. I am certain I would remember that."

Alex was struck by the General's last statement. It was almost as if he was trying to convince himself. Alex made a mental note to touch base with Buxton about this before she left for Egypt. Maybe he could use his deft abilities at getting information out of people on the General to find out exactly what he might know about any artifacts Herr Schliemann might have mentioned. Her stomach rumbled, reminding her that it had been quite some time since she'd eaten. "I think I'm going to head to the kitchen and grab some grub, then settle in for the night." She could feel Niles's pointed stare. It was hard not to look back at him.

The General stood. "Let me show you the way. Your personal belongings should be in your room shortly." And with that, the General offered his arm to Alex. It was an odd gesture, but also in line with his general old-school gentlemanly countenance. He patted her hand when she linked arms with him and led her into the foyer.

Alex stopped to take in the cuckoo clocks as they ticked away. "I can't believe how many there are."

"Herr Schliemann was quite the collector, and craftsman."

"He made some of them?"

"He started out collecting already made antique clocks in the beginning. As his obsession grew, he paid handsomely for rare examples. I think he may have amassed the largest collection in the world. It became a hunt he never tired of. Once he'd collected the rarest of the rare, he started to make them and became manic about it."

The General pointed upward. "The clocks toward the ceiling are the older purchases. The ones in the middle area are his rarest examples, and the others nearest us are clocks he made. If you have the time, you will want to peruse them. There is a rollable ladder he installed that allows a person a grand tour of them. He was eclectic in the themes of the clocks he made. There is one where a prisoner gets his head chopped off at midnight, another is oddly clown-themed."

"Clowns?"

"Yes, that one took him an especially long time to make. For each hour it rings, a different number of clowns escape from a very small circus car. I think in the end he felt it was his masterpiece."

Alex wasn't sure which fact surprised her more—that there was a clown car cuckoo clock in existence, or that it would be anything like a masterpiece. The General must have read her mind.

"I'd have to say I agree with him on that assessment. Figuring out the logistics of how to hide the noontime and midnight clowns and have them come tumbling out of the car was indeed a master-level challenge."

The General led her away from the foyer and into a long wood-paneled hallway, the end of which opened to a bright kitchen. From a distance the fifties chrome and Formica decor stood out. "If I remember correctly, there is an Egyptian-themed one that might be of interest to you. You might want to make a point to check it out. It has a huge scarab that rolls the sun out every morning at six a.m."

"He certainly was a man of many interests." Alex mentally rolled her eyes, wondering why it was that every hobbyist, no matter what their interest, always had to create something Egyptian-themed. "Herr Schliemann was allowed to live out his life here? Isn't that unusual?"

The General stopped in front of the large pass-through leading to the kitchen. "Yes, it was part of his agreement. After his top-secret project was deemed a failure, he spent the rest of his days here in a less than official capacity." It was as if the General was trying to find the exact words he was supposed to say. He put out his hand. "Well, I've got to get back to the main base. Make yourself at home. It's been a pleasure to meet you."

As the old man turned and walked away, Alex couldn't stop wondering what the General was hiding about Herr Schliemann and an ancient Egyptian artifact he may or may not have owned before his death.

CHAPTER SEVENTEEN

Venus, Minerva, and Paul kept their end of the deal. They brought Hattie and the boys back to the Luxor hotel and to the portal in Horatio's suite of rooms, so they could return to Egypt quickly. Thabit and Zuberi had been unusually quiet since their return. Hattie guessed they were probably a little hurt that after all this time the first words spoken from her about their creator came in an explanation to strangers.

Standing on the deck of her dahabeeyah, Hattie stared at the Nile as a strong sense of foreboding washed over her. She was correct in her assumptions regarding Narmer's connection in the mortal world. She looked at the calling card that was left on her bedside table. It wasn't just the name on it that sent waves of revulsion through her, but the thought of the great deceiver or one of his minions encroaching on her sleeping chamber.

"The great deceiver" is how Hattie liked to think of Rekhmira on the rare occasions she did. Ingrained in her was the concept that speaking one's name gave them power. She refused to think or speak his actual name for many centuries.

It began so innocently when Rekhmira was a youth in her court, a magical prodigy wearing the sidelock of youth. He was an apprentice to her high priest of Amun, Hapuseneb. He wasn't raised to the highest level of the priesthood because his father was a part of Hatshepsut's court. It was because he possessed impressive magic.

Hatshepsut enjoyed having his boyish innocence and exuberance within the jaded halls of palace life. He became a fixture in her inner circle. His name meant *knowledge like Re*. However, she favored him with a nickname. He was her little Rekhyt, as he constantly flew around her in energetic and worshipful circles. The term was an endearment, a loving poke at his station as a nonroyal, and a play on words with his name. The hieroglyph for *rekhyt*, an abundant bird species, was depicted on temple walls as a bird praying in adoration.

Many years after she gained her immortality and was living in a self-imposed exile in Greece, she ran into him. He was a foe masquerading as a friend, who set a trap to settle his revenge upon her. She was an easy target, as the crimes he blamed her for were beyond her knowing. It wasn't until after the dust cleared that she understood how long he had been plotting his intricately planned reprisal.

The way he savored his revenge still burned at the edges of her soul. With her unaware of his claims against her, he made a fool of her with the secret smugness of a thief who had yet to be discovered. It shamed her to this day how she let a commoner bewitch her and become more than an element of her personal life—an equal.

The one good thing that came from that time were her companions. She never mentioned their maker or the complicated past she had with him. It was the very night Rekhmira cast the spell bringing breath to their stone bodies that Hattie cut her ties with him forever. Many times she thought of telling Thabit and Zuberi about him as their bonds grew, but she never quite found the words.

As time passed she would hear snippets about a powerful magician, allowing her to loosely keep tabs on where he was so she could avoid him. Hattie went out of her way to banish him from her life and thoughts—to expel the unworthy man, relegating him to the realm of the forgotten. But she knew it was inevitable their paths would cross again one day.

A flock of birds erupted from the river grasses nearby, drawing her away from her thoughts of the past.

Hattie slipped the calling card emblazoned with the name of Rekhmira's shop into her pocket and went to collect the boys. It was time for her to do the unthinkable and stand before the great deceiver once again.

~~~

As she passed under a large wooden gate in front of the centuries-old souk, she wondered at how fate had drawn her to him again. Rekhmira's shop was located near the main entrance of the market. Down the way, pashmina scarves flowed from display racks, as shimmering waterfalls of rainbow-colored fabric billowed at the motion of passersby. Countless woven carpets were strung along the covered alleyway to appear as if they could be commandeered and flown away in an Arabian night's fantasy, for a well-haggled price. Hattie passed by two behatted tourists standing near a tangle of dusty brass lanterns, negotiating for objects they probably assumed were handmade in Egypt, but were most likely mass manufactured in some far-off country.

Hattie recalled the glorious time before the invasion of easy travel, when visitors from far away would have to journey for months to arrive at this sacred city. A time when the music of the streets was filled with braying donkeys and the hubbub of the market as shopkeepers hawked their wares, and not the continuous buzz of cars and motorbikes outside the walls of the market. When the stalls held the bounty of the land, the handcrafted goods that were needed for use instead of mass-produced souvenirs that would only collect dust on someone's mantelpiece in a distant land.

A few stalls down was the entrance to Rekhmira's shop. Above the doorway was an out-of-place neon sign with the words *Apophis's Cave* in an exotic-looking font, and a rather large cartoonish snake. It didn't surprise Hattie he named his shop in honor of the serpent god that was a primeval force of darkness and chaos. Rekhmira's store had a dubious reputation. He was known to the locals as a trickster to avoid, but the tourists flocked to his shop. His eccentricities only added to the magnetic draw for visiting foreigners. Over time Rekhmira became somewhat of a mythic being among those of Luxor. There were stories of tourists seeking magical wishes who were never seen again. It was said that sometimes the marketplace echoed with the lamentations of their ghosts.

Before she knew it, they were at the threshold of Rekhmira's shop. Hattie opened the door and stepped inside. It was like entering a space in which a whirlwind collected all the Egyptian-themed trash and trinkets from around the world and deposited them there in multiple massive piles. Every square inch of the space was mounded with Egypto-junk. Hattie was surrounded by every type of cheap scarab, colored stones with symbols carved on their surface, and—resting precariously on random peaks of junk—brass jewelry boxes. One mound was topped with a ceramic tray displaying several tiny rubber God talismans in front of a small plastic pyramid. Random strings of beads rained down from one shelf to another, creating unintended adornments for the objects below them. Brass lanterns, wind chimes, scarves, and rugs reached toward her from above. This shop was exactly what someone would imagine as the hoard of a Jinn who was treasure-blind and collected every shiny thing they'd ever come across. Beyond the strange landscape of souvenirs was a lit glass case in the rear of the room, on which rested an ornate cash register.

The helter-skelter nature of the space sent Hattie's head spinning. Aside from the bizarre wonderment surrounding them, there was a huge load of powerful magic buzzing around. Hattie was certain all this detritus was a clever camouflage for what most likely were the true treasures of Apophis's Cave. It made sense a trickster like him would get a rush out of hiding things in plain sight.

The lights overhead flickered off. Unnatural darkness surrounded them. Not even the light from the street beyond reached into the room. Hattie grabbed one of the large carved stones from the pile next to her just in case a ready weapon proved necessary.

The lights flashed on. Rekhmira stood behind his counter with a greasy smile. "I've been waiting such a long time for you to jangle my shop bell." He looked at the stone clutched in her hand. "I wouldn't have thought your highness would be interested in such things. Take it. That stone of pure lapis is my gift to you, your eminence."

Rekhmira's self-satisfied tone sickened her. By entering his domain, she was handing him a victory he'd waited centuries for.

The stone in her palm was most definitely not lapis, but colored cement created in a mold with a crudely rendered ankh on its surface. "A cheap fake, just like the shopkeeper." She tossed it back onto the pile.

"I see you are still as charming as I remember." His gaze moved past her to Zuberi and Thabit. "I see you are still enjoying some of my earlier gifts to you."

"Cut the crap. You know why I am here." Hattie walked to the counter with the boys in her wake.

"Returning faulty goods?"

The boys grumbled behind her. Hattie put her hand up to silence them, then reached in her pocket and grabbed his calling card. Hattie slapped it onto the counter. "As we both are aware, your friend Narmer sent me. I believe you have some accessories for me."

Rekhmira reached into the glass case in front of him and pulled out a large leather box with brass findings. The lid creaked as he lifted it.

It was strange to see the awakening sense of awe transforming his face as he gazed at the contents of the box. The softness in it made Hattie remember him as a child in her court and how he treasured magical relics.

He turned the box around so Hattie could see the cuff bracelets. The broad jewelry shone with the silvery-gold glow of electrum. All along their surface ran horizontal lines, and in between them were depictions of feathers representing the feather of truth. Alex wondered what Narmer had on Rekhmira to get him to hand over something like this.

"What are you waiting for? The sooner you put them on, the sooner we can be done with each other."

"Thanks for the reminder." Hattie reached in and grabbed one of the cuffs. Intense magic thrummed within the metal. She eased it onto her wrist. As soon as the metal touched her flesh, it glowed red with an intense heat that burned her wrist as the cuff shrank against her skin. Hattie shook her hand.

Rekhmira sneered at Hattie. "What, you can't take a little magical heat?"

Hattie ignored his bait and took the second cuff as the first one began to cool.

"So don't you find this even the smallest bit funny?"

"Having to be in the presence of a great fool?"

"That you are now in the direct employment, or shall I say subordination, of the very pharaohs you have loathed for ages. You've even let them cuff you." Rekhmira laughed. "Oh, how the mighty do fall."

Hattie reached over the counter and grabbed his shirt, jerking him close. "One of these days I'm going to find a way to kill you." The cuffs glowed with a bright blueish-white light against his pallid complexion. Hattie let go of him.

Rekhmira stepped backward as he fiddled with his collar. "Looks like those cuffs are working."

Hattie let go of him. "These things light up when I say something I really mean?"

"They reveal if your intentions are true of heart." Rekhmira brushed his hands together. "So, darling, it looks like our business has concluded. Don't be obliged to stay and catch up."

"You wish."

Zuberi looked as if he was going to say something. Maybe he thought Hattie had forgotten about their friends. "I am not finished with you, Rekhmira."

Pleasure washed over his face like a crocodile as a tasty gazelle entered the water. "Interesting turn. Your highness needs something from this commoner? Your little Rekhyt am I once more?"

Hattie wished she could magically call up all the stones and junk around her and bury him alive under their weight. Her blood boiled at having that term of endearment thrown in her face. She bit the inside of her cheek to refocus her thoughts. "I met some statues while I was in Vegas recently. They said you brought them to life. I want you to free them."

"Free them? Why would I spend the magical energy to do that? I kind of like having creatures that are compelled to adore me in my presence. It's a good feeling, am I not right, dear one?"

She clenched her fists at her sides. "I will pay." She hoped this detour from her current mission could be kept as transactional as possible, and if she knew one thing about Rekhmira, he always had a price. She could kill two birds with one stone and do the pharaohs' bidding and a favor for the boys.

He set his ring-studded hands on the glass and leaned in. His breath smelt of stale coffee. "I will make a fair trade. Your two, for the three in Vegas."

"I am not offering mine for trade. I have another offer. Something that will appeal to your greedier self."

His expression changed from mocking to interested in a flash. Hattie knew him well and would use her knowledge of his unending appetite for power and wealth to pull him into doing what she wanted.

"Ever hear of the lost army of Cambyses?"

Rekhmira rolled his eyes. "You know I have."

Hattie had no way of knowing how much Narmer told Rekhmira about why she needed the cuffs. However, taking into consideration Narmer's tendency to embrace the power dynamics of conservative hierarchies, she figured it was likely Rekhmira was more of a servant than a confidant. "I am looking for it. I need a few inventory items for my auction house. I possess an object that might let me find it. I don't need all the hoard. I would be willing to split the take with you if you free your servants in Vegas." The cuffs glowed brightly.

"People have been looking for the hoard for centuries. What makes you think you can find it?"

"Didn't the glow of the cuffs convince you enough that I believe what I say?"

The familiar glint in his eyes betrayed an interest in her deal. "Sixty-forty split."

"Fifty-fifty even split."

"And I free them after you deliver?"

"Sixty-forty. With one catch."

"What is the catch?"

"You free the Vegas triad now."

"Seventy-thirty. And I will up the ante with an object that will all but guarantee you will find the hoard you are looking for."

"Why would you want to help me?"

"Don't fool yourself, sweet cakes. I am a businessman. I want those magical objects. Imagine how much more power I can attain with seventy percent of the Karnak hoard." He held up his hand. "I'll be right back." He disappeared behind a black curtain and reappeared holding an opaque white-yellow mass which he unceremoniously tossed at her.

She caught the rock and studied it. There was something about it that was familiar, but Hattie couldn't quite place it. On its bottom there were indentations where it must have been attached to something.

"This will help you find the hoard, although it was never a part of it. I can see that you recognize it but can't remember where you've ever seen such a large desert opal." He reached under the counter and pulled up an ornate electrum rod about three feet in length. "Maybe this might help."

All the pieces fell into place. It was the stone that sat atop the fabled ceremonial smiting stick of Narmer, the first true pharaoh. The stone in her hand was made by a meteor that slammed into desert sand millennia ago creating this glass-like formation. Narmer's high priest imbued the massive stone with powerful magic. It was said that this smiting rod enabled Narmer to unite the Two Lands of Egypt. The powerful artifact was long lost by the time Hattie had ascended to the throne, but many fantastical stories about it fed her childhood imagination.

"How on earth did you get it? It has been lost for centuries."

"Let's just say I've had a lot of time to look. And as you know, I have deep connections in the Netherworld."

His self-satisfied smile made Hattie regret letting her awe at seeing the artifact break through her intentionally placed down-to-business demeanor with Rekhmira.

"It will help you in a more direct way than using whatever mysterious object from the hoard you have and won't tell me about. You may like to think me dense, but even I know the story about the objects in the hoard and how they are attracted to one another. I've yet to find one. And I am willing to guess you have no idea how to use the object you have to guide you to its spell-mates. The stone will allow you to see what you most desire. You will need to take it to the sacred pool at Karnak, to the spot where the treasure was originally dumped. There it will reveal where you can find the hoard."

"Why haven't you used it already?" Hattie removed the cuffs and placed them in the small box.

Rekhmira looked as if he'd just imbibed a large glass of bile. "I have no royal blood. And you are the only one left with the pure blood of the pharaohs."

CHAPTER EIGHTEEN

N o sooner had Alex settled into a puffy chair by the fire than a soft knock came at her bedroom door. She set her bourbon down on the small side table and extracted herself from the chair's cozy embrace. Niles promised to find a way for them to spend time together without attracting the attention of the others. And now, close to midnight, the time had come. Her pulse quickened at the thought of being all alone with him. She was suddenly self-conscious of her wardrobe choice as she padded to the door. Alex wondered if she would find herself sitting on the chair once again, fidgeting with the lace trim of her peignoir, embarrassed by her assumptions, or if the fancy lingerie would end up as a pile of forgotten silk somewhere on the floor.

Alex was never a buyer of lingerie and tended to purchase more utilitarian cotton undergarments and sleepwear, but that changed when she met Salima. When Alex was first called to duty by KHNM, her luggage was dragged across the tarmac by a baggage cart and caught fire. All her personal items were a complete loss. Buxton sent Salima on an errand to pick up some new things for her. Salima bought her an expensive silk night-gown Alex would have never looked twice at in the department store. That gown opened Alex's mind to the attraction to fine fabrics, and how good they could feel against her skin. The violet-and-blue art deco set Alex was wearing felt vintage without being fussy. It was ludicrously expensive, but its fabric glided over her skin like a cool enchantment.

Alex pulled the door open. Instead of Niles, a sour face stared back at her. Gwen was standing in the darkened hallway with her hand raised as if to knock again. Her expression softened to something akin to entertained as she took in Alex's attire. "You brought that from New York? Expecting someone?"

"This old thing?" Alex shrugged her shoulders and tried to act nonchalant but wasn't altogether sure if she pulled it off.

"I just wanted to see if you had the chance to talk to your mother about your father's reburial. If I'm going to put my energies toward it, I'd rather start sooner than later."

Alex knew it was inconsiderate that she hadn't taken the time to call her mom. With everything happening it was easy to pass it over. Especially since she knew her mother was most likely going to internally combust, spewing out all manner of toxic barbs when the topic was broached. Alex was one hundred and ten percent certain Roxanne would not take the suggestion of digging up her dead husband and reburying him in a calm and pleasant manner. And now Alex stood in a drafty doorway in lingerie in the dark of night facing the repercussions of her inaction. "Sorry, Gwen, I've not been—"

"Honestly, I don't care why you haven't. I need you to do it, and soon. Again, I am not doing this because we are friends, or because I like you. Because I don't. The only reason I am asking is because I promised Jorge I would. So, please be kind enough to ring mommy dearest and find out. Okay?"

"I will. Sorry, Gwen."

"Again, I don't need your apology. I need your answer. Good night." Gwen swung around and stomped off, leaving a trail of angry energy in her wake.

After closing the door, Alex returned to the fireplace and gazed at the lively blaze as small starlike embers floated up from the glowing coals within. The bearskin rug at her feet felt soft yet prickly against her bare skin. She breathed in the scent of the blazing wood. Wood fires always made her feel cozy and safe, hearkening back to a time when she was young and her family was still intact. Every winter around the New Year, they would rent the same cabin next to a frozen lake and spend days exploring the surrounding forest. The three of them would gather by the hearth each night, making up stories to tell one another.

The clown car cuckoo clock above the mantelpiece read ten o'clock. It wasn't too late to call her mother, but since she was an early bird whose song was most pleasant in the morning hours, Alex would wait until tomorrow.

She was taking another sip of her bourbon when a large thud on the balcony made her jump. She moved to the light switch and dimmed it before investigating. If someone was out there, it would be best to not be seen brilliantly lit from behind. At the far edge of the door, she peered into the darkness. Big fluffy snowflakes floated down, thinly dusting the balcony with white. She squinted to see if there were footprints, but there were none. The curtain of hot-pink geraniums and ivy in the planting boxes in the far corner twitched violently. Alex leaned into the glass door, her breath fogging it.

Two hands shot out and pushed away the snow-laced green-ery. Niles was sitting with an avalanche of flowers and white flakes cascading down his hand-tailored suit. He blew out a puff of air from the side of his mouth to detach a bloom from the tip of his nose. As Alex glided the door open and stepped out, she was surprised Herr Schliemann's fake flakes chilled her bare feet.

Niles brushed himself off as he stood. "And here I was trying to be inconspicuous," he mumbled. His voice trailed away as his gaze shifted from his jacket to her. Niles was at a rare loss for words. It was as if a Jinn had frozen his tongue. She shivered against the artificially cold night air and realized exactly how much of her was exposed and pulled her robe tight around her.

Niles stepped toward her, his eyes sharp with desire. "You look . . . amazing."

"This old thing?" She laughed. "You look ready for a boring board meeting." He was stunning in his suit and tie, but he was dressed for a different kind of liaison than what Alex had in mind.

"I was called to report to the other Gods with Salima and didn't want to waste time changing into something more comfortable. I'd rather spend as much time as I can with you. As an odd aside, for some reason the Gods think KHNM will recognize our authority better if we are in suits."

Alex thought Niles looked tired, like he hadn't had a good night's sleep in a while. "As if being Gods weren't enough?"

"Exactly. Osiris thinks that humans only understand structures they experience in their realm, like corporate hierarchies." Niles tapped his hands against his suit pants.

Apparently, Alex wasn't the only one with a case of nerves. They were parted for so long neither seemed certain that they were still fluent in the language of their love. It was one thing to shoot meaningful glances at each other or to pine away for an unseeable future together, but quite another thing to suddenly be inches apart from one another.

Alex glanced up at Niles. The look of longing in his eyes

erased any lingering uncertainty. She was drawn to him by the internal ribbon that entwined their hearts. Alex slipped her arms through his and rested her head on his chest. The thrum of his God powers surged under the cool cotton of his oxford shirt. Niles's grasp tightened as he pulled her close. His strong embrace was everything. To be this near him was a moment she had anticipated for what felt like a lifetime. Alex never wanted to let go of him as they held each other in the silence of the snow falling around them. It was as if they were two castaways who finally found land and neither was willing to let go for fear that an errant wave might pull them back to sea.

He pulled away slightly and cupped her chin. His eyes were bright with passion, and something Alex couldn't quite read.

"Is something wrong?" she asked.

"I can't believe we are together and alone. You can't imagine how many nights I have dreamt of this. Us. Together." He pulled her to him and scattered kisses along her neck. Her body shivered at the featherlight touch of his lips, making her giggle.

"Something funny?" Niles grinned as he stroked the rim of her ear.

"Only that we are still standing here in this snow."

He leaned in and kissed her. He tasted of salt, snow, and the metallic tang of magic. It was an elixir melting her heart that had been frozen in place for so long.

Alex pulled back just a little so she could see him. She wanted to make sure this wasn't a cruel dream. The snowflakes dotted his raven-black hair. Alex ran her fingers through it, melting the flecks with her body heat. Grabbing his hand, she led him into the room and slid the glass door home.

He made a little bow and kissed her hand. "My lady." Then with an overdramatic flourish, he spun her around. She laughed as he pulled her to him. Niles's hands glided down to the small of her back. His keen interest pressed against her.

Alex wanted to slow things down a bit. She had waited for this moment for so long and wanted to savor it. She didn't want this to be like Christmas morning, with her presents open five minutes after waking. They had all night, so why rush things? She pulled out of his embrace and sauntered to the bar cart. "Bourbon?"

"Elixir of the Gods."

Alex poured him two fingers of the golden liquid. "You'd be the one to know." She handed him his glass and then retrieved her own. She sat on the bearskin rug in front of the fire and rested her back against the settee. The tile near the hearth made a perfect place for her drink. Niles joined her.

"I have something for you."

Alex smiled. "I know, I felt it earlier."

He rolled his eyes. From his jacket pocket he pulled out a small burgundy velvet pouch and handed it to Alex.

Inside the pouch was a dark-red carnelian heart amulet on a thick gold chain. The heart was rendered in the shape of the ancient Egyptian hieroglyph *ib*, the word for *heart*. It resembled a rounded vase with two handles on either side. The amulet glowed faintly from within. Looking closely, Alex could tell the glow came from a gold sphere deep inside the carnelian heart. Carved into its surface were tiny hieroglyphs.

"The text on the exterior is a spell of protection for the wearer."

"It's beautiful. Thank you, Niles." She unclasped the magnificent work of art and secured it around her neck. Alex placed her hand over the pendant. "I love it."

"Back when the first people lived in the Nile valley, they believed their heart was the seat of all knowledge and feelings. It was your essence. To them, the brain was a useless grey mass only worthy of being whisked out from the skull before completing mummification. To call someone your heart meant you loved them like no other." His voice trailed off as he gazed into the dancing flames of the fire. He turned to Alex with the intensity of the crackling blaze. "You are my heart, Alex. And will forever be."

Alex stood. Holding her hand out, she drew Niles up to her and kissed him, tasting the trace of bourbon on his tongue. She gently broke away and looked into his ember-like eyes as she slid her robe down her body. It felt like a cool river against her skin, making her shiver. It was as if Niles had stopped breathing for a moment. He stood awestruck as if he was in the presence of a goddess. As he moved near, Niles's eyes lit with the desire of a devoted acolyte in a state of ecstatic passion. Niles traced along her thin strap, causing it to cascade down her shoulder. As he teased the second strap down, he scattered a line of soft kisses as it fell. The sensation of his tender lips gliding across her skin quickened her desire. As if bending to her unspoken wish, the negligee slipped over her body and pooled around her feet.

Alex stepped backward over the negligee so he could see her fully. She took his hand and led him to bed.

~~~

Draped over his bare chest, Alex woke with a start.

"Did you hear that?" Niles slipped away from her and out of the bed.

Even in a lingering sleepy haze, Alex could appreciate his fine naked form as he stood in a shaft of moonlight. Alex didn't hear a thing, but she knew as a God his senses were more fine-tuned. "It's probably the cuckoo clocks."

As if on cue, the clown car cuckoo clock on the wall commenced its midnight performance, accompanied by circus pipe organ music from within. Niles watched the tiny clowns pile into a garishly colored car. "No, not that. I could have sworn I heard a howling sound." Niles made his way back to the bedside.

"Maybe it is the ghost of Herr Schliemann."

"Oh, ghosts! Scaaary." He smiled, then leaned down and kissed her.

As the clowns completed their nightly task the music died away. This time Alex heard the sound. She pulled away from Niles. "I hear it now. It sounds like a strange moaning and scratching."

"It is getting louder." Niles went to the heating vent and leaned down. "It must be coming from the furnace room." His expression turned mischievous. "Let's go ghost hunting."

Alex got up. "We are forbidden to go into the basement."

"That will just make it all the more exciting."

She shrugged her robe on while Niles threw on his crumpled suit. On the way out she grabbed an amber colored beeswax candle from the mantelpiece and lit it. She handed it to Niles and then lit its mate for herself. "If we're doing the whole haunted house vibe, we might as well go all the way. Besides, I couldn't find a light switch in the hallway to save my life."

They exited into the darkened hallway and crept down the stairs. The flickering light of the candles and the strange house made Alex feel as if she were in an animated Scooby-Doo caper as they slunk down to the basement.

The scratching and sharp cries were becoming louder as they reached the bottom of the stairs. Niles grabbed her hand as they passed into the darkness toward the sound. It was as if they were right upon the source when the thud of feet rushed toward them. Niles gripped Alex's hand a little tighter.

With the flick of a switch, the room was filled with bright white light. Alex dropped Niles's hand to cover her eyes. Once the floaters stopped progressing across her vision, she saw Luke, who was at the top of the stairs with an exasperated expression. "Oh, Jeeves." Luke's voice was filled with disappointment as he brushed past them.

Jeeves had trapped a small cat in an air vent, who was scratching and yowling in alarm.

"Bad, Jeeves. Back." Luke pointed behind him. The little dog lowered his head and complied. Luke squatted and undid the top latch to the wall vent. The cat sprung away and sped toward the stairs. Jeeves moved to follow but stopped at Luke's stern expression. "The cat must have run into the vent, and it closed behind him."

Alex visually explored the large room they now stood in. At its center was a massive clockwork ticking away. Aside from the large mechanism, the only other element was a floor-to-ceiling bookcase spanning the entire perimeter of the room. From the looks of it, there were no vacancies at this literary inn. "This is the forbidden basement?"

Luke picked Jeeves up and wandered to the bookshelves nearest them.

Niles went to the clockwork and leaned on the large bronze rail surrounding it. "Yeah, I don't get what the big deal is."

"Maybe they are afraid someone will mess up the timing of this whole Schliemann-created system."

Jeeves's head cocked to the side as if he was contemplating the title in front of him as Luke spoke. "Yes, because mechanized snow is so important to the stability of the universe as we know it."

Niles was inspecting the brass barricade. There was a glint in his eye Alex read as a desire to dive deep into the restricted area.

They'd only been guests here for a few short hours and already broken the one rule laid down for them. She whispered into Niles's ear, "Let's go back and finish what we started."

Niles stepped away and spoke in an overloud voice. "Well, I guess we've seen enough here. I'm going to my room to get some shut-eye. Alex, you might want to do the same. We have that flight to Luxor tomorrow. We'll need all the beauty rest we can get." Niles winked at her and blew out his candle. "Good night, Luke and Alex." He strode briskly up the stairs.

Alex wandered over to Luke, who was still perusing the books. "Looking for a little bedtime reading?"

Luke's expression morphed from perplexed to knowing as he took in Alex's nightwear for the first time. "No, I was curious to see what books were here. It looks like a mix of many subjects. Engineering, astrophysics, woodworking, ancient myth, history, key making, boat building, and metalworking, I mean this guy was into just about everything. I think if you look long enough, you might find a how-to book on macramé."

"Yes, he certainly had eclectic tastes."

Jeeves jumped out of Luke's arms and onto the floor. The dog started sniffing a rather large leather folio. He pushed at the book with his nose as his stub of a tail twitched back and forth furiously. Luke squatted to pull the book from its shelf then blew a cloud of dust from its cover. "It looks like Herr Schliemann's diary."

CHAPTER NINETEEN

T he visit to Rekhmira's shop took far longer than Hattie had anticipated. The boys refused to leave until they had assurances that their three newfound friends in Vegas were given their freedom.

Thabit and Zuberi were silent as they exited Apophis's Cave and made their way through the souk. Hattie guessed they were waiting for her to broach the subject of their maker Rekhmira, but she wasn't in the mood, and she didn't relish airing her dirty laundry in such a public arena. They had gone this long without answers and could wait another day until the task at hand was completed.

When they arrived at Luxor Temple, Hattie sent the boys on an errand to grab a few things from the boat. There were several objects she needed for her spell-work tonight at Karnak Temple. Between having to deal with Rekhmira and the sour mood of the boys, Hattie was looking forward to time alone to clear her mental vessel for the magic she would be casting later.

The desert opal's presence felt heavy in her pocket. She couldn't believe the pharaohs managed to twine her life with

Rekhmira's once again. Were it not for the love she held for her beloveds and her desire to save them from returning to the eternal void of nothingness, she would never have allowed this entanglement to happen.

Hattie stood alone in front of the massive statue of Ramses II. Its pharaonic gaze followed the Avenue of the Sphinxes, which stretched outward as a broken pathway to Karnak Temple. The Egyptian Department of Antiquities had been excavating the avenue between Luxor and Karnak Temples for over a decade to make the entire three-mile stretch walkable. After razing many buildings and pulling up streets, it was yet to be completed. She wondered if it ever would be.

In her experience, the modern-day government of Egypt was a many-headed snake that couldn't ever decide on a way forward. As a king, her word was that of a God, which had kept things clipping along.

The sistrum jangled in her other pocket in time with her foot-falls as she walked the sphinx-lined promenade. She hadn't gone far when she needed to cut into an alleyway as a detour. At this point the restoration was more of a patchwork than a completed avenue. She assumed there would be more detours ahead. Not only was the avenue itself a dashed line, but the sphinx sculptures were in various states of survival. Some were nearly whole, and others resembled an unrecognizable lump of beige stone.

She always found the efforts modern humans put into ancient places odd, and she was constantly confounded at their misplaced sense of discovery. It was as if it was solely their modern gaze that validated its worth. How can something be discovered if it was never lost, only buried by the sand? The ancient people they sought were lost to those who knew and loved them, but these places of stone and worship were never lost. They had always been exactly where they were. It also amazed her how the modern man managed to feel justified and righteous at unearthing the dead, who only wished for the blessed sleep of eternity. In her day as a mortal and a pharaoh, archaeologists would have found their heads on a spike and not talking about their crimes on celebrated television programs.

Every once in a while Hattie would find herself reflecting on her days as a mortal in ancient times. It never lasted long. Most people of today live with far greater ease than the greatest pharaohs of her time. Modern medicine and dentistry would have been powerful magics any noble or king would have traded a fortune for. At a time when a small infection could quickly end your days or leave you racked with pain, something as simple as over-the-counter painkillers or readily available antibiotics would have been nothing short of miraculous. Not to mention indoor plumbing and jetted tubs, both of which were modern favorites of hers.

Whenever her antiquities business lagged a little and no adventures were to be found, Hattie would fall into a general malaise in the many cycles of her life. At times Hattie would enroll in Egyptology classes. She favored ones focused on the translations of religious texts. They were always good for a deep belly laugh. Or, if she needed some quick humor, she would tuck in with a bottle or two of wine and binge-watch well-meaning archeology documentaries. It tickled her to no end to watch the talking heads wax poetic on their newest hypothesis on the meaning or use of any object they found.

The default for perplexing objects was usually to classify them as an object with possible religious significance. These especially amused Hattie, especially when she knew they were broken household items. She likened it to a future scholar finding a suburban North American house buried under layers of ash, like a modern Pompeii, and having all the preserved stuffed canine squeaky toys classified as sacred fetishes.

Hattie gazed toward the west. The light around her was starting to soften as the sun set. Not too far in the distance was her destination, Karnak Temple, the precinct of Re. But the boys were nowhere in sight.

Between Hattie and the temple lay a vast parking lot where tourist coaches were loading to take their human cargo to their hotels for dinner. A couple in the distance had stopped to take a picture. The woman was laughing as she climbed up and flung her leg over a crouched sandstone sphinx. She jerked to and fro as if astride a bucking bronco. Her hands flew in the air. She whooped triumphantly as her Stetson-hatted boyfriend snapped a picture. This raised the attention of the Egyptian tourist police kibitzing not too far away. They quickly made for the couple and were politely waving at her to get down.

Hattie shook her head. As pharaoh she constructed this sacred way for the holy procession for the annual Festival of Opet. It took place during the summer months, when the mighty Nile crested. It was a wonderful celebration that brought the holy statues of the Theban triad of Amun, Mut, and Khonsu and of the king from Karnak Temple to Luxor Temple. The effigies would travel the sacred route in golden barques, hidden from the view of commoners who would line the streets for this joyous procession.

When she had the avenue constructed, it wasn't lined with sphinxes. That was added by a later pharaoh. Her creation was intended to ease the way of the sacred travelers and allow everyday people to share in the celebratory rapture of renewal. Along the road she ordered sacred kiosks to be constructed. These stopping places were intended for priests who carried the heavy gold-laden ceremonial boats in the blazing sun. These gave them a chance to stop and rest along the processional way and allow commoners to approach the enshrined vessels. The Gods' likenesses were always hidden from the gaze of everyday people. However, if a wayward breeze gifted a glimpse of the golden statues within, the viewer was celebrated as blessed.

When the sacred effigies would arrive at their destination, dancers, singers, and musicians gave of themselves in rapturous movement and sound to honor the holy day. The Festival of Opet had been Hattie's favorite celebration, imbued with the joy of new beginnings, rich pageantry, and feasting, making her feel blessed and connected to her land and its people.

Hattie looked around at the tourists piling into their air-conditioned coaches, complaining about this or that while they checked this temple off their must-see list of sacred sites, without lending a second thought to the thousands upon thousands of humans who had worshiped and passed through the sacred space.

In between a couple of large white coaches with matching florescent-pink swoops of color strode the boys, making their way to her. They were obediently carrying the items she requested. As they approached, she was unsurprised they were still wearing their stern frowns. Neither would look her directly in the eye.

"What next?" asked Zuberi.

"The site is about to close for the night. We need to sneak in and stow away until we are alone and can work the magic needed." The two tourist guards were still engaged with the young American couple. Seizing the opportunity, she motioned to Thabit and Zuberi. "Follow me. I know just the place."

At least, she hoped it was still accessible.

Hattie had a few great advantages in her acquaintance with this site. She possessed an intimate knowledge of it from the perspective of a princess, priestess, and king, and as a modern who was drawn to its sprawling splendor. At times she felt as if the temple complex was calling to her as an ancient and kindred spirit.

She wondered if the Bas of the ancient ones who worked and worshiped in these spaces were hovering above her and wondering how she, a former king of the red and black lands, could choose to live in exile from her exalted afterlife and in the disharmony of forever walking among mortals.

It didn't take them long to reach what tour guides refer to as the eighth pylon. Hatshepsut had it built during her reign. It was meant to replace a simple mud-brick structure at the southern entrance with a grand sandstone gateway. Like all Egyptian pylons, this one was fashioned after the hieroglyph for the horizon, akhet. This symbol resembled two hills between which the sun rose and set. The pylons, by embodying this symbol and its association with re-creation and rebirth, made them more than mere passageways for the devout. They were a means to transition into the holy space.

Unlike other Egyptian pylons, this one held a secret buried deep within.

The irony wasn't lost on her that the magicked hidden space she planned to hide in was created for her by a young, mortal, and at the time unjaded Rekhmira. When he brought it forth, he was a powerful magical prodigy with a singularly large crush on the king. He witnessed her struggles and made for her a magicked space perched on the side of the pylon, where no one could see or hear her. A place she could escape the courtiers and nobles who not so secretly thought her rule was a blight on the land. He made it a refuge in which she might be able to enjoy the peace and ponder the night sky.

Initially, she was livid that he presumed to know her heart or needs, but the pride in his young eyes when he revealed it to her during her Heb-Sed festival made her hold her tongue. It wasn't long before she made more trips to Karnak than was her custom, under the guise of religious rites.

Hattie located the cartouche of her father that Rekhmira had chosen as her keyway. The sandstone warmed at her touch. "I am here, hear me, so that no one may." She smiled at the memory of how funny Rekhmira thought those words were. An archway appeared in the sandstone, revealing a dark void. She motioned the boys inside. "Once inside, wait for me. I alone can open and close this portal."

The portal closed behind her when she stepped inside. Magicked torches flamed up, illuminating a staircase ending with a drape of deep-blue fabric that shimmered as if it was adorned with thousands of tiny stars. At the top of the stairs, Hattie parted the curtain with one hand and looked down the sharp drop to the stone path below.

CHAPTER TWENTY

J am-packed flights to Luxor made it impossible for Alex to sit next to either Thorne or Niles, which was fine on both counts. After spending the previous night with Niles doing everything but sleeping, she was a little tired. She caught some shut-eye and read a large portion of Herr Schliemann's journal during the flight.

Before leaving Area 51 that morning, Alex told Luke she wanted to bring the book with her to Egypt in the hopes of finding any information in it that might be about artifacts from the hoard. He acted a little deflated at the prospect but handed it over. She had the impression he was a little in love with the idea of reading through the intimate thoughts of the mad scientist and didn't want to give it up.

She decided against mentioning it to Buxton. As a part of Schliemann Haus, she assumed it was the property of the US Government. Although he would have most likely gone along with it, for the good of the order, she figured it would be better to do it and ask forgiveness later.

Alex had high hopes of finding an entry about artifacts from

Cambyses's army in Schliemann's possession, but so far, there was nothing. There were vague references about objects that were once in his ancestor's possession, but nothing like an inventory or random list. Most of the journal entries consisted of vast amounts of clock building and a smattering of scientific theories.

She experienced a strange and nonsensical dream while they were in flight. It featured Niles counting an unseen commodity on a scroll of papyrus in the presence of the Goddess Maat. She was blathering on about nothing while the other Gods danced in a circle around them. When the music and dancing stopped, the text appeared stating it was going to be a very favorable day. Alex sure hoped it was true.

They were scheduled to arrive in Luxor close to the deadline for getting the book of magic to Nun and Naunet at the lost oasis. Alex knew they would have to hit the ground running. When the clock struck midnight, the fortnight time limit would be over, and the primordial magic within the book would be lost forever. She and Niles would go with Thorne to Chicago House to drop off their bags and then start their search for the lost oasis.

The streets of Luxor were relatively deserted, but their driver still found a way to make the trip frenetic. He was driving impossibly fast and, for some odd reason, tailgating the occasional car they came upon. He took turns as if an afterthought, making Alex clutch the door handle. In a few hours the sun would rise and this small, glorious city on the Nile would start to wake. The hustle and bustle of tourist buses, hansom cabs, and automobiles would drown out the early morning birdsong.

As they pulled up to the long drive in front of Chicago House, Gini, the resident librarian, had not only left the lights on but was standing outside the main entrance waiting for them.

The residence held a special place in Alex's heart. It was affili-
ated with the Oriental Institute of the University of Chicago and
was founded in 1924. Their mission was to produce photographs
and precise line drawings of the inscriptions and relief scenes on
major temples and tombs at Luxor for publication. It continues
to this day as a working residence where Egyptologists, linguists,
and artists do this work. The epigraphic staff who lived at the
residency on a seasonal basis were not aware of the reality of
KHNM. To all but a few, they believed the comings and goings of
a few familiar faces had to do with a long-standing arrangement
with a high-dollar donor who helped keep the lights on. That
wasn't far from the truth. KHNM paid a large sum over the years
for the ability to do their work in secret.

This was the third time Alex stayed at the residence, and in
that short time she had come to think of Gini not just as a co-
agent, but as a friend. The librarian was the only KHNM agency
staff who worked at the residency full time. Gini was a magical
being, directly from Jinn stock. They have lived for eons and
move fluidly from male to female over time. To stay incognito
they put in their notice from time to time, take a bit of a vaca-
tion, and return as a completely new persona. Currently they
were a small-but-mighty, campy woman who wore cat-eyed
glasses and turquoise eyeshadow.

When the car pulled to a stop, Alex bounded up to Gini and
was immediately encased in one of their powerful hugs. Their
strong signature spicy-sweet perfume burned Alex's nose.

Gini squeezed Alex hard. "Glad you are here."

It was a relief of sorts when Gini released Alex from their iron
embrace. Alex did her best to regain her breath after separation.

"I told Maspero he should wait for you to get here, but he
was in a hurry to get to the airport."

"Maspero was still here in Luxor? I thought he was supposed

to set off ages ago. Arriving now is a day late and a dollar short as far as the move is concerned." Buxton had granted agent Maspero time to take care of some personal business here in Egypt. He'd been off the agency's radar for about three weeks. This unfortunately coincided with the last-minute all-hands-on-deck move. The absence of another body was keenly felt.

Gini's shrug said volumes about how much they'd enjoyed his company. "Why don't you guys get settled in? I know you want to head out, but you should take a moment to refresh your minds and bodies." Gini shot a meaningful look at Alex and Niles, then shepherded Alex into the building. Niles and Thorne followed behind them.

Alex didn't know the extent of Gini's powers, but apparently Gini must have sensed a change between her and Niles.

They passed through the main foyer to the courtyard with the small apartments of the residencies above it. The pre-dawn still-ness made the usually popular social space feel oddly vacant. This was where the staff enjoyed afternoon tea and conversation, and the traditional happy hour before dinner. Seeing the empty tables in the space, Alex felt like she was wandering through an empty set.

She paused a moment to gaze at the sky above. The stark night sky was softening into bluish silver light as the morning approached. She shivered against the morning chill. "I gather Maspero was heading to the new temporary headquarters."

"I think that is the plan eventually," said Gini.

Thorne crossed her arms and frowned. "Eventually? Where else does he have to go? He's been gone long enough from his responsibilities at KHNM. He should have had plenty of time to square away any personal business he needed to take care of."

"That weasel-man has a personal life? Good on him." Niles broke out a high-wattage smile.

Thorne shot him a disapproving look. "I'm going up." She marched off to her room.

"He was planning on making a stop at the European head-quarters to clear some things up before heading to Area 51," Gini said. "Any more information about the stolen artifact? Was Ms. Winifred able to find out anything more before you left town?"

"No, they were going to check in the database to see if they could find a collar necklace they thought was in the agency's possession," said Alex.

Niles cleared his throat. "I'm going to head to my room and freshen up. Come see me when you are ready to depart."

"Will do." Alex smiled as she watched him and his broad shoulders walk away.

"It's so weird."

Gini's comment pulled Alex's mind out of a pleasant Niles-themed gutter. "What's that?"

"The sistrum. Why would somebody all of a sudden decide to steal it?"

"Not to mention somehow knowing exactly when it was in transit after being in European storage for all these years."

Gini looked a bit sheepish. "Seems like it might be . . ."

"An inside job. I know. I too hate the thought it was one of us." Alex didn't think it would be wise to point her fingers in any one direction within the organization, but the one person who rose to the top of mind for her was Gwen. She needed to keep those thoughts close to her chest until she had proof and not just a latent suspicion. It wouldn't be a good look to accuse their current benefactor of insider stealing.

"My long life has taught me many things. One of those things is that when harm comes, you typically need to look to the ones closest to you first."

"Speaking of which, I have phone calls to make." Alex

dreaded calling her mother about Gwen's offer for a proper ancient Egyptian reburial for her father. She knew it would go over like an emotionally loaded shit show. It was telling that the past few times Alex had something disturbing to tell her mother, she waited until she was out of the country to do so. Her relationship with her mother was beset with numerous painful barbs, but that didn't diminish her love for her.

Alex touched Gini's arm. "I'll come check in with you before we head out."

"If you don't, I'll come after you."

"All the way to the lost oasis?"

"You know me." Gini brought Alex in for another hug. Without the excitement of arriving, this one was a tad less vise-like. When they parted, Gini's face brightened as if they'd just solved an ancient mystery. "Does the rail yard where the artifact was stolen have surveillance cameras? Maybe our thief was caught on camera."

"Great thought, it might help the others identify the thieves. I saw them, but you know how faulty witness memories are. I'll mention it to Buxton when I check in."

"You actually ran into them?"

"I assumed it was Freddy and her assistants. It wasn't until later I found out that wasn't the case."

"What did she look like?"

"She wasn't what I would imagine an artifact thief would look like. It was as if she just stepped off a Paris runway—she had long jet-black hair and was stunningly beautiful. Her companions had the classic chiseled facial features and solid bodies representative of whatever classical Greek or Roman statue might come to mind."

Gini had a far-off look in their eyes and sighed. "Michelangelo's *David*. I knew him, you know. I mean *knew* him."

"Michelangelo?"

"No." Their voice went soft, as if they were caught up in a blissful memory.

Alex touched Gini's forearm. "I'm heading up now."

Gini snapped back to the moment. "Did the woman you meet have wide brown eyes that made you want to stay a while?"

"Why do you ask?" It wasn't exactly how Alex would have described them, but there was some truth in the description.

"You might want to have a chat with Maspero when he gets to Area 51. I think he may have been working with someone who fits your description. Her name is Hattie Shepard, and she runs an antiquities house as a front. He was hanging around with her at the National Museum of Egyptian Civilization when the pharaonic mummies arrived. I wondered about them being there together at the time but chalked it up to the eclectic guest list for that soirée. But now I think about it, there was something strange going on between them."

"What is her shop a cover for?"

"You're not going to believe this."

"Hit me."

"She is the Pharaoh Hatshepsut."

CHAPTER TWENTY-ONE

Hattie's stomach flipped as she stepped out onto the invisible platform leading out from the pylon. It had been centuries since she visited this place. Apparently, after such a long time her body questioned the sanity of stepping from a perfectly good staircase into nothing. The boys followed her into the small space, their expressions uncertain as they stepped onto the unseeable surface.

There was a time when she would sit there for hours in quiet contemplation, casting her gaze over the sprawling sacred site, connecting with the heavens above, or watching the sunlight reflected from the electrum caps of the obelisks. It hadn't been a complete fabrication that she came to Karnak for religious rites. The time she spent here with her thoughts protected her from corrosive intentions and the weight of ruling. There were times in this space when she felt connected to the holy.

Now, it was decidedly strange to be in this tight space with Thabit and Zuberi. Especially given their current mood toward her. The space was created to allow her to sit, stand, or lie down, but not much else. The three of them stood shoulder to shoulder.

Thabit was in the middle and looked a bit stupefied as Zuberi visually explored the boundaries of the space around him.

"I hope neither of you suffers from claustrophobia."

Thabit thrust his arms out, pushing Hattie and Zuberi against the pylon wall. The bag of ceremonial items he was carrying whacked against the wall. "Watch out. There are people down there. They might see us."

A few stragglers were meandering below them by the sacred lake and were in the process of getting escorted out. "Don't worry. They can't see or hear us here. This is a space created with a powerful spell from the ancient book of Amun and Amunet, the hidden ones." She pushed herself away from the wall and started to undress. "How about we get me ready for the ritual?"

Thabit dropped the bag and then squatted to unzip it. The small space filled with the fragrance of scented oils that the ceremonial linen sheath dress was saturated with.

Hattie stood naked to the night sky in her magicked private space overlooking the sacred temple complex of Karnak, unseen by all but Thabit and Zuberi. She lifted her arms so they could pull the fine linen shift over her body. They had soaked it in aromatics of camphor and myrrh. The mentholated coolness made her shiver against the still air of the small space. Zuberi gently tugged the garment around her hips as its pleated fabric expanded to hug her curves. As Zuberi was making final tweaks to the garment, Thabit bent to retrieve Hattie's diadem from the large bag they brought from the boat. It was a thing of beauty, fashioned from the purest of gold and adorned with brightly colored stones. Front and center, cobras reared back as if about to strike. It was given to Hatshepsut when she was anointed as the God's Wife, the most powerful position a woman could hold in the court at the time.

The crown was one of the few things she owned as a mortal that she was able to locate and steal back for herself. It had been a long time since she wore it, and now having it placed on her head, it felt like a beautiful beacon of light calling to all things Holy.

The boys were achingly silent as they dressed her. Hattie had been mulling over where to start her explanation about how they came to be in her life. She promised to tell them, but she had no idea where to start. Most likely her hesitation was rooted in the guilt she felt for not telling them sooner. Each moment of quiet became louder and more uncomfortable as the minutes ticked by.

Zuberi stepped back to assess their work. "It might be time to anoint her and take her to the lake." Disappointment laced his words.

"Thank you both for this, and everything else good you have brought into my life."

Thabit retrieved a case holding small alabaster vessels filled with sacred oils. He made a stiff bow. "We are here at your command." He dabbed his finger in the first pot and rubbed myrrh oil into her hands. His expression was uncharacteristically dour.

Hattie stilled his hand. "I have done you both a great disservice by not telling you about my past with your maker. It must have felt like a keen betrayal for me to talk about it so freely with complete strangers when I never shared anything with you, even after all this time together."

Zuberi grabbed a second pot. His eyes avoided hers as he knelt to anoint her feet. "You owe us nothing, mistress." His clipped tone sent the opposite message.

"Okay, stop."

They continued the work of massaging the sacred oils into her flesh.

She sighed. "I command you to stop and join me." Hattie stepped back from them, hiked up the linen shift, and sat down.

The boys followed her lead and sat on the transparent platform beneath them. Zuberi leaned against the pylon wall and crossed his arms.

"As you know, life isn't cut and dry. There are many reasons I never told you about your maker."

Zuberi bristled at her stern tone. It had been a long time since she used a voice of command with them. The three of them shared so much over the centuries. Over time a strong familial bond twined them together. Long ago the original bindings of master and servant had almost entirely diminished. Both men treated her with deference out of respect and trust.

Thabit looked at his feet, staring beyond the clear surface and into the sacred pool below them. His voice was soft. "You don't have to tell us anything."

Zuberi shot Hattie a sharp glance, his words sharper still. "Yes, mistress, my brother is right. You owe us nothing. It is for us to serve you."

Hearing Zuberi lash out by denying their close ties, Hattie realized how hurtful this was to them. An unfamiliar sensation passed through her. It was shame. The shame of hurting the two entities in her life that she not only owed the most to but loved deeply.

The moonlight danced on the sacred pool below. Her nephew added it to the temple complex after her transition as an immortal. She keenly felt the wheel of time moving forward without care or whim for her or anyone else's problems. "At first I didn't tell you because it wasn't your place to know. You were given to me as servants by my lover."

Zuberi tilted his head. "Rekhmira?"

"Lover?" Thabit grimaced.

"Yes. During that time, it was only a couple hundred years from my kingship. I still held my identity as a past royal and ruler close to my heart. Although I lived among the everyday people in my self-imposed exile, I awoke proud in the knowledge that I was once Lord of the Two Lands and Horus-on-earth. To me, you were simply objects. Living ushabti helpers to ease my life as an immortal."

Thabit and Zuberi looked away. Although she couldn't see their pained expressions, her heart felt them.

"I have known Rekhmira during two different periods. The first time he was a youthful apprentice to my high priest of Amun. He was allowed entrance into the courtly life, as he held powerful magic. Believe it or not, it was he who created this secret space that now holds us above the sacred pool. It was a gift for his king as a place of refuge. A place only I could access." The vault of stars glimmered above them in the night sky. The same stars she used to contemplate when visiting the space as pharaoh. "The second time I knew him, centuries had passed. He was a grown man and had found his own path to immortality. He sought me with a hidden agenda—to woo my heart, take the pleasure of my body, and make a fool of me. It is sad when the sweetest of pleasures turn rancid."

Thabit leaned nearer and caressed Hattie's chin. "You need not tell us more. I can see how this pains you."

Zuberi sighed. "You have always had a tender heart, brother. I wish to know more of this. We three have welcomed countless sunrises together. I feel this explanation isn't owed but should be offered in the sanctity of Maat and the love we have shared."

"It pains me to bring up these old ghosts, but maybe in the telling, you will be able to find the answers you have longed for about your creator and how you came to be in my life. I owe this to you both not for your service to me, but for the love you've continually shown me." Thabit and Zuberi were on either side of her, sitting cross-legged with their hands resting on their thighs. Hattie clasped the hand nearest her for each of the stone brothers. The coolness of their touch anchored her as she continued.

"In that first knowing, when Rekhmira was a lad at court, all the nobles, myself included, were swept up with his innocence and enthusiasm. I let him tag along for some of the ceremonial rights, and eventually, he became a pet in the throne room. I had no idea at the time he was infatuated with his king. I excuse myself for this lack of awareness, as everyone in proximity to me played the courtly game of holding the king close in their hearts. It was this love, unseen by me, that would sow the seeds for his future hatred toward me."

"When did the bad blood come between you two?" asked Zuberi.

"It started with unrequited love and betrayal. One of which I am guilty of and he the other. I had ruled for several years. My homeland was flourishing, and my nephew Thuthmosis had grown into a fine man and was ready to rule. I spent a lot of time in this space, hungering for freedom. My lover Senenmut had flown West years before. Although he was dead, I was able to visit him in visions. During one of these visitations, he explained how hellish the Field of Reeds was for him. As a commoner, the pharaohs treated him as an outcast. He knew they would treat me as a pariah too and advised me to avoid the afterlife by finding a path to immortality. Although he would be sacrificing eternity with his beloved, my eternal happiness was his chief concern. He told me of a potential pathway toward avoiding the Field of Reeds."

"But what does that have to do with Rekhmira?" asked Thabit.

"I asked him to use his magic to help me fake my death. That way I could freely go on my journey to find my path to immortality. Looking back, I must have known how Rekhmira felt about me. Otherwise, I wouldn't have thought to ask him and been confident he would take part and keep quiet about it." A small flare of guilt lit within her. It was easy to continually fault Rekhmira for everything that happened, but in reality, she knew what she was doing. "I made up a story for him. Telling him I needed this magic as I was departing for a secret state journey."

Hattie let go of the boys' hands and leaned toward the invisible barrier, gaining strength in the sacred landscape as she recalled her past. "One of my beloved caretakers died on the day I left. I asked Rekhmira to create a glamour, in which whoever gazed upon her would think she was me. I let him believe at the time that I would take him with me, but I never had any intention of doing so. Looking back on it, the fact I entrusted him with such a sacrilegious task probably led him to believe that I not only trusted him but felt the same as he did. Even if I did know of his love for me, I don't think it would have stopped me. I had far greater concerns than that of a tender young heart. I made an excuse of needing to be ready for my journey and left in the dark of night without him. This abandonment was the ember that sparked his hatred for me.

"Many years later, as an immortal, I returned to the land as a commoner to partake in an Opet festival. The draw of my homesickness was great. At the time the land was under the rule of my nephew Thuthmosis. I took great pains to stay in the shadows and be unseen, but I must have been careless. After the festival, I returned to self-exile in Greece, unaware that I had been seen.

"When Rekhmira spotted me, he guessed at my true reason for leaving him all those years ago. He used his magic to sense the immortal within me. He whispered into well-placed ears my heretical actions. Of my affront to the Gods who had birthed me in choosing immortality over the blessed afterlife in the Field of Reeds. Gossip needs no wind to spread in palace life. This information fanned the flames of hatred many priests already held for my rule as a woman. It didn't take long before the priests pressured Thuthmosis into scraping my memory, my rule, and my work from the logs of history. In one stroke Rekhmira found a way to strip my life's work, legacy, and identity from me.

"It gave me cold comfort to know later that my nephew Thuthmosis banished Rekhmira for his treachery. This banishment had consequences as well. It spurred Rekhmira toward his path of immortality and revenge upon me.

"My second knowing of Rekhmira was at that agora in Greece where we ran into each other. It wasn't until I saw him that I realized how I longed for understanding and companionship. I didn't know it, but all he wanted was revenge while he sang to me songs of love and lulled me into believing him to be true of heart. We spent many days making love and eating honeyed cakes. At the time I reveled in having someone around who knew me back when I was mortal. After I learned the completeness of his deeds, it shattered me to know he must have mocked me while I mooned over our love. He made the once pharaoh, Child of Amun, a fool."

Hattie stood and leaned forward, pressing her hands against the transparent barrier. "It wasn't until the night he breathed life into your stone bodies that I came to know the full extent of what he had done.

"That day Rekhmira wanted me to meet him at the Temple of Amun at midnight, where he planned to give me a gift. He said he would have to get there early and set up the surprise. I expected it would be another one of his elaborate romantic evenings. Before leaving I decided I needed to find a particular book of poetry we liked to read to each other."

The boys shared a revulsed look.

"As I searched, a book fell to the floor and a many-folded document flew out from within its pages. It was an old papyrus that spelled out his banishment and the reason for it. Rekhmira was exiled by my nephew the king for letting it be known that I had faked my death and sought immortality, becoming anathema to all things Holy. I knew that the priests and nobles who hungered to erase my rule must have pressured my nephew to wipe me from the annals of history. Everything I had done, every good I had done, made into dust. Rekhmira must have thought himself clever, but only earned himself banishment from this foul deed.

"To say I was furious would be a vast understatement. My entire body burned with hatred. All those years of wondering why my beloved nephew would do such a thing. To curse my name and rule.

"To know Rekhmira caused my erasure from history. Well, you can imagine how angry I was. When I arrived, he had already created you from two statues that adorned the temple. I can't tell you exactly how it happened, because I was taken over by a rage so intense that I went berserk, and all I saw was red as I rained my fury down on him. I recall seeing him standing in front of you two. I caught him unaware, and the rest is a blur. The next thing I remember is looking back and seeing Rekhmira tied to a pole as I took you both away. I'm not sure if either of you recall it. You both were probably overwhelmed by inhabiting your new forms."

Zuberi and Thabit stood next to her, each placing an arm around her waist.

Thabit leaned in. "My first memory is of the next day, upon waking."

"I have only brief flashes of what you describe, but I have always wondered," said Zuberi.

"I have intentionally not allowed these thoughts to cross my mind for a long time. I hope this revival of the ghosts from my past will strengthen my spell casting tonight. The sacred waters are calling to me. I think we should go down and see if we can figure out where to find this lost army of Cambyses and get the pharaohs the artifact they desire."

Zuberi caught Hattie's glance with his warm brown eyes. "I am glad you told us, mistress."

"It is good to know of our creation story," said Thabit.

Both men leaned in close to her in a half hug.

Thabit broke away and retrieved the duffel bag.

Zuberi took her hand, leading her to the stairway. "Let's go make some magic."

At the bottom of the stairs, Hattie opened the door for the boys and let them exit before her. She gazed back in wonder at the unseen pocket of space Rekhmira created for her and thought about how it might have been the gift of headspace that led her to this very moment.

She followed the boys across the sandy walkway to the stone stairs leading down to the water's edge. The strong aromatics the boys had saturated her garments with wafted up in the late-night breeze as it skimmed across the sacred pool. The fragrance enlivened her senses, making the magic within her start to dance. The full moon was bright and illuminated her white linen garment as she stood at the water's edge.

Thabit and Zuberi continued to anoint Hattie as they chanted in low harmony. They sang in praise of Amun as they gently spread the fragrant oils over her exposed flesh. Their baritone hum reverberated with the strong emotions that were exposed tonight, redoubling her connection to the holy. Thabit paused in his application of the sacred oils and handed her the sistrum she had retrieved from KHNM.

Hattie gently shook the instrument. The small metal disks jostled and chimed against each other as she held her free hand out, palm up, to receive the desert opal. With both objects in hand, Hattie waded into the pool. The water was cool against her skin as it drank her in. She walked in as deep as her thighs then stopped, and the water stilled.

Shaking the sistrum in time with Thabit and Zuberi's chanting, she held both objects up to the heavens above. She joined their chants of adoration to Amun by calling out to him, her higher tones shimmering over their baritone.

Eldest of the Gods of the eastern sky
Amun Kematef, he whose time is over
Lord of the throne of the two lands
O hidden one, my father
Reveal to me that which is concealed.

Wisps of fog circled within the opal, gaining in density as the power of the ancients thrummed through her. The air around her crackled with the sharp scent of magic. Hattie squinted into the opaque rock, expecting to see a vision, but there was nothing. She was left to wonder if the Gods had abandoned her as she had abandoned the rites of her bloodline.

The power around her was unmistakable but no path had been revealed to her. It made her wonder if Rekhmira was wrong about the opal or about her blood connection to it. Could it be that her hereditary access to the powers within it were severed by her sacrilegious choice to live as an immortal?

A bright glow in her peripheral vision caught her attention. The desert opal in her hand was projecting a scene onto the placid water in front of her. The landscape was otherworldly, and yet very familiar. It was comprised of surreal white chalk formations jutting out of the crust of the desert. In the distance a pastel-hued sunset painted the entire scene in tones of pink and orange.

She knew exactly where to start her search for Cambyses's army.

CHAPTER TWENTY-TWO

When Alex opened the door to her room at the residency, she was glad her things had been brought up. There wasn't time to unpack. She only had time to squeeze in a couple of phone calls and a quick shower to rinse off her travel residue before leaving for the lost oasis.

Although she slept during the flight, the bed was calling to her. Her body must be responding to the O-dark-thirty hour. She hoped a shower and a large tub of coffee would help clear the fog. Then she thought better of it. Long roads and not any restroom choices would make for an uncomfortable journey. A couple shots of espresso from the kitchen before they hit the road would have to do.

She decided to call her mom before taking her shower. That way the powerful stream of water could wash away the toxicity of whatever dysfunction she might plunge into during the conversation. Alex threw her scribe's bag on the bed and rooted around for her phone.

While Alex was growing up, her mother went out of her way

to keep KHNM far away from the bubble she created for her daughter and made sure no one from the agency could contact her. It was a shock for Alex to find out her father had been an agent in a secret society her family led for centuries, and that she was entangled in a prophecy stating she needed to join KHNM in the fight to save humanity from an unhinged God.

Alex's gaze wandered around the small space. This was the same room from which Alex called her mother from the first time she stepped foot in Egypt. It was one of the many times her mother had checked in at a recovery center. Alex had a hard time getting a hold of her. But once she did, the sparks flew. That call was to get answers from her mother about why she kept everything regarding KHNM from her for all those years, putting not only herself but also all of humanity in danger.

Alex loved her new life as an agent of KHNM. Her mother just had to deal with it. Once this world of living Gods and magic was opened to her, there was no going back. Working for the agency also allowed her to work with others who knew and loved her father. These colleagues, like Buxton, made her feel connected to him even in his absence. Their friendship helped fill the void that the loss of her father created. There were other benefits to working for a supernatural agency, like being able to see him in the Netherworld while joining the seer Akh-Hehet on a visioning. At the time, they were on the hunt for lost primordial books of magic.

Alex swiped her phone to life and took a deep breath. She knew this was going to get real very fast. On a logical level, she understood why Roxanne had kept her in the dark, but Alex wasn't quite at forgiveness yet. As of late she and her mother were doing better due to some virtual joint counseling sessions now that Roxanne had moved back to California. As the ring chimed, she reminded herself with each sound that she had much to be thankful for. At least this time Alex was calling her mother's home number and not a recovery center.

"Awww, my little Magpie has reached out to mama bird." There was a happy lilt in Roxanne's voice. Alex knew it wouldn't last.

"Hey, Ma." Alex paced the floor.

"I'm glad you called. Bernadette is in town visiting from Chicago. She's been asking about you. Since I've not heard from you in a while, I was falling short on any answers as to what you might be up to."

The passive-aggressive opener sent a well-placed wave of guilt through Alex. There was truth in it, though. Alex had been far less attentive about staying in touch with her mother now that she'd moved back to California. Her mother followed Alex to Chicago when she accepted the position at the Oriental Institute that led to her work with KHNM. Her mother always felt like a fish out of water there. Both the counseling and the move were working wonders for her mother, but nothing would most likely ever change her professional-grade passive-aggressive tendencies.

Bernadette had been Roxanne's housekeeper who became a dear friend over time. Alex was glad her mother had Bernadette's sympathetic ear around to help smooth out the blows to come. Discussions regarding Alex's dearly departed father always triggered her mother in a big way.

"I've been meaning to give you a call, but there has been a lot going on with the move of our headquarters." Alex cursed herself for mentioning the agency right off the bat.

Roxanne sighed heavily, then mumbled something Alex couldn't catch.

"What's that?" Alex asked.

"Oh, nothing."

"You remember we've agreed not to brush things aside anymore."

"I was just thinking about the hubris of youth. And how people your age think they are bulletproof and think they have all the time in the world with the ones they love. I know I sure did." Roxanne's voice went soft.

Alex knew that wasn't what her mother had been thinking. It was more likely some sort of a curse against KHNM. She scrambled to think of something upbeat to say. "I am in Egypt right now." As soon as the words trailed out of her mouth, she whacked herself on the forehead.

A loaded silence hung between them.

"I had to come and return the book. You know it's something I have to do. As soon as you and I hang up, Niles and I will head out to return it." Alex had just unintentionally thrown down her third emotional land mine in so many sentences.

"Interesting. So the great God Thoth has deigned to return to you and your little mortal life."

Although her mother was holding a phone and couldn't have made them, Alex knew her mother was mentally putting air quotes around the descriptor of Niles. In the spirit of sharing truths in their joint counseling sessions, Alex had talked about her feelings for Niles. She couldn't say she outright regretted it, but it sure didn't make things any easier.

"I mean after all that has happened . . . I can't believe you are hanging out with that charlatan." Roxanne's tone was razor sharp.

Alex wished she would have thought to lay out a conversation strategy before dialing her mother. The conversation was tanking, and she hadn't even gotten to the part that was really going to piss her off. Alex walked to the window and tried to let the view calm the rising tide of emotion welling up inside her. Out beyond the wide Corniche lay the ink-black Nile. "I am not calling to talk about Niles, or KHNM for that matter. At least not directly."

"There is nothing about that agency that is direct. I can't see why you put your life on the line for that bunch of fools."

"If I didn't, you would most likely be a subject of an unhinged and cruel God ruling creation with a heavy hand." Although Alex understood where her mother's trauma came from, it hurt so much that she couldn't see past her old fears to understand and even celebrate the accomplishments of her daughter—like saving humanity.

"Alex, you know how I feel about that . . . story."

"You still don't believe me?" Alex sat on the bed as tears threatened to erupt—she thought they'd made a breakthrough with this recently.

"You mean all the nonsense about magic and the Netherworld?"

Alex's body hummed with anger. How could it be that someone she loved so dearly, had known her every second of her existence, could not believe her? Time to change the subject, before returning to the subject with hopefully cooler minds. "What have you and Bernadette been doing? It is wonderful she came to visit you."

"Cut the bullshit, Alex. Why have you called me? I'm guessing there is some emergency. Otherwise, you wouldn't have bothered. Let's just have it out, so we can both go on with what we were doing. You have a supposed lost oasis to find, and Bernadette and I have dinner plans."

Roxanne's tone suggested no safe escape, no pools of calmer waters. It was time to ride the tsunami and hope for the best. Alex took a deep breath and dove in. "I think I might have mentioned the agency has a benefactor who is helping us stay afloat while we battle the ongoing lawsuit."

Silence filled the line.

"The benefactor happens to be Gwen Pendragon. She was involved with Jorge Trinculo, who escaped the Netherworld with Buxton."

"So you say."

"I am sure you will remember in my telling that Dad helped—"

"Alex."

"Mom."

"Maybe we should pause and have this conversation during our next session."

"If this were a normal circumstance, I would be supportive of that. However, I need to give Gwen an answer."

"No. See how simple that was?"

"But you've not heard what I have to say."

"Don't need to."

Alex cupped her head in her hand. "Mom, please hear me out. This is something I need from you. This is important to me." Alex let the silence stretch between them, knowing how much her mother hated dead air. She wasn't going to say a word until Roxanne agreed or hung up.

A resigned sigh broke the silence. "Tell me what she wants so we can be done with this."

"Jorge promised Dad that if he and Buxton escaped the Netherworld, he would pay for a proper ancient Egyptian burial for Dad with all the ushabtis and grave goods needed for his time in the afterlife. Gwen promised Jorge she would ask you."

"But Jorge is dead, right?"

"Yes."

"Then how did she promise this to him?"

"She has visitations—"

"Oh god, you have to be kidding. My husband has been dead for many years, and he's never visited me. Why do you think that might be?"

Alex hadn't thought of it before. "Maybe it might be because he doesn't currently have a false door."

"A false what? Jeez Louise, Alex. The reason is he is dead, d-e-a-d. I knew once those crazies got a hold of you . . ." Roxanne's voice trailed off.

"Mom, this conversation has gone sideways. All I ask is you do this for me. I know you don't believe me, but I've seen Dad in the Netherworld, and he has a great house, but there isn't anyone living in his village, he has no helpers, no companions. He is alone without the supplies he needs for his afterlife. As much as I don't like Gwen or having to deal with her, this is something he needs."

"You truly believe all this, Magpie?"

Alex wished she could somehow magically make her mother see the light. There might have been several things an outsider could say about their mother-daughter relationship, but up until Alex worked for KHNM, trust was never an issue. It broke her heart her mother actually thought she was delusional. "You know if I had a way of making your life better, you know I would do anything to make it so, right? I would travel to the ends of the earth to make it happen." Alex had countless times saved her mother from the emotional abyss.

"I know, dear."

"Hold that in your heart, Mom, because I know you would do the same for me. If you truly don't believe me, please at least try to understand how important this is to me. No matter how I feel about Gwen, I want this for Dad. What if I am right, Mom?

About the eternal situation you are leaving him in . . . if you pass this up?"

"You want me to dig up my dead husband, and what?"

"Have him reburied in a tomb. Let's say for the sake of argument you're right, and I am wrong. What is the worst that will happen?"

"Alex, I just can't."

"It'll give us a chance to celebrate his life again, Mom. I was so young when he was buried. This could be a healing moment for us, and a chance for us to mourn together."

"You know I'm going to say no."

"Please give it a think. That is all I ask. Hash it out with Bernadette if that makes you feel better. I will call you when I get back."

"Be safe."

"You too." Alex stood and walked to the window. Dawn was starting to break. The Nile was turning a pale silvery blue with long clouds of mist hovering over it.

Alex could hear gentle sniffles on the other end of the line.

"Love you, Magpie."

"You too, Ma."

Alex tossed her phone into her bag and then grabbed a few items before heading to the shower. With the new day rolling forward, they were running razor close to the return deadline for the book of magic. If she failed, the book's ancient powers would be lost forever.

CHAPTER TWENTY-THREE

It was just past dawn when Hattie and the boys left Karnak Temple. When they arrived at her dahabeeyah, she was exhausted from the spell-work, making Hattie realize the drive to the White Desert would have to wait a little longer. The boys, knowing her ways, drew a warm bath for her. Floating rose petals danced on the water's surface as she gazed at the early morning Nile as it started coming to life. In the distance were small wooden boats where fishermen stood, casting their nets into the bounty of the great river. Thin strips of fog lay across the water, adding a dewy glow to this breaking of a new day. Her heart soared like marsh birds taking flight. This land never ceased to entrance her.

She stood, sending rivulets of the lotus-scented water cascading down her body. Stepping onto the soft patterned rug, she reached for a thick towel made from the finest Egyptian cotton. The soles of her feet padded along the cool tile floor to her chamber, where she slipped into her silken sheets, certain sleep was not far off. As she lay in the nest of modern textiles, she wondered at the luxury available to the average person. Her head rested on a pillow that would fool the sky as a cloud. Nothing she experienced as a pharaoh was as sumptuous as this.

The satisfying tug of a well-earned sleep pulled her into the void of dreamland where she found herself walking along the Nile of her youth. Soft waves of the mighty river lapped against the shore near the palace grounds. Today was the beginning of the Opet Festival, her favorite time of the year. Brushing her hand against the marsh grasses sent a clatter of squawking waterfowl into the air. Gazing down at her ceremonial garb, she knew she had to be careful. She wouldn't hear the end of it from her father if she muddied them before the sacred parade.

Hatshepsut breathed in the earthy smell of the surrounding marsh and the rich black soil. Contentment filled her breast. She closed her eyes and listened to the sounds of nature surrounding her.

Upon opening her eyes, her gaze landed on her father standing nearby. However, it wasn't the living father of her childhood who looked at her with deep concern, it was her long-dead father currently residing in the Netherworld. Disappointment settled in at the realization this was only a dream, and she hadn't been magically transported to the time of her youth.

"They sent you to check up on me?"

"They figured they'd have far more success if they sent me and not your husband."

"Ha!"

Her father's expression plummeted. He knew her better than most anyone. If he didn't want her to laugh, he should know better than to use such a dry delivery on that particular topic.

"You know I love my brother in an I-wish-I-hadn't-had-to-marry-you kind of way. And it makes sense they chose you over Senenmut to meet with me. I guess it wouldn't do to send a commoner as an emissary for a bunch of dead pharaohs."

His expression shifted from disappointed to disapproving. "They thought you might be too . . . distracted if they sent him."

Hattie let the loaded comment slide. Her father never met her lover in life, and he never liked him in death. Aside from the fact that probably no man would be good enough for his daughter, even his own son, it didn't make things any better for Senenmut, considering he was the one that looped Hatshepsut in the scandal that landed her father in the eternal clink.

Hattie did everything in her power to try and unmake those repercussions. For centuries, she scoured the world to find a way to free him, her husband-brother, and lover, but with no luck, until now. "What did you have to do for them to free you from your bonds? A promise of fealty to the grand schemers of this new harebrained escapade of the royal departed? Hadn't they learned from the past?"

What warmth his eyes held was gone in a flash. "I am no one's vassal, daughter."

Hattie realized instantly she had gone too far. "Sorry, Father, I meant no insult. Let's walk. It has been a long time since you and I have had a nice stroll along the Nile."

She hooked her arm in his and walked along the riverbank. A flock of marsh birds erupted from the cluster of reeds nearby. They both ducked as the waterfowl flew over their heads. The bucolic scene made her realize that if she had to have her rest interrupted, walking along the Nile with her dear father wasn't so bad. "It is good to see you, Father. Although I don't see much sense or success in this proposition to rein in the Gods by your pharaonic brethren, I am relieved it could return you to your well-earned eternity in the Field of Reeds."

"I can hardly believe I'm free. I never thought this day would come." He looked down at his hands. "They unbound me so I might meet with you here for a status update. Hopefully, my freedom won't be temporary. I have faith you'll be able to find the artifact the pharaohs are looking for, freeing all the captives permanently. If not, we will be sent to the eternal void." He grimaced at the thought. "Can you imagine how it was having all those kingly Bas trapped in one stone shaft for centuries on end, with all those other pharaohs?"

"You must have been cursing my name the whole time. If I hadn't gotten caught up in that ill-fated scheme to bar Ramses the eleventh from the afterlife, you wouldn't have been punished."

"I know you, daughter, and you are true of heart. You would never have intentionally harmed me. What was done is done. You did what you thought was best at the time. Take peace in knowing the time passed as if I was lost in eternal dreamless sleep, albeit in a drafty and dark chamber roughly hewn from the mountainside."

Hattie leaned into her father and breathed in his familiar scent. Even in death he managed to smell of myrrh and mint. She knew the source of the myrrh scent. He was a stickler for fresh breath and consistently had a ball of resin in his mouth, but she was never sure where the mint notes came from. "Thank you, Father, for your kindness to me in your forgiveness."

He chuckled. "Well, I wouldn't go so far as to say you are completely forgiven. Maybe after you do this task we've asked of you, we can clear the slate."

"We?"

"Although still a captive, I am a part of the plan now. This situation has real stakes for me and the others. I too am a dead pharaoh, and once free would have to live under the current sub-optimal conditions of the Field of Reeds. I don't think you understand how bad it is."

"You mean your regal selves are being asked to do some

work. How bad is that? I would think you might love to have something to do. Given that none of you are anything less than type-A personalities on steroids."

"Type-A?"

"Sorry, modern lingo. It means you overachieve with great gusto and will smite anyone who attempts to hinder your way."

"I miss smiting." His voice trailed off dreamily. Anyone else might have thought he was being silly, but Hattie knew her father did fully enjoy raining justice down on those who endangered his beloved land.

Her father's presence flickered as if it was a projection whose light was on the fritz.

"I am guessing our time is short, as you appear to be fading, Father. I should get down to business and update you. I know Cambyses's army was lost somewhere near the White Desert. As soon as I am rested from the magic I cast, my companions and I will be setting off for that destination. I am hoping once we get close enough to the hoard, the sistrum can lead us to it. By the way, did your new pals ever enlighten you about what exactly I am looking for?"

"They said it was something that could bring the Gods to their knees. Make them negotiate a little. They seemed to think it would become obvious to you as you go through the hoard."

Hattie shook her head. "A wish and a prayer are all that is holding up this grand scheme."

"Sometimes in life, you have to follow the wind and hope it brings you where you need to be, daughter. This is something we need. I will be double blessed if you are successful, and if not, maybe we can find another way. But right now, all we can do is try."

"So off to the desert for me."

"My heart will travel with you, my beloved. Stay safe."

Hattie hugged her father, who was somewhat taken aback by the sudden contact. "This I will do for you, Father."

Thuthmosis stepped away from her embrace. "Until next time." A mischievous smile pulled across his face as he turned and walked down the slope to the river beyond. He mounted a large hippopotamus that turned and swam away. "It is wonderful what can happen in dreams," he yelled as he disappeared into the marsh.

⌇

She slept for a while and awoke to find the boys had prepared for the upcoming desert trek and packed the Range Rover. By the time she was dressed and fed, they were ready to roll. As they drove through the town of Luxor, Hattie happened to notice a familiar face outside the Chicago House complex. It was that woman who ran into her at the train depot after stealing the artifact. Hattie was stunned to see her walking alongside a God. Her heart sank. KHNM must be on to her. Had Maspero squawked and led them to her?

"Boys, our timeline just got tighter. Put the pedal to the metal."

"Of course, mistress," Zuberi said from the passenger's seat.

Hattie reached into her bag and pulled out her phone. Unfortunately, she would have to call Rekhmira and ask a favor of him. Setting out to find Cambyses's army and its hoard, while KHNM agents seemed to be on her trail, she needed to be sure Maspero was kept quiet about her and the Tears of Isis he had procured for her. She would ask Rekhmira to find Maspero and put him on ice for a bit. She knew he'd be game. He would see the value in protecting his cut of the hoard. For all she knew, Maspero might have already made his way to the new KHNM headquarters.

Lucky for Hattie, she had three newly freed friends in Vegas who owed her big time.

As her Rover passed the woman and the God, inspiration struck. "Boys, on second thought, we have a pit stop to make." All she needed was a distraction and two seconds to put a kink in their plan.

Hattie wondered if the God's father ever taught him to change tires.

CHAPTER TWENTY-FOUR

Alex sunk into the embrace of the fine leather seats in the ultraluxe Range Rover. Niles was perched in the driver's seat, expertly cutting in and out of the chaotic Luxorian traffic. He was fluent in the language of the Egyptian car horn—whether they were short staccato sounds or lengthy moaning calls, he knew how to translate the strange music around him into quick forward motion.

Although his driving skills were steady, it seemed like forever since they'd stepped foot on Egyptian soil, Niles was on edge. She wondered if it had anything to do with the meeting with Salima and the Gods the other night. That night he happened to show up on her balcony wearing the incongruous suit, covered in snow and flower petals. She caught a glimpse of this type of reaction just before they got into the Rover. Niles paused and looked over his shoulder as if someone was watching them. The expression on his face instilled a deep sense of foreboding in Alex.

Niles glanced over at Alex. He must have felt her gaze upon him. "What are you looking at? And why such a sad expression?"

"Oh, I don't know . . . I wasn't really looking at anything."

"Gee thanks." His mouth quirked up.

"What I meant was I was thinking."

"Well, maybe you should stop thinking about whatever it is. It is obviously not making you happy. You must have been thinking of Thorne. Banish ye, scorpion, from my house!" His voice boomed like an overeager and undertalented thespian.

Alex chuckled. "Actually, I was thinking about you."

Niles's eyebrows knitted together. "And that made you sad?"

"No, I have this feeling you are keeping something from me."

"What would give you that idea?"

Alex played with the heart pendant he'd given her at Schliemann Haus. "I've noticed you looking over your shoulder a lot lately. Like you know something is coming and you aren't telling me."

"What would I have to keep from you?"

"Oh, I don't know, maybe something that came up during your meeting with the Gods the other night."

"It is just a little bit of Salima troubles. You know how she can be."

"Don't I ever." There was a time when Alex had been abducted by Salima and her father, Raymond, and left in an abandoned tomb in the middle of nowhere. Before they left Alex there to die, Salima left her with a parting gift. A lie she hoped would torment Alex's last moments of life. She told Alex that Niles had betrayed her, and he never cared for her. That he had only been toying with a mortal for fun.

"So, what did the she-of-three have to say that was so troubling?"

"Don't put words in my mouth. I never said 'troubling.'"

"I think you kind of did."

Niles huffed, then acquiesced. "Salima was making it sound like I was keeping information from the Gods about your powers.

She kept at it until I ended up telling them about your dreams. The ones you told me of when we met in the Netherworld. Which frustrated me, because it ended up looking exactly like I was keeping things from the Gods, thanks to her."

"Well, you kind of were, I guess. What did they say?"

"You know I can't tell you that. Have you experienced any more of them?"

"I did on the flight over."

"Talk about keeping things from one another."

"It just seemed so innocuous."

Niles was fuming in the silence that stretched between them. Alex felt bad for not telling him, but it wasn't easy to know what to say about this whole superpower thing. She never knew what small thing might push the balance over and end her life.

"I am sorry I didn't say something sooner. The dream featured you counting an unseen commodity on a scroll of papyrus in the presence of the Goddess Maat. She was talking endlessly while the other Gods danced in a circle around you. When the music stopped, the hieroglyphic text appeared to reveal it would be a very favorable day."

"This is happening frequently?" His nonchalant tone belied the concern in his eyes as he asked the question.

"Almost daily."

"There is something about this thing that is happening to you that feels somewhat familiar to me, but I can't put a finger on it, exactly. It seems prophetic in some way. I am scheduled for another check-in when we get back to Chicago House. You know I'm going to have to tell them about this."

Another silence filled the car.

"You know I would do anything I can to protect you, my heart." His voice trailed off as he concentrated a little too intensely on the road ahead.

"I know. It is so hard not knowing what might be the thing that sets the Gods off to call for my blood. Knowing that your entire family has it in for me. By the way, I think Salima is on the top of the Gods-who-have-it-in-for-me list. And I think that Gwen might be playing at being an entry-level sycophant to her."

"What makes you think that?"

"On the train, when I belatedly went to relieve Salima from guard duty, I passed by Gwen, who was leaving the cargo hold with a self-satisfied look. Salima and I had a typically intense conversation, and before I left her, she told me she was watching me. It seemed plain as day they are in cahoots, and it made me wonder what exactly Gwen told her."

"And you didn't bother to tell me this?"

"We were a little busy the other night." Alex flushed at the memory of waking in his arms back at Herr Schliemann's Haus. Nestled against his broad chest, his strong arms encircling her as she breathed in his woody-spicy scent of myrrh and smoke. She pushed the memory aside. "And, what would it matter anyway? It's not like you have any control over either of them."

A shadow crossed over his face. "Please, my heart, whatever you do, don't hold anything back from me. Any piece of information you share with me could mean the difference between your life and death."

Alex stared out the window, contemplating her precarious situation with the Gods. The landscape ahead of them was quickly becoming more rural once they departed the city limits. Large mud-brick dwellings were scattered along the road. On Alex's side of the car a low patchwork of verdant fields bordered with date palms scrolled by. The other side was a vast expanse of rock-strewn desert. Now that they were out of town, it was probably a good time to test her theory on finding the lost oasis so they could return the book of magic before it was lost forever. Alex was ready for a change of topic.

"Could you pull off the road up there?" Alex pointed toward an area free of houses on Niles's side of the road.

"Before I do, promise me you won't keep anything from me again."

Alex looked at Niles and his worried expression. "Of course. Now pull off the road, please."

He turned the Rover onto the rocky surface. The cab jostled as they drove over the uneven landscape. "Why turn off a perfectly suitable road?"

"Find a place where we can stop. I'll need to get out of the car."

"I told you that espresso was a bad idea."

"Very funny. I'm going to try and find our way to the lost oasis."

"Do you have an ancestral divining stick you plan on using?" Niles stopped the car not far from the roadway.

Alex hopped onto the sandy ground, scoping out the terrain as Niles made his way to her. She opened the clasp on the gold chain around her neck, holding her new heart amulet as she slid a small bird-shaped pendant off that was next to it. Its two black eyes glinted in the midmorning sun like diamonds in the palm of her hand. She refastened the chain around her neck. "I am hoping this will work."

"A pendant?"

"It is more than just jewelry."

"As if that is not enough?" Niles's tone held a mock-philo-sophical tone to it.

Alex pushed the small white bird around in her palm. "This bird led me to the lost oasis from a cave that Gormund, Luke, and I took shelter in from a sandstorm. When I returned the book, it brought me back to that cave and then turned into this pendant. The lost oasis stays lost by casting about the red and black lands. Even if I could find the same cave, I don't know if the entrance to the lost oasis would present itself there. I am hoping that this little guy and my connection to the oasis through the blood of my lineage will lead me to it."

She tossed it into the air, and it plummeted into the soft sand at her feet. She sighed.

"Now what?"

"I don't know."

"You mean that was the only plan you had?"

"Maybe."

"I'll take that as a yes."

"I guess I thought my intention of seeing my ancestors Nun and Naunet in the lost oasis would be enough. That was how it worked last time. I must have missed something." She knelt to retrieve the pendant, but it was gone. She pushed the sand around frantically, trying to find it. "Damn, now I've lost it."

"Um, Alex."

"Magical objects are so unpredictable. Don't just stand there —help me find it."

Niles pulled her up and then pointed to the sky above them. A bright-white bird was playfully darting and dancing through the air above them.

"It worked!" Relief flooded through Alex.

"Let's get going before it decides to leave us behind." Niles dashed to his side of the car.

As soon as Alex slammed her door shut, Niles pulled out and followed the bird. It lowered its altitude so it would be easy to follow.

"When we get to the oasis, I will return the book. You probably won't have to wait long, unless of course Nun and Naunet want to catch up with me. The last time I was there I had the sense they suffer from a heavy dose of isolation. Now that they have their servants back, maybe it has changed. But if they do want to chat, I am sure you can amuse yourself."

"It is kind of you to think about their being lonely. Time is a little different for Gods. We do have impossibly long lives, and as a survival instinct, we do find ways to amuse ourselves. Ways that would never occur to mortals. I am willing to guess they are fine no matter who may or may not be spending time with them. But no matter, I have no intention of staying behind."

"How will you get in? I thought the oasis was only accessible to those of my lineage." She frowned. "Are you trying to tell me we are related somehow? Because that would be . . . uh, gross."

"Really?"

"Well yeah, just because the ancient royals did the marry-your-relative hoedown doesn't mean—"

"We are not related. But that is the reason you think I would be barred from the lost oasis? There is another more obvious reason why I am not."

"Oh, yeah. You are a God."

"I love it when you say that."

Not too far ahead of them, a small desert fox darted out and jumped onto an outcropping of large rocks near the Rover. Its long snout moved around as it tracked the movement of the magicked white bird. Its head tilted sideways as if it occurred to him magic wouldn't fill his belly, and he scampered off.

Alex was struck by this. "How would the fox have known?"

"Creatures of the wild have an innate connection with the magical, my heart."

"Since you are planning on joining me, how do you feel about seeing Nun and Naunet? Aren't they distant relatives of yours?"

"I guess you could say they are my great aunt and uncle, but not by birth."

"There are so many different renditions of Egyptian myth. It makes it hard to know who they would be to you in your family tree."

"Myth?"

Alex was used to her thinking of ancient Egyptian beliefs as a myth. She still hadn't gotten used to the reality of it all. "Sorry, my dear, religion."

"I prefer *consort*." Niles laughed.

"Of course you do." In a grand voice, she exclaimed, "O divine and heavenly consort . . ."

"That is more like it."

"Okay. Let's see if I can follow the straight trunk of your family tree. First, there were the eight Gods of the Ogdoad to which Nun and Naunet belong. Their child Atum emerged from the waters of chaos onto the primeval mound and created the first Gods on land, Shu (air) and Tefnut (moisture). They begot Geb (earth) and Nut (sky), whose incestuous relations brought us the mighty four, Osiris, Isis, Nephthys, and Set?"

"Why do they get to be mighty all the time? I am the God of writing, knowledge, and the moon for heaven's sake."

"But you aren't blood-related to them, right?"

"What do you mean? We all come from one another somehow or other. Are we not all stardust?"

"No evading of my question with cosmic platitudes allowed."

"But there is a kernel of truth in that saying. That is why it has become overused. Mortals like to think of themselves as having always existed in one form or another. Although it isn't at all true, it comforts them."

"Again with the mortal-shaming and question avoidance. Yes,

those of us who must one day die have more of an emotional issue with nonexistence. But back to you."

"One of my favorite subjects."

"Speaking of self-love. Aren't you known as the self-created one or something? I mean how does *that* work?"

"I'll give you two guesses, but I think you'll only need one."

"Very funny. No, really. I know there are a couple of stories out there. Which one is true?"

"How about you guess. If you choose correctly, you could win big." Niles wiggled his eyebrows.

"One." She flicked out her index finger. "There is the story you were self-created as an ibis and you laid the egg of creation."

Niles smirked.

She flipped up her middle finger. "Two, that you emerged from the lips of Re."

Her ring finger was next. "And three, you were created from the head of Set during his famous brawl with Horus in which Horus became aroused and Set accidentally swallowed some of Horus's semen."

"Which do you think was true?"

"Knowing you and the trouble you tend to get into, I would think number two, about emerging from the mouth of Re, was probably made up by you to appease him." Alex tapped her chin while she thought. "I am guessing number three was something you made up to piss off both Horus and Set."

"We Immortals have to find ways of entertaining ourselves, as you are well aware."

"So, you did lay the egg of creation?"

"Do you see me as a layer of eggs?"

"If the nest fits."

"You are right in the story about Re. I did make it up to

appease him, because the actual story of my creation had nothing to do with him, which hurt his feelings."

"You did lay the golden egg?"

A loud thump came from the rear of the vehicle. "Oh damn." Niles stopped the Rover and got out. In a few shakes, he returned. "It looks like we have a flat."

Alex slid out of the cab and walked to where he was assessing the issue.

"How on earth did that happen?"

"I won't know for sure until I get the tire off. I am guessing we drove over a nail or something."

"Perfect timing. There isn't anything around for miles."

"Well, it shouldn't take me too long to get the spare on." Niles opened the back of the Rover to an empty compartment. His shoulders sagged. "It looks like we are in for a delay. Our spare is gone too."

"Great." Alex's phone rang. "Maybe it's Gini, and she can send another car or something." They only had a small window of time to reach the lost oasis and return the book of magic. How were they going to make it on time? Sweat beaded down her neck as she grabbed her phone. "Hey, Luke, how are things over there?"

"I have some bad news for you. You know the artifact that was linked to the stolen sistrum that we thought KHNM had?"

"The collar necklace?"

"It hasn't been in the possession of the agency since the 1950s. It was stolen around about that time. I guess that puts a crimp in your plans."

A bead of sweat burned her eye as she wiped her forehead with the back of her hand. The fates appeared to be working against them on many fronts. "Well, thank you for checking. By the way our Rover had a flat in the middle of nowhere. I'd like to save as much of my phone battery as possible, since we are out here with no spare. Could you ring Gini and have her send another car?"

"No spare?"

"No spare."

"Double damn. Certainly, I will get her on the horn and have her work her magic."

"It better be strong magic. We are running out of time."

"Roger dodger." Luke hung up.

Alex dropped the phone into her scribe's bag and gazed into the empty sky. The situation had gone from bad to worse. It appeared their feathered guide had abandoned them.

CHAPTER TWENTY-FIVE

Zuberi was driving and Thabit was in the navigator's seat, which left the entire back of the Rover to Hattie. She bought the Rover not too long ago, thinking it would be a good purchase for herself and the boys. Apparently, the agents of KHNM had the same taste in cars. It wasn't surprising they chose the expected secret-agent black. Hattie selected a rich, vibrant green. She almost went for a sinfully rich red, but the green spoke to her, reminding her of the dense vegetation lining the banks of the Nile. The lush paradise that supported a multitude of life-forms was only a thin strip edging the vast desert. The contrast was a daily reminder of the tenuous line between thriving and desolation.

Stopping to pierce one of KHNM's rear tires was a detour in their plan. It was a big gamble. If they were caught, Alex would most likely recognize them. However, Hattie needed to find a way to slow them down. The opportunity presented itself and allowed Thabit and Zuberi to exhibit their masterful skill in creating a leak slow enough so it would flatten when the mortal and her God were out in the middle of nowhere. She thanked whatever God or Goddess was looking out for her, as Zuberi had the forethought to remove the spare from the back too. It was rare for things to work out perfectly, but in this case, they did.

Hattie pulled her phone out of her bag and dialed Rekhmira. There was one loose end she had to tie up. The thought of talking to him again was about as attractive as taking a huge whiff of a low-budget mummy, but she knew she would have to suffer through the rot.

He picked up after the seventh ring. Hattie wasn't sure why she counted, but she did.

"You couldn't stay away, sweet cakes?"

Back when they were together, he used to call her honey cake. She didn't like it two thousand years ago, and this rendition was less palatable, but she would never let him know it got under her skin. "How right you are."

"To what do I owe this pleasure so soon after you have departed from my loving gaze?"

"I need something from you."

"Another favor?"

"No, not quite. This is something to protect both our interests. I need you to stop someone."

"Stop as in forever, or for now?"

"For now. I think KHNM might be on to me. One of their agents is returning to the bosom of the agency, and he possesses information that could spell our downfall. If he isn't stopped, he will most likely call in the cavalry and you can kiss your treasure from the hoard of Cambyses's army goodbye."

"How may I be of service?"

"It is the three you freed in Vegas that I need help from. Do you still have a way of contacting them?"

"Does a hippo crap in the marsh?"

Hattie rolled her eyes. "The target is a KHNM agent C. C. Maspero."

"Gaston Maspero? Is he immortal too? I thought he died in 1916, or thereabouts."

"Not the same person, although he is a distant descendant of that archeologist. I was working with Maspero to get the sistrum." It was a lie, but Hattie didn't give two shakes about lying to Rekhmira. "I think Maspero is on his way to the new headquarters at Area 51. I need them to keep an eye out for him and apprehend him if possible. He'll probably show up in the train yard waiting for the Area 51 transport train to bring him in."

"Area 51? How do you happen to know where a secret society has its headquarters?"

"I have eyes everywhere." It was another lie. It couldn't hurt to make him think she actually did.

"What does he look like?"

"He looks like a twitchy white rat who hasn't seen the light of day in ages, and his eyes are continually in a squint. He will stand out against the backdrop of the freight yard, as I believe he was born wearing an ill-fitting suit." Hattie wished she would have snapped a picture of him on the sly. It would have come in handy now. And since KHNM was a secret agency, it wasn't as if she could point Rekhmira to the agency's web page for head-shots. "It may be a fool's errand. For all I know, he may have already returned and shared too much, but until I can get your goods to you . . . you must have those three keep an eye out for him."

"And eliminate him?"

"No need for rough sport. If we are lucky enough to catch and detain him until I can locate and clear out the hoard, we will be doing well. We don't need any blood on our hands."

"Okay." He sounded dejected at the thought of a no-kill order. "But you know mistakes do happen."

"I don't want him killed. End of story."

"Bring me what's mine. End of story."

The line went dead.

"Your father sends his love, boys."

Silence filled the car.

"Too soon?"

Thabit looked back, his nose wrinkled as if he'd smelt something bad. "Too soon."

She had done what she could to slow KHNM down. It was out of her hands now. All she could do was find the hoard. Hattie gazed at the sandscape punctuated with dark-brown rocks and boulders scattered around. In the distance towering cliffs bordered mountainous peaks. There were only nine hours left of driving in this repetitive landscape before they got to their destination.

⌇

Hattie's head knocked against the Rover's window, waking her. Sugar-white chalk formations carved into surreal shapes by eons of wind erosion jutted up against the pastel-painted sunset. Surrounding the bases were large patches of rippled brown sand. Zuberi stopped the vehicle next to a large formation topped with a large mass resembling a sphinx's head. The column of chalk beneath it looked far too thin to bear its weight.

"I'll start looking around before we lose the light. I think you two should set up the tent while I do a little recon."

Hattie hopped onto the sandy ground and took in the glorious sight before her. It had been a long time since she traveled to the White Desert. When she was a mortal, there were some strongly held superstitions about this place. It was a place most people avoided. Some thought it was inhabited by the followers of Set, making it a cursed land, a place from which no good could come. It was one of the reasons she loved to trek out here and camp. Its reputation ensured peace and quiet.

Zuberi came from the other side of the vehicle holding a wooden box. "Here is the sistrum. It might aid you in your search."

Hattie flipped it open and retrieved the golden instrument. The pierced disks chimed pleasantly. It always surprised her the instrument didn't survive as a popular choice into the present day. It always seemed more sophisticated and elegant than its distant modern cousin the tambourine. It was obvious this sistrum was crafted by the highest-ranking court artisan. The carnelian and turquoise inlaid handle bulged out slightly in the middle for a perfect hold. At the joint between the handle and the U-shaped instrument was a magnificent head of Hathor, her bovine ears peeking out from finely rendered hair.

"Thank you." Hattie held it close to her chest and bowed slightly to Zuberi. Holding this object made her feel underdressed in her jeans and tank top. Hopeful, she held it up to the setting sun and focused her thoughts on finding the hoard. She strained her ears to hear the smallest of noises, but there was nothing. "I wonder how this is supposed to lead us to the hoard. That box doesn't have any instructions, does it?"

Zuberi laughed. "If only we could be so lucky. Maybe it is like a dowsing stick, and you have to walk around." He snapped the box shut.

"I'll take it around and see if I get any sounds."

"Of course." Zuberi went to help Thabit to set up the tent.

She was glad they brought it and supplies for a few days. From the looks of it, this might take some time. There was a lot of ground to cover. Scholars and adventurers had spent fortunes searching for the lost army of Cambyses over many centuries to no avail.

Up ahead was a rather large mound. Hattie figured she should scale it to get an overland view. She hoped one of the land formations would jump out at her. Sistrum in hand, she climbed to the top. Holding it in the air, she walked in a small circle, pausing in each of the cardinal directions. Nothing.

After slipping it into her back pocket, Hattie shielded her eyes against the setting sun. As luck would have it, nothing strange stood out among the decidedly odd land formations around her, and there were no obvious signs of a lost army either. Her heart sunk at the possibility that since the treasure was lost thousands of years ago maybe someone quietly found it and melted it down.

She turned away from the western horizon. Soon the dusk would turn to night, and not many things were darker than the remote desert. They would need to find an activity to pass the time. She smiled. *Maybe it would be a lucky night after all.*

She pulled the sistrum out of her back pocket. If it was a dowser of sorts, who knew how fine-tuned its receptors were? She shouldn't keep it stowed away; every step might lead her closer to her quarry. A sudden gust of wind blew past her making the sistrum sound. The air smelt of the sharp electricity of magic.

She turned and what she saw stunned her. At the bottom of the hill, as if appearing out from the setting sun itself, was a high priest with a shaved head and leopard-skin pelt slung across his body. He was accompanied by an entourage of soldiers in ancient Persian battle armor.

CHAPTER TWENTY-SIX

Alex and Niles sat on a large boulder in the vast open desert. The bright midday sun beat down on them. A bead of perspiration rolled across her skin, making her wonder if her sunscreen was truly sweatproof. "I hope Gini will get a car here soon. Once they arrive, we'll take the car they bring." Alex glanced at her wristwatch. Time was ticking away. They were already cutting it close, and now this. Failure had always been a threat, but it felt closer with each moment.

Niles leaned in. "Makes sense. Why wait for them to change the tire on the Rover?"

When they left the Chicago House residence, they had until midnight to find the lost oasis and return the book. They'd already burned half the day, and she had no idea how they would locate it. She didn't like to think of the repercussions of failure. Not only would she let down Nun and Naunet, but it would be heartbreaking to be the one responsible for losing the ancient book of magic she was entrusted to protect.

The problems were piling up. Even if someone immediately showed up with a workable car and a spare, they had lost their little white guide. It was strange the bird left them. If its job was to guide her back to the oasis, why would it abandon her? But she knew magical creatures were unpredictable at best.

Alex reached for her phone. Niles covered her hand with his. "I am sure Gini has it under control. They know you are working against the clock. I think it'd be best if we don't waste our batteries in case something goes really sideways. The desert isn't exactly known for its charging stations or hospitality centers."

"You don't consider this really sideways?"

He shifted off the rock to stand behind her and rubbed her shoulders. "Things could always be worse."

"Great words to live by." Alex leaned against Niles and closed her eyes. The prickling heat of the full sun raining down on her actually felt good as he dug deep into her stiff muscles.

A trilling call sounded in the distance. She squinted in the direction it came from, where blurry waves of a heat mirage appeared. Their winged friend was coming toward them at a fast clip.

"It looks like our guide has returned." Niles's hands stilled.

"I think the patch behind it might be a portal to the lost oasis." Alex grabbed a pen and paper from her scribe's bag and jotted a quick note. *Found a way forward. Leave the fixed car here.* She quickly moved to the Rover and grabbed the book of magic from behind her seat, then placed the note on the dashboard. After slamming the door shut, she and Niles ran toward the bird and the shimmering haze that trailed after it. When they got close to it, the bird did a one-eighty and disappeared into the cascading pocket of air.

Alex grabbed Niles's hand and pushed forward into the void. The sharp buzz of magic charged through her as she emerged into a deep and narrow ravine with a small rivulet running through it. Although the cleft of rock they stood in was dark, she recognized exactly where she was. Without the aid of a flashlight, she knew the rock walls on either side of her were filled with intricate bas-reliefs depicting an Egyptian creation myth.

She dropped Niles's hand and followed the sound of their guide's flapping wings toward a bright light in the distance. Alex wasn't far behind when it disappeared around a bend she knew would take them to the oasis.

The rock corridor opened to an idyllic landscape. The stream from the cavern burbled along a path of impossibly fine sand, leading to a mother-of-pearl temple. It was the residence of the primordial Gods Nun and his wife, Naunet. They were one pair of four who made up the Ogdoad, or The Eight. Before earth and the heavens were created, the four couples appeared out of nothingness. The other three couples each represented the elements of space, darkness, and hiddenness. Nun and Naunet's purview was of water. Alex believed theirs to be the most important element. With no water, there is no life.

Alex wondered what type of greeting she might receive from Nun and Naunet as she walked down the path of sand as fine as caster sugar. After all, the book of her ancestors that she was returning now held an impurity. Trapped inside it was the powerful magician Idris Niru. Alex needed to think fast to stop him from gaining the powerful magic within. She still thought she made the best and only choice. Alex guessed Nun and Naunet might feel very differently.

It wouldn't be long before she would know. At the massive abalone doors, she held her hand out, palm up. The little bird's claws tickled her skin as it landed and turned back into its amulet form. It was warm against her skin as she brought it near the keyhole. The ivory figure shifted again into a key form which Alex slid inside. A loud clockwork sounded from within. She jumped back quickly as doors flew outward.

When the doors swung open, the key returned to its bird form, flying away into the pale blue sky overhead. Niles walked next to her as they came into the large hypostyle hall. It was filled with many rows of black stone guardian statues. She glanced up at the stalwart soldiers, each wearing the full kit of an ancient Egyptian warrior, including the large curved khopesh, or sickle-sword, clutched in one of their hands. The statues leaned against massive stylized papyrus bundles rendered in stone which were the support columns for the temple.

Unlike last time, this hall was not empty. The statues were festooned with flower garlands, and the air was thick with the fragrance of myrrh. The temple was abuzz with the anticipation of a grand event. Serpent and Frog, Nun and Naunet's servants, were scurrying around adding final touches to the elaborate decorations. Beyond the main colonnaded hall, Alex caught a glimpse of Nun and Naunet standing near the large pool in their open courtyard, presumably presiding over the work of their servants.

"Wow, they must like you, Alex." Niles looked suitably impressed. "I don't know the last time I've seen preparations like this for someone's arrival."

Alex breathed a little easier, glad to know they weren't mad at her after all. That would come later, probably, when they heard about their inconvenient bookworm.

One by one the others took notice of their arrival. Nun and Naunet dropped what they were doing and made their way over, but Serpent and Frog sagged a little at seeing her. It didn't surprise Alex that her ancestors' servants were less than happy to see her. They had betrayed her after she rescued them from being trapped within the book of magic. Nun and Naunet revealed their true names to Alex as recompense for their disloyalty. Knowing someone's true name was to hold an undeniable power over them. Alex didn't know when, but she knew someday the knowledge could be valuable in getting her out of a tight spot.

Naunet wrapped Alex in a warm embrace. "Oh, dear one, it is good to see you."

Alex breathed in her Godly scent which always reminded her of a metaphysical bookstore that used to be in her neighborhood in Chicago, a heady combination of every available incense.

Over Naunet's shoulder, Alex could see Nun standing with his arms crossed and leveling a sharp and appraising eye Niles's way. "Do you have the book with you or just your special guest?"

"Good to see you as well, Uncle," said Niles.

Alex broke from Naunet's embrace. "Yes, I wouldn't show my face around here without it." She gazed at her surroundings, taking in all the lovely efforts put forth in welcoming her back. Frog and Serpent slowly made their way to the pool. "These decorations are beautiful, but you shouldn't have gone to all this trouble."

Frog's bulbous eyes widened even more and Serpent's angular features sharpened. "You think this is for you?" Her tone held non-veiled mockery.

A deep flush ran up Alex's neck and spread to her hairline.

Naunet shot her servant a disapproving look. "I think you both have a sacred pool that needs dredging before our son arrives. Hop to it." She sharply clapped her hands.

With heads hung low, both servants left the room.

Naunet patted Alex on the hand and half-smiled. "They despise cleaning the pool. Although these decorations aren't for your arrival, it is good to see you, dear one."

"Not to be the foul southern wind in this warm reunion . . . the book, if you will." Nun held his hand out.

Alex pulled it out of her scribe's bag and handed it to the God.

"We have little time to waste. Come with me, Alex." He carried the book across the courtyard and into the small Holy of Holies that lay beyond. Within the sacred space lay the ceremonial boat that was the home of the book of magic.

They followed him to the small room, beyond which lay the grand library she desperately wished to peruse at her leisure someday. When Alex initially came to retrieve the book, the library was hidden away, only revealing itself when she took the book from its secured enclosure.

Nun gave Alex the book. "You were the one to take it. Ancient law dictates you must be the one to replace it."

Alex hesitated. "Do you need to retrieve anything from the library?"

Naunet's elegant eyebrows pulled together in confusion, then returned as the reason dawned on her. "Oh, you think once you replace the book, the library will disappear. I can see why you might think that, but the only reason the library was hidden was a security measure. You see, Nun and I had—"

"Sorry, again—let's get the book back, and we can explain later. The grains of sand left are but few, my love. I will feel more at ease when the book is in place."

"But there is something I must tell you." Alex had to come clean about the book's new stowaway.

Nun crossed his arms. "Return book, then talk." His tone brooked no argument.

Alex climbed the large wooden boat, placing the book back in the small shrine at its top. As she neared the cache the book pulled toward its home as if both objects held rare earth magnets. The book fell into place with a satisfying snap. She stood on top of the wooden barque and breathed a sigh of relief now that the book was safe once again.

While climbing down, she noticed Nun and Naunet were giving Niles a hard time.

"It has been quite some time since you have graced us with a visit. How long would you say it has been, my love?" Admonishment sharpened Nun's tone.

The observed guilt-tripping comforted Alex in that you don't have to be human for your relatives to be disappointed in you.

Naunet appeared to be taking on the role of peacemaker. "I don't think it has been that long . . . really."

Niles seemed a tad uncomfortable at the familial prodding. It was a look Alex didn't ever expect to witness from him. She broke into the uncomfortable silence. "What were you saying about the library? Glad it didn't go anywhere. It is a beauty; it would be a shame to not be able to access it." She stepped out of the small Holy of Holies and into the library, allowing the others to follow.

The inviting space boasted several oversized chairs with soft velvety cushions. They were supple delights that would beckon you to sit and read for hours on end. Scattered about were long worktables where one could camp out and pleasurably plummet into the rabbit hole of research. Encircling the room were large mahogany bookcases filled with jewel-toned treasures. A large dome capped the room that held thousands of small nooks containing papyri scrolls. The multitude of documents was held aloft by an unseen force. Small tags hung from each scroll. The gold and silver medallions twinkled in the brightly lit room like the sun against shimmering water.

Naunet leaned against one of the high tables, crossing her slender arms over her chest. "When you came here last time,

Nun and I were trapped in our sacred pool. We were freed when you took the book from its shrine."

"How can it be you were trapped in there? Who would have that kind of power?"

"It happens from time to time." Naunet's gaze moved beyond the courtyard, her voice even further away.

Nun shot Niles a look of open scorn. "There was a long expanse of time in which we didn't have any visitors, and for us, that can be particularly hazardous."

"Since we are part of the original eight, it is harder for us to maintain our corporeal presence. As you know, Alex, in our religion an entity continues to exist by the speaking of their name and the worship from others. Although the traffic in worship has slowed for all Gods in modern times, some Gods like your Niles there still have their names spoken and receive praise on occasion."

My Niles, is that how they see it?

Nun walked over to his wife and took her hand. "Being more obscure, our names are rarely spoken."

"We need those of our line to come visit." Naunet looked at both Alex and Niles with a hopeful smile. "With a lack of visitors, we go into a sort of stasis, reverting to our water forms, and we are relegated to the sacred pool."

"And as guardians of all of this." Nun motioned to the library around him. "This treasure is hidden as a security measure when we are sequestered in the pool."

"Of course, so the treasures within stay safe." Alex's gaze roved around the magnificent space. For the first time, she noticed the large relief on one of the walls. It depicted Nun and Naunet in a sacred procession. Unlike the beige bare reliefs at a ruin site today, these were painted in vibrant colors. In them both Gods were wearing their Sunday best. Naunet was depicted wearing her ceremonial garb complete with formal headgear and adorned with a beautiful suite of jewelry including a gorgeous broad collar necklace with a large scarab at the center.

Alex concluded they would have to make a point of coming to visit her elders more often, making a mental note to visit whenever she was in Egypt. She was also going to make damn sure Niles's Immortal ass would put a little more effort into his elders too. It was a shame to think of these beautiful Gods imprisoned in the pool for an indeterminate amount of time.

"What is this news of the book?" Naunet asked.

"It has an impurity now."

Nun let go of Naunet's hand. "What exactly do you mean?" Both Gods were now standing at attention.

"Alex had to take unfortunate measures to stop the magician she was after." Niles stepped forward, standing between Alex and the other two Gods as the tension rose in the room.

"He's in the book," said Alex.

Nun and Naunet's complexions blanched, then flushed with anger.

Alex stepped back as the Gods came nearer. "It was the only possible choice."

"There are always other options than damaging an ancient wonder." Nun's tone was sharp.

"I thought it wouldn't matter much, as your servants had been in there so long—" Alex's phone buzzed in her scribe's bag. "What the hell? How on earth am I getting reception here?" She fumbled to grab her phone. "Sorry, I have to take this. It's Luke."

Both Serpent and Frog had returned with their arms full of cleaning equipment. "How rude," croaked Frog.

Serpent dropped the buckets she was carrying and put her hands on her hips. "The gall of it. Taking a call in the audience of a God."

Naunet spoke loudly. "Get to work, Serpent, you have much to do before our son arrives."

Alex held the phone close to her ear to block out the noise. She could barely hear Luke. "I can't believe I've received your call here. Niles and I are in the lost oasis."

"I wonder if it might have to do with why I was able to enter with you last time. Maybe descendants from the four lineages might have access to it."

"Might be. What's up?"

"I thought it would be best to call you ASAP. Maspero showed up at headquarters and had a strange story to tell. Apparently, people tried to abduct him on his way to Area 51. Luckily, he was able to evade them and get here. He believes this has something to do with the stolen sistrum."

Maspero always struck Alex as a self-important prig. It was likely he was just trying to make himself feel like a part of things after being gone for so long. "It seems a stretch to me those two things might be related."

"I wouldn't be so sure, Alex. He came forward with new information. He admitted he helped Hattie Shepard with a little light thievery of an unguent from the KHNM storehouses."

"What? He stole from the agency?" Alex was completely floored by the thought. He was a by-the-rules bureaucrat. What would entice him to do something like that to an agency he'd worked for his entire adult life? He wore his position at KHNM like a badge of honor. It would seem completely against his DNA to do so.

"It is a long story. After he came clean, Buxton asked Colonel Sanderson to lock Maspero up in one of his barracks until he decides what to do with him."

It was hard for Alex to imagine Maspero in lockdown. He was

probably shivering in a corner in a cold sweat, awaiting whatever punishment his employer might mete out upon him.

"I have to tell you, though, this has put Buxton in a smiting mood."

"I bet. He is calm as a temple cat, but threaten his agency, and the claws come out."

"Maspero was offered information about his ancestor for an obscure item from our holdings. He swore up and down he didn't think it was anything of importance."

Nun was impatiently tapping his feet.

"Was Maspero able to identify this person he believed might have stolen the sistrum?"

"Yes. Once we processed the information that someone tried to abduct him, we told him the details of the robbery. I'd given him your description of the thief and he went sheet white. That was when he told us about his indiscretion. He believes it was the same person who you ran into at the rail yard."

"Indiscretion? I would say what he did was far more than that."

"Agreed. The person who Maspero was working with was Hattie Shepard."

"You know Gini mentioned to me that she believes that Ms. Shepard's true identity is the immortal Pharaoh Hatshepsut."

"No way."

Gini's hunch was spot on. Aside from running into her at the train yard, Alex never met the woman. She was well known within the Egyptology community, and not for good works. Her long-standing business was known for working in a very grey and murky side of the antiquities world. "What did she want from Maspero?"

"A small vessel that held the Tears of Isis."

"Wait—what? We had Tears of Isis?" She immediately regretted saying it out loud, knowing if the Gods around her weren't already listening to the conversation, they most certainly were now. The agency was in too much trouble with the Gods to let a big thing like this slip in front of two of them. Although Alex didn't think Nun and Naunet would go out of their way to undermine Alex and KHNM, she knew it was hard for the Gods to resist internal gossip with the Others. Also, she knew she might be a little bit in the doghouse with her ancestors at the moment.

"Unfortunately, the artifact was mislabeled, stating that the small vessel held unspecified ancient unguents. It took a bit of digging to understand what it contained."

Alex shook her head. It was a shame their collection had never been well documented. The next time she spoke to Buxton, she needed to argue the point of how unsafe it was to have a holding of magical artifacts and a patchwork approach of recording them. They needed to employ a larger number of registrars within the agency. "Even if he thought it was a useless token, it doesn't absolve his betrayal of the agency."

"I know, but like I said, Buxton has it in hand," said Luke.

"I wonder what the connection is between the tears, the sistrum, and Cambyses's army?"

"I'm working on it. There is the legend that the items from the hoard are magically linked to one another. Just not sure about the tears. That seems to be an outlier."

Now Naunet had her arms crossed.

"I gotta go. Thanks for the info." Alex averted her gaze from the angry Gods, allowing it to land on the beautifully colored relief. A thought struck her. "Hey, Luke. Could you find the Egyptian-themed cuckoo clock at the Haus and give it a look? If I recall correctly, it features a scarab that rolls the sun out every morning at six a.m. I am wondering if the beetle might be a missing element from the collar necklace that disappeared from KHNM in the 1950s at the same time Schliemann was living at the Haus and building those clocks—he certainly had dubious connections. It might be a stretch but check it out. If you can remove it, see if any identifying markings might tell us if it is modern or an artifact."

"The General isn't going to like that."

"Then make sure he doesn't see you." The words came out sharper than she intended, her stress starting to show. "Let Buxton know what you are doing first and come up with a plan to do the work unseen."

"Will do."

The line went silent. Alex dropped her phone into her bag.

All five beings stood around her with varying degrees of shock on their face.

Nun was the first to speak. "I am sad to say, but I think your agency is doomed. You can't be trusted to care for the objects in your care. Tears of Isis in the hands of . . . that woman."

"You know of her?" It was stunning to think they would be aware of Hattie's existence. The Gods normally didn't concern themselves with the likes of non-Gods.

Naunet sat in one of the plush chairs. "What you said to your friend was true. This Hattie was a pharaoh at one time."

"It's true?" asked Alex.

Niles's face scrunched up as if he was trying to make an impossible calculation work. "Oh, this can't be good at all."

The Gods looked at him knowingly and nodded their heads.

Alex plopped onto one of the cushy chairs. "Could someone please share whatever insider God moment you are all having?"

All the Gods, Niles included, looked uncomfortable. It was Frog who broke the silence. "She is an immortal. She decided to insult the Gods by choosing a life among mortals instead of taking her place with the other pharaohs in the Field of Reeds. She has walked the earth since she faked her death and took on a new persona, living in a different place and changing every life span."

"But why is that a problem for the agency?"

Naunet shifted in her chair. "It isn't her existence that is the problem, it is what I think she is after. The Tears of Isis have the power of resurrection, and there is an obscure prophecy about the hoard and the end of the Gods. Without specifically knowing what she is up to, I have to side with the worst possible scenario. Could it be possible she is trying to bring down the Gods? She was involved in a similar misfortune centuries ago which caused a great deal of pain for many, including a number of her family members." Her expression hardened. "Dear one, you know we must report this to the other Gods. This is far too dangerous."

Alex needed more time to figure out what was going on. "Please, I ask of you, just a little more time. I can find her and sort this out."

Nun shook his head. "You ask too much."

Alex locked eyes with Naunet. "Two days. That is all I ask. Then if I've failed, you can move this up the chain as fast and as furious as you please. I need to fix this." Alex hoped she might be able to talk her ancestors into some leeway. Niles would always be on her side, but the Others were an open question.

This issue was larger than the potential fallout for the agency. Since the Gods returned to the Field of Reeds, magic was now back in the realm of mortals. Humanity had yet to discover the power that lay just beyond their known reach. Once mortals were aware of the presence of magic, all bets were off. The world needed KHNM around more than ever before.

If the upper echelon of Gods were informed of what was happening, it wasn't as if they would step forward and help sort things out. They held no care for mortals any longer. Back in the day when they were routinely worshipped, humans had a value to them. After changing the Gods' temples into ticketed show-places, mortals became more like a reality program for the Gods; lots of drama, no substance, only sheer entertainment value. "Please."

"Okay, two days." Nun looked none too thrilled about it.

"Can you give me a hint about your suspicions of what this Hattie is trying to do?"

"If my wife and I are going to play dumb for forty-eight hours, I think we should end this conversation now. Your clock is ticking, Alex."

Alex hugged them. "It was good seeing you. I'll come back before I leave for the States."

"If you are successful."

Alex didn't like the fact that Naunet's words sounded more like a question than a statement.

"I understand. If I'm not, everything is uncertain."

"'Tis the way of life," said Naunet.

Alex and Niles exited the library. When they reached the entrance to the Holy of Holies, Naunet called out to Alex, "You might want to check in with your friend Akh-Hehet. It is likely her boyfriend might be in another pickle. I doubt she will be able to save him from the Gods' wrath twice."

CHAPTER TWENTY-SEVEN

Hattie gazed in wonderment at the small party kneeling in deference to her at the bottom of the hill. A priest was surrounded by ten Persian soldiers in ancient battle regalia. Behind them was an empty gilded palanquin. She had found a remnant of Cambyses's army, or, more correctly, they had found her.

Thabit and Zuberi had stopped setting camp and scrambled up the hill to stand by her side. They must have sensed the magical energy.

A silence stretched between both parties, reminding her of her time as a ruler. In her experience, when people prostrated themselves facedown in front of her, it meant they were waiting for her to speak. In this instance she had no way of knowing how to address them, as she didn't know who they were. Many centuries ago, she heard whispers about a cult hidden in the Western Desert who were coincidentally banished as a punishment for their participation in the failed attempt that caused her beloveds to be severed from their afterlife. She wondered if the cult members had joined forces with Cambyses's army and were kneeling before her now.

Hattie cleared her throat, hoping her pharaonic voice wasn't too rusty. "O priest who kneels before me, pray stand and report your business."

The priest slowly stood but kept his head bowed. "O mighty Great One, I have been sent to take you to our humble city of Bakhu, to visit our Holy of Holies. We have brought a litter to bear you to our sanctuary." He motioned to the gilded conveyance behind him.

Hattie was intrigued by the thought of visiting this unknown city, but she was here on a mission. She had no intention of making a pit stop. Not only did she want to get this mission for the pharaohs over and done with, but she knew that KHNM might be close at her heels. "I thank you for your kind offer to visit your fair city, but I am here to find Cambyses's army. I need an object from their hoard. I will pay you handsomely if I shall find it."

Hattie knew this would piss off Rekhmira, the fact that she would try to find the object the pharaohs required and renege on the deal she made with him, but did she care? No. If he wanted the treasure so badly, he could fight all the Persian warriors he wanted to get it.

The priest raised his head but still would not make eye contact with her. "We will take you, Great One, to the hoard. It rests in our city." Four of the soldiers made their way to the palanquin and stood on either side. The priest waved toward it. "Your transport awaits. Your companions will walk."

Thabit and Zuberi's faces showed concern. Zuberi nodded toward the entourage before them. "We can stand on either side of you until we arrive at this city. If a problem arises, we can protect you from without."

"I appreciate the sentiment, but as you are both aware, I can hold my own in a fight."

"Yes, but we will let no harm come to you."

"For which I am ever grateful."

She gazed down upon the waiting party. "I and my companions accept your gracious offer."

The small priest bowed as she strode down the small hill. Standing in front of him, she said, "You may rise, priest."

He stood, keeping his eyes averted. "As you wish, Great One."

"May I have a name to call you?"

"I am Sabu, high priest of the Holy of Holies."

"Take my hand and lead me to the palanquin."

He gently took her hand, leading her to the gilded conveyance. He slid open a side panel that was finely carved with a rendition of the snake God Apophis, the enemy of Re, its long curvaceous coils creating a screen where the negative space allowed for the passenger to see out yet be obscured from prying eyes.

Hattie stepped inside. It smelt of cedar and was built for the creature comforts of one. Around three sides ran a bench with plush cushions to sit on as well as pillows to adjust as needed. This interesting U-shaped bench allowed the passenger to either sit or recline in comfort. The box was enclosed to provide shade from the sun and also allowed for a cross breeze through the intricately crafted snake emblems. Hanging from the ceiling was a small lamp to illuminate the darkness within.

The priest slid the door shut. Hattie braced herself in expectation of the motion of the guards lifting the carriage, but the maneuver was so smooth it was as if it were lifted by a swell of air. Hattie noticed the middle portion of the bench pulled out a little to form a bed of sorts, allowing one to recline in more comfort. She settled in for the ride, checking on both sides to make sure the boys were there. Their presence allowed her to let her guard down, just a little.

She peered out the side Zuberi was on. The priests were walking toward one of the chalk formations near to them. The main priest knelt in front of the towering white pillar and chanted in a low voice, making a door appear. As they carried her through the large entrance, the carriage angled downward as if they were descending a sharp slope. Close to the elbows of Thabit and Zuberi were gleaming white walls of narrow chalk tunnels.

Hattie motioned to Zuberi. "Please request the priest attend me here. I'd like to ask him questions while we are in transit."

"Of course, mistress."

In a few short minutes the priest was by her side.

"Of what service may I be, oh Great One?"

"I am curious about your city. What can you tell me regarding its origins?"

A troubled look passed over his face. "I fear that is for another's mouth to tell. I am commanded only to convey the transportation of your sacred self. All will be explained by others."

"How did you know my companions and I would be there?"

"As I said, all will be explained—but not by me."

"What about these tunnels? Can you tell me of them?"

He lightened up with a smile. "Of course. I am free to talk about the natural formations around us. These tunnels were created by the Great River of Apophis that snakes through the ground far below the blessed land of the white sands."

"Where is this great river now?" The area around them looked pristine and dry, with not a watermark to be seen.

"The river was tamed by our predecessors and is the milk of our existence. It nourishes our community."

As they passed through the underground tunnel, she saw

many smaller passages leading away from the main one. "Were these corridors created by the tributaries of this great river?"

"Some were made by the rushing waters; others were carved over time by our predecessors. The area between the entrance and the city is a maze of tunnels and dead ends."

Hattie hoped one if not both of the boys were committing their path to memory in case a hasty exit was necessary. "Were they dug as a mining interest, or something else?"

"I must take my leave of you now. We are near the city gates. I must confer our passage through the guard station. Do please forgive me, oh Great One." With a minute bob of his head, he was gone.

Hattie leaned into the side panel in an attempt to get a better view of what lay ahead, but she was unable to see much of anything. Several soldiers stood in front of a large stone gateway. After a brief conversation, the entourage was ushered through. Passing through the gate, they entered a massive domed cavern. Peering down, she could see a white river rushing through its basin. The high walls of the cave that reached up to the dome appeared to be made of sturdier stone.

The city below clung to the white canyon carved from the chalk. Above in the city were the more formal temple and palace structures carved out of more solid sandstone. This hierarchy of materials paralleled the construction approach in ancient Egypt where the houses were made of mud brick and the temples of stone. The entire cavescape resembled a mash-up of modern-day Santorini, with its maze of white domiciles clinging to a steep edge, and the rock-hewn temple structures of ancient Petra hanging above it.

The massive space was surprisingly bright. Hattie would have expected the city to be entirely in darkness, as it was located in a subterranean cave. A large metal disk hung from the cavern ceiling and reflected the torchlight from the city below. The quality of light made her think of how snow illuminates a nightscape under the moonlight. Being born in Egypt, Hattie never experienced snow until she became immortal and traveled to the northern lands. She was amazed by the beauty of it. It was like a strange dream to wake up to a white world and step into the frigid cold and experience the muffled sounds of walking in thick snowfall.

Much like the tunnels they emerged from, the space in between buildings was very tight. It appeared that the builders of this city had to be efficient in their use of materials. The pathway was so narrow the boys had given up walking directly next to her when they entered the urban center. She tried in vain to see the residents she could hear going about their business, but the alleyway walls were well above the palanquin's screens. The walls were decorated with large inscriptions written in gold hieroglyphs.

HE has seen
HE has known
HE will be
SHE has come
SHE will know
SHE will be

Once the cycle ended, it was repeated. There were many of these repetitions before the landscape changed. They were making their way to the temple precinct high above the white city.

The palanquin came to a stop in front of what Hattie guessed was a palace cut deep into the rock face. The exterior boasted two rows of columns, which spoke of the grandness of this building to afford so much real estate for decorative purposes. Sabu slid open the palanquin's door and held his hand out for Hattie to take as she descended.

The guards moved to stand in equal numbers on each side of the doorway.

With a sweep of his hands, Sabu motioned toward the palace. "Oh Great One. Please honor me by allowing me to show you to your chamber."

As someone who had ruled over Egypt, Hattie recognized the way she was being treated. Like a visiting head of state, and not a prisoner. It didn't mean they shouldn't stay at the ready in case trouble should arise.

Thabit and Zuberi came to stand on either side of her. "Keep your eyes peeled, boys."

The priest led them through the palace via the main hall that stretched on forever. This long corridor made it so the builders didn't need to dig deep into the cliffside, lessening the worry of an internal collapse. The long hallway was decorated with finely rendered painted reliefs. It appeared to be telling a creation myth, but it wasn't one she was familiar with. Finally they arrived at a large wooden door. It looked as if it was made from an ancient cedar tree.

Sabu opened the door and ushered Hattie and her companions in.

The room was large and well-appointed. One entire side of the long room was a balcony overlooking the canyon below. The wall facing it contained more reliefs like the ones in the passageway.

"As you can see, there is plenty of accommodation for your

entire party. If you prefer your attendants to have other quarters, I can arrange it."

"They shall stay with me."

The priest made a quick bow. "Please make yourselves comfortable. The servants will bring a meal shortly. After you've had time to refresh yourself from your journey, you will go through purification rites and witness the Holy of Holies."

CHAPTER TWENTY-EIGHT

Alex and Niles returned to Chicago House fully aware there was no time to waste. Her ancestors were generous in allowing them the time to try and sort this all out before reporting to the other Gods. If this went sideways, it would add yet another chink in the Gods' view of Alex. It made her wonder—if Niles did end up having to kill her for some supposed superpower, what were her chances of being welcomed into the Field of Reeds? Would they weigh her heart and find it wanting? Would she be fed to the Devourer of Souls, Ammut? Realizing the thought experiment would likely end in a non-optimal answer, she instead focused on searching the compound for Gini.

It was well past dinnertime. Alex first checked the courtyard, thinking Gini might be enjoying an after-dinner cocktail with colleagues. It was their favorite part of the day. Alex peeked in. There were many others in convivial conversation, but the librarian was absent. Alex headed to the library, thinking they might be working late, which was a rare occurrence. The magical being was dedicated to their work but also dedicated to enjoying every minute of their long life.

Before entering the library, Alex was able to pick up the scent of their perfume. The plume of fragrance was something Gini used to overpower the scent of magic emanating from their Immortal body. Over time they lived in every skin and gender. The rest of the staff at Chicago House were unaware of their magical status, so they would occasionally cycle out old personas and return as a brand-new hire. The only consistent trait was the strong cloud of scent orbiting around them. It was a lucky thing no one to date complained regarding a sensitivity to their cologne.

Upon spotting Alex, Gini dropped the document they were holding and ran to Alex and enveloped her in a big hug. Gini released Alex from their tight embrace. "Glad to see you made it back safe and sound. I was worried when I didn't see you anywhere in the vicinity of the vehicle. Thanks for the note."

"Thank you for saving us. I was so glad to see the new tire on the Rover sitting there waiting for us to drive it away."

Gini's expression turned dreamy. "How I love a tire change . . . noncerebral, hands-on, physical work." They snapped back into the moment. "Were the Gods cheesed about the new book stowaway?"

"They didn't seem happy about it, but I think they believed me that there was no other choice. I can see how one might feel a little weird with an unknown magical parasite in a sacred book they are protecting. But in reality, their servants were in the book for years. I guess there isn't any harm in it. I am sure Hapi the bookkeeper is at least a little happy at having someone new to toy with. We didn't have much time to hash it all out. Niles and I had to jet out of there."

Gini crossed their arms. "They ran you out? They were that mad at you?"

"Oh, it wasn't the issue of the hidden magician that made us hightail it out of the lost oasis. It looks like we have yet another red-hot crisis on our hands."

"Please tell me it doesn't have anything to do with the Gods. Buxton called me today, and the lawsuit is not progressing well at all."

"Damn it. I should check in with him about that. But now, we've got much bigger fish to fry. I am sure Buxton told you about Maspero."

"I can't believe it. Any of it. I never liked being around the little weasel, but the one thing I respected about him was his loyalty to the agency. To say I was shocked would be a gross understatement."

"Ditto. I think he has unwittingly gotten us caught up in another extremely problematic situation with the Gods. I can only imagine if this Hattie—"

"I know, right? I mean, the real-life Hatshepsut." Gini's face lit up as they made excited little claps.

If the situation weren't one that could potentially upend reality, Alex would have been just as excited. One of the tricky things about working with Immortals is they don't have the same high priority of death avoidance that mere mortals do and therefore can find humor and thrills in otherwise perilous situations. "She is someone I always thought would be fascinating to meet, but not like this for sure. She is putting the mortal realm in grave danger."

Gini's excitement dulled a skooch. "Such a party pooper."

"I guess that happens after you save humanity a couple of times." Alex puffed her chest out and spoke in a voice of grand self-importance.

"Oh, you." Ginny playfully swatted at her.

"I don't know the why of it yet, but the fact that Hattie Shepard procured a vial filled with the Tears of Isis and is scrounging around to find Cambyses's army . . . Well, it spells out trouble no matter what letters you use."

"Is she trying to raise a magical army? To take over the world or something? Trying to relive her past glories on a much wider scale?"

"We don't know the specifics yet. Nun and Naunet suggested I talk to Akh-Hehet for some reason. Niles and I are going to pay Auntie a visit to her shop soon. Hopefully we will be able to get more answers out of her."

"It's so strange. The fact there was magical residue all over the Rover's trunk makes it more so."

"Magical residue?"

"Yes, the whole scenario felt awfully convenient. That your tire had a slow enough leak to land you in the middle of nowhere and the spare was gone. It seemed too intentional to be an accident. Before leaving to fix the flat, I glanced at the record books and saw the Rover was serviced no less than a month ago. When I arrived at the abandoned car and knew you were both safe, I ran a magical diagnostic on it. Both the tire with the hole and the trunk were coated with magical residue. It was anything but an accident."

"Looks like we are being pulled into another dangerous scheme." Alex paused. "Speaking of which, I promised my mom I would call her when I returned. I best get at it."

"Good luck. I know that is never easy on you."

"Thanks. Maybe I'll see you in the courtyard later for a drink."

"I will be there awaiting you, ready to enable decompression session mode."

Alex mock-saluted Gini and turned to leave.

"Oh, Alex, I forgot to mention Luke called."

Alex spun around. "What did he say?"

"He mentioned something about a scarab, said you would know about it. He was in a big hurry—there was a flight he needed to catch."

"A flight?"

"Yes, he was flustered at what he'd found. Apparently, it had an inscription with both Ahmose-Nefertari's name and a newer inscription written in Elamite with the names of one of Cambyses's wives. He said he figured you'd need help. From the sounds of it, both he and Gormund are on their way." Gini's expression warmed with the mention of the latter. Alex had a hunch the librarian and Gormund were entwined in a longtime fling.

Alex wasn't certain how she felt about the reserves trouping in. They didn't know what they were dealing with. She didn't like the idea of everyone jumping ship on Buxton's plans, but it would be nice to see the two of them. Hopefully Gwen was staying back in Area 51 to help Buxton.

"Thanks for the info. You'll know where to find me when you are ready for a drink." Alex made her way to the courtyard. It was located at the heart of the Chicago House compound, where staff could congregate for after-dinner cocktails after a hard day of work unveiling the mysteries of ancient Egypt's past. As she walked through the arched entrance, a breeze rustled the greenery climbing up the trellised walls. Alex picked a table away from the others to call her mother from.

Phone calls between them didn't have a great track record for staying on the positive side of things. Usually Alex would hide out in her bedroom upstairs to make the call. Lately she wondered if the seclusion didn't enable the negativity to run wild. This time she would try the call from a more public place in the hope it might enforce a cooler head on her part.

She sat down and dialed her mother.

"Hey, Magpie."

"Hey, Mom, how's it going?"

"Bernadette and I are having a marvelous time. It's been fun for me to play tourist in my own town, showing her all the sites that are fit to see."

Alex breathed a sigh of relief it was Bernadette and not she who was being dragged along to Roxanne's favorite sites. Alex knew from pained experience her mother would sprinkle in a couple of destinations her companion might enjoy, but aside from that, it was the Roxanne show.

"I am glad to hear you are having a good time." Alex was relieved to hear a happy lilt in her mother's voice.

"I think I will need to cut this call a little short. We have a tee time at the country club."

"Golf?" Alex was taken aback. Her mother never showed any interest in golf. Unless making fun of it counted. Her favorite way to rib those who partake in the sport was to brush it off as the best way to ruin a good walk.

"The other day we were at the museum looking at some rather fine oil paintings and Bernadette kept noticing a distinguished gentleman who kept looking our way. A very handsome man . . . Anyhow, over the course of our journey through the exhibit, we kept on meeting in the same rooms and looking at the same paintings. He commented about it to me after the third or so occurrence, and before you know it, we were all taking lunch together . . ."

Her mother was dating? Albeit with a chaperone, but dating, nonetheless. For the many years since her father's death, her mother didn't so much as look at another man. This last round of counseling had really worked at pulling down the protective emotional walls her mother built around herself.

". . . and he belongs to the country club. When he found out I'd never been, he invited us both for a game. He said he could teach me how to swing."

Alex didn't doubt it was true. It was surprising to hear her mother go on in such an excited manner. "Well good for you. I am glad to know you've met someone intriguing. I won't keep you from your exciting social liaison. Have you given any thought to Gwen's proposition?" Alex felt her body tense in expectation of the foul wind about to blow her way.

"Tell her yes."

Alex looked at her phone to make sure it was her mother's number on the call display. "Are you sure?"

"Yes, I have made up my mind. We should go for it. It is a kind offer."

This complete one-eighty blew Alex's mind. She hated to prod further, but she needed to know. "What changed your mind, Ma?"

"It was something you said about how you would do anything for me to make my life better. I know in my heart it is true. And I thought if there is the slightest chance that you are right, I would be a horrible person for not allowing this if it would make his life in death more comfortable."

"I am so glad to hear it." Her entire body unclenched.

"It is funny in a way. Once I made the decision, I was filled with a strong sense of peace. It feels like I am ready to move on. It gives me comfort to think this reburial might allow him to live as he should in the Netherworld you speak of. It makes me happy to think there is the slightest possibility he is still some-where and isn't lost forever."

"But you still don't believe me?"

"I want to believe you. I've literally known you all your life. You've always had an active imagination, but never lying. I like the thought that there is an afterlife. Let's just say I am working on it."

"Love you, Mom."

"I love you too, Magpie." And with that, her mother hung up.

Alex hummed a happy tune as she walked to the bar to make herself an old-fashioned.

With cocktail in hand and things sorted out with her mother, Alex was feeling a surge of good luck. She dialed Gwen to let her know her mother agreed to the reburial. Gwen didn't answer. Alex didn't want to leave a message, figuring she would try later. It felt a little strange to talk out loud to a voicemail recording about re-entombing her departed father.

After some time Gini joined Alex for drinks in the courtyard in the cool night air. Although it was nice to catch up with them, Alex couldn't help being disappointed that Niles didn't make an appearance. It made her wonder if he was held up in his meeting with the other Gods. Maybe it wasn't going well. The thought of it had her tossing and turning all night.

At breakfast Alex was surprised to see that Luke had arrived already. He had the scarab from the cuckoo clock at Schliemann Haus on the table next to his plate that was piled with mostly bacon and sausages. He must have felt her gaze. "What? I have to keep my strength up. Who knows what sort of battles we might be getting ourselves into with this Hattie Shepard? Besides, I've been cutting back on carbs lately."

"Feeling a little defensive about our food choices, are we? I wasn't looking at your breakfast selections. I was just checking out the scarab you personally couriered here. Thank you for bringing it." She had been judging him but didn't want to admit it. His comment from the train about how she'd been acting lately was ringing truer than she liked.

He picked up the scarab. "Yeah, as soon as I connected it with the hoard, I figured you might need it right away. Buxton agreed, so here I am." He tossed the stone beetle to her.

Alex barely caught it as Niles strode into the room. She slipped the artifact into her bag. It might prove valuable during their visit with the seer. Alex hoped she might be able to tell them more about the scarab.

Niles grabbed a pastry from the sideboard. "We'd better get going to Akh-Hehet's."

"Looks like yet another walking breakfast." Alex grabbed a croissant and followed Niles out of the residency and onto the wide Corniche. As they walked, he kept glancing at the heart amulet he'd given to her. She couldn't shake the feeling something was bothering him.

"How'd your meeting go last night? I am guessing that is what kept you away."

"Things are definitely heating up."

"How so?"

"One thing I can tell you is undercurrents are getting stronger by the moment. It may not take much to turn the tide in an unfortunate way. One of the Gods inferred that your dreams are tied to the Egyptian horoscope calendar. Right now they think the power might be one of foresight."

"What else?"

"We cannot talk about this any further. There is nothing more I can say. I know I have said this before. But you know I will do anything in my power to not let them kill you."

"Let them? What do you mean by that?"

He shook his head. "Slip of the tongue. I meant I will do anything to not have to kill you."

Alex looked up at him with a dubious expression.

"Really, Alex. Let's keep moving forward. It is all we can do now." He grabbed her hand as they passed through the entrance of the souk.

She stopped in front of a shop filled with T-shirts emblazoned with pharaonic faces. "But this is my life we are talking about."

Niles gazed into her eyes. "I know. And I am doing everything I can to keep you safe, and alive. One way to work toward that end is to figure out what is going on between the pharaohs and the Gods. Who knows what favor we might gain if we find out what mischief they are up to." He pulled her into his embrace.

It wasn't until he held her that she realized she had been shaking.

He held her tight and stroked her hair. "My heart. I love you so. I will never let anything happen to you. No matter the cost."

She didn't want to move out of his protective embrace even as a stream of irritated humanity flowed around them. She pulled away then and took his hand, pulling them both deeper into the souk and her uncertain future.

CHAPTER TWENTY-NINE

Hattie stood on the long balcony outside her chamber overlooking the hidden city of Bakhu. As it would be night in the world above, so was it here. The metal disk suspended over the city was tilted at an angle so no light from the valley would be reflected, allowing the cavern to be shrouded in darkness. The city below was dotted with hundreds of lamps resembling an inverted night sky. It was impressive that these people learned to manipulate their environment down to the detail of human circadian rhythms.

In the chamber behind her there was much commotion. The clamor of servants laying out food on a long table at the center of the narrow room filled the air. They had brought in enough food to satisfy a small army as they worked diligently to set out a long train of edible delights. The linen-clad workers were plying the table with roasted ducks, sweet dates, and steaming hot flatbread.

She wandered into the room feeling a little more than hungry. There was a surprising amount of fresh fruit on the table. The scent of freshly sliced watermelon filled the air, making her mouth water and her stomach growl. It was quite some time since she had eaten.

The stream of servants bearing trays had come to a halt. The ones who remained were positioning the food to optimize visual appeal. Hattie wondered where the bounty came from. She approached one of the servants who was securing a large slab of honeycomb. When Hattie came near, the woman's chin dipped to her chest.

"Does your fair city have a subterranean farm?"

The poor thing was quaking but provided no answer. The priest who escorted them here was reluctant to talk. Maybe the servants were on strict orders to not engage with their guests. All the servants except for the woman standing in front of Hattie were filing out of the room. "You may go." The woman set down the plate of honeycomb and scurried out in haste. Hattie made a mental note to inquire about this with Sabu.

The boys were seated on either side of the chamber door. They'd taken on the role of sentries since they arrived—at the ready in case a threat walked through their threshold.

Hattie popped a large grape in her mouth. It gave off a satisfying crunch as she bit into it. She grabbed another, enjoying the sweet juice running down her throat. It had been a long time since she was waited on hand and foot, and Hattie had forgotten how glorious it was. She could get used to this, once again. She grabbed some grape clusters and then made her way to the wall running the length of the room to examine the stone reliefs. They were like the ones in the main corridor in both style and the myth they were telling.

She handed a clutch of grapes to each of the boys. "Have either of you made heads or tails of this?"

Zuberi popped one in his mouth and came to stand beside her. "It isn't a telling I am familiar with."

The panel directly in front of Hattie depicted a priest facing what appeared to be a deified scribe standing under the sun. It resembled the artwork one might expect from an Amarna period relief. Except in this case instead of the rays of the sun showering down on him ending in small hands or ankhs, these had a stylized depiction of Apophis the snake. This was interesting, as Apophis was the enemy of Re. It was peculiar that the rays of the sun would end with such a symbol. Hattie wondered if it could be a depiction of the actual sun and not have anything to do with the God Re.

In the next panel the same priest figure was prostrated with its forehead resting on the ground before one of the chalk formations in the desert. Hattie drew in for a closer look. Under further inspection, it looked as if he was digging, not praying. She read the hieroglyphs above the pictorial depiction. "Looks like this guy's name was Apepmosis, Apophis is born."

The large chamber door yawned open. Hattie turned to see the priest Sabu enter. This time without a regiment of Persian soldiers. His eyes were lowered to the ground as he spoke. "Oh Great One, I hope you have found comfort and refreshment here."

"I and my companions thank you for your gracious hospitality."

Sabu dipped his bald head in acknowledgment. "It is our hope you find rest tonight. Tomorrow preparations will be made for you to visit the Holy of Holies. For now, rest and rejuvenate your souls." As if on cue, a golden harp was rolled into the room, pushed by another priest who Hattie assumed would be its player. The new arrivals made their way to the balcony. The musician softly strummed his instrument, filling the room with its light music.

"At either end of this chamber are sleeping couches and bowls with lotus-scented waters for your evening ablutions." Sabu clapped his hands and three servants arrived with fine linen robes draped over their forearms. Behind them were yet more servants who entered holding intricately woven slippers made from palm leaves. He dipped into a shallow bow and motioned at the garments. "Fresh vestments."

They placed three sets of clothes on the floor in front of her and backed out of the room. At the doorway, his chest swelled with pride at the offerings for his guests, but his eyes were still cast down to the chamber floor. "Tomorrow before Nut gives birth to another day, you will break your fast and be ritually cleansed so you may be present for the Holy of Holies rebirth. I shall take my leave for you to take your rest. Send the musician away when you tire of his songs. Is there anything more the Great One requires?"

A million questions were swirling around in her head. "What are these reliefs depicting? It isn't a story I am familiar with."

He lifted his gaze and looked past Hattie into the distance. She sensed his thoughts went to a place of holy reverence. "Those panels tell the story of the Holy One, Apepmosis, and how he was lost in the desert and was blessed by a holy vision just as he was certain to die. Many things were revealed to him. Things of the future to come and where to find the sacred river of Apophis."

The priest-harpist halted their playing and stared gap-mouthed at Sabu.

Sabu dipped into a deep bow, avoiding Hattie's eyes. "I have spoken too much. All your questions will be answered tomorrow." And with that he left the room, closing the door behind him.

The harpist started to play again as Hattie returned to inspect the reliefs. The boys reclined on the large cushioned benches on either side of the door. The grapes must have whetted their appetites; they were both tucking into large plates piled high with all types of delicacies.

With the small amount of context Sabu provided, Hattie was able to intuit a little more from the reliefs. She moved on from the panels depicting Apepmosis alone in the desert having visions and digging for water. The next scene resembled a cross section of an ant colony with an abundance of belowground tunnels, the highest of which reached up into a desert landscape. At the center of this warren of corridors was a large oval. Inside the oblong circle was a small figure of Apepmosis, who was kneeling in prayer in front of a shrine within a temple. In this depiction, he was surrounded by others, each with a shaved head and wearing priestly garments.

She moved on to the next frame. In this relief, there were fewer priests around Apepmosis. The sun above penetrated through the subterranean area and shone upon him. Scattered around the narrative depiction were figures shown in a horizontal position which seemed to indicate mass deaths had taken place. Hattie wondered if this community experienced a plague.

The next scene took place aboveground with the ever-present sun radiating light on the chosen one once again. Apepmosis's hand was raised, holding a mace in the typical smiting pose. Rendered in a smaller scale were Persian soldiers that he was crushing under his stride. Piles of corpses littered the desert floor. Did Apepmosis fight Cambyses's army? It was impossible he would have had the manpower to succeed in defeating fifty thousand trained soldiers.

Hattie continued on. The next relief appeared to be a glory shot of Apepmosis basking in the light of this strange snake-rayed sun. She recognized it as the "All glory to me and my conquering ways" panel every pharaoh wanted regardless of how the battle played out in reality.

She wasn't sure what to make of the next panel. On it was a symbol she had never seen before. It made sense after all these centuries of isolation that these people would have deviated from the long-standing traditions of Egyptian society. Hopefully, tomorrow would shed light on the strange subterranean community. Hattie wondered how long they had inhabited this underground city. Cambyses's army was lost in 524 BCE. By Hattie's calculations it was most likely they had lived here for over twenty-five hundred years.

She walked to the panels at the far end of the chamber, the ones she had yet to inspect. These reliefs appeared to precede the one by the doorway depicting Apepmosis's vision. In it one of the figures was that of a woman who looked vaguely familiar. She was standing far away from several mummies who were laid out horizontally with their arms crossed, like those of dead pharaohs. Above their prone forms were depictions of Ba birds hovering over them. Next to the bodies stood a priestess holding a scythe of sorts.

Her pulse raced as it dawned on her. She glanced up at the cartouche of the first female figure she spotted. Her two cartouches read Useret Kau, Wadjet Renput; Mighty of Ka's, Flourishing of Years.

She knew why the woman looked familiar. Once upon a time, those were her names.

CHAPTER THIRTY

T he marketplace was in the heart of Luxor. Alex did her best to push away the fear of what the Gods may or may not have in store for her. If she were to die now, it would do her no good to spend her last moments worrying.

She allowed herself to get visually lost in the magic of the souk. She paid close attention to the strange mix of vendors who sold their wares to passing tourists. The bright morning sun raked against the bazaar's ancient beige walls. The screened windows of residences above the small shops and stalls looked down upon them.

She marveled as she passed by one shop front with a multi-tiered table holding countless mass-molded statuettes of goddesses, pharaohs, noble cats, and pyramids. They were packed together in tight rows as if waiting in a mini-amphitheater for a performance to start on the walkway below. Clusters of intricate brass lanterns hung over these unlikely spectators like an impossible cloudscape against a sky of dusty teal and bronze of the antique rug draped behind them. The shop next door was choked with boxes of all sizes and shapes made of inlaid mother-of-pearl. Unlike most shops, this owner decided to focus on one specialty instead of a dizzying array of inventory.

As they moved deeper into the market, they passed by less-touristic fare intended for the traveler with deeper pockets who didn't mind shipping home massive marble antiques or fine inlaid furniture. The twists and turns of the corridors drew closer together and the ceiling lowered. An occasional lantern graced corners where deep shadows persisted although it was daytime.

They turned a corner Alex recognized. She knew to look away from the blinding light emanating from Akh-Hehet's chandelier shop. To call it a shop was an untruth, as nothing was for sale within, but it was packed to the rafters with chandeliers of every type and style. The first time Alex saw the space it blew her mind. Each fixture dripping with crystal globules was reaching out to its neighbor, much like a tree canopy in a dense ancient forest. Walking underneath them, one needed to dip their head or else send a cascading tide of crystalline music to announce one's presence.

Akh-Hehet used the crystals for her visionings. As she aged, the seer found them necessary to focus her visions. She was a literal old soul with a bulletproof Ba who lived and died within each host she embodied. When transitioning to a new life, she was careful to select a host who just passed, occupying the corpse seconds after its soul fled. This was a process she refined over the centuries. Now her host body was no longer young and was experiencing the limitations of age.

With the lights on, Alex wondered if the seer was using her visioning abilities.

Niles moved to rap on her door. Alex stilled his hand. "Let's let ourselves in. I fear she might be in the middle of a visioning."

She felt bad about barging in, but they didn't have the time to spare for coming back later. They needed answers and needed them fast. Alex gently pulled the door open, hoping to avoid making its ancient hinges squeak. She slipped in, and Niles followed close behind her. They carefully made their way down the few awkward steps into the shop. Alex dipped low to avoid creating a tsunami of tinkling crystals. If Akh-Hehet was in the middle of a visioning, she would be sitting under the large inverted pyramid that lay at the center of the chandeliers.

They moved in closer and could hear the old woman speaking in a low, seductive tone. As Alex neared the center, she wondered what the seer might be doing. Casting a visioning or— Alex straightened to standing, jostling a gigantic chandelier hung with hundreds of heavy crystal pieces. A startled specter that Alex guessed was the naked Horemheb disappeared with a gasp into thin air, leaving a disheveled seer lying alone on the floor au naturel.

Alex grabbed Niles by the shoulders and turned him around. By the looks of his expression and the deep blush overtaking his face, she realized she didn't act quite fast enough. She had never seen him blush before. Alex didn't think he had it in him.

"Oh dear," exclaimed Akh-Hehet as she quickly threw on a silken garment that lay on the floor next to her. Alex turned around, joining Niles with her back to Akh-Hehet, who was grumbling about youth as she was angrily tying her robe. "You may turn around now."

Alex turned around. She had never seen Akh-Hehet this mad before.

Niles's back was still to Akh-Hehet. "Sorry, Auntie, for disturbing you. We just thought—"

"I know exactly what you thought. You thought, Let's barge in, I am sure the old woman has nothing going on."

Niles turned around. "We wouldn't have ever intruded like this, but time is of the essence."

"Nun and Naunet said you might have information that might be helpful," Alex added.

The old woman shook her head. "The arrogance of youth. Not only do you visit only when you need something, you barge in as if I have no life and all I do from day to day is wait around for visitors to just drop by." Her eyes were bright with anger and laser focused on Niles.

Niles jangled more crystals as he walked to the seer and gently took both of her hands in his. "Please, will you ever forgive us?" He flashed one of his sweetest smiles. "And I must say, dear lady, your natural beauty is anything but shameful."

"Oh pshaw." Akh-Hehet swatted at him. "Well, at least you both learned a big life lesson today. I can forgive you, but I don't know if Hormey will, and that man has quite a memory . . . among other things." Now it was the seer's turn to blush. "Never underestimate your elders, as you never know what they are getting up to. You know how the saying goes about assuming?" Akh-Hehet smiled back at Niles. "You make an ass of yourself and get to see mine."

Both Alex and Niles laughed. It seemed they might be emerging from the doghouse.

The seer played with the tie of her robe. "I am getting a bit drafty, though. How about you come into my quarters? I will put on something a little less comfortable, and you both can make me tea."

"You've got it." Alex fell in line behind Niles, who followed Akh-Hehet through the black curtained-off space that was the seer's living area.

The space was small and sparse in furnishings. Akh-Hehet lived in what most would think to be a life of monastic deprivation. Living life through many different corporeal hosts might have cured the seer of inclinations toward material possessions.

THE MUMMY CACHE 293

Although, like most, Akh-Hehet was full of contradictions. Alex knew that the seer's longtime love, Horemheb, once a pharaoh and now living in the Field of Reeds, managed to procure trinkets of luxury for his beloved. One such item was the delicate hand-painted china set both Niles and Alex were handling with great care.

Alex filled the kettle with water and set it to boil, while Niles gathered the necessary accompaniments on the small table near the makeshift kitchen. He even set out the marginally sweet biscuits Akh-Hehet favored. With the tea things ready, Alex and Niles waited at the table. The seer was taking an inordinate amount of time. Alex figured it was part of their payback. She glanced at her watch. They were already twelve hours in and didn't have much to show for it.

Alex was just getting ready to call to Akh-Hehet when she emerged from the bathroom. The seer was decked out in a fine linen dress and had adorned herself with a suite of jewelry, including a majestic collar necklace whose fine beadwork screamed Middle Kingdom workmanship. The seer swept into the room and sat directly across from Alex. "Why did you come to see your auntie today? I hope it has nothing to do with the lawsuit. I cannot talk about that."

"Not directly. It has to do with the dealings of the agency but not the lawsuit in particular." Alex poured tea into each of their cups.

"Two sugars, please." Akh-Hehet lifted her cup and saucer in Alex's direction.

Alex used the tiny silver sugar tongs to drop in the requested amount. "What do you know about Hattie Shepard?"

"She is Hatshepsut. That, I know."

"Well, the agency certainly did not. A few recent occurrences have brought her into our sights, so to speak. She was implicated in the theft of an artifact from KHNM. She also made it her business to corrupt one of our agents into acquiring another object for her. These two things added up together are concerning. We don't know exactly what she is up to, but we think whatever it is might be calamitous."

Niles leaned back in his chair. "The items she took were quite potent. Taken separately it wouldn't seem dangerous, but together it is an entirely different story."

The seer sat in silence.

"I ran into her just after she stole a sistrum we were transporting to the new temporary KHNM headquarters. At the time of the theft, I mistook her for someone else, but now we know it was her."

The seer took one of the biscuits. "What do you think she wants with a sistrum of all things? Does she want to start an ancient Egyptian revival band?"

Alex sipped her tea, taking strength from the double bergamot fragrance. "It was one of the objects from Cambyses's hoard. We've dug into it, and the objects from the hoard are magically linked and could be used to find one another."

"What is the big deal? It makes perfect sense she would want to find the army. You know she is in the antiquities business. If KHNM knows she stole it, why are you bothering me? You should be gathering evidence to prosecute."

There was something in Akh-Hehet's matter-of-fact reply that made Alex suspicious she was hiding something big. "That may be true, Akh-Hehet. However, the other item she acquired through nefarious means from the KHNM stores was a small vial filled with the Tears of Isis."

Akh-Hehet's complexion paled.

"Now what would she need with the Tears of Isis? Nun and

Naunet mentioned you had firsthand knowledge of something that might help us."

Niles leaned in toward the seer. "They said you were there and that we should ask you. Whatever that means."

Akh-Hehet dropped her teacup, and it shattered into a million pieces on the floor. "Leave now. I cannot help you."

Niles got up and grabbed a long-handled brush and a bin propped against one of the cabinets and worked at clearing away the tiny porcelain pieces.

"I am sorry, Auntie—you must help us," Alex pleaded.

"And why is that?"

"If we can't stop Hattie at whatever she is doing, Nun and Naunet will report this to the other Gods. It was their opinion that Hattie is attempting to somehow undo the Gods."

Akh-Hehet sat up straight. "And why would that matter to me?"

"To save your boyfriend's skin." Niles dumped the broken pieces in the trash bin. He grabbed another cup and set it in front of the seer and poured in some new tea.

The seer's shoulders slumped in defeat. "I didn't want to see it. But I had this sneaking suspicion he's been keeping something from me. You can't know someone for thousands of years and not be able to sense these things. If Naunet thinks he's tied up in this . . ." Akh-Hehet's voice trailed off as she gazed into the distance.

"What was it you saved Horemheb from in the past? That is one of the cryptic things Nun and Naunet shared with us before we departed." Alex poured herself more tea.

"I haven't thought of it in ages. I intentionally buried the memory in the furthest corners of my mind." She took a sip of tea. "Back in what is now known as the twenty-first dynasty, Hormey got caught up in a scandal with a bunch of other dead pharaohs in the Field of Reeds. All were enjoying their afterlife until one of them got a bee in their bonnet. Ramses the tenth, or was it the ninth? Who cares, right? It was so long ago I guess it doesn't matter. It boils down to the fact that one of the Ramseses with a very fragile ego took exception to a later pharaoh of the same name besmirching his reputation. The dead Ramses conspired with a cadre of other dead pharaohs to bar the recently dead king from an afterlife by disabling his false door. Hormey and the others brought the outsider Senenmut into the deal to use his one connection still out in the mortal world to help facilitate the plan. That was the immortal Hatshepsut, or Hattie as she is known now. In case you are taking notes." She shot a look at Niles.

"I may be the God of writing, but this is all going up here." He tapped a finger to his head.

"To make a long story short, they were caught, as was Hatshepsut. I was able to plead a case that Hormey wasn't one of the ringleaders. The pharaoh in charge at the time, Smendes, said they would let him off the hook if I did one thing." She shuddered.

Alex scooted her chair next to the seer and held her hand.

"Smendes espoused the idea of poetic justice being meted out."

"An eye for an eye?" asked Alex.

"Close enough. He decided I would need to work death magic on the Bas of the involved pharaohs and deny them their after-life. And Hatshepsut, but since she was an immortal, they couldn't do anything to her, so they made me sever the Bas of her father, husband, and nephew, along with her guilty lover."

"And you did this?" asked Niles.

"I had to. There was no other way. As a high priestess of Hehet, it went against everything I believed in, but I had to save

Hormey. Not long after this justice was enforced, several priests thought to be a part of this whole conspiracy were banished to one of the far-off oases."

Alex's Egyptology antennae pricked up. "Would these have been the same priests whose exile was commemorated on the banishment stela from the twenty-first dynasty?"

"The very same."

"Naunet said you wouldn't be able to save him a second time. But what if things go down in a less-than-optimal way? Maybe if we could prove to the Gods that you were helping us stop this, you might be able to save him again from a potential eternal banishment from the afterlife, if the others are caught. Or an even worse end if the Gods are so inclined."

"But how can I do that?"

"I think a visioning is in order." Alex dug into her bag and placed the scarab Luke gave her that morning on the table. "This was a part of a collar necklace from the hoard. Maybe if you do a visioning, you can tell us where we need to go."

CHAPTER THIRTY-ONE

Hattie awoke to the sound of the gentle strumming of a harp. Servants were standing in front of her, their arms laden with ceremonial vestments. An elder priest stood in front of the servants, extending his hand to her. Hattie reached out and allowed him to help her stand. The sandstone floor was cool against her bare feet as he led her to a room hidden behind a heavy curtain. In the middle of the small room was a square sunken tub surrounded by blue tiles decorated with lotus flowers. Thabit and Zuberi tried to follow her through to the room but were blocked from entering.

The priest dipped in a shallow bow in front of Hattie. "Your companions must stay behind while you are purified. His grace will see only you, Great One."

Hattie didn't like not being able to bring her two large security blankets with her, but so far she hadn't sensed the slightest of threats to herself or them. She nodded at the boys. "Be refreshed as you stay behind."

She turned back into the chamber.

The old priest clapped his hands twice. The vestment-carrying male servants set down their loads and vacated the room along with the priest, leaving Hattie surrounded by four female attendants. Their languid movements were beautiful to witness as they divested her of her clothing. The woman who stood in front of Hattie appeared to be the senior member of the group, as the others looked toward her for silent cues. This woman wore a large collar necklace with snake forms radiating from its center. Each of the finely crafted creatures had small carnelian eyes that glowed in the low light of the bathing room. She pulled her shift down around her body and waded into the pool, beckoning Hattie to do the same.

The water was perfectly warm. Pink and red flower petals danced away as Hattie sunk into the bath. The other three attendants knelt by large gilded towers, each crowned with small ornate jewel boxes encrusted with floral decorations in lapis lazuli and turquoise. Fragrant incense emanated from these beautiful spires. The three women each took a small boar's hairbrush and a vessel that lay on the tiled floor and waded into the water. As their matron chanted in a low and sultry voice, the three attendants all poured a golden liquid onto their brush and gently scrubbed every inch of Hattie's flesh. The bristles were soft, yet delightfully scratchy. The strong scent of honey and myrrh wafted up from the water, mingling with the smoky cedar oil fragrance of the incense.

Hattie closed her eyes and breathed the heavenly combination in. It had been a long time since she experienced the joyful sensations of a formal purification rite. Back before she was pharaoh and served as the High Priestess of Amun, this was her favorite part of the job. She reveled in the sensations and the expectation of what was to come . . . her feet. Oh, how she loved her feet to be rubbed. Knowing the drill, Hattie knew she would have to be seated for this part, as she was certain these women were not amphibious. She opened her eyes and saw the lead attendant motioning Hattie to sit on a seat submerged in the scented water. One of the three attendants exited the pool and squatted behind Hattie. Her strong fingers worked at massaging the flesh of her shoulders as the other two attendants in front of her gently rubbed her feet.

Hattie lay her head back and let out a soft moan of pleasure and drifted off to a dream state of relaxation. After a while the head attendant stopped chanting and the others stopped their work. The matron was motioning for Hattie to stand. The attendants exited the bath and each retrieved a new large vessel that appeared next to the pool. They stood above her and slowly poured warm honey-scented milk over her. Once empty, they dipped the vessels in the fragrant water and rinsed her off. Hattie stepped out of the pool as the attendants each grabbed a large palm frond jutting out from an alabaster vase. The women flicked the greenery against her skin, invigorating her.

After returning the fronds to the vase, they retrieved the garments left behind by the male servants. Hattie slipped her feet into stiff golden sandals as they wrapped a fine linen sheath around her. It was scented with cooling and purifying camphor. They adorned her with weighty golden jewelry, a fine collar necklace that had a counterbalance in the shape of a great snake. On her wrists they placed thick metal cuffs with depictions of Apep along the surface. The snakes's gleaming eyes were picked out in the reddest carnelian, much like the matron's collar necklace.

Once clothed, the lead attendant motioned Hattie to follow her to the wall which had a detailed naturalistic mural of the Nile. The woman knelt in front of the artwork and then bowed, placing her head against the floor. Unseeing she reached out with knowing hands and pressed a lotus symbol. The stone wall slid back revealing a dark corridor lined with flickering torches.

Hattie followed the attendants into the passageway leading into the long, narrow columned corridor spanning the length of the palace. Outside the columns Hattie could see the canyon and lights of the city below. At the end of the corridor, they took a sharp turn to the left, moving deeper into the cliff. The further they traveled, the lower the ceiling became. Hattie guessed they must be nearing the Holy of Holies, the most sacred space in any temple. It was where priests and priestesses would maintain a golden effigy of the God, changing its clothing throughout the day and making offerings.

The attendants stopped in front of a doorway with a lintel plastered with hieroglyphs and motioned for Hattie to proceed through without them. She was amazed at how these women were able to communicate without saying a word. It made her wonder if they'd taken a vow of silence.

She ducked as she entered the space, not wanting to ruin the delicate diadem adorning her hair. Once inside she was surprised to find herself completely alone. The only other thing in the room was a life-sized statue resting in the nook of the main altar at the back of the small space. The walls surrounding her were carved with reliefs telling the same story she had seen all over the palace. Whoever ran this place was in lockstep with the Ramses-the-Great-Battle-of-Kadesh messaging approach of making something true by simply repeating it over and over again.

The deep reliefs in the walls came to life by the flickering light of the torches around the room. The person who built this temple surely spared no expense for the artwork. The large granite altar in the back of the Holy of Holies resembled every other she had ever seen, except this one was much larger. Instead of a smallish fetish of a God, this figure was life-sized. The grand statue stood in a large granite box festooned with hieroglyphs and topped with a pyramidion pointing up to the heavens.

Whoever this statue memorialized, it wasn't a God, or at least not one she was familiar with. Instead of wearing a complex headgear signaling a God, this figure wore a clean-shaven head and a leopard-skin pelt of a priest draped over its body. A buffet of morning delicacies lay at the statue's feet. She leaned in close and peered into its stone face.

"The insolence!"

Hattie jerked up and bashed her head against the top of the shrine. She rubbed the newly thudding spot on the crown of her head as she backed away. The immediate tenderness telegraphed there would be a large bump to remember the moment by. Glancing behind her, she couldn't see anyone else in the chamber who might have spoken. Sometimes temples had holes in the walls to enable a priest to speak for the Holy One. Hattie searched but found none. She knew that was the trick of it. The builders would have gone to great lengths to conceal them. In some chapels, they added hidden levers so the priests could manipulate the God's body forward or backward to show approval or disapproval to any questions posed to the God.

"How dare you come so close to the Holy of Holies!"

Hattie made a small bow. The voice seemed to be coming from the statue somehow. "I mean no offense. I am merely a visitor in this great and noble house. Please offer my greatest of apologies to this enshrined Holy of Holies." Hattie moved to the back of the shrine to check for speakers or other contrivances to project a voice from the statue.

"Face me! You do not have permission to leave."

Again she could see nothing. Hattie returned to the front of the statue. "I apologize. O priest of the deity before me, please—"

"You are misinformed, Hatshepsut. We two are but alone."

"You have me at a disadvantage. I know not your name."

"I am Apepmosis, Holy of Holies, seer of the hidden city of Bakhu."

She dipped her head so that this Holy of Holies couldn't see her stifling a laugh at the awkward word play of him being called that. The fact that this cult leader referred to themselves as the Holy of Holies showed how much they'd deviated from the norms of ancient Egyptian religious life. All this time she'd thought they were taking her to a place and not a trumped-up cult leader who had the ridiculous presumption of taking the title of the most sacred of spaces. "I am blessed to meet you, o seer of Bakhu, Holy of Holies. I am here in your great city to locate a powerful object. I was told you could show me the lost hoard of Cambyses."

"You are mistaken."

"You can't tell me where it is?"

"It isn't that simple, immortal Hatshepsut. You may believe that is why you are here, but your arrival was foretold for countless generations, and now this blessed day has arrived."

He seemed to think Hattie was involved in a prophecy. This was not exactly something she wanted to get wrapped up in. She had one thing to do and one thing only—find the object in the hoard for the pharaohs. It was just her luck that instead of finding the thing she was looking for, she happened to step into a delusional cult mistaking her for someone who was a part of whatever story they'd told themselves over the past twenty centuries. The desert had a way of warping the minds of those living in its endless desolation. "I thank you for the hospitality for myself and my companions. But we are mere travelers looking to locate a specific artifact. Is the hoard I speak of unknown to you?" Hattie contemplated the unmoving stone face in front of her.

"Again, you are mistaken. You are here to fulfill my destiny and bring the Gods to their knees. The hoard was only a ruse to get you here."

The problem with dealing with delusional priests trapped in a statue for a few thousand years is that their delusions become deep truths over time. Hattie struggled to find an argument to send his spoken truths away. "I fear it might be you who is mistaken. I only come for the hoard."

The statue made a soft sigh. "Of course, you are denying the words I speak. You know not the truths I have seen. As you witness, I am immovable and cannot take you anywhere. When my emissary returns from his tasks out in the world, he will take you to your hoard."

"When do you expect them to return?"

"Soon, with the last sign of the prophecy. Then you will believe." Two sharp claps echoed through the stone room. "Sabu, escort the Great One to her chambers."

The nervous priest scurried through the chamber and stood next to Hattie. Sabu quickly knelt before the statue, lowering his head just over the food offerings below. "As you wish, my Lord."

"And share with her the prophecy, or you will join the speech-less ones. You may leave."

Sabu stood, then backed out of the room.

He was waiting for her in the doorway. She made a slight bow. "Again I thank you for your gracious hospitality, and I look forward to the arrival of your emissary."

Turning to leave, Hattie's gaze landed on a section of the narrative relief. It depicted the ritual severing of the Ba-souls inflicted on her beloveds centuries ago. Although she didn't want to extend this interview any longer, she couldn't help herself.

"You mentioned being here for such a long time, Holy of Holies. How did you come to be here in the city of Bakhu?"

"Take your leave and Sabu will tell you all. I grow weary and must rest. I leave you with great thanks on this blessed day of your arrival. It is good to see you again."

Hattie stared at the statue. Whatever presence enlivened it was now gone. She joined Sabu at the entryway, knowing that she had forgotten many things throughout her long life, but she had never met anyone named Apepmosis.

CHAPTER THIRTY-TWO

Alex and Niles put the tea things in order while Akh-Hehet prepared herself for a visioning. The old woman had disappeared some time ago behind a large black curtain that hid her sleeping area. From previous experience, Alex knew there were several things the seer needed to do to be spiritually cleansed before peeking into the plethora of possible futures, but this time it was taking an abnormally long time.

"I'll go see if she needs any help." Alex peered behind the curtain. She was shocked to see the seer was fast asleep on her bed. Her wig had become skewed off-center as she slept. A strand of hair puffed up as the seer exhaled. Alex gently nudged her.

The seer stirred slowly, then shot up like a bolt. "Oh bother, I've done it again." Her frown pushed against her deep smile lines. Akh-Hehet tidied herself and shifted her wig into the proper position. "I am sorry, I get so tired nowadays. I start my meditations and just flat-out fall asleep. I think Hormey wore me out." The old woman gazed into the distance and sighed.

"That is all right. It gave us time to see to the tea things."

Alex held her arm out for Akh-Hehet to grab so she could lean on her as the seer rose from the bed. Alex placed her other hand against the seer's back. Her bones felt like those of a small bird. Alex had no idea how frail the old woman had become.

Akh-Hehet swayed a little as she stood. "Oh, dear."

"Are you sure you are up to this?" Alex held her steady.

Her posture stiffened. "I am." She breathed in deeply and flung the curtain open with a flourish. "For I have a second wind for my second sight. Besides, I have boyfriends to save." She winked at Alex and then marched through the small apartment area and into the canopy of chandeliers beyond. Alex and Niles followed her into the visioning area. It was located in the center of the crystals with a large antique woven rug strewn under a large, inverted crystal pyramidion hanging from the ceiling.

The three of them sat cross-legged in a small triangle, their knees nearly touching. Alex placed the scarab Luke brought with him in the center. Alex gazed around the space and could see that Akh-Hehet had added not only more chandeliers but also mirrors on the walls and ceilings. She must have needed to boost her powers more.

Alex held Akh-Hehet's hand, once again struck by the delicate bones under her soft skin. She grabbed Niles's hand to form a chain of connected energy between them.

"I can see you have noticed my new additions. My visionings are less clear as of late. The extra crystals have helped."

"I see you are using mirrors as well."

"I have you to thank for that. The reflection of the crystals boosts my powers without having to add more light fixtures. I think if I add any more, I might blow out the whole city's power grid."

Niles chuckled. "I think you may be right."

Alex was glad to see that the emergency measures they had

taken to enable a visioning from Akh-Hehet during a time when her crystal field was inaccessible worked out as an unintended boon now. At the time the old woman's safety had been compromised. Alex had whisked the unconscious seer from her shop in the souk to the residence. When Akh-Hehet gained her strength back, a visioning was needed to help Alex attempt to fool the powerful magician Idris Niru. However, since they were at Chicago House, they didn't have the seer's vast array of crystals to assist her. The idea of extending the power of the crystals through mirrors was inspired by an art exhibition Alex went to in which an artist placed many lights in a small, mirrored infinity room. "I am glad it is working for you."

Akh-Hehet squeezed Alex's hand. "Let's get started. I presume you will want to join me. Niles, of course, will need to stay behind and mind the store, so to speak."

Alex nodded. In the past she joined the seer during her visionings. Her experience was always far less defined than the seer's. It was like traveling to a country where only your companion spoke the language. You get a lot out of the experience, but not as much as your partner.

"As you both will remember, I need absolute silence." Akh-Hehet closed her eyes and chanted.

A soft breeze sent the crystals into a bright melody. Alex focused on the sound, letting her mind clear as she concentrated on the delicate music. As the seer's chants became louder, the wind picked up, tossing Alex's hair around her head.

The seer's voice raised above the clamor. "O mighty Hehet, Great Goddess of the Immeasurable, please show this one, Daughter of Truth, what she seeks."

Alex focused her thoughts on the scarab lying in front of her and the connection it might have to the lost army of Cambyses. A lightness filled her as she took to the sky in her bird form,

Akh-Hehet flying alongside her. They were gliding over the Western Desert for what felt like a very long time, when they picked up speed, moving faster than Alex thought was possible for their tiny bird bodies. The ground below was beginning to blur as they skimmed over it. They must be far from Luxor, judging by the distance they'd traveled. She wished there were a landmark she recognized nearby instead of miles and miles of sand, rocks, and hills. Then, as if her unspoken wish had been heard by unseen powers, she could pick out white surrealistic chalk formations in the distance. They were nearing the White Desert.

She followed Akh-Hehet's starling form and flew amongst the surreal shapes. The seer seemed to be looking for something specific. She must have found it, as she dove down and landed atop one of the formations.

Akh-Hehet's voice spoke in Alex's mind. "This is where you will find the end of your search."

The starling inched close to Alex and placed its clawed foot atop hers. Alex's eyes opened to the crystal filled room at the pressure of Akh-Hehet's hand closing around hers. "It looks like we'll be visiting the White Desert, Niles."

The old woman was white as a sheet. The visioning must have taken much out of her. Alex made a mental note. Asking Akh-Hehet for help in the future might not be an option. She didn't want to be responsible for causing the death of this host, forcing Akh-Hehet on a yearlong quest for another.

Alex stood and helped Akh-Hehet to her feet. "Niles, could you grab her some water?"

"Of course. I'll be right back."

Akh-Hehet grabbed his arm. "Be a dear. Make it a gin."

Niles disappeared through the sparkling crystal canopy.

"There is a shadow around that one, Alex."

"Niles?"

"Yes, I fear there is something he is keeping from you."

"Join the crowd. He claims he isn't holding anything back, but I don't know that I believe him."

"Why would he lie?"

"I think he has a masculine savior complex, and he thinks he is keeping me safe by keeping me in the dark."

Akh-Hehet shook her head. "We all do strange things for the ones we love, right? While we are alone, I wanted to know. Did you see what I saw in the vision, Alex?"

"I saw a whole lot of desert and not much more."

The seer looked as if she was weighing her words. "Don't go on this mission."

Alex put her arm around the old woman. "You always say that. You are like an old mother hen, clucking every time a chick tries to leave the henhouse."

Akh-Hehet locked eyes with Alex. "I saw that you will die there."

"You have seen my death before, and yet here I am. Like you said when we first met, you can see many different possibilities. I am willing to guess what you saw was no different from the potential of death you saw for me last time. Nothing is written in stone, right, Akh-Hehet?"

"You are being glib."

"Thank you for your concern. I will be careful." Akh-Hehet's worried look sent a clear message that the old seer wasn't messing around. The fear Alex felt earlier about the Gods scenting on a potential latent power within her grew stronger. She knew her future held many perils, and she wouldn't let this warning stop her from moving forward. She didn't want to hide from her fate, whatever it might be.

"This had to do with a prophecy—"

"That I resolved by sending the Gods back to the Field of Reeds." Alex quoted from the prophecy that brought her to this new life with the Keepers of the Holy and Noble Maat. "Fights to save the cause divine, may you banish the God's abomination and ensure man's salvation." Alex squeezed the seer's hand. "I did that. I saved humanity from Raymond. Prophecy done!"

"I don't know, Alex. I believe what I saw."

"'Tis the life of a KHNM agent."

Niles swept into the room, holding three neat gins.

Akh-Hehet tipped hers back and emptied her glass in one go.

CHAPTER THIRTY-THREE

Hattie followed Sabu out of the Holy of Holies and to the long corridor. She had never seen him move so fast. The small priest flew out of the room as if Apepmosis's threats were chasing him. Carved on either side of the passageway were the strange symbols she saw before but didn't recognize. It was a depiction of a snake coiling itself around a flagpole. It was a strange mixing of symbols. The flagpole represented the Gods or the holy. To have a snake twined around it seemed a defilement of the sanctity of the Gods and their sacred omnipotence. Hattie paused to contemplate it.

Sabu stopped and turned toward her. He was trembling.

Hattie moved away from the symbol to the panel adjacent to it. This part of the story wasn't depicted in her room. On it, there was a palanquin, much like the one that conveyed her on the shoulders of a platoon of ancient soldiers. "Sabu. What does it depict?"

"Oh Great One, it is telling of the vision from the Holy One, Apepmosis, who foresaw the coming of the Great Change, the Destroyer of Gods."

Hattie hadn't seen that coming. She wondered what misguided things this strange desert cult had in mind for her. "Pray tell me more. What is this Destroyer of Gods?"

"That specific information is for the Holy One or his emissary to tell you."

"Are you certain? You wouldn't want to join the speechless ones, would you?"

He blanched. "You may trust I would never risk that."

Hattie continued down the corridor. Sabu trailed behind her at a slower pace. She stopped in front of a relief depicting many bodies lying horizontally as if a sudden tragedy with great losses had depleted the city. "What is happening in this scene? Was your city overrun by a plague?"

The priest brightened a little as he slipped into a role of an ancient-garbed tour guide pleased to share what he knew. "This was the time of the great blight or the great questioning. It is known by both names." He paused as he reverently studied the wall. "This was the time before the Holy One's visions were vindicated and before the faithful were glorified in the truth of his light. In the first vision of Apepmosis, he saw a great army come to the city. This foreseen coming was key to the prophecy. Many years passed and for some followers it was too many years. Those of weak faith were afflicted with sickness and died. It was a time of deep questioning and tests of faith for our community. Only those who were true of heart and believed were rewarded with the glory of truth when the army eventually arrived as the Holy One foresaw. Apepmosis bested the army and then imprisoned the soldiers. He sacrificed those who would not comply, and those who did were indoctrinated. When they joined us, our numbers were replenished from those we lost during the great blight."

"But how was this force of fifty thousand men brought down by the members of a depleted city?"

Sabu made a small bow toward the figure of the prophet. "The power of Apepmosis is strong."

"It must be." Hattie wasn't altogether sure she succeeded in keeping her sarcasm in check. From her time as a king and engaging in a battle or two, Hattie was well aware the numbers just didn't add up. There was no way a small number of priests and believers could take down a highly armed and trained army like Cambyses's. The Holy One must be prone to exaggeration, a common affliction of leaders in general. Most likely the army was half-dead from exposure or lack of supplies by the time they reached the White Desert. As foreigners they would have been at a great disadvantage in the unforgiving red land of the Egyptian desert.

As they passed through the corridor they traveled back in time via the long carved mural. Hattie stood in front of the panel showing the priest digging in the sand near a chalk formation. Initially she assumed it was Apepmosis. But now standing before it, she realized the figure had a different name written in hiero- glyphs above it. It was one she recognized, Shedsu-nefertum. He was the priest who turned in the guilty pharaohs from the Field of Reeds as well as herself all those years ago. A vision flashed in her mind of the caskets dragged out under a full moon, the priestess of Hehet calling forth the Bas of her beloveds and severing them from their long-dead bodies, relegating them to the dreaded limbo of nothingness. How was he involved with this cult? The same name identified the same priest figure who was facing a deified scribe. Hattie pointed at the hieroglyphs. "Who is this?"

The priest spoke low and soft. He placed his hands behind his back as he continued down the hallway. Hattie joined him.

"Shedsu-nefertum was a high priest banished by the unjust King Smendes along with many others. After the king punished the criminals to keep balance in the scales of Maat, he banished those who brought the knowledge of the crime before him. Also, at the time false whispers were floating up to the king's ears that some priests were involved in the scandal.

"During his long desert trek, Shedsu-nefertum became lost in the desert. Near death, he experienced a vision of seeing the Destroyer of Gods. In the vision his emissary came to him, showing him where to find life-sustaining waters and leading him to the underground riverbed which became the city of Bakhu. He was instructed to wait there until this blessed time."

They passed the scene in which the name Apepmosis first appeared. "So Shedsu-nefertum was renamed Apepmosis, by this emissary?"

"He was reborn. Shifted into the form you see now, to withstand the storms of time for this blessed moment." He motioned toward the door to Hattie's chamber. "I must return you to your rooms, where you may refresh yourself and await the return of the emissary. He will have in his possession the treasure of the final prophecy. Then all will be clear."

Sabu opened the door. The harpist was accompanied by two other musicians. One played the lute and the other shook a sistrum. The room was filled with delicate music. The long table in the center of the room was piled high with freshly laid offerings. Thabit and Zuberi were filling their large plates up with delectables. Hattie wandered through to the balcony and leaned against it. Below, the bright-white city sparkled in the reflected light from above. It looked as if their mission was taking an unexpected turn. Instead of artifact recovery, it looked like she had managed to get them tied up in a religious prophecy cooked up by a centuries-old banished priest. She didn't buy the vision story. It was probably a daydream by a near-dead priest who was allowed to stew for a few thousand years in their own brand of condensed crazy.

Whether the prophecy was true or not, there were some alignments between Hattie's needs and those of the cult. It never hurt to have a crazy desert cult be in your debt. Hattie was enjoying being worshiped once again. She could easily slip comfortably into the raiment of a Great One. This was the kind of living she could get used to. Although she wasn't sure she could ever get used to working alongside the stone priest, Apep-mosis or Shedsu-nefertum, whatever they wanted to call him.

They could call him whatever they pleased, but Hattie wasn't sure she could ever see him as anything but a traitor.

CHAPTER THIRTY-FOUR

A s soon as Alex knew where they needed to go to find Cambyses's army, she and Niles left Akh-Hehet to get some rest. While they wove through the mazelike souk, Alex called Gini. She hoped they would be willing to get the vehicle packed with gear while she and Niles made their way to the residence. They would have to go prepared for anything with the limited amount of information they had. They might be out there for hours or days. The White Desert stretched over many miles, and she had no idea about where to start looking except for what was in the seer's vague vision. She and Niles had already nearly burned half of the time they were granted by Nun and Naunet before her ancestors spilled the tea about this latest agency kerfuffle to the other Gods. The clock was ticking.

They stepped from under the large wooden entrance of the souk and onto the bustling main street. The moment Alex's foot hit the curb an old tourist carriage stopped in front of her. "Would the lady like a ride? My horse Rambo is the best in all of Luxor."

Alex was ready to say no and walk away but changed her

mind. If Akh-Hehet was right, this was at least one thing she should tick off her bucket list. "I would like nothing more."

Niles eyed the ancient black carriage with suspicion.

Alex linked arms with him. "Oh, it'll be fun."

The wiry man jumped down from his tattered burlap seat and then held out his hand. Alex grabbed it and let him help her inside. The driver pointedly smiled at Niles. "Happy wife, happy life . . . No?"

"She's not my wife."

The man gave him a wink and a broad smile as he motioned Niles to join Alex. "All the more fun then."

The carriage shifted as both Niles and the driver ascended. Small silver charms hanging around the cab's hood jangled. The black canvas hood shielded them from the view of others.

"Where to, miss?" The driver turned to face them.

"Chicago House, please."

"Hup, hup," said the driver as he tugged the reins of his white steed. The horse clip-clopped through the main street and then turned onto a narrower, more residential-looking street. Along the road were shops with large, colorful swaths of fabric hanging overhead, creating sun shields for the vendors and their customers. Strung across one shop was a long line of bright and playful children's pajamas. The small street teemed with people going about their daily errands. Above them on both sides of the street were apartment buildings with small balconies, forming a vertical beige canyon.

"I've always wanted to ride in one of these." Alex was drawn into this scene of everyday life on display before them. It was interesting how quickly the streets transitioned from touristic to lived.

"Somehow I'm not surprised." Niles put his arm around her, pulling her close.

"I love the ordered chaos of these streets. One of these days I would love to find an apartment around here and just live my life like a normal person."

"Do you mean not as an agent of KHNM? I thought working for the agency gave you . . ." His voice trailed off.

"The family I wish I had. Yes, there is that. But sometimes it seems like ever since I've jumped on the KHNM train my life has been a nonstop adventure, which is great, but I wonder if I am missing the simple everyday moments of life by moving from one magical emergency to another."

"Maybe when this is over, you and I can find a piece of normal somewhere. I think you've earned yourself a little time off after saving humanity more than once."

"If I survive." Alex laughed and caught his gaze. She leaned into him, her lips grazing his as he pulled her close.

A motorcycle buzzed by, startling Rambo. The carriage jostled as the horse went into a trot that sent the metal fetishes chiming. "Damned fools!" The driver shook his fist.

They were nearing Chicago House.

Niles was gazing into the distance. "When I left to get the gin, what was it Akh-Hehet said you were being glib about?"

"Take your pick." It was a little more than slightly irritating when Niles thought questions being answered were always a one-way street.

"There you go again."

"It's nothing really."

"I think the last time you said something along those lines, the world was about to be taken over by a power-hungry family member of mine, so don't get upset if I don't believe you."

"She warned me against going to the White Desert. She said I would die."

"You are still up for it, right?"

Alex felt her expression sour. "What, you want me gone that bad?"

"No, that came out wrong. I just wanted to know how you felt about all of this. I mean, with the Gods starting to take notice and then this advice from Akh-Hehet. We didn't have the chance to talk about the Gods earlier in the market. So I thought I should check in with you to see if you wanted to stay back and let Luke and Gormund hunt down the treasure seeker, Hattie Shepard. I of course would have to stay with you."

"My personal Ba-die guard." Her attempt at humor fell flat. "I guess no matter how you cut it, I can't avoid what is coming down the pike for me. If I stay, I could be killed by the Gods' emissary." Alex shot Niles a meaningful look. "Or get killed by some unknown force out in the middle of nowhere. Maybe it is unavoidable, and they are the same. But, I am sure you noticed Akh-Hehet's visions are becoming less clear to her over time. Honestly, I think she was conflating information from the past with the future. She thought it had to do with the prophecy, but we all know it was resolved."

"We do, do we?"

"I sent the Gods back to the Field of Reeds."

"Yes, but I certainly didn't see a big sign with blinking lights that dropped from the sky saying, *Good job, Alex—prophecy managed!*"

"Of course not. Now who is being a glib ass?"

"I'm just saying Akh-Hehet may not be wrong. You don't know your prophecy was a one-and-done type. Prophecies are vague for a reason. They are like horoscopes for the entirety of humanity, written so anyone can see themselves within them."

"Nothing is certain and safety is never guaranteed?"

"Exactly."

"You know, there was another thing the seer said while you

were gone. She said there was a shadow over you and that you were keeping things from me."

"Who, me?" Niles said overdramatically.

Alex playfully whacked him against the chest. "Yes, you. Are you?"

"There are things I cannot tell you. That you must understand. I'm not lying to you. I just cannot speak of it, as part of my oath to the other Gods."

The carriage conveniently pulled up the long drive to Chicago House. Alex jumped out and paid the driver. She held her hand out for Niles to disembark the cab.

"What a gentleman." Niles laughed as he stepped out of the carriage.

Alex looked at her heart amulet. It was glowing. "Niles, why is the pendant you gave me glowing?"

Niles blanched as Gini came running from the residency toward them. "You both need to head straight to the car. It's been packed. Luke and Gormund are waiting for you."

Alex put her arm around them. "What is the matter? Has something happened?"

"Buxton called to warn you Salima is on her way. The Gods have sent her to do Niles's job."

CHAPTER THIRTY-FIVE

Hattie was summoned again to the sacred chamber of the Holy of Holies by Apepmosis. She was surprised to be called so quickly after he feigned fatigue in their earlier meeting. The ablutions to spiritually cleanse her before the meeting lost their glow and weren't nearly as enjoyable as the first time around. Now that Hattie knew more about who was running the show, she was far less enamored by the hidden city.

She had spent the past few hours in a contemplative stew that got thicker over time. The whole romantic idea of this city of Bakhu felt tarnished by the fact that it was built around this ridiculous soul who spent the last few thousand years stuck in a statue, who also just happened to be the self-important dill weed who ratted on her and the dead pharaohs all those years ago.

Hattie was practically seething as the silent handmaidens massaged sacred oils into her freshly bathed flesh, but did her best to stay calm. If she was going to get revenge on behalf of her beloveds on his silly stone ass, she would need to make herself appear amenable to his plans, whatever they may be. The camphor-infused garments invigorated her humors as she was marched through the palace and into the Holy of Holies by Sabu. The priest waited for her to enter the chamber and stood resolutely by the door.

She flung her shoulders back, channeling her inner pharaoh as she walked to the large stone altar housing Apepmosis's black diorite statue. Upon seeing the life-sized statue of Shedsu-nefertum, an unwelcome surge of anger rushed through her. Banishing her instincts, she knelt in deference and bowed her head. Not only was it the expected thing for her to do, but it also ensured the statue's inhabitant couldn't see the seething fire behind her eyes. "O mighty and wise Apepmosis. I and my companions thank you again for your generous hospitality."

"It is I who must thank you. Your arrival brought forth the foreseen and the blessed day when I will once again roam free from my stone bondage."

"You shall be freed?"

"Yes, my emissary has returned. He reported that all is as it should be. Before the new day has dawned, I will walk as freely as you do. Maybe not with such grace, though."

Hattie faced the statue and hoped her red flush of anger would be read as a blush of modesty to Apepmosis. "Your kind attention honors me."

"It is the day I have waited for all these years. This day is a day of the great convergence. The day I will be reborn, and the Gods themselves will be brought to their knees."

"And how will these great wonders happen?"

"My emissary will make the knowing clear to you. He has all matters in hand."

"As always, my Lord."

Hattie swung around at the sound of the familiar grating voice coming from behind her. Her stomach clenched at the sight of Rekhmira and his crocodile smile. Now the chamber contained two great weasels from her past.

CHAPTER THIRTY-SIX

A lex fumed as she and Niles walked toward the Rover. Gini trailed in their wake, keeping a fair distance from them. Alex hadn't known a time she was this angry, and it must have shown. Alex grabbed the front passenger side door and shouted, "Luke, you're driving. I'm taking shotgun. Niles and Gor can take the back."

Niles sidled near her. "Alex, we need to talk."

"When exactly were you going to tell me this? That Salima was on her way to kill me? When exactly did it seem like it would be a helpful thing for me to know my certain death was tracking me as we speak?"

"You've got to believe me. I didn't know it would happen so fast."

"So you did know?" Alex huffed as she pulled the car door open.

Niles grabbed her arm. "Alex, please hear me out. I didn't know this, but I had an inkling the other Gods were getting impatient with me and were starting to feel like I was dragging my feet. When I brought up your last dream, well, some were calling for your death immediately."

"Some?"

"Since it wasn't a complete vote of no confidence, I figured I had more time to sort all this out. Now in hindsight, maybe I should have taken it differently. Maybe I was in denial and didn't want to see the writing on the wall. But apparently something has changed if they are sending Salima."

Any hope Alex was holding on to spilled away. She would receive no quarter from Salima, who was charging toward Alex in her embodiment of Sekhmet as the lion-headed Goddess and Destructor of Re. Alex spun around and pushed him backward with both hands. "You are unbelievable. You have continually gaslighted me on this. How could you?" Hot tears threatened to erupt.

"I was trying to buy us more time. More time to try and get at something that might solve this for us. There were things I couldn't tell you. Until now."

Niles pulled her into a hug. She almost let him—until her fury reignited, and she shoved him back. "What do you mean by that?"

"Now that I'm unseated as your executioner—"

"Well, whatever *us* you were trying to save, I would like to point out there is only one person Salima is after, and that is me, Niles. You are an Immortal—this is just a game to you."

Gormund stepped forward. "He hasn't told you?"

Alex closed her eyes. "What now?"

"Gormund, mind your own business. This is something between me and my family."

Alex slapped Niles. Everyone stared at her in stunned silence. "And I am not? You bastard."

His hand rubbed the red spot where she hit him. "What I meant is this isn't something you need to know about."

Stepping around Niles, Alex confronted Gormund. "You will tell me."

Gormund gazed at his feet as he pushed around a small grouping of pebbles. "If he should fail to kill you as the Gods willed, he will have a punishment worse than Prometheus's. His powers will be severed from him for eternity, and instead of a bird flying in daily and eating his innards, you will be strapped to a rock on which he will have to execute you by a thousand cuts each time the sun rises anew."

She spun around to face Niles. "So in putting off the inevitable, you've managed to make both my death and your eternity worse. That is grand. Why didn't you just kill me?" Alex fumed as she stalked to the Rover, pushing Niles aside. As she climbed in, he touched the back of her arm. "Alex, please listen to me. I can explain."

She flicked his hand away, then slid into the seat and slammed the door shut.

Gini, Luke, and Gor stood around them in a stunned silence.

Gini clutched their clipboard close to their chest. "You better get moving unless you want to see Salima sooner than later."

Luke took his place in the driver's seat and Gormund and Niles slipped into the back. Niles was trying to make eye contact with Alex via the rearview mirror. She pointedly ignored him. An overlarge sadness settled on her as she looked out at Gini. What if it was the last time she would ever see them?

Alex rolled the window down and reached out to the librarian.

"If Salima comes a-knockin', I will do everything in my power to waylay her. You know that, don't you?"

"Don't put yourself in danger, Gini. She is a God and will be in her most powerful form."

"You forget, I am a Jinn, and a strong one at that. I've learned a few tricks over the past few thousand years. I will be fighting for you."

They clasped Alex's hand.

"Thank you, Gini." Alex breathed in the Immortal's strong scent as they squeezed her hand.

Tears were spilling over Gini's face as they stepped away from the Rover.

Alex rolled up the window. "Let's get going. We've got to stop this Hattie Shepard. Maybe if we do so, I will find a way out of this mess."

⌁

Dawn was breaking on the horizon that was lit with a hot-pink blaze against the silvery morning sky. A residue of stars lay overhead as Nut readied herself to birth the sun from her celestial body. In the distance lay the surreal chalk formations painted in the bright colors of the new day. A new day that could end her life and ruin the agency.

To say the drive to the White Desert was quiet would be a vast understatement. After a time, Luke did his best to lighten the mood, but to no avail. There were too many grave thoughts hanging heavy in the small space of the Rover. It gave Alex time to think. Her mind kept fluctuating between the internal and repetitive dialog of how pissed she was at Niles, and the disbelief that these hours might be her last. She was riding an emotional swing, tilting back and forth between her anger and hurt and a tired hopefulness of figuring a way out, or at least not spending what little time she might have being angry.

Although she didn't agree with Niles and how he handled the situation, she wondered what she would have done were the tables turned. Would she ever be able to give up hope of saving him? Alex was uncertain, but she hated how he was continually keeping things from her, even if he thought it was for her own good. As if she couldn't handle the truth.

She grabbed her scribe's bag and pulled out the carved beetle that used to grace the diadem from the hoard. Since it was taken from the crown many years ago, Alex wasn't sure if it would work anymore in finding other objects from the hoard. But it was all she had. That and a vague memory of what the chalk formation Akh-Hehet's bird form landed on looked like. She remembered it as having a large bulbous top resting on a thin column. She recognized that that information wouldn't be much help, as there were a million such formations in the countless miles of this strange landscape.

Luke continued to drive as gentle snores emanated from the back seat where Gormund was apparently fast asleep. Niles sat next to him and was staring out the window. Alex hadn't slept, her mind preoccupied with what was to come.

Alex was glad when they arrived. She rubbed her tired eyes to scope out a good place to stop. "Luke, why don't you pull up under that large formation ahead, and we'll do some exploring? See if anything jumps out at us." Alex was disappointed. None of the formations stood out as the ones from the visioning.

When the Rover came to a stop, Alex grabbed her scribe's bag and jumped out onto the soft brown sand. The strange landscape surrounding her looked as if she was standing atop an extra frothy latte with towers of whipped cream. She knew a fellow Egyptologist and partner who spent their honeymoon glamping here. It took a lot for the couple to get the permits to camp at this national park, but it must have been well worth it. It would be a delight to see the colors of the day and night painting these windswept shapes. A pang of loss echoed through her, knowing she would most likely never be able to experience it.

Everyone gathered in front of the Rover. "It's now or never, guys. Let's take a look around."

They walked down a brown wave-patterned river of sand leading to the field of bright-white formations. As they came upon a bend, Alex stopped in her tracks.

They were surrounded by soldiers in ancient Persian battle gear. An Egyptian man with hair as black as a raven's wings stood before the platoon, wearing jeans and a burgundy silk button-down shirt. Gold rings adorned his hands. One held a lit cigarette between his fingers, its smoke snaking up from the red-glowing tip.

Before her mind could process the bizarre scene, everything went black.

CHAPTER THIRTY-SEVEN

Hattie stood in the sanctuary in between Apepmosis and the newly arrived Rekhmira. Her blood ran cold with the clarity of the moment. She was standing in the temple of a mad and ancient priest, not of her own free will, but on the whim and machinations of the great deceiver. How blind had she been? Why had she thought Rekhmira was done with her?

Apepmosis's voice boomed through the hall. "Excellent. As you can see, my emissary has arrived. Please take the Great One to the Place of Sacrament and enlighten her about our plans."

Rather than street clothes, Rekhmira wore priestly vestments, with one exception. Instead of a clean-shaven head, his lustrous jet-black hair flowed to his shoulders. It didn't surprise her he would insist on keeping his hair. It was always one of his weaknesses of vanity. He strode toward her with a distinct look of pleasure and made an ever-so-slight bow. "Oh Great One, follow me. I have much to tell you."

Apepmosis's voice boomed through the hall. "You both may leave. I must take my rest and ready myself for our ritual."

Rekhmira grabbed Hattie's arm, in a tight grip. "I will make sure she understands."

"So let it be done."

Rekhmira dragged Hattie out of the chamber.

Hattie tried to twist from his clawlike hold on her. "Unhand me!"

"If I recall correctly, you like it a little rough." He pulled her along to the corridor where Sabu was waiting.

"I will escort the Great One to the Place of Sacrament. You stay here and see to the needs of the Holy of Holies."

Sabu bowed. "Of course, my Lord."

"But before you go, make sure the Great One stays put while I gain entrance."

Sabu stood at the ready, blocking her egress.

Rekhmira let go of Hattie and stood in front of the relief depicting the unusual symbol Hattie couldn't identify of a snake twined around a flagpole.

Hattie had many questions and was beyond pissed that the one who held the answers was Rekhmira. She loathed him for many reasons, but one of the qualities she most hated about him was his unabashed know-it-all approach to everything under the sun. It was just her luck to be in a position where he would be able to joyfully expound on a grand explanation to her. To say she was not looking forward to it was a vast understatement.

Rekhmira knelt before the wall and mumbled words. The wall opened with a grinding sound, making the floor vibrate. Beyond the entrance lay a winding spiral staircase. He grabbed her wrist and pulled her in.

"Let me go."

His eyes grew sharp. "You find my touch offensive? I remember a honeyed time when that wasn't so."

She jerked away from him. "I can walk on my own. I am not a

captive here, so don't treat me as one. I am the guest of Apepmosis."

"Are you certain about that?" The stone door shut behind them. As it closed, torches came to life and illuminated a large tower. Rekhmira released his grasp on Hattie and climbed the stairs. "Come, follow me. All the answers you seek are waiting."

Hattie followed him up the wide, curving staircase that wound itself up the tower. The rounded walls were made of sandstone, but as they progressed, it changed into the chalky white material of the aboveground formations. As they approached the end of the staircase, it occurred to her that they were climbing through the interior of one of the chalk structures.

They entered a brilliant white room carved from the interior of a massive formation. Above, the ceiling contained a large oculus opening to the desert sky. A broad band of gold panels stretched around the room, retelling the story of Apepmosis. In the center of the room was a large object resembling a gigantic pearl suspended over a golden disk. The disk was inscribed with hieroglyphs on its surface. The pearl was pulsating with a strange and bright blue glow.

"What is this?"

"It is the hoard. Or more accurately, it was the hoard. Minus a couple of pieces."

He reached into the leopard skin slung over his body and pulled out the sistrum. Hattie cursed herself. With everything happening she forgot to keep an eye on it.

"I had been looking for this for a long time." He gazed at it for a moment, then tucked it into his garment.

"Are you going to melt it down too?"

"In a fashion. But it is far more complex than that. What you see before you is pure unadulterated magic that was extracted from the hoard of artifacts. Most of the objects dumped by the priests of Karnak were coated in thick magical residue, as they were used for centuries in sacred rites. The disk amplifies the magic, making it far more powerful than it would be by itself. We will extract the magical residue from your offering and add it to the orb for our ritual tonight. The gold itself most likely will be used in an added adornment for our temple." He puffed his chest out as he wandered around his creation.

"The disk is a mirror of sorts?"

"Only if your mirror makes you look one thousand times more youthful and beautiful before obliterating you."

"What do you mean?"

"Don't you sense the sharp bite of magic around you? If anyone were to get near its power, it would vaporize their flesh." He tapped his chin, thinking. "Actually, now that I think on it, you would be safe, as you are immortal, but even with that, I think after your exposure you'd never be quite the same."

"Why did you need to build a magic amplifier? Were you finding you were having magical performance issues as you got older?"

"Very funny." His tone was flat as he gazed at his creation. "I never knew you possessed such comedic talent. When I realized its potential, I knew it was a game changer, something that would enable me to take my place among the Gods. Then it occurred to me how messy things could get when you tried to crash their party, so I decided to annihilate them. Seemed far more efficient."

Hattie noticed Rekhmira had slipped from the plural to the singular. "Why the stooge?"

"Whatever do you mean?" His smile revealed he knew exactly what Hattie meant.

"Shedsu-nefertum or Apepmosis, whatever you want to call him. Why would you hook your star to that particular bag of useless flesh? Even in the day when he was the high priest at the Temple of Amun, he was a self-important ass kisser."

"That was exactly why he would work for my plans. As you know by living forever, time has a different meaning. It gives you the ability to plan things out, way out. The long con takes on a whole new meaning. I stumbled on our priest friend when he was on the verge of death in the desert. It seemed fair game if I saved him to have a bit of fun with him. I cast a spell to have him see himself as Apep, an opponent of Re. Although in the state he was in at the time, it might have been overkill. It is likely a mere suggestion might have done the trick. I fed him some nonsense about a prophecy."

"This whole cult is something you started on a lark?"

"Remember the long game, dearie. I have planted many seeds over time that are waiting to sprout. This seedling has grown and thrived and has branched out in unexpected and fortunate ways. If you scatter many seeds, some will take root. This flower of mine once suffered from a major plague. I thought this was going to be the end and it would fade into the desert around it. Just when the population and true believers dwindled to almost nothing, Cambyses's army strode past the front door, breathing new life. Its arrival fit the loosely worded prophecy I put forth to Apepmosis long ago. Before you knew it, the numbers swelled."

"With the soldiers?"

"That accounted for some, but the real jump in population came from the recruitment process."

"Recruitment?"

"Stealing of children from cities and towns. Apepmosis may be a dullard, but he has a true gift of cruelty, which has proved invaluable for keeping the cult going. Like the genius idea of removing the tongues from the serving class. So useful. Not only does it eliminate the ability for them to speak their minds but also cubs the transmission of any rebellious thoughts regarding the Holy of Holies and yours truly. Quite the effective."

The thought that every servant had been mutilated in this way disgusted Hattie but didn't surprise her. Not with Rekhmira at the helm. Although he gave the credit to his partner, Hattie guessed the idea was planted in Apepmosis's head by Rekhmira. She couldn't believe that all this time she thought the servants taken a sacred vow of silence. "I am guessing you have no intention of freeing Apepmosis from that stone body you must have imprisoned him in."

"You know me too well, dear one. There is no way I can. I told him that so he would stick by me. At the time, I didn't know if or when his cult would become useful to me, and now those actions are bearing their long-awaited fruit and are ready for harvest. Tonight, I will have Sabu wheel Apepmosis up to witness the hope he's held on to for centuries evaporate before his eyes as I realize my full glory and bring down the Gods themselves." Rekhmira's eyes shone brightly.

"The sistrum was the piece you were missing to complete the hoard?"

"Yes, I was missing two of the three artifacts Cambyses took for his wives. Or at least I thought that was the case."

"You didn't know how many of the three you had? I know you can be an idiot, but I was certain you could at least count that high."

Rekhmira pointedly ignored the barb and paced in front of her. "Cambyses removed three objects from the hoard. I found the diadem centuries ago. It belonged to a Persian noble. I bought the collar necklace from an eccentric German in the 1950s. At the time it was missing a carved scarab. I brought both the collar necklace and the diadem here and scraped all the magical residue they contained. All this time I thought there was one more relic to be found from that object. But with the arrival of our newest guest, I know the scarab is worthless. It is made of stone and not gold, the flesh of the Gods. Although it was a part of the hoard, it was made of a different material so it hadn't absorbed the magical residue like the rest of the treasure. If it were introduced to the hoard, it would have created an imperfection." He gazed through the oculus to the daylit sky. "But as luck would have it, she is the treasure which makes all these little bits of gold, like your sistrum, look like mere tourist trinkets."

"Why are you telling me this? Aren't you afraid I will run to Apepmosis and tell him your plans?"

"I know you won't, and if you try, you will fail for three specific reasons. First off, you can't. You have no access to him. The Holy of Holies is secured for his purification rights, and no one has access. Although I don't think it would matter if you did. Everything is in motion and Mr. I-can't-move-my-legs has no way of stopping it. Second, the scarab my new guest brought is useless, but when I looked upon her, I knew what she was, a mortal who defeated a God. She knows his true name and that, dearie, will make me more powerful than I'd ever imagined. And I have made sure you have no access to her either. You will be under lock and key until our ceremony is to begin."

"Who is this guest?"

"Alex Philothea."

"The KHNM agent?"

"The very one."

"What's number three?"

"What do you mean?"

"The third reason you know I won't stop you."

"Oh, how could I have forgotten my most delicious reason." He clapped his hands twice. "Thabit and Zuberi, tie her up."

She turned around to see her companions walking toward her as if in a daze holding lengths of rope.

"I look forward to tonight when you can see me in my regal glory. To witness the day I became a God." The boys roughly grabbed her hands and tied them behind her. "Long game, Hattie, remember the long game. Take her to her room."

As they grabbed her, Hattie caught a glimpse of her companions. Their eyes glowed a bright violet color. Breathing a sigh of relief, she relaxed into their firm hold as they dragged her from the chamber. The protective wards she cast on them many moons ago had worked. Once alone, she would break Rekhmira's hold on them and use them as cover to find Alex.

It's the long game, dear one.

CHAPTER THIRTY-EIGHT

On the edges of Alex's consciousness, she heard harp music. *Am I already dead?* The strange thought floated through her mind as her body became aware of the soft downy substance supporting her and the throbbing bump on her head. She cracked her eyes open a smidgen to make sure no one was looming over her. When she felt the coast was clear, Alex sat up. The fast movement made her head swim. She rubbed the spot where the unseen attacker whacked her on the head. Alex guessed it was the handiwork of one of the Persian soldiers. Which was odd in and of itself. What were troops dressed in ancient Persian armor doing in the Egyptian desert? It was unlikely they'd been roaming the White Desert since Cambyses's time. But then again, Alex knew all too well nothing was truly impossible. Could they have something to do with Salima? If so, Alex figured she would already be dead.

Niles, Luke, and Gormund were still out cold. Presumably, they were bashed in the head as well.

The soft music was painful to hear as it pinged through her

wounded head. The sound was coming from a large balcony stretching across the long and narrow chamber. She slung her feet over the bed and walked to the others. After checking their pulses, she breathed a little easier in the knowledge they would eventually wake.

Alex wandered to the balcony and immediately sick, heaving up whatever remained of her last meal. She grabbed onto the railing to steady herself as she was overcome with dizziness. After a few deep breaths, her body stabilized. Alex opened her eyes and peered over the steep bluff the balcony was perched on. Down past the lethal drop was what looked like a white Greek village clinging to the sides of the canyon below.

There weren't any musicians on her balcony. The offending noise was coming from another one down the way. It was surprising that the sound was coming so strongly into her room. She guessed that the canyon probably made sound jump in unexpected ways.

Unable to stop the music, she staggered into the chamber and stood over her sleeping companions. At the other end of the room, there was a bathing chamber. She grabbed a large amphora and filled it with water and doused them with it.

All three of them sputtered back to life.

"Where are we?" Niles stood and grasped his head with both hands. "And what is that horrible music?"

"Apparently a neighbor of ours has a penchant for the harp."

Luke walked to a chaise lounge and sat down, cupping his head in his hands. "My head feels like it was hit with a sledgehammer."

"Most likely an ancient cudgel." Alex laughed at her joke and instantly regretted it.

Luke rubbed his head. "Yeah, what is it with those ancient soldiers, anyway? Do you think we found Cambyses's army?"

Alex set the amphora on the floor. "I thought that too, but I wondered how they could still be around. Niles, is this a place that is connected to the Gods? I mean, have I been captured by Salima?"

"No, I've never seen this place before. Also, Salima's orders are to kill on sight, not capture."

Luke glared at Niles. "Thanks for the reminder."

Gormund sat next to Luke. "It would make sense that it is Cambyses's army. They must be under a magical enchantment to have survived all this time." Gormund's tone was light, as if pointedly changing the topic.

Alex grabbed onto the change of subject matter like a life raft. She didn't have the energy to be pissed anymore. "Or maybe they have recycled the gear over the years."

She spotted her scribe's bag lying overturned on the floor. "It looks like somebody took a brief tour of the contents of my bag. But nothing seems to be missing."

"The scarab is still there?" asked Luke.

"Everything. I wonder what they were looking for?" asked Alex.

"Well, they obviously didn't find it," added Gormund.

It was noticeable that Niles hadn't jumped in with his two cents. Luke's comment must have sent him back into the doghouse.

The distant harp music stopped. The silence was a great relief. Alex walked to the balcony to take in their surroundings in case they needed to exit quickly. Since they were all unconscious when they arrived, they were under the unfortunate circumstance of not knowing where they were.

As she stepped onto the balcony, she realized they were in a massive cavern. She didn't recall any landmasses in the desert landscape that could have had such a large space within them.

She deduced they might be underground. She was impressed with the unusual beauty of the city in the canyon below them and how ingenious the inhabitants were. They managed to create their own sun of sorts to light their everyday lives.

Niles stood near to her and leaned onto the balcony wall. Alex kept her gaze trained on the city below. She could feel the frizzle of her anger between them, like an unseen barrier he dared not to cross. The silence gathered between them as they gazed outward, pointedly not looking at one another. Alex wondered what the occupant of the room with the harp music would think if they stepped onto their balcony and saw Alex and Niles. Most likely they would assume a lover's spat. In that they would be right, however this wasn't an ordinary spat. It felt unfair they had to continually tangle with supernatural perils. Alex sensed her anger starting to dull.

"Alex, I love you."

"I know you do."

"And I am sorry."

Alex wasn't sure what to say next, but she knew it wasn't going to be something like "It's okay." She was glad his apology didn't come with a side order of excuses.

"There is something I need to clarify."

Disappointment filled her. "That didn't last long."

"What?"

"Oh, now you are going to tell me how everything was very much out of your control. And I don't want to hear it."

"You are right, I've been guilty of doing that on occasion. But that is not what I want to tell you now. I need to let you know what Gormund told you wasn't true."

"Are you saying he lied to me?"

"Just hear me out. Please."

Alex sighed. "Go on."

"If I failed to kill you, it is true the other Gods would strip me of my powers and make me kill you into infinity, but you will be dead. They will wipe the memory of your death from me. They will make it so I will experience killing you each day as a continuous experience with each sunrise. The Gods have no intention of letting you live."

"Not even tied to a rock and killed each day?"

"The Gods want to be certain there is no way you could escape somehow and live. So, you will be very much dead when I serve out my eternal sentence."

"And why are you telling me this?"

Niles turned to face her, placing his hand on her forearm. "I wanted to ease your mind. If you die today, you will not be tortured into infinity."

"But you will be."

"It is the price I was willing to pay for the chance of saving you, my heart."

Niles pulled her close, and she let him. His warm embrace brought her comfort. She leaned her head against his chest thrumming with his God power.

"It just didn't work the way I hoped." His voice grew soft.

Alex pulled away as a thought crossed her mind.

"Niles, if I die today, we can hold in our hearts that it will be a farewell and not a goodbye. Maybe we will meet once again in the Field of Reeds." She toyed with the heart amulet he'd given her.

A shadow crossed over his face as if he didn't think it was likely but didn't want to say so out loud. "The amulet has a protective spell. It contains strong magic, but nothing that can stop Salima in her Sekhmet form. If anything, it might buy us time. I love you, my heart, and will forever."

Alex let go of the amulet as it suddenly burned against her skin. Its inner core glowed with a hot brightness.

Niles blanched. "It looks like Salima is on her way."

CHAPTER THIRTY-NINE

Hattie was unceremoniously tossed into her chamber by Thabit and Zuberi. Their eyes still glowed purple with the protective spell she cast on them years ago. After securing the door behind them, they each took their place on either side of the entrance. They stood there motionless, as if awaiting orders. That is until Hattie tested it and tried to get past them. They pushed her back and returned to their still stance as sentries.

The ceremony Rekhmira and Apepmosis talked about would happen shortly. She didn't have much time to remove the veil of power Rekhmira cast over Thabit and Zuberi. Once she did, she could use them as a shield to search the palace for this Alex person.

The pharaohs in the Field of Reeds who sent her on this fool's errand wanted the Gods brought to a place of negotiation, to make their life in the Field of Reeds better—to bring them to their knees, but not to destroy the Gods. The pharaohs were conservative royalists at heart who spent their lifetimes worshiping and paying homage to these Gods. Despite their current dispute with the Gods, they would never want to destroy the cosmic order set in place since life emerged from the waters of chaos. They were looking for contract negotiations, not to burn down the entire enterprise.

Even if there were a rabid few in their numbers who did want to take the Gods down, they were fools. They would just have to eat the buffet of disappointment Hattie hoped to hand them by stopping Rekhmira.

In addition, there was no existence Hattie wanted to live in where Rekhmira held the power from the hoard and the knowledge of the true name of Re himself. It would be insanity to replace the Gods, however capricious they might be, with that self-serving fool Rekhmira. He would be the one and only God power once he succeeded in destroying the entire Egyptian pantheon.

Hattie strode into the bathing room where the servants had purified her. She scanned the room to find anything she could use to amplify her spell work. On a far wall was the painted Nile scene that the priestesses had led her through to the main hall. Hattie hoped there might be a preparation room in that hall where she might find some sacred oils and unguents. She placed her hands on the exact spot on the wall with a depiction of a lotus. It was where the priestess touched it earlier to open the passageway.

Nothing happened.

Hattie made a circuit of the room, looking for anything to help her. Placed at three corners of the pool were large vessels. They initially struck her as decoration, until she remembered what they were for. She peered into one and smiled at its glorious contents. It was filled to the brim with sacred honeyed milk. The attendants must have prepared the room for tonight.

Leaning over one of the large vessels, she murmured the

incantation to wash away Rekhmira's spell. She grabbed the amphora and made her way through the sleeping chamber to where the boys were standing like silent soldiers awaiting orders. She repeated the incantation to free Thabit and Zuberi as she neared them.

You shall not be imprisoned
You shall not be restrained
You shall not be fettered

She splattered the honeyed milk across their faces. The purple glow slowly faded from their eyes as the spell retreated. They woke with an astonished expression as they sputtered at the honeyed milk dribbling down their faces.

"You've missed a lot, boys. We've got work to do."

CHAPTER FORTY

There was a heavy knock at the door of the chamber Alex and the others were in. She turned around to see the two buff men she ran into at the rail yard. One stepped forward and spoke. "The Great One, Hatshepsut, Useret Kau, Wadjet Renput—Mighty of Ka's, Flourishing of Years—requests an audience." Hattie Shepard stepped into the room. Her companions shut the door behind them.

Alex strode over to the woman who she'd knocked over in the Vegas warehouse. This situation was getting curiouser and curiouser. "Do you have the KHNM property you stole?"

"Not on me, but it is here. Listen, I don't know how much time we have before the person you need to really be worried about figures out that I've sprung his trap."

"You are being held captive?" Alex was a little more than shocked. She assumed since Hattie stole the sistrum that she was in cahoots with whoever abducted them.

"Trust me, it's a long story, one that we don't have time for. I came to warn you that you are in grave danger."

Niles put himself between Hattie and Alex. "Who is this 'person' you are referring to we should be worried about?"

"He is an immortal magician named Rekhmira. He has used his long life to acquire the three gifts to Cambyses's wives from the hoard in order to amplify his own powers. He has stripped the magic from the hoard artifacts and created a large magical mass and amplifier for it. And now that you've arrived, you've added an unexpected boon to his bounty. A chance to eliminate the Gods."

Gormund gritted his razor-sharp pointed teeth. "Let the insect try."

"I wouldn't be one to discount him. I have paid the price of underestimating him more than once. He knows you have defeated a God, Alex, and he plans to use your power for himself."

Alex was feeling suddenly off-balance and leaned against a column behind her.

Hattie paced the floor. "Time is wasting. I came here to help you. You need to hear what I have to say. I signed on for a little light larceny, but not this. I can't allow Rekhmira to gain the power to have dominion over all things mortal and immortal."

Alex moved closer to Hattie. "We came here to find you and the sistrum, and to figure out what you were up to. We were working under the impression you were trying to bring down the Gods. Up until now, we've never heard of this Rekhmira. When we arrived at the White Desert, we were ambushed and knocked unconscious. I assume by his people."

"The sistrum is the least of your worries now. I have an escape plan to offer you." Hattie motioned to the two large men standing behind her. "Rekhmira needs you, Alex. He thought the scarab you were carrying would complete his set from the hoard. After examining it, he realized the scarab was made of a base material. It would be an impurity that could damage his newly created orb of magical power. It was useless for his purposes. But he recognized in you the magical force of someone who has defeated a God. Now he has readjusted his plan for an optimal payout."

"And what is that?"

"To make you reveal the name of Re. This would give him power the likes of which no one has ever contemplated. Power that could end the Gods themselves. But if we hurry, you can escape. At the moment Rekhmira thinks my two companions are under his magical thrall. We could use them as a shield to leave this place unmolested."

"And why are you helping us? And how can we trust you? You did after all steal the sistrum from us."

"All I can say is I stole your artifact for another group who has its own interests."

"And what are those interests?"

"They want to bring the Gods to their knees, but never would they want to wipe them away."

Niles blew out an exasperated breath. "Are you telling us you were dumb enough to get involved with another pharaonic uprising in the Field of Reeds? You know how well that went last time."

"This time it is different."

Gormund came close to Hattie. "That is what they always say. Maybe I should rip you from limb to limb, and then you'll see how it is to live through eternity as an immobile stump."

"You have no idea how randomly appropriate your threat is. No matter what you think of the old codgers I was working for, they respect the Gods—"

"Enough to try and take them down?"

"They wanted a bargaining chip, to improve their situation, that is all. Not like Rekhmira, who wants to end them."

"Well, that settles it. There is no way I am going to leave. We need to stop him," said Alex.

Hattie huffed. "But you *must* leave."

Alex glanced at Niles. "There is no escape for me. There is only one silver lining for me now—to stop this Rekhmira, and in doing so possibly gain favor from the Gods. I am staying." She walked over and grabbed her scribe's bag.

Niles caught her eye. "I will stay with you to the end, my heart."

"Luke, Gor, you should leave with her," said Alex.

"Never," they both said in unison as the door swung open, revealing the priest with raven-black hair who captured them in the desert. He was surrounded by Persian guards. "Take them to the Place of Sacrament."

Many guards filed into the room, vastly outnumbering Alex and her companions. They made quick work of securing everyone. Alex struggled against her guards. Each squirm earned her a tighter grip from the hands holding her.

The guards dragged them through the palace, arriving at a strange door with a symbol of a snake twisting around a flagpole. Alex was shoved through the door, then prodded up a grand circular staircase. It opened to a large, glistening white chamber. Around its perimeter was a broad gold band covered with reliefs.

Adrenaline surged through her and brought forward a sharp clarity of mind. The odds were piling up against her, and she saw no way out. They were completely outnumbered and surrounded in a compound within a city they had no logistical knowledge of. And if that weren't enough, Sekhmet was on her way.

Alex took stock of the situation. In the center of the room was a massive disk and suspended above it was a large blue orb. The gold disk must be the amplifier of magic Hattie mentioned, and the orb must be the receptacle for the hoard magic. On the left side of the disk lay a table with leather straps. A diorite statue of a priest stood before the orb.

Alex grabbed the strap of her scribe's bag. Its familiar leather case brought her a sense of comfort. The scarab was pulling toward the orb from inside her bag. Was it trying to join its brethren? She held the bag against herself to still its motion.

The guards made Alex, Niles, Luke, and Gormund stand in front of the statue.

Alex glanced behind her and saw that Hattie and her two companions were surrounded by a flank of soldiers in the back of the room. More soldiers filed into the space, creating a secure perimeter around it.

"Welcome honored guests to our blessed celebration." The voice emanated from the immobile form in front of the orb.

Alex was taken aback to hear the statue speak. "Who might this be who is addressing us?"

Rekhmira strolled to the diorite statue. "This is my, uh . . . partner Apepmosis, the prophet of the City of Bakhu. Yes, welcome to our honored guests. One of you will be receiving the honor of our great attentions." He motioned to Luke. "Guards, take her mortal friend to the table and strap him in."

Alex struggled against the two soldiers who held her fast, but there was no use in trying to escape them.

The soldiers lifted Luke and carried him to the table. He kicked his legs wildly as he yelled for them to let him go. Three more came to the table and stilled his legs so he could be strapped down.

"Unfortunately for your friend, he is the only mortal in this room aside from you, Ms. Philothea. May I call you Alex?"

"Ms. Philothea will do just fine."

"Of course. Well, Ms. Philothea, your newfound friend Ms. Hatshepsut got my plans wrong in her retelling." He looked pointedly at Hattie. "Yes, I need you to speak Re's name. But my plans for you don't end there. After you share his name with me, I can use it when I have everything in place. I will sever your Ba and keep it in this little alabaster container. I will then add your magical energies, which are very potent, to the orb, and then use the God's name myself. If you are wondering why I am telling you this, it is because I thought you might like to know what will happen after you are sacrificed. With your energies added to the orb, I will cast the spell on the surface of the disk, then speak the name of Re. I will use this new power to annihilate the Gods." Rekhmira scratched his chin. "I wonder what this might do to these second-tier ones who are always casting about with you?"

"How dare you, a once and banished servant of the pharaohs, pretend to be greater than the Gods?" Niles surged forward. His captors reined him in.

Rekhmira's eyes burned with fury. "Guards, shut him up." He signaled to a group of guards who surrounded Niles. The soldiers holding him let go so he could be more easily beaten by the gang of warriors who now surrounded him. Niles gasped as the punches and kicks rained down on him.

Alex twisted against the grip of her captors. Her heart was aching with each blow landing on her beloved. "Make them stop!"

The magician only smiled as the violence against Niles continued. "Oh, you'd like me to stop, I am sure. But I am finding this rather entertaining. To see his Immortal greatness taken down a notch or two. As a matter of fact, I think your friend could lose a few more notches. Lieutenant, please assist your men."

A giant man holding a large khopesh sword moved from the back of the room toward Niles.

"One day I will see you pay, magician," Gormund hissed

through his clenched pointed teeth.

"Is that so, little man? Maybe I should send the lieutenant to do some work on you."

"If you want to continue negotiations, you need to call off your guards," shouted Alex.

"Very well. I was starting to tire of it anyway. We have business to take care of, and I can always resume these entertainments later if you don't do as I ask." Rekhmira waved his hands.

The guards made a few parting kicks as they stepped away from Niles. His original captors grabbed his arms and lifted him to an approximation of standing. His body sagged between the two who held him. Golden blood ran from his nose and down the sides of his mouth. As Niles straightened up to stand, he lacked his usual grace. His movements were erratic as if he were struggling to move with all his newly acquired injuries.

Rekhmira had a self-satisfied grin as his gaze moved from Niles to Alex. "I do find it a little precious that you think of this as a negotiation. Nothing could be further from the truth. Your future is certain. Die now with a fully intact friend or die later with a very much damaged friend." Rekhmira glanced at Luke, who was strapped to the table.

"And why should I volunteer to do any of this for you, if you plan on killing me either way?"

"If you do not give me the God's name, I will torture both you and your friend. I will make you endure your own and witness his. I have had many centuries to perfect my approach to the art of prolonged suffering. It can go on as long as you like— until you give up the God's name, that is. As you are aware, I have all the time in the world, unlike you."

Alex couldn't believe the deadly ironic parallels of it. "But what of the Gods? What makes you think I am in favor of ending them?"

"I know you have certain . . . relationships with them." Rekhmira glanced at Niles and grimaced. "But would the modern world really care about the end of a bunch of has-been Gods?"

"Coming from a has-been priest," Niles yelled.

Rekhmira waved his hand at the guards restraining Niles. They pushed him to his knees and held him there. "Hit a sore spot, have I? It's time for you to get used to kneeling before your betters."

Niles glared up at the magician.

Alex needed to shift the conversation away from Niles and buy time to think. "But mortals would celebrate having one named Rekhmira take the old Gods' place?"

"It is not of your concern. You will die today or the day you agree to tell me Re's name. What hangs in the balance is the life of your friend here."

From outside the chamber came an incredible roar that shook the entire space.

Rekhmira looked uncertain.

A bloodied guard slumped into the room. "Master. There is a lion-headed beast making ribbons of your guard."

Alex knew what she had to do. Even as a lifelong optimist, she could see there was no way out. If it were only that they were all surrounded and outnumbered by a company of guards controlled by a powerful magician with delusions of grandeur, she could still hold on to a tenuous hope. But Sekhmet was on the way to kill her. The Goddess was the destructive Eye of Re and destroyer of mankind, whose legendary fury had made both the mighty Set and Apophis run from her wrath—the situation doused any hope Alex had. She didn't want to die. She wanted whatever was coming next to be her choice.

"That fierce fighter who is tearing through your guards right now to get to us is the Goddess Sekhmet. Free me and Niles, the God Thoth, so we may intervene with his sister. She will annihilate you and your men to rescue us. Save yourself and unbind me, and I will tell her of your deeds, so she might find mercy for you and yours." Sekhmet was there for anything but a rescue, but Alex was certain Rekhmira had no idea of the God's price on Alex's head.

"What if I hand you over to her and let you all go on your merry way?"

"She will not rest until she has eradicated those who acted against her beloveds. Without our intervention, she will kill you and all of your followers in retribution."

"I am immortal; she cannot kill me."

"She can tear your limbs from you so you may live through eternity as your stone friend there. Ever tried to work magic without hands?"

Screams of Rekhmira's followers echoed up the circular staircase.

Rekhmira's complexion paled. "So be it." He nodded. The guards let go of her and Niles.

Alex removed the glowing protective amulet from her neck and handed it to Niles. "Tell Salima you made me do this. Have Gor back you up."

"No, Alex. I cannot let you do this."

Alex pressed the carnelian heart into his hand. "You know this is the only way."

His fingers curled over the amulet as the truth of what she said dawned on him.

"Farewell, my heart," Alex whispered to Niles, and walked to the magic orb. The scarab inside her bag thrust itself against her as if it wanted to fly through her flesh and bone to join the magic within the orb. She gazed at the great ball and was awed by its beauty. Being close to the swirling mass of magic was like standing on the edge of a universe.

The sounds of death and destruction from below were getting louder every second. Another roar shook the chamber. She hadn't much time left. She turned to look at Niles one last time. His gaze sharpened with emotion. In that moment, she knew he was hers and always would be.

She pulled the scarab out of her bag. Her hand jerked up to the orb. Alex's muscles burned as the force between the objects pulled against her. The tension quickly became unbearable. The scarab and the orb's deep attraction demanded that the space separating them be closed. Nausea welled up within her as the flesh of her shoulder threatened to rip from its socket. The two magical objects had no desire to take Alex along for the ride. She had to hold on as best she could until the attraction of the two objects overpowered their refusal of this impurity. She ignored the excruciating pain and redoubled her grasp of the scarab. The force between the two objects continued to strengthen. The scarab was slipping from her hand. She flung her other hand over it and held tight. The magnetic pull between the two objects gave way, sucking Alex up into the ball of magic.

Searing heat burned her flesh as she passed through the magical membrane. Struggling against the intense pain, she gazed down at Niles, Luke, and Gormund. A surge of emotions welled up within her—love, longing, and sadness in the knowledge her time with them was at an end.

A blood-covered Sekhmet burst into the room just as a bright-white inferno erupted around Alex. Her body was immolated by the sharp light of a thousand tiny stars burrowing into the hidden places between her flesh and bone and exploding in one simultaneous flash.

She never felt such pain or freedom.

EPILOGUE

Alex felt buoyant, as if she were floating weightless on the surface of the Dead Sea, but instead of a brilliant Jordanian sun above her, she was suspended in a soft, murky darkness. She had no memory of how she arrived. Her thoughts were fuzzy and unfocused as she tried to grasp any clues about where she was.

An excruciating jolt charged through her as memories returned, and she flashed back to the moment after she breached the orb and was consumed by the magic around her. Alex recalled floating above everyone for an instant. The orb shattered into infinite shards, showering the chamber in bright prismatic color just as a bloody Sekhmet burst into the space.

The darkness around her was fading, and she could make out a flickering light below. She wondered if this was the tunnel of light everyone speaks of.

A force from below pulled her down through the beige fog. The color gradation of the substance, along with its pits and depressions, made her think she was traveling through a mass of rock and into a tomb.

Torches flickered against painted scenes of the Egyptian after-life gracing the tomb's walls. The torchlight gave the impression of movement to figures who were hard at work in the Nether-world. Thorne, Gwen, Akh-Hehet, and others from KHNM were also in the room, seated on gilded straight-backed chairs set in rows in front of the altar.

Niles, Luke, and Gormund were standing near a stone altar piled high with food offerings and garlands of fresh flowers. Her heart lifted at the sight of them.

Her mind was having a hard time keeping her thoughts straight as impressions floated through her consciousness in a slow, rosy-hued chaos.

Buxton stood behind the altar between a propped-up coffin and a large Ka statue. A small gasp escaped her, but no one in the tomb seemed to hear it. He was in full high priest regalia, draped leopard skin and all. He had even shaved his silver hair away. The golden ceremonial adze he held glowed in the torch-light as he moved from the statue to the coffin.

Alex floated down, hovering over the beautifully decorated cartonnage that was a masterful likeness of her father, Phillip. Her heart swelled with the knowledge that he would no longer be bereft of his well-deserved grave goods. She quickly scanned the room but didn't spot her mother. Apparently she okayed the reburial but declined to come.

With the detachment of a waking dream, Alex had no idea why she was there. Was it possible KHNM had pulled strings in the afterlife so she could be a part of her father's funeral?

She glided over to his Ka statue and stopped cold.

The granite face was hers. The rosy disassociation cleared away and it was crystal clear. This wasn't only her father's funeral. All at once the small stone room felt like it was closing in on her. She darted out in a panic and flew down a corridor leading to a large bright space. Although it was also cut from the living rock, its high-domed ceiling and rounded corners felt less oppressive. At its center lay a massive crystal sarcophagus.

Alex circled it a few times until it hit her. She was in the burial chamber of her ancestor Alexander the Great. It rested upon a huge stone plinth, taking on the appearance of a giant jewel case made from large slabs of moonstone. The semi-opaque material reflected and refracted a rich rainbow of colors and made it appear as if it were covered with frosted glass. A thick band of gold incised with hieroglyphs encircled both its lid and base. She hovered above it and gazed into the lifelike painted eyes of her forefather's cartonnage. His beatific expression filled her with a sense of peace.

Buxton must have been using the adze in performing the opening of the mouth ceremony on her statue and that was what called her forth from whatever limbo she had been occupying. She found it strange that she was here to witness the burial rites for both her and her father. Alex had always assumed that once the opening of the mouth ceremony happened the deceased would be sucked up into the Netherworld for their weighing of the heart ritual. Alex didn't know how long she'd been in this state or how long she had in this plane of existence. She decided to pull up her dead-girl pants and go return to the funeral in progress. It would be good to spend what time she had with those who came to honor her and her dad.

As she left Alexander's tomb, she wondered if all of those who served KHNM were buried here in a sort of family crypt. Given the length of time KHNM had been in existence, it would have to be a massive warren of tombs rivaling the hundreds of chambers built for the many sons of Ramses the Great in the Valley of the Kings, known as KV5.

Once she returned to the tomb where the ceremony was

taking place, she floated back to where Buxton, Niles, Luke, and Gormund were still standing at the end of the offering table. They all had dark circles around their eyes like they hadn't slept in ages. As she came closer, Alex caught a glimpse of red carnelian peeking out of Niles's shirt. It made her happy to see him wearing it, but the sight of it sent a flood of memories through her, filling her with a weighty loss. She lowered herself to the ground and tried to touch him. He shivered as her hand pushed through his body.

She returned to hovering above them so she could gaze on each of their faces a little longer.

"So, Niles. Any word on the state of Rekhmira and Hattie?" asked Buxton. "The Gods have been particularly tight-lipped about it."

"They've been imprisoned ever since they were captured, awaiting their sentences. But then again, I'm not up to speed on most things. I'm not exactly a favorite of my family at the moment."

Gormund had his arms crossed over his chest. "So, I guess Salima must have believed us."

"You think she did? I had the feeling it wasn't necessarily her decision to make. I didn't think she bought our story at all. I think it came down to the decision of the sensational six," said Niles.

"You mean Re, Isis, Osiris, Set, Nephthys, and Horus?" asked Luke.

"The very same. I think they didn't care how it happened, so long as the result was that Alex was very much dead." Niles's tone held a broken quality.

"And they had a reasonable excuse to not punish one of their own," Gormund added.

"Yeah, if only they would have that same empathy and good-will toward others outside of their little circle." Luke nodded toward the Ka statue of Alex. "I mean, why did she have to die? Because she could tell you what the ancient Egyptian horoscope calendar said for a particular day? What a waste."

"She scared my family because she knew Re's true name by defeating him. Although it pains me to say it, I think the death of Alex was always their endgame."

Luke flushed with anger and edged closer to Niles. "Well, that is mighty grand of you to say. An Immortal throwing around the concept of death lightly at a funeral that is happening because of him."

Alex dropped to put herself between them. Then it occurred to her that in this form she wouldn't be able to stop them if they came to blows.

Buxton moved close to Luke. "That is not entirely true, and you know it. Let's not fight today of all days. I think if Alex were here, she wouldn't want to see a show of anger between the two of you."

"Luke, this isn't at all how I wanted this to end. I would have done anything to have her back with us. You don't have to like me. Let's just try and get through the day as two people who loved Alex very much." Niles looked away from the others with tear-filled eyes.

Luke stepped back a little as his complexion normalized. "It's the least I can do."

Alex breathed a sigh of relief and floated back above them.

Buxton's voice cracked with emotion. "Today is a day to remember Alex. I have mixed emotions about today. On one hand, I feel I've lost the daughter I never had, and on the other, I have hope in the possibility that if she is admitted into the

Netherworld, her death will allow her to spend time with her father, Phillip. Maybe if we are lucky, we will all someday see her again in the Netherworld."

Alex wished so much she could hug the old man.

Niles brightened a little. "There is that hope at least. At least it is what she believed. Before she sacrificed herself, she told me this was a farewell and not a goodbye."

"We can only hope it is the case. I guess we should go ahead and move Phillip into his sarcophagus," said Buxton.

They walked to her father's propped-up coffin, carried it to a large stone sarcophagus, and gently lowered it in. The massive stone lid lay beside it. Thick ropes were secured around the lid, connected to a pulley system to lift it and forever seal away her father's mummy.

The guests were milling around the tomb enclosure with small plates of food as they grazed over the altar of offerings buffet style. Gwen had piled up honey cakes and roast duck. Since she probably paid the bill for this entire shindig, Alex did her best not to judge.

"So her mom didn't show?" asked Gwen.

Apparently, the sweet cakes hadn't sweetened Gwen's personality at all.

Thorne took a sip of wine. "She doesn't believe Alex is dead."

"What in sweet Horus do you mean by that?"

"She thinks it is all a fake. Anything and everything to do with KHNM. It's a shame, but then again, she was never . . ." Thorne's voice trailed away.

"What?"

Thorne looked around the room as if she could sense Alex's presence. "It just feels weird talking about it here at her husband's re-internment and her daughter's funeral." Alex was

THE MUMMY CACHE   369

surprised to witness Thorne actually having possession of some emotional competencies. "But I always felt like Roxanne was unworthy of Phillip—weak, really. And her weakness is evident in her not being here today."

Alex instantly regretted giving the old bitch any credit as a hot rage ran through her. She thrust herself down, wanting to punch Thorne, but only managed to knock wine all over her shirt. Alex figured the dead had to take their victories where they could. Her blouse looked to be white silk and expensive.

Thorne grabbed a napkin and was furiously trying to blot the large red stain.

"It is time." Buxton's voice brought everyone to attention. He nodded to Meyret and Akh-Hehet, who were standing together in the far corner. Until that moment Alex hadn't noticed they were both dressed in their fine priestess vestments and were draped in gold, lapis, turquoise, and carnelian sacred jewelry. Meyret wore the stepped crown of Isis, and Akh-Hehet wore the raised basket headdress of her sister Nephthys. Both made their way to Buxton. Akh-Hehet stood on the far side of Phillip's sarcophagus, and Meyret took her place next to Alex's Ka statue.

Thorne stopped wiping at the stain and tilted her head at Gwen. "I don't know if it was worth the trouble and expense of doing this for her too."

"Alex? I know she didn't have any remains, but the statue should work as a stand-in."

"That's not what I meant."

The two priestesses chanted as Niles and Luke pulled at the rope, lifting Phillip's sarcophagus lid.

Gwen raised an intrigued eyebrow.

"Do you think after all she's done, the Gods would ever allow her to step foot in the Field of Reeds? I think her heart will be found wanting against the feather of Maat. Most likely she's destined to be a tasty snack for the Devourer of Souls."

"Oh shit." Alex's last words went unheard as she was sucked back into the dark haze.

CHARACTER GUIDE

Ahmose I: Founder of the eighteenth dynasty, pharaoh.

Ahmose-Nefertari: Eighteenth dynasty queen, Great Royal wife of **Ahmose I**; Hatshepsut's great-great-grandmother.

Akh-Hehet: Seer, high priestess of Akh-Hehet during the reign of **Akhenaten**; longtime girlfriend of the dead Pharaoh Horemheb.

Alex Philothea: Agent of KHNM, descendant of Alexander the Great, parents are Roxanne and Phillip Philothea. Has a hereditary connection to the Keepers of the Holy and Noble Maat (KHNM).

Apepmosis: The immortal form of Shedsu-Nefertum, an eighteenth dynasty high priest of Amun.

Bradley: Ms. Winifred's assistant and companion.

Buxton (Charles, Dr.): The director of KHNM.

Colonel Sanderson: An officer at Area 51.

Djoser: Third dynasty pharaoh during the Old Kingdom, builder of the first pyramid in a stepped format.

Frog and Serpent: Servants of Nun and Naunet.

General, the: General at Area 51, friend of the dead Jorge Trinculo.

Gini T.: Librarian at Chicago House; of Jinn heritage.

Gormund: The God Bes in anthropomorphic form, protector of Priestess Meyret, liaison between the Gods and KHNM.

Gwen Pendragon: KHNM's new financier; was a journalist in the past; the girlfriend of Jorge Trinculo.

Hattie Shepard: Shady antiquities dealer, the immortal Hatshepsut, fifth pharaoh of the eighteenth dynasty, daughter of Tuthmosis I, sister and wife of Tuthmosis II, aunt to Tuthmosis III, lover of Senenmut.

Horemheb (Hormey): The last pharaoh of the eighteenth dynasty, longtime lover of Akh-Hehet.

Idris Niru: A power-hungry magician, Immortal, born a mortal (*Gift of the Sphinx*).

Jeeves: A miniature schnauzer belonging to Luke.

Jorge Trinculo (deceased): Adventurer, lover of Gwen Pendragon (*Daughter of Maat, Gift of the Sphinx*).

Meyret: Ancestor of Alex, a priestess under an enchanted sleep in a tomb located in New Mexico, lover of Alexander the Great.

Minerva: Statue who comes to life in Las Vegas, modeled after the Roman Goddess Minerva.

Narmer: The unifier of Egypt and founder of the first pharaonic dynasty.

Niles Greene: The God Thoth in his anthropomorphic form, watchman for the Gods, heartthrob to many, including Alex.

Nun and Naunet: One pair of Gods that are a part of the Ogdoad (eight) primeval Gods. This couple represents the primeval forces of water.

Phillip Philothea (deceased): Alex's dad, former KHNM agent. Was killed by Raymond Sol while on a KHNM assignment.

Bernadette: Alex's mother's former housekeeper and friend.

Herr Schliemann (deceased): A scientist who worked at Area 51 on a top-secret project, collector of cuckoo clocks.

Horatio Diogenes: The God Horus in his anthropomorphic form, a talent agent who split his time between Las Vegas and Egypt and now resides in the Field of Reeds.

Luke: The head archivist with KHNM.

Maspero: Agent of KHNM, descendant of Gaston Maspero (Director-General of Excavations and of the Antiquities of Egypt from 1881 to 1914).

Paul: A statue who comes to life in Las Vegas, modeled after the Roman God Apollo.

Ramses the ninth (IX): The eighth pharaoh of the twentieth dynasty of Egypt.

Ramses the eleventh (XI): The tenth and final pharaoh of the twentieth dynasty.

Raymond Sol: Re in his anthropomorphic form; tried to kill all other Gods and attain Aten-hood (*Daughter of Maat*); now resides in the Field of Reeds.

Rekhmira: Powerful immortal magician.

Roxanne Philothea: Alex's mother.

Sabu: A priest of the lost city of Bakhu.

Salima: Goddess triad of Sekhmet, Hathor, and Bastet in her anthropomorphic form; daughter of Re; watchman for the Gods and sometimes a liaison for KHNM.

Senenmut: Eighteenth dynasty ancient Egyptian architect and government official, lover of Hatshepsut.

Smendes: The founder of the twenty-first dynasty of Egypt.

Sneferu: Fourth dynasty pharaoh and builder of the first true pyramid.

Thabit: A Greek statue brought to life; Hattie's porter and companion.

Theo: Ms. Winifred's assistant and companion.

Thorne (Roberta, Dr.): Buxton's assistant.

Tuthmosis I: Third pharaoh of the eighteenth dynasty, father of Hatshepsut and Tuthmosis II.

Tuthmosis II: Fourth pharaoh of the eighteenth dynasty, father of Tuthmosis III.

Tuthmosis III: Sixth pharaoh of the eighteenth dynasty, son of Tuthmosis III, nephew of Hatshepsut.

Venus: A statue who comes to life in Las Vegas, modeled after the Roman Goddess Venus.

Winifred Soane: Freddy to her friends. KHNM registrar, European branch. Buxton's old flame.

Zuberi: A Greek statue brought to life; Hattie's steward and companion.

AUTHOR'S NOTE

I had loads of fun writing this novel by incorporating historical events and personages that spanned thousands of years. Of course, one personage is the woman who ruled ancient Egypt as its divine King, Hatshepsut. She has always been one of my favorite figures in ancient history, and I just couldn't resist bringing her into the KHNM fold. It was such a delight to spend time with my character Hattie and imagine what it might have been like for the great Hatshepsut to live in modern times.

TT320 or DB320 is what the actual cache of mummies featured in the story is commonly known as. About fifty mummies of Pharaohs, Queens, and other royals were moved to this unmarked cleft in a mountainside in the twentieth dynasty to protect them from tomb robbers. My more scandalous and fictional reason for this mummy movement sparked the inspiration for this book.

The banishment stela I refer to in the novel is in the collection at the Louvre in Pairs. This document in stone is from the twenty-first Dynasty. In this story, I attribute its creation to Pharoah Smendes. In my novel, this stela memorializes his

banishment of priests to a far-off oasis for their alleged involve-
ment in my fictional conspiracy.

Both legends exist about the priests at Karnak Temple
stashing away holy treasure in the sacred lake in anticipation of
Cambyses taking Luxor and Cambyses losing an entire army. It
is told that Cambyses quickly found the loot soon after taking
control of the temple. When he left Egypt to quell a rebellion in
Persia, Cambyses sent an army of 50,000 men to the Siwa Oasis
from Luxor. The entire army was lost and has yet to be found.

Many of the ancient Royal mummies from the cache were
transferred from the Old Cairo Museum to the National Museum
of Egyptian Civilization in April 2021. They departed from their
old home with much pomp and circumstance. The evening soirée
at the NMEC with the perilously open mummy coffins is
completely from my imagination.

If you would like to learn more about ancient Egypt, I would
suggest going to the American Research Center in Egypt (ARCE)
website and joining a local chapter. It is a wonderful national
organization that supports research on all aspects of Egyptian
history and culture and hosts in-person and virtual lecturers
featuring top-notch Egyptologists. And speaking of top-notch
Egyptologists, there are several video classes from The Great
Courses featuring Bob Brier that are so very worthwhile watching, and re-watching. He is an enthusiastic and engaging teacher.
Bob's classes were the spark that lit within me the desire to learn
more about ancient Egypt.

Also by Sandy Esene

The KNHM Series begins with Alex Philothea in Daughter of Maat followed by Gift of The Sphinx and The Mummy Cache.

But, the adventure isn't over—it has only just begun.

Alex stands before the Gods, who demanded her death, in the weighing of the heart ceremony. Will her soul be found in balance with the feather of Maat, or will she be tossed to the Devourer of Souls?

Join Alex Philothea when she battles for her very existence in the Egyptian Netherworld in the fourth installment of the KNHM Series.

ACKNOWLEDGMENTS

Thank you, readers—everyone who has joined me on this journey with Alex and the Keepers of the Holy and Noble Maat. I thank you from the bottom of my heart for reading my work. Like the ancient belief in speaking one's name, I believe the final act of being read breathes life into my characters and their stories. If the ending of this book made you want to hurl the book or e-reader across the room, please keep in mind what Seneca the Younger is attributed to saying: Every new beginning comes from some other beginning's end.

My husband Rob deserves piles of thanks for all his continued support, endless reads, and sympathetic ear in sorting out story issues. I feel so lucky to have someone who is a wonderful partner in crime and a willing victim in my journey as a writer. I couldn't do it without you. Love you to the moon and back.

To my pod, fellow writing addicts and friends; Heidi Hostetter, Ann Reckner, Laurie Rockenbeck, Heather Stewart-McCurdy, Liz Visser, and Michael Gooding. I am truly thankful to have such a wonderful, talented, knowledgeable, and supportive writers group. You are my unlikely herd of unicorns bestowing your magic along the tangled pathway of my writer's journey. A very special bonus thank you to Laurie for helping me tie up everything at the end of it all. I so appreciate you.

Thank you to Ann, Heather, Liz, Michael, Melanie Henry, and Pat Remler for being early readers as this novel found its way. All your comments and insights were invaluable in making *The Mummy Cache* the absolute best it can be.

I'd like to thank all my colleagues at the Office of Arts & Culture for how supportive you've all been throughout the years. A special thank you goes out to Blake Haygood. I very much appreciate your continuous understanding and flexibility in the sometimes-sudden needs of publishing.

Thank you to Egyptologist Dora Goldsmith for having such wonderful online workshops and inspiring me to incorporate the scents of ancient Egypt into my writing.

To my Mummies, Bob Brier and Pat Remler, I continue to learn so much from you both! Bob's *Ancient Egyptian Magic* and Pat's *Egyptian Mythology from A-Z* were constant companions as I wrote this novel.

Thank you to Kristin Carlsen for your brilliant copy-editing skills, and to Mariah Sinclair for your spectacular cover design.

In this novel, I endeavored to represent the ancient Egyptian pantheon of gods and their myths as accurately as I could. Any missteps were completely my own.

ABOUT THE AUTHOR

 Sandy Esene is a self-professed ancient cultures geek. Traveling to ancient ruin sites around the world is one of her great passions. Over the years, she has traveled to over twenty countries including Greece, Malta, Jordan, Turkey, Belize, Peru, Thailand, Japan, and of course Egypt. When not traveling or writing, Sandy enjoys making jewelry, going to museums, and taking long walks in Seattle parks with her husband and their two miniature schnauzers Ozy and Mandias.

In addition to her creative pursuits, Sandy is the registrar for a civic art collection.

Sandy loves hearing from readers. Connect with her on Facebook @SandyEseneAuthor or at www.sandyesene.com.

If you enjoyed reading *The Mummy Cache*, please leave a review or rating on your favorite bookseller's website.